# Keturah II to None

*Book Two*

*Vickie L. Mosley*

HerBet Publishing

All Contents: Written by the Author
Published By: HerBet Publishing
Editing: Susan Keillor
Wendy Bray
Book Cover Design: Rebecacovers
Book Cover Image: Getty Images

Biblical scriptures throughout this book are found in the King James Version

ISBN: 13: 978-1-7327964-0-9

# *Dedication*

To my father Herbert D. Mosley. A man who has consistently demonstrated the importance of being a person of integrity and a man of his word. At ninety-one years old, I look forward to seeing you reach one hundred plus years. May your faithfulness to God and your family be rewarded.

Love you!

# Prologue

"I testify that there is no god but God, and Muhammad is the messenger of God, and the Holy Quran is the authentic expression of God, revealed by Him," Ishmael Taylor professed before all of his family and guests at his wedding ceremony.

"You've failed him!" An inner voice taunted Abraham Taylor while standing as part of the wedding party looking stylish in his white black trim tuxedo. He needed air but his throat continued to tightened as he tried swallowing past the fire burning within his body. His shaky hand fumbled with his bowtie as he attempted to loosen his collar.

"Just breathe." a soft whisper admonished.

Taking a steadying breath, Abraham exhaled, letting his head roll from side to side trying to alleviate the tension building in his neck and shoulders.

"Dad, are you, all right?" Isaac Taylor murmured.

Turning towards his youngest who was also dressed in a tux similar to his, he saw the unshed tears glisten in his son's light gray eyes. Even Isaac recognized the severity of his older brother's decision. Placing a reassuring hand on his son's shoulder he smiled. "I'll be alright, son. Don't worry about me." He assured. In that moment he wanted to pull Isaac in for a hug...for that matter he would have like to charge to the front where Ishmael stood, grab him and rush off with both of his sons taking them somewhere safe out of harm's way.

*"Train up a child in the way they should go and when they are old, they will not depart from it."*

"But I didn't train him Lord, his step father Hassin did and as a result...." Abraham didn't finish his thought. He was seeing the result of his absence from his eldest son's life.

Watching Ishmael's convert to Islam was like witnessing his first wife, Sarah's death. The hurt reached deep within, shattering his heart. In fact, it was harder watching knowing the damage this would ultimately do to his son's soul.

"I just can't believe this?" Isaac shook his head, swiping at his eyes. "Why is he doing this, Dad. Why?" Isaac clenched and unclenched his hand then halted feeling his fiancée's fingers caressing his hand. Turning he smiled down at Rebecca Reynold who gazed lovingly up at him.

Looking at his youngest and his future bride gave Abraham some comfort. He hadn't totally blown it as a father. Needing to reassure Isaac he whispered to him. "It's my fault, Zac. I should have been there for him, done a better job of staying connected…keeping you both connected with each other. So, this is my burden to bear."

"No, Dad, not true! Mael is grown, he's—" Isaac stopped as his father held up his hand. He knew Isaac loved him and merely wished to support him, but this dilemma was his responsibility, and he would carry the burden alone.

As the conventional Muslim marriage ceremony ended, the new Mrs. Marlana Taylor, in her shimmery gold accented cream-colored gown, took her beloved Ishmael's hand as he led them towards their awaiting guests. The large group began shifting towards the *Walimah*, the Muslim's rendition of the wedding reception. As everyone began to shuffle outside where the festivities were to commence, Abraham turned to Isaac. "I need you and Becca to travel back home and run interference before this makes its way to the press. If possible, try and get ahead of this."

"Why!? This won't harm us," Isaac declared, his confusion at his father's request evident on his face. "This is Ishmael's debacle, one that reflects on him, not us or Canaan."

Abraham sighed. Both of his boys were still green when it came to business. They didn't consider how a decision like this could reverberate through the entire network. "Son, it's already hurt us." Abraham gave him a stiff smile then swallowed, knowing there was really no way for Isaac to get ahead of the backlash sure to follow Ishmael's conversion. "With the takeover completed and the announcement of Ishmael heading the international office, do you think Canaan's business associates will believe I didn't know my son would convert to Islam or the meaning it would have for our Christian constituents?"

Isaac sucked in a loathing breath. "This was his intention all along. He deceived us!"

"Not us, Isaac, just me. I was the one duped as I'm sure Aunt Sari will remind me." He rolled his eyes heavenward. "I had assumed I could make this work by my sheer will. But I was mistaken. I'm just thankful I had the foresight to name it Taylor International and keep Canaan Enterprise as a separate entity. At least it presents us some degree of separation," Abraham responded gruffly. "Look, son, get Aunt Sari to help convince our shareholders that everything is going to be business as usual for Canaan."

"When will you come back?" Isaac's brows furrowed with apprehension.

Placing his palm on his son's shoulder to comfort him, he replied, "I'm not sure, Zac. But I know with you at the helm and this beautiful woman at your side," he gave an affectionate hug to his future daughter-in-law Rebecca, "everything will be fine. Besides, something in my gut tells me I'll be back soon." He pulled his son in for a hug, then released him. "Now, go and congratulate your brother and sister-in-law."

"Sure, thing Dad." Isaac grinned then turned toward his fiancé retrieved her hand, and they disappeared into the crowd of well-wishers.

As Abraham watched their retreating forms, a sinking feeling engulfed him that somehow this would be one of many defining moments that would generate a rift in his household for generations to come.

# *Chapter One*

*The same day...*

"AGH!" Clutching her swollen belly, Keturah Taylor fought to stay alert as her contractions intensified. "I can do all things through Christ, who strengthens me," she cried out while trying to remember the visualization techniques her Lamaze instructor taught her.

*"See the white crest of the blue ocean wave crashing onto the waiting sandy seashore. As you visualize the water receding from the sand in your mind, let the intensity of your contraction slowly fade away."*

"What a load of crap!" an exhausted Keturah dropped her head back onto the hospital pillow. Her black curly hair matted against her sweaty face while the blue gown provided by the nurse clung to her dampened skin.

"You're doing great, honey; it won't be long now." Carlton Parson pressed a gentle kiss on her brow and smiled.

Maybe it was the glare from the hospital's light or just her own weary state, but for a moment, Parson looked like Abraham... she jerked her head away, not sure if it was Abraham or Parson's caress she was evading. "I can't...I can't do this," she muttered as her head rolled from side to side. "I think I want an epidural now." She panted while grabbing at Parson's arm.

"Honey, remember you said you wanted to deliver the babies without it," Parson reminded.

"Don't remind me of the dumb stuff I said, Parson. Please tell the doc I want some drugs...NOW!"

"Okay, Tourie. I'll go and find your doctor."

Within seconds another contraction came barreling down on her. "PARSON!!!! Don't leave, please don't go!" She held out her hand and immediately felt the strength of his clutching hers.

"I'm right here, Tourie." He took her hand and pressed a soft kiss on it. "I'm not going anywhere. Just breathe honey...remember to inhale through your nose, exhale in quick breaths making that ...he-he-he sound," Parson encouraged.

"I AM BREATHING!" She snapped.

"I know you are sweetheart, and you're doing a great job." He patted her brow with a damp cloth. "I just wish there was something I could do to make things better for you," he confessed.

"How about having these babies for me?" She chuckled wearily, dropping her head back on the awaiting pillow, still breathing heavily and sweating through her hospital garb. "Parson!? I..." she felt a catch in her dry throat. "I'm being awful to you.... I'm so sorry." Her face contorted with emotion that had nothing to do with her oncoming contraction.

"You get a pass sweetheart...today is special. You're about to bring new life into this world, it's the only thing important right now." He gently patted her mouth with a moisten towel.

"But I la...aaagh!!!" Keturah's words came to an abrupt halt as she bore down on his hand as the pain took the words from her mouth.

"Nurse, is there anything that can be done to lessen her pain?" Parson pleaded as worry lines shrouded his handsome face.

Keturah looked over at him and smiled. She was beginning to care deeply for his mild manner nature. He was her Clark Kent but very capable of changing into Superman when she needed a hero. Much like today, he was being Superman right now, but gentle like Clark. She sighed looking away thinking at times he also reminded her of …once again, it was Abraham's face she saw. Blinking the sweat out of her eyes, she tried to refocus, but an even stronger contraction came, blinding her mind to everything but the pain.

"It won't be long now, Keturah, the babies are in the right position. Just hold on a little longer," her doctor who had just walked in the delivery room informed them.

"But I need to push," she blurted weary of the process and ready to get through it.

"Not yet," the doctor ordered.

Keturah rolled her eyes heavenward but obeyed. How any woman survived this process was beyond her. As she looked up at the textured taupe colored pattern in the ceiling, she felt herself coming unglued, then Parson's face came into focus. His mouth was covered and he had a cap on but she could imagine his brown curly hair and how his well-trimmed beard with just a hint of gray outline his amazing smile. She wondered what a true kiss from his mouth would feel like. Would it forever rid her of the memory of her husband Abraham's gentle caresses?

"Squeeze down on my hand as hard as you need too. I can take it Tourie," Parson encouraged.

His voice shook her out of her delirious fantasy. "Oh, Parson." Her voice wobbled as shame for her thoughts and harsh tone, convicted her. He was so sweet and attentive. He seemed to know just what to say and how to support her when she needed it the most.

"It's okay sweetheart…I'm here and I'm not going anywhere." He promised pressing his cloth covered mouth to her right temple.

Without doubt, he was the type of man she wanted to be married to. His actions towards her spoke volumes. He had walked through the fire with her, had been her strength and comfort while Abraham remained distant. Parson's love was what she and her babies needed and deserved.

*"What about Abraham?"*

God's gentle whisper caught her off guard. As a coppery taste filled her mouth, she moved her tongue around then winced at a tender spot on her lower lip. "I bit my lip," she mumbled.

"Here, let me help," Parson responded by dabbing the area carefully, not putting too much pressure on it.

"Lord, if Abraham was half as considerate as Parson is right now," she thought inwardly, this time biting her lip on purpose to keep thoughts of her husband at bay. But it was no use. His face kept drifting in and out of her mind. He wasn't the man she initially thought he was, or she at one time declared to love. She would likely never feel the love and support from him that Parson gave. "I don't want my children to grow up in a dysfunctional home. Our marriage was a mistake, and I'll have to live with it, but our children don't." Her heart acknowledged with an exhale. The truth hurt, but it was time she faced facts and moved on.

*Is divorce what you really want?*

"Does it really matter?" Keturah closed her eyes to shut out the voice, trying to reason with her.

*Does my will matter?*

A catch in her voice was the only sound she made. As always, the whispers of God still took her breath away. In the past eight months, she'd given voice to every negative emotion inside her mind, from her hurt pride to her rejected inner child, yet God's voice remained silent until today. Dangling between the border of relief and mounting tension from her next contraction, within that small space of time, she had an encounter with her first love. "Yes, Lord, your will matters to me!" she acknowledged as tears and sweat flowed down her face.

*"Then call your husband!"*

Shutting her eyes, to the voice of her protest, Keturah, to the surprise of every one, pushed herself up on the birthing table until she was in a seated position and turned towards Parson. "Give me your cell, I need to make a phone call." She stuck out her hand towards Parson.

"You want my what? Honey, no, you're about to give birth," he said gently, trying to push her back down.

"But I've got to call Abraham. P-Please Parson, I have to let him know he's about to be...to be—" A grimace crossed her face as she did her best to steady herself for the contraction bearing down on her.

"Keturah, I need you to concentrate," the doctor ordered.

"Yes, darling, we'll call him after the delivery. Just concentrate on your breathing," Parson whispered while swabbing the perspiration off her forehead.

"No, you don't understand. I promised God...I..." Reaching for his hand, she squeezed it hard as she tried to muddle through the pain while talking.

"Keturah, you need to relax. The babies are in position, but you've got to focus," her doctor coached.

"Keturah, if Abraham were here, he'd want you to concentrate on bringing these babies into the world," Parson reasoned.

"But he's about to become a father *again,* and he doesn't know it." She let out a strained sob. "I've been so angry with him, but God has been dealing with me to call and tell him, but I…" She swallowed hard, trying to control her breathing. "I want him to at least know. I owe him at least that," she begged.

"All right, if it means that much to you, I'll call him myself okay…just lay back, relax, and breathe and I'll step out and make the call… okay?"

"O-okay…thank you, Parson." She panted heavily, relieved that Parson was going to lift a tremendous burden off her shoulders.

Parson gave the back of her hand a quick kiss and squeeze. Nodding to the doctor, he moved back and left the room.

***

Outside the delivery room, Parson gave a quick jab of his fist to the hospital's oatmeal-colored walls. "Always Abraham…Always!" Parson growled while rubbing his tender knuckles. "He is an undeserving jerk. God, how is it that you could continue to bless a man like him?" He accused, rapidly pacing back and forth just outside the delivery room doors.

"Carlton… what in the world is the matter… is Keturah okay?"

He jerked around in time to see Tippany Jaymes, Keturah's sister, hurrying towards him, concern whittled in her features. As she came up to him, he placed both hands on her shoulders and smiled.

"Everything is fine, Tippy. Don't worry. The doctor says the babies are in position and will be here at any minute."

"Whew! You scared me for a moment." Tippany placed her hand over her heart and steadied her breathing, then just as quick, her face broke into a grin. "We're about to become an aunt and uncle." She grabbed his hand and pranced around like a schoolgirl.

Her enthusiasm was too much to ignore. He smiled at her as she twisted and turned causing her wavy mahogany-colored hair to flow freely around her oval-shaped face. It was amazing to him how she and Keturah looked so much alike but were in many ways, so different. Shaking his head to bring his thoughts back to the present, he motioned with his thumb towards the delivery room doors. "Well soon-to-be Auntie, you better get in there. I think Keturah could use your moral support right about now."

"Oh yeah... right!" She giggled as she turned and marched towards the room then made an abrupt stop. Raising a well-sculpted eyebrow towards him, she inquired, "Aren't you coming?"

"Yeah, I'll be in after I make this call," he said, punching in the numbers forcefully.

"So, she roped you into calling him," Tippy smirked as she made invisible quotation marks to emphasize her words.

"No, I volunteered." He glared at the phone, his thumb still hovering over the send button. He took a quick glance at Tippany.

"Oh...I see," Tippany said, then pursed her red colored lips, cutting off all other comments.

"No, you don't. Keturah was fit to be tied in there. She couldn't concentrate or focus on her breathing. I told her I'd call him just to keep her calm." Tilting his head to the side, he asked, "How'd you know I was calling Abraham anyway?"

Playing with the buttons on the sleeve of her shirt, Tippany, not looking directly at him, spoke. "Do you know what you look like every single time Keturah mentions Abraham's name?"

"No!"

"Pretty much the same way you're looking right now...ticked off....and I love you for it," she said, moving closer to him and planting a small kiss on his bearded chin. "You have been an amazing friend to me...and Keturah." She gave a timid smile.

"Well, thanks for that." He ran his hand through his brown curls. "If only those divorce papers had come as we expected, things would be so much easier. "

"Umm...maybe and maybe not," Tippany said.

"Of course, it would Tippany. If they were already divorced instead of her worrying about Abraham's precious feelings, she could move on with her life. But no, here we are on one of the greatest days of her life, and she's trying to chase down that self-absorbed..." Parson let his words trail off to keep from messing up his Christian witness.

"Carlton, Keturah is angry, hurt, even confused, but also in love with her husband." Tippany shrugged her shoulders. "I know it makes little sense, but deep down, she still loves Abraham."

"Are you sure about that?" He raised a questioning brow.

"Sure, about what?"

"Sure, about her still being in love with Abraham?" Parson asked, still looking at his nemesis' phone number.

"Maybe forty percent sure." She shrugged her shoulders as she twirled a strand of her hair in thought. "But I'm one hundred and one percent sure calling Abraham is the right thing to do. He deserves to know he's becoming a father again."

The muscle in Parson's jawline twitched as he tried tempering his anger. "He deserves to be beaten to a pulp the way he's treated Keturah during their entire marriage. As her sister Tippy, I, for the life of me, can't understand how you can defend his behavior?" He turned away from her, shaking his head. "What is this sick hold Abraham has over the two of you that commands such loyalty?"

Tippany put her hands on her hips and gave him a challenging glare. "First off, he doesn't have some sick hold over me. I'm very much aware of his faults and flaws, and yours. It's called being human. But unlike you, I'm willing to give him the benefit of the doubt," she contested. "After all, it hasn't been that long since he lost his first wife, so cut him some slack. Besides, what's the old saying…the heart wants what the heart wants."

"Yeah…if you say so."

"Well, I do, and so do you. After all, the only reason you're struggling with all of this is because of your own feelings for Keturah." She smirked.

"Well…I…" he faltered.

"Don't worry, your secret is safe with me." She held up her hand to his lips, stopping him before he could finish.

"How long have you known?" he asked, unable to make eye contact.

"Since Keturah and I got back from Paris."

"Do you think she knows?"

"Yeah, why else would she be struggling like this?" Tippany shook her head as if he were daft. "Do you know how easy it would be for her to keep her mouth shut and allow you to be the man of her dreams?"

"If I was a different man, I'd encourage her to do just that." He exhaled with bowed head. God knew he wanted to push the issues with Keturah and would've, but it pricked his conscience. *'Thou shall not covet!'* The bible verse would ring in his ears for hours. Although his feeling ran deep for Keturah, he'd never dishonor God that way. A hand on his shoulder caused him to turn towards her.

"Carlton, Keturah knows the type of man you are, that's why she trusts you. She knows you'll always put God first." Turning towards the delivery room door, she squeezed his shoulder. "Look, we have two babies waiting to be born and a mother who needs us both, so make your call," she said firmly before walking towards the delivery room as a loud wail from Keturah greeted both their ears. "Hurry!" She commanded, disappearing through the doors.

His thumb tapped the send button. He would honor Keturah's request. By the fifth ring, his mood grew darker. He was about to hang up when a woman's nasal voice said hello.

"Yes, I need to speak to Mr. Taylor... please?" He spoke in an even tone.

"Who's calling?"

"Carlton Parson. I'm calling on behalf of his wife, Keturah. Now is he there or not?" His tone mirrored his impatience.

"Unfortunately, Mr. Taylor is out of town. Would you like to leave a message?"

"This is extremely important. I need to get in touch with him now concerning his wife."

"I'm sorry, he is unavailable. If you leave a message?" she said in a no-nonsense tone.

A million things came to mind as he tried to keep his anger in check. "No message." He hung up on her. Maybe he should have told Abraham's secretary the circumstances of the call. Perhaps it would have provoked her to call her boss. "You did what she asked…besides if Abraham is too blind to see what a good thing he has, his loss will be my gain." Parson powered down his cell phone.

"PARSON!!!" Keturah shrieked.

Jerking his head towards the delivery room doors, he shoved his cell in his pocket and made a beeline towards the door. He'd repent later for his attitude towards her deadbeat husband, but right now, Keturah needed him.

# *Chapter Two*

The breeze off the shoreline of Barcelona was refreshing on the hot midsummer afternoon, ideal for an outside reception. It had rained for two weeks straight in the city so in celebration, the sky exiled all clouds so everything could bask in the sun's glorious rays…everything but Abraham's mood.   Plastering a fake smile on his face he greeted business associates and the other wedding guests, making small talk of how the wedding planner out did themselves in pulling off the well-orchestrated event.  He smiled and posed, stood where he was instructed by the photographer but the entire time his mind was far from the joyous festivities going on around him.

Watching his son take pictures while holding his wife close for a minute, made his mind drift across the ocean to where his own young wife resided. "Ahh, Keturah!" Just saying her name caused a yearning for her gentle caress. Her beauty caused his heart to ache even further. He discovered that he was more miserable without her than he'd ever thought, and now with this mayhem on his hands, his desire for her presence overwhelmed him.

*"Come unto me all who are weak and heavy laden, and I will give you rest."*

The scripture was like a balm to his bruised soul.  He didn't even know where to start. His burden had been so heavy. "Father, why?" Abraham whispered the simple question while wrestling with his wayward emotions. "I did what I felt was right back when Ishmael was a youth. I sent him out of my home and now…" Abraham sighed, uncertain if his forever Friend had somehow neglected to take care of Ishmael like he vowed.

*"If we are faithless, God remains faithful, for He cannot disown himself."*

The scripture rose within his spirit. Like a lifeline to a drowning man, Abraham clung, to the promise, yet his mind was still restless. "I should have done better by him." Abraham, desiring his reconnection with Ishmael to go well, had never thought to witness to him about the love of God. He didn't realize he needed to. For the first time, he had both of his boys working by his side. He cherished it and didn't wish to make waves that could disrupt the bonding he was experiencing with them. Perhaps his euphoric state caused his guard to slip. He never imagined that Ishmael's uncle Hassin Zarah's Islamic beliefs would have such a profound impact. "I should have known... or been told," Abraham muttered in indignation.

"Abraham, is something the matter?"

He spun around just as Hagan Zarah's came to his side. She looked radiant in her royal blue pant suit, with gold lace emborded on her sheer outer jacket. Her brilliant hazel colored eyes were dim with concern at his brooding demeanor. Seeing her caused the muscles in his jaw to clench. For the last two hours, he wanted to unleash his fury on someone, and Hagan's proximity made her the unknowing target. "I need a word with you," he growled, moving in front of her and away from the crowd partaking in the festivity. Once out of earshot, he drew a deep cleansing breath to purge himself of the offense in his soul.

"Abraham, what in heaven's name is the matter with you?" Hagan frowned at him as she came near, flipping her long black mane off her shoulder.

"What's the matter? Are you serious?" He gave Hagan a peeved looked. "Our son, in the midst of his wedding, converts to Islam, and you're asking me what's the matter?"

"Oh, that." Hagan made a face waving off Abraham's concern with her hand, then snagged two glass of champagne from the waiter who passed by them. "Here darling, let's share our own private toast, to our son and his new bride." She held out a glass to him but he refused it.

"Is that all you're going to say about this matter?"

"Ishmael is a grown man, competent enough in making his own choices. What are we expected to do, lock him in his room? Now listen Abraham, stop all this brooding and enjoy yourself. Your son has just gotten married for goodness sake."

"I should have known this kind of thing would mean nothing to you. It's not like you concerned yourself with the type of Christian example you placed in front of him all these years. No wonder he switched to your husband's faith," he accused.

"How dare you Abraham!" Hagan's lips quivered. "My Jamal, God rest his soul, and his family was anything but perfect, yet they were there for Ishmael. Jamal was the only father figure Ishmael had because you drove us out." Hagan poked a hard finger in Abraham's tux clad chest. "You are his father and the Christian. If Ishmael remaining in your faith meant so much, then where in heaven's name were you?"

Her words stung like a fresh slap to the face and simply reaffirmed what he believed. He failed his son. Sobered by her indictment with a hand to her shoulder, he ushered her towards a more secluded area on the terrace. Once at the edge of the balcony, he acquiesced. "Hagan I'm sorry, I didn't mean to blame you."

"No, that's precisely what you meant to do, blame me. When are you ever going to accept responsibility for what you and your precious Sarah have done to our son? How long will you turn a blind eye to the repercussions of your abandonment? How your constant exclusion of him and his feelings have resulted in his rejection of your so-called loving God." Her eyes blazed. "If anybody is at fault here, it's you and Sarah."

Abraham rubbed his jaw with his hand, while the words failure like a neon light flashed in the blackness of his mind. Hagan had given her best. She had to be the mother and father before her husband Jamal came along. The guilt gnawed at him like an excruciating toothache. Had he been there for Ishmael, he wouldn't have been a witness to what just transpired. "I would have come if you'd have called." He gave a feeble appeal as an attempted to alleviate some of his culpability.

"Call you?" With hands-on-hips, she squinted up at him, a tinge of red rising to her cheeks. "I have something to show you Abraham, stay right here," Hagan commanded, storming off in the opposite direction from where they entered.

Something about her precipitous departure made his heart tense. The intensity in her eyes and the energy in her stride made him wish he had held his temper in check.

"Dad, is something the matter?"

Startled, Abraham turned to see Ishmael coming towards him. His son's face wore a frown as he watched his mother's retreating form. "Ahh... no, nothing's wrong, Ishmael." Abraham lied, while gathering his thoughts to assure his son and himself all was well. Looking again at his son's profile, his heart swelled with pride, as he was reminded of his and Sarah's wedding day so many years ago.

"What?!" Ishmael asked.

"Nothing really. Just funny how history repeats itself. I wasn't' that much older than you, when I first got married. I'm blessed to be able to witness you and Marlana begin your journey together.

"I believe we'll do fine granted Marlana understands her role as my wife and plays it well." Ishmael spoke casually clasping his hands behind his back as he walked to an opening in the balcony. Looking like a royal prince in his custom-made gold colored Sherwani wedding suit he gazed down over his guest and in the process caught the eye of his bride...he extended her a chivalrous bow.

This was their day, Abraham would spare him the, *'marriage is work speech'*. Besides, this generation was more into appearances and throwing a memorable party for their guests than wanting sound marital advice. *"If you wanted him to learn your Christian principles, you should have been here to teach him."* Hagan's words rose up in his mind. Sighing inwardly, he knew he owed her a huge apology. Her remarks were accurate. If he wanted Ishmael to embrace Christian beliefs and principles, he should've guided him. He blew out a breath and tried to prepare the words in his mind to say when Ishmael spoke up.

"So… did you enjoy the ceremony?" Ishmael raised an eyebrow at his father as he waited for his reply.

To be critical of his decision would be a mistake, but to pretend as if he was okay with everything that had transpired would be a lie. Not wanting a skirmish in front of the wedding guests, he remained on impartial ground. "I treasured watching you marry the woman you love. I'm proud of you, son," he replied, clapping his hand on Ishmael's shoulder.

"Thanks, Dad, although I expected you'd have issues with me converting to Islam. Although I don't know why I never intended to accept Christianity," Ishmael said, a hint of pretension in his tone as he strolled away from his dad looking down at one female party guest in particular and raised a glass to her. "Christianity is ineffective, in my opinion," he suggested gripping his glass of alcohol in his hand. His tone was casual yet challenging.

Abraham perceived that Ishmael was trying to provoke him to debate the issue, but he wouldn't be baited. Stepping forward to where his son stood, he looked down at the woman who caught his son's attention. It was his office administrator Kayla Meyers. He gave her a curt nod. With a timid smile she nodded back and quickly exited out of their view. Noting the exchange, Abraham frowned, then spoke.

"Son, many individuals I meet don't share my beliefs. It's a part of life, and I respect it. My faith teaches me and has made me who I am. Perfect, not by a long shot, but the God I serve is perfect, and he makes up the difference." He then turned toward Ishmael and held his son's gaze. "And for the record, son...trust me when I say, there is nothing feeble or passive about my God."

The grin on Ishmael's face faded as he bent his head, unable to match his father's fierce glare.

"Listen, Mael, you're a man now with a wife and one day a family. I haven't been there for you when you needed me, but I hope you'll permit me to be here now." Abraham extended his hand.

Ishmael stared at him for a long moment, then broke out in an earnest smile and accepted the hand extended. "I'd like that, Dad... I'd like it a lot."

***

"How dare Abraham insinuate that it's my fault Ishmael has changed faiths!" Hagan fumed, shaking with indignation as she jerked open the door to her loft. "Besides what type of benevolent God would have us put out in the street?" She stalked towards her wardrobe doors and flung them open. Like a thief in search of quick cash, Hagan, pushed pass the expensive purses and shoes, throwing clothes with price tags still on them to the floor all in searched of the infamous tote. There it was snuggled in between her old fur coats; immediately her blood burned in rage.
Pulling down the offending box swelling with Abraham's betrayal, she lifted the lid off smelling the stale aroma of paper and ink. Years of unopen and unanswered letters scrawled in her son's handwriting at various stages of his life. She shook her head with the hurtful memories. What started out as a shoebox turned into a clear rectangular tote that showed decades of Abraham's negligence. Her heart constricted, looking at the heaps of unopened letters.

"My baby's childhood is all right here in this crate, and you missed it, Abe… you missed all of it." Eyes blurring, she swiped at the rogue tears that refused containment. Now grown, Ishmael didn't recall half of the stuff he sent to his father, but she remembered every bit. 'Return to sender!' was on every letter scrawled in Sarah's writing. "You witch!" she yelled, digging her hands into the letters crumpling as many as possible. Abraham never wrote his son, not once in all those years they'd been apart, making the injury even worse. The only thing she received from them was a monthly child support check. As generous as it was, it could never make up for Abraham not being around. It crushed Ishmael… and devastated her. "How can you forget about your child?" she voiced.

"Oh, Hagan… honey, when are you going to let all this suffering go!" A feminine voice spoke up.

Startled, Hagan jumped and twisted to see her sister-in-law Darma Zarah standing in the doorway. The woman of middle eastern descent looked striking in her ruby red Anarkali pantsuit she had designed for the wedding. Hagan turned aside and fisted her hand. "I can't, and I won't. He wronged us, Darma. He and his precious Sarah wronged us."

"Ishmael is an outstanding businessman, has adopted the Islamic way, and even as we speak, celebrates a new life with his bride. All praises to Allah," Darma said, raising her hands towards heaven, then strolled over to the bed, clasping her sister-in-law's hands that were clenching the letters. "Let this heartache go and live. Enjoy your life, discover love… travel, pick up a hobby."

"It's not that simple, Dar. I wish I could just move on… forget the past, but I can't." Hagan hissed, feeling her yearning for revenge burning within her soul. "These letters are the evidence setting the record straight once and for all. Abraham will have no choice but to confront Sarah's treachery."

"What has happened has happened. Burn these letters. Be free of this dreadful misery Hagan." Darma stood beside her, took hold of her by both shoulders, and compelled her to comply.

"No, I can't!" Hagan hugged her sister-in-law, letting out her grievance in tears. "I realize I should, but I just can't." She broke down in violent sobs. "Abraham needs to see the squandered time robbed from his first-born. Sarah was never wrong in his eyes, but here is the proof."

"Okay, even if Sarah did all those things, she was a wife with a remarkable husband and did what she considered best to preserve her marriage." Darma shook her head as she wandered towards the windows to watch the festivities. "The other woman never realizes how hard it is to keep a good man happy."

"What!?" Hagan's mouth hung open in disbelief of what Darma had just stated.

"Men become restless and like to challenge themselves with something new. Abraham saw you as inexperienced and innocent and took advantage of the situation. A brief affair occurred, culminating in a baby, it happens." Darma consoled, shrugging her shoulders.

Hagan grabbed Darma's arm and turned the woman around. "What are you saying? That's not how it happened between Abraham and me, not at all." Hagan shook her head, unable to comprehend how Darma could reach such a conclusion. It was not some unplanned fling she and Abraham had.

"Your father explained everything to Jamal and the rest of our family when we all met for your engagement party. He informed us how your situation with Abraham came about. Jamal understood and readily took you and Ishmael in," Darma stated. "Jamal, my Hassin, and Abraham are men who are very much alike with capturing the affections of a youthful woman." Darma bowed her head, looking somewhat disconcerted but then waved her hand as if swatting at a pesky fly. "It is harmless and means nothing."

"You're saying my father told you Abraham and I had a simple affair?" Hagan gave Darma a grim look, unable to accept what she was hearing.

"You were young, and Abraham was an affluent businessman who, in an hour of weakness, turned to you. Maybe it was just a fling while Sarah was away. Who knows why men do what they do? You, like many other women, assumed there was more to your time together than there actually was. Like I said... it happens."

"You don't understand," Hagan said with a bent head as selective memories of that time rose to the surface of her mind. It wasn't a foolish affair on her part. It was the only way to ensure her family's passageway to America. Looking at a picture of her parents on the mantle of her fireplace her mind took her back.

*Her homeland of Egypt continued to suffer from political controversy. She wanted her family to be away from the fighting, so when Sarah offered to bring her entire family over in exchange for her being Sarah's surrogate, she had agreed. However, surrogacy didn't work, so Sarah upped the ante by suggesting she and Abraham have a child the natural way. It was a bizarre request, and she wanted to tell her no, but how could she refuse? Her family's lives were at stake. To be together with her family was well worth devoting a few nights with Abraham so they could be parents. So, Sarah stayed out of the country for a few months, while she and Abraham tried to conceive. During those months, Abraham was gentle with her and spoke in a tender and kind way in the wee hours of the night. She became accustomed to his caresses, the laughter, and the pillow talk that they shared. He seemed to care for her. No man had ever cared for her with such sweetness and revere. Then she learned she was pregnant and suddenly everything changed. Abraham was to come back from a business trip that day, and she was thrilled to tell him the glorious news, but instead of Abraham, Sarah greeted her. It was apparent she already was aware she had conceived. From that time on, Sarah's cold, impersonal tone towards her never changed.*

*Once she returned to the states living with Sarah was a nightmare. She was cruel and abusive. Abraham never showed her cruelty, but still, he was as much at fault as Sarah. So glad for his wife's return, he never interfered in how Sarah treated her. He also spent no alone time with her.*

As a stray tear slipped from her lashes, she tried wiping the hurtful memories from yesteryear out of her mind. Walking away from her sister-in-law, she went back to her bed. Bending over, she picked up the box. She planned on throwing it at his feet or, better yet, dump it over his head. She hadn't decided yet.

"This is silliness, Hagan!" Darma asserted. "So, what if this is proof of how cruel Sarah had been? What makes you think he doesn't know? Sarah is dead, and Abraham has moved on. It's time that you do the same."

Hagan shook her head no. The acknowledgment was only the first of many things this man owed her and their son. As the letters on the bed stared back at her speaking of the years of hurt Abraham and Sarah caused, Hagan moved passed Darma into her bathroom and grabbed a clear plastic trash bag from under the sink determined to make Abraham see how his neglect had played a role in why Ishmael had done what he did today. "Darma, you think Sarah was a drama queen, well honey, you have seen nothing yet," she vowed, filling the bag with the letters then turned ready to exit the room with the bag in tow, when she happened to glance out her window and saw on the balcony below, Abraham embracing Ishmael. Her mouth hung open as the bag slipped from her hand. Her feet felt like lead as she watched them. Tears formed in her eyes as she stepped back to find herself right in Darma's arms.

"I realize I might not understand all the nuances of your relationship with the Taylors," Darma spoke in hushed tones. "But one thing I believe is clear, today is not about your history with Abraham but your son's future with his new bride. So maybe for today, allow your son his happiness."

Hagan bowed her head in submission. No matter how she wanted, Abraham to suffer, it would never be at the expense of her son. So, for now, she would heed Darma's advice and wait.

# Chapter Three

*Two months later…*

"Keturah, I'm so sorry to back out on you at the last minute. But mother saddled me down with some unexpected business to attend to," Tippany complained.

"Don't worry about it, Tippy. I appreciate the offer, but I understand." Keturah said while heading for her bedroom with her laundry basket in tow. It was Wednesday, that meant mid-week house cleaning. "Gretta, you'd be proud," she thought, looking at the picture of the two of them hang on her wall. She smiled at it then turned around looking satisfied at the other furnishings that nicely decorated her bedroom. The sandstone and burnt orange colors gave the room a sense of warmth and calm. The only other room she loved being in more was the nursery. Although most of her things were still in boxes at least those two rooms were complete. *"Child…any time you move always get your bedroom together first, that way you will always have a place to lay your tired head."* As the memory of her grandmother's words of wisdom played in her head, she grinned.

"Keturah are you listening to me?"

Her sister's voice snapped her out of her daydream. "Yeah…Tippy I heard you. Your mom saddled you down with some last-minute work, so you can't come by…no biggie. Like I said, I understand."

"Well, I don't." She sucked her teeth in the receiver. "Why are we responsible for cleaning up Ishmael's mess? Abraham should cut all ties with him and his momma and stay stateside where he belongs." She then gasped in the phone. "Keturah, I'm so sorry. I didn't mean to go on and on about them to you."

"Tippany, really, it's okay. I'm not crying or waiting on pins and needles for him to call. He's made his choice, and there is no changing it."

"Do you want it to change?"

"Honestly, I'm not sure," Keturah said, looking out her bedroom window, while putting away the last bit of laundry she had to do for the week.

"I don't mean to bring you down sis. I'm just frustrated, and you must be too. After being cooped up in the townhouse for six weeks. You must be going stir crazy," she sighed. "Oh...by the way, did you speak with Carlton by any chance?" Tippany charged ahead, not giving a moment's break in the conversation. "I called to tell him my plans had changed, but it went straight to his voicemail."

"Don't worry, if he calls, I'll tell him you won't be able to make it." Keturah rolled her eyes at how her sister insisted on calling Parson by his first name.

"Oh, okay. I just hate for him to make a trip up there for nothing."

Keturah scrunched her face up at the phone. Her sister was mighty concerned about Parson's welfare as of late. As to why, well, Keturah had her on theory about that but wouldn't give voice to it. They all had grown closer over the summer. Parson had even said Tippany was like the kid sister he never had. Keturah smirked, wondering what Tippy would think knowing Parson only saw her as his kid sister.

"Keturah...are you still there?"

"I'm here, and don't worry about Parson. He's been itching to spend some time with the twins anyway, so it won't be a total loss if he still stops by.

"I think he's more inclined to spend time with the twins' mother if you ask me?"

"Well, no one is asking you." Keturah rebutted as she did a closer inspection of her face in the mirror. She pouted at the dark circles she saw under her eyes thanks to Kamara's crying spell last night.

"Whatever!" Tippany chuckled. "What's up with you two anyway? Are you guys going steady?"

"Of course not." Keturah adamantly denied.

"Okay, okay…no need to be so sensitive about it. If you're not dating, then what do you call what you two are doing?" Tippany pressed.

"Well, we call it being friends, and until my divorce is final, that's all we are to each other."

"Well, I think you're crazy if you ask me."

"Well, no one asked you. But that never stopped you from putting your two cents in." Keturah huffed moving from her window and sat on her bed.

"Exactly. All I'm saying is if I had a man like Carlton coming after me, divorced or not, I'd go after him."

"Tippy, that's not the Christian way," Keturah admonished.

"Ughhhh!!! You and those Christian principles of yours."

"They are not my principles, they're God's. His word teaches Christians how to please Him, not ourselves and I'm committed to live by His rules."

"And if *His* plan for your life is to stay with your husband, then what?" she countered.

"I'll have to cross that bridge when I come to it." Her heart betrayed her as it fluttered to life in the hope of being reunited with her husband. It was a foolish dream. "For now, I'm moving forward, trying to get my life back on track."

"And the two men in your life? What are you going to do with them?"

"I only have one man in my life, Abel, and I plan on giving him all the love, affection, and cuddling he and Kamara can stand." Keturah chuckled, imagining her sister's eyes rolling.

"But after you cuddle them, who is going to cuddle you, Keturah? I know you're putting on this noble act now. But when your stitches come out, and the feeling down in your nether parts comes back alive, you're going to want more than Abel's bubbly smile for comfort."

"Well, I guess that's another bridge I'll have to cross." She ebbed at her bottom lip, ready to end this line of questioning.

"With all these bridges you're crossing, I sure hope you get to your destination," Tippany mocked.

"Tippy, I realize you don't see things in the same way I do. But honoring God is important to me."

"But Carlton adores you, and I think his feelings should be considered in this equation," Tippany pointed out.

"Tippy, let's drop it," Keturah spoke with finality in her tone. There was nothing she could do about Parson's feelings, and she dare not act on hers. She didn't want to talk about her need to be held or comforted because, as things stood, the only man who had those rights was halfway around the world taking care of his other family.

"No Keturah, you're going to have to deal with this sometime. Now Parson, he is a good man, and if you are going to keep him in limbo until you figure this thing out with Abraham, maybe the best thing for you to do is let him go, so he can move on with his life."

Keturah remained quiet. She would have given serious thought to what Tippany was saying if she was certain her reasons were pure. Tippany's feelings for Parson were evident to everyone but Parson. In a heartbeat, she was sure Tippany would peruse Parson. The only thing holding her back was the fact they were sisters, making him off-limits...well, at least it should as far as the sister code went.

*"If she does peruse him, what will you do? Is it right to hold on to Parson's affection when you still are in love with your husband?"*

The soft whisper of the Holy Spirit caused her pulse to quicken. She could deceive others, even herself, but never the Lord. Was she doing Parson and herself a disservice allowing her heart to be divided between him and Abraham? "Tippany's right. I'm going to have to deal with this sometime," she spoke to herself as a voice in her ear began intruding on her thoughts.

"Keturah, where is your mind today? Did you hear me?"

"I'm sorry Tippy, I do have a lot of things going on, so if I'm a little scattered today I apologize. What did you say?" Keturah inquired.

"I asked about Abraham, has he called you yet? I'm sure he has to know about the twins. I was sure he'd have phoned by now?"

"Well, he hasn't," Keturah spoke with a harsh tone. This was her greatest struggle when trying to forgive Abraham. Ignoring her was one thing, but neglecting their children—that, was unforgivable. Daily she had to go to God and release all the pent-up anger and resentment she felt towards him. Every time she looked at her beautiful children, she thought, *you're missing this!* and anger would swell up in her soul.

"This is so not like him," Tippany muttered her disbelief in the phone. "I found out that the day you were in labor was the same day as Ishmael's wedding from what Becca told me."

"Did she say anything to Abraham about me?" Keturah's heartbeat quickened as she asked.

"No, they flew in for the wedding ceremony but abruptly came home the same day. Apparently, Ishmael's conversion to Islam threw everyone off. Abraham asked them to come back home so they could do damage control. All she said was Abraham looked heartbroken."

"I see. Well, did she say if he looked okay? I mean, is he well?"

"I knew you still cared for him," Tippy retorted.

"Care, of course, I care!" Keturah fisted her hand to keep her temper from erupting. "I've always cared. He's the father of my children, but that's apparently not enough to keep us together, or him in the country."

"Well, it's a start. I think if Abraham saw the children, he'd—"

"Abraham doesn't have time for Abel and Kamara because he's too busy changing the diapers of his adult children," Keturah interjected her tone full of spite.

"Be fair, Keturah. It was a shock that Ishmael converted, and it definitely hasn't been a cakewalk at Canaan since that announcement. I can't tell you how many questions the staff has had to filter because of the ties Canaan Enterprises has with Taylor International."

"Be fair? Excuse me, how am I not being fair?" Keturah jerked her body off the bed and paced back and forth.

Remembering the twins were still sleeping, she lowered her voice. "I've called several times, and not once have I been able to get through to him. His assistant keeps stonewalling me, and I'm tired of it."

"Tourie, things are not always black and white when it comes to Abraham. He has been under a huge strain with the announcement of Ishmael's conversion to Islam. It took everyone by surprise, and it is making a lot of our stakeholders nervous. We all have had to do a lot of damage control and calming others' concerns. So, calling you back probably..."

"Is not a priority...trust me, I am very much aware of that fact." She crossed her arm in front of her.

"No...that's not what I was going to say," Tippany defended. "It probably slipped his mind."

"Oh, so that makes me feel a lot better." Keturah stopped herself knowing her anger was beginning to shift towards her sister. She realized Tippany meant well, but her constant dismissal of Abraham's insensitive behavior towards her was getting on her nerves. If anything, she should be defending her. They were, after all, sisters.

"Keturah, I'm just saying maybe you should wait and hear Abe's side of the story before you go severing ties."

"For me to hear his side, I have to hear from him," Keturah charged. "Parson ran into the same interference the day he called when I was in labor. So maybe the birth of our son and daughter got in the way of his eldest's nuptials—fine, I'll give him the benefit of the doubt, but it's been six weeks Tippy. What excuse can he possibly give for not calling me, or checking on his children?

"Well, honestly Keturah, you should have called him before the actual delivery. Besides, I know Abraham, and he would have blown a gasket if he'd have heard this information from anyone but you. That could have really made things awkward for Carlton."

"Hold up, Tippany, are you saying this is my fault?" Keturah fumed. "You must have forgotten how I made every attempt to see him before we left for Paris last year. It was my plan to tell him about the babies, the way I felt, everything. Yet his secretary let me sit in his office for almost an hour before I was told he already left for the airport."

"Keturah listen, calm down. I'm not blaming you. I'm just saying…Oh, I don't know what I'm saying. I just feel you're at a very vulnerable place in your life right now, and you shouldn't make any rash decision you might end up regretting."

A doorbell rang, effectively interrupting their conversation of which Keturah was glad for. "Hey, Tippy, someone is here, so I'm going to let you go," she interjected as she walked from her bedroom to answer the front door.

"Hey, don't hang up yet. Let me know who's there, so I know you're okay," Tippany admonished.

"Oh… probably just the mailman. You know it's that time of day. Talk with you later. Bye." Keturah hung up, knowing Tippany was only trying to find out if it was Parson. Taking a quick check of her appearance in the mirror by the door, she took a deep breath and opened the door, greeting her visitor with a welcoming smile. "Hey, Parson."

"Hey yourself." He smiled back. "Don't you look all bright and sunny." He walked in the door, giving her a one arm hug.

"Thank you, you don't look so bad yourself. Playing hooky from work must agree with you." She smiled, noting his carefree look in his worn jeans and green fitted crew neck shirt that showed off his biceps. Keturah sighed inwardly. It had been a long time since arms like that had held her. Hearing him clear his throat made her jump a little.

"Everything is alright, isn't it?" His face scrunched up with a look of concern as he looked at the phone in her hand.

"Oh…yes, everything's fine." She waved off his concern. "I was just on the phone with Tippany, who by the way, is not going to be able to come, so I guess lunch at the Mocha House is off."

"You can't call off a lunch date when your date is standing in your doorway Keturah."

"Oh…I see. Well, what would my date suggest that we do?" She crossed her arms and looked at him with a flirtatious smile.

*"Do friends normally flirt with each other?"* A quiet whisper inquired.

She knew she probably needed to take heed to the voice, but after the conversation she just had with her sister coupled with this week marking her first-year wedding anniversary minus her husband, attention was something she wanted lots of.

*"He probably didn't even remember it."* A dark thought screamed in her ears caused her mood to sour.

"Keturah…honey, are you sure you're alright"?

Swallowing hard to keep the lump of emotions in her throat down, she looked up at Parson and gave him a fake smile. "Sure…I'm fine." She waved a hand in front of her face to rid her of unwelcome thoughts. It was then she noticed the picnic basket in his right hand. "What's this!" She motioned towards the basket while moving aside to allow him full entrance in her home.

"Something always seems to come up whenever we try to go out together, so I took some initiative and decided to bring lunch." He smiled, walking straight to the kitchen, sitting the basket on her kitchen island. "I like what you've done in here Tourie." Parson complimented looking at the furnishings. "You're really getting things organized I see."

"Well thank you for noticing." She smiled. "But I can't take all the credit, you and Tippany were a huge help in getting my things situated and then setting up the nursery. I can't tell you how much it meant having everything done when I brought the twins home."

"Hey that was all Tippy's creative genius, I was just the hired muscle." He smiled at her for a long time looking as if he wanted to say more but instead said, "So, where do you want to have it?"

"Have it?"

He pointed to the basket. "Lunch."

It was a warm day, even though it was mid-September. Taking a quick look at the blue sky, "Why don't we go out on the deck?" She smiled.

"Excellent choice. Lead the way, my lady," he said, moving out of her way so she could pass by him. "You do smell wonderful, by the way. What are you wearing?"

"Lavender-scented baby lotion." She chuckled at his surprised look. "I didn't have a chance to run to the store to pick up some personal items, so I improvised."

"Well darling, it works on you."

"I'm glad you think so. I guess I'll wear it more often." Again, she flirted. Staring at him a little longer than she should, she bowed her head and cleared her throat. "How about you set things up out here, and I'll grab the baby monitor and something to drink and be right back," she said while moving towards the hallway. Once out of sight, she steadied herself on the hallway wall, placing a hand on her chest and the other on her head. "Just breathe, Keturah." What was she doing?

*"Shamelessly flirting with Parson is what you're doing."*

Continuing to hold her head as she pushed off the wall and slowly walked back to the nursery, she felt conviction pressing in on her every step of the way. Didn't she just tell Tippany that she wasn't free to engage in a relationship with anyone until she was legally divorced? Yet before her words could grow cold, she was already crossing the line. "It's just harmless flirting." She pouted.

*"Is it? But more importantly, does your behavior honor God?"*

She huffed a deep sigh. She knew how Parson felt about her, but as Tippany had stated earlier, was it right to keep him in limbo when she knew her heart wasn't healed? "God, this is so unfair. Abraham is off doing as he pleases. Why should I have to honor my vows when he's not?" She fussed, walking over to the cribs to check on her babies. "Sound asleep as usual." She sighed, gently touching Kamara's soft crown. Checking the receiver, she picked up the other monitor and crept back out of the room.

*"Your vows were to your husband and me; honor them."*

It was pointless to continue to try to win an argument with God. Sulking, she looked up at herself in her hallway mirror and smiled despite herself. Turning from side to side, she gave herself a playful wink. "It's nice to have someone notice me for a change." She smirked at herself. She was slimming down in all the right places. Well, she might not be able to date Parson or flirt with him, but she was determined to enjoy his company for the afternoon. Walking away from the hall, she headed for the kitchen when her phone rang.

"Hey, you want me to grab that?" Parson hollered from the kitchen.

"Nah... let it go to voicemail." She waved a dismissive hand as she reached the kitchen smiling at him wearing her apron. "Don't you look domestic."

Holding his hands away from his side, he flashed her his one-hundred-watt smile. "What can I say? I am a man of many talents."

*"No, flirting!"* she admonished herself. "Well, I guess you—" She abruptly ended her sentence as she quickly spun around to give her complete attention to the message being left.

"This is Sari Jaymes' office, you must return this call immediately."

In an instant, her happy world tilted. Not sure why, Keturah hurried to the phone and picked up the receiver before the woman hung up. "I'm here, this is Keturah Taylor," she answered, giving a nervous look back at Parson, who was mouthing the words *what does she want?* Shrugging her shoulders, she turned from his frowning face.

"Please hold while I place Ms. Jaymes on the line?

"Yes, I'll hold," Keturah stated, turning as she felt Parson's presence nearing her.

"Why in the world would she be calling you?" Parson questioned.

"I have no clue."

"Well, put her on speakerphone so I can hear too."

Nodding in the affirmative Keturah did so, then whispered, "I pray nothing happened to Tippy." Inwardly she was praying nothing happened to Abraham. It seemed like forever before the woman came back on the phone to connect her to her estranged stepmother.

"Mrs. Taylor?"

"Yes, I'm still here."

"Ms. Jaymes is on the line."

"Okay, thank—"

"Well, I'm surprised that you still answer to your married name." Sari Jaymes' brash tone rang in her ear.

Keturah looked at Parson, who rolled his eyes, almost causing her to giggle, but she managed to hold her peace. She didn't even know why she bothered picking up the phone in the first place. "Ms. Jaymes, is there a reason for your call?"

"Of course, there's a reason for my call. I wouldn't call you just to shoot the breeze." She sounded affronted.

"Ms. Jaymes, I'm in the middle of my lunch, and I…"

"Keturah, my time is money, and I have way more business to do than you. But I'm making an effort, so the least you could do is try as well."

Keturah blocked Parson's hand as he tried to grab the phone. Shaking her head, no, she moved out of his reach. "Ms. Jaymes, I—"

"I would prefer you call me Mother Jaymes from now on. After all, you are my stepdaughter, and I think we need to display an appropriate image to the public."

"What?!"

"Look, your brother Malcom is running for governor. Therefore, our family has to be above reproach. That means all of us. This, in part, is why I am calling. I know you've been seen with that Parson fella, and as a married woman, it is inappropriate, and I insist you stop it at once."

"What?!... Wait… how do you know who I'm out with?" Keturah's face twisted into a scowl as she dodged Parson's hand.

"Little girl, I make it my business to know what is happening in my family. Now the second reason I'm calling is for an update on how the children are progressing and for you to discuss with my secretary when we can schedule a family photo-op."

Keturah stood frozen in disbelief at what she was hearing. Sari Jaymes hadn't asked about her welfare during her entire pregnancy, she hadn't called to see about her or the twins even after they were born, but now she wants an update so she could look good for the press. "Ms. Jaymes, I don't think that's a good idea."

"What do you mean, it's not a good idea?" she challenged. "You should be thankful that I'm even considering it."

Looking at Parson, Keturah was baffled beyond words as to how to respond.

Moving forward, Carlton reached for the phone, and this time Keturah didn't object. "Ms. Jaymes, this is Carlton Parson, and I think you have a lot of gall to request anything from—"

"Keturah!" Sari yelled in the receiver. "Do you mean to tell me you have that Neanderthal in your house? What in heaven's name are you thinking? If the tabloids get wind of this, it will reflect badly on Malcom's campaign. Not to mention what will your husband think when he returns home next week?"

"Ms. Jaymes, first off, my name is Carlton Parson. Secondly, Keturah is a grown woman and can have whoever she chooses to have in her home and doesn't need your permission."

"Boy, are you still there? I am clearly not talking to you, so mind your business and put Keturah back on this line at once."

"Ms. Jaymes, I'm still here, I have you on speaker," Keturah spoke up.

"What!? Keturah, you mean to tell me that boy has been listening in on our entire conversation! Lord, this generation is so uncouth. Look, I have another appointment to attend to, but I'll be calling back this evening, and I expect him to be gone so we can have a private discussion regarding family matters, and I mean private."

A sharp click in Keturah's ear signaled Sari had hung up.

"That woman has more nerves than a bull and just about the same amount of tact." Parson slammed the receiver back in its carrier and ran a frustrated hand through his hair.

Keturah listened to Parson continue his rant, but her mind was far off hovering around the Mediterranean Sea where Abraham was. *"He's going to return."* She wrapped her arms tightly around her stomach and sat quietly on the couch. For the longest time, she kept the thought of his return at the furthest place in her mind. In theory, she believed the longer he was gone, the stronger she became. "I guess it's time to put this theory to the test," she reasoned within.

"Keturah, are you listening to me?" Parson was looking down at her with concern.

"I'm sorry, what did you say?"

"The divorce papers, have you heard anything back from your attorney?"

"I didn't contact an attorney about the divorce yet."

"What?! Keturah, why in the world not?"

"Parson, I didn't think I had to. Abraham had left me the papers some time ago. He already signed the papers. After I signed them and gave them to his secretary, I assumed it was a done deal."

"But you didn't follow through to make sure things were filed or finalized." His voice rose in irritation.

Feeling her own frustration rise, she stood up, placing her hands on her hips. "Look, it's not like I file for divorce every day, Parson. I was too busy trying to get over a broken heart while my body was being twisted out of shape carrying his babies. So, excuse me if I didn't have all of my I's dotted or my T's crossed." She walked away from him but then felt a hand on her shoulder, restraining her.

"Tourie, I'm sorry." He let out a frustrated sigh. "I was hoping for closure. So, you could move on with your life, so we..." He turned away and rubbed his jaw hard.

She held on to the hand he placed on her shoulder. "Parson, I want closure, too, so..."

A small whimper followed by loud squawking came from the nursery room, causing them both to look in that direction.

"How about we adjourn this conversation for another time and have lunch with the twins?" Parson offered.

Keturah chewed on her lip momentarily then turned, smiling at him. "Sounds like a plan." She squeezed his fingers before letting them go. "You get lunch, I'll get them." She pointed, heading in the direction of the nursery.

# Chapter Four

*Later that afternoon…*

"My son and I are looking forward to having Davenport's support this coming election year John," Sari Jaymes stated as she dabbed her lip with her linen napkin. It wasn't a request as much as a statement. She needed him to confirm. Placing a piece of her smoked salmon in her mouth, Sari then looked up poised and ready to receive his endorsement.

"Well… about that, Ms. Jaymes… I've got to be honest, there are a few concerns many of our stakeholders and I have about backing Malcom."

The fish tasted as dry as his words. With a wine glass in hand, she tilted it towards her plum colored lips and sipped, letting the sweet liquid coast down her throat. She lowered the tall glass, looked at her lunch companion, and spoke. "John, we go way back, so I'll ignore that comment after all the time the Taylor Jaymes family has bailed you and your constituents out. Not to mention the numerous discrepancies Canaan Enterprises has absorbed on your behalf because, as we promised when you join our family, you become a part of it."

"Ms. Jaymes, Sari, I don't dispute your words, and please understand, as a corporation, we would not be where we are today without the influence and provision of Canaan Enterprises. But you have to admit, the last couple of months, the quality of care received under Isaac's leadership hasn't been great. The abrupt change in management has a few people on edge, myself included." John mopped his brow with his handkerchief feeling the intensity of Sari's heated gaze. "But that's not all. The new merger with Mosaic International has thrown us all. Many of us prided ourselves in sharing many of the same values and principles with Abraham. But now with Ishmael becoming Muslim and Abraham not addressing it… I'm concerned."

"John, Taylor International and Canaan Enterprise are two separate entities. And your right, Isaac is young and lacks the experience of his father, but the variations have been minor. Every firm goes through transitions, and Canaan is not exempt. But the bottom line is family sticks together through thick and thin. When Davenport is in a fight, Canaan is still the team you want as an ally. I need to know that I can count on you John...can we?" Sari's no-nonsense tone came through loud and clear as she saw the man agree with an affirmative nod. "Good, now how is that adorable grandbaby of yours?"

An hour later, lunch was over, and Sari was back in the car headed towards the office. Momentarily she allowed the car's soft leather headrest to support her weary head. "If my family only knew the lengths, I go through to keep our social standing in this town." She fussed then allowing her well-manicured hand to cradle her forehead. "Oh, good lord, I almost forgot..." she said hitting the intercom button on the door panel to speak with the driver. "Carlos make sure you go by Bishop Robertson's church. I need to speak with him today."

"Yes ma'am. Do you still need me to take you to the museum for the benefit at two thirty?

"Oh, lord I forgot all about that." Sighing heavily, she rescinded her last directive. "Take me to the museum now, I'll have to find another day to speak with the bishop".

"Yes, ma'am...right away."

"What a day." She fumed still peeved with how things went at lunch with Davenport. Of course, she got what she wanted, but still, her mind was ill at ease. She shouldn't have had to play hardball, not as long as Canaan and the Davenports had been in business together. "Just goes to show you how much of a toll Abraham's shenanigans are taking on the company. This has to stop before we're all in the poor house." Sari sighed, resigned to what her next move had to be. Rummaging through her Louis Vuitton Alma bag, she found her iPhone and hit three on the speed dial then waited. In a few moments, her cousin's familiar tenor answered.

"Well, I didn't expect to hear from you this late in the day. What's happening?" Avery Jaymes asked.

"It's not late here; it's only lunchtime, and to answer your question, what's happening is chaos, sheer and utter chaos. It's time for the commander in chief to come home," Sari said forgoing any greeting.

"Sari, things can't be that bad. Besides, why is it so important for Abe to return?"

"What do you mean, why? Why do you think! He's needed here. He has to stop playing nursemaid to his eldest and take care of his responsibilities stateside." Sari ordered as she picked up her compact and refreshed her lip stick, then smoothed out her dark forest green suit.

"Sari, what are you talking about? Isaac is in charge. You were the one who encouraged Abraham that he was ready for a more visual position in the company."

It pained Sari to have to admit this, but if it got her what she wanted, so be it. "Isaac's not as ready as I hoped to take over the executive chair. He requires more of his father's guidance, which is why Abraham has to come home."

"Sari, Abraham is aware of what is happening at Canaan. He is keeping abreast of our shareholders' concerns and Canaan holdings."

"That's not the only issue needing his attention," Sari retorted. "This new partnership with Taylor International is wreaking havoc at Canaan. Our business partners are beginning to believe Abraham is supporting other religions."

"Not true, Sari. If there is one thing Abraham is solid on is his allegiance to Christ."

"But didn't he just support his son's conversion to the Islamic faith?"

"It was a surprise to us all. I'm sure Isaac informed you Abraham was not pleased."

"Yet he's still there," Sari accused.

"Yes, he is."

Sari rolled her eyes. Although Avery was a Jaymes, he was always more loyal to Abraham than to his own family. "Listen, Avery, our family's reputation is on the line."

"What are you talking about?"

"Just today I had to strong-arm John Davenport into supporting Malcom for this approaching election," she spat out.

"Ahh...finally, the cat is out of the bag." Avery gave a sarcastic chuckle. "You want Abraham to return to endorse Malcom for governor. You'd do anything to get him into the governor's mansion."

"He deserves it," Sari fired back. "He's worked hard to help the citizens of North Carolina, and it's time they acknowledged it by electing him as their governor."

"I'd suggest you not use that line for his campaign slogan." Avery said with sarcasm.

"Look, Avery, my son is going to win this election, and I will not have anyone keep him out of it, including Abraham."

"How can Abraham, who is halfway around the world, possibly impact Malcom's run for governor?"

She pinched the bridge of her nose. She was getting nowhere with this Neanderthal, time for a new approach. "Did you get a package I sent to you a week ago?"

"No, I haven't."

"Well when you do, I trust you'll handle things on your end. After all, you're still a Jaymes, little though it might mean to you."

"Yeah, Sari, I'm family when it's convenient. Otherwise, I'm an outcast to the Jaymes' clan," Avery snapped.

"Ugh…Avery, this is ancient history. What's it going to take for you to get over it and move on?"

"When are you going to get over the fact that Keturah's mother was not the reason for your failed marriage with Kedron?" Avery insinuated.

The silence on the other end of the line lasted a long time.

"Sari, are you still there?" Avery inquired.

"Listen to me, Avery, and hear me good." Her voice quivered with contempt. "I don't need you to lecture me about a moral-less hussy like Pamela Birch. To be honest, I'd think you'd have grown tired of defending gutter trash."

"Don't even go there with me, Sari," Avery growled.

"No, let's travel down this road a bit Avery." Sari sat back poised in her seat as her leverage in the conversation spiked. "You should thank Sarah and me for intervening before you made a complete fool of yourself following after Hagan like some love-sick puppy. She was a leech, just like Pamela."

"No… not true Sari, it was you who brought Pamela to your husband's bed, and Sarah brought Hagan to Abraham's. Stop playing the victim. Both of you were responsible for the problems in your household because you didn't trust God, and the repercussion have affected everyone.

"Avery, you're right," she said unexpectedly.

"Oh…okay, well, it took over thirty years, but at least you're finally admitting the truth."

"Yes, Sarah and I invited those trollops into our homes to help rid us of the shame of being barren. Was it a mistake? Perhaps. Now it's your turn to be truthful, Avery. You're not mad that Sarah brought Hagan to Abraham. You're angry that Hagan gladly went, and even after all these years, she still prefers Abraham over you," she said in a nasty tone right before hanging up.

*** 

Avery sighed, listening to the dial tone in his ear. Sari always went for the jugular. Reaching in his suit pocket, he pulled out the roll of Tums for his upset stomach, only wishing he had a pill to take for his troubled thoughts.

*If you need a pill, try the gospel.*

He chuckled as Abraham's little phrase rose in his mind. He shrugged it off. "Maybe later," he thought. "Wonder what the bible says about a meddlesome seventy-five-year-old cousin who never learned how to keep her big mouth shut or mind her own business?" Taking a deep breath, he sighed. "Awe well," as he looked at the mounds of paperwork on his desk. Shoving the pile away from him caused some of the files to spill onto the floor. He could sum it all up to being tired and keeping late hours. Abraham had been out with Hagan, Ishmael, and Marlana every night last week. It seemed they had developed a new bond after Ishmael's wedding, leaving Avery as always to pick up the slack.

*"You're angry because, after all this time, she still prefers Abraham to you."* Sari's words continued to linger over him like a bad odor. What bothered him more was the accuracy of her comment. Although his feelings for Hagan were a thing of the past, it irked him to no end that she still looked at him as if he were nothing but Abraham's errand boy. He threw his glasses onto the desk. He was the CFO of Canaan Enterprise and Abraham's friend. The years had been good to him in Abraham's employment. He had status, wealth, and business prowess.

*What profits a man to gain this whole world but lose his soul?* A soft voice spoke.

His eyes widened as he spun around, expecting to see Abraham, but he was alone in his office. His heartbeat quickened as a bead of sweat rolled down his forehead. Swiping a hand down his moist face, he looked around the room again. He had been hearing God's voice calling to him for months, encouraging him to come closer, but he held back. He had one more goal to achieve; then he'd focus more on his relationship with God.

*Come to me all who are weak and heavy laden, and I will give you rest. Take my yoke on you and learn of me.*

His fingers massaged his closed eye sockets as he tried ridding himself of the emotion threatening to seep through. It wasn't only Abraham that God had been a friend to. Avery knew, without a doubt, how good the Lord had been to him. He had been father and mother to him when his natural family turned their back on him. Avery sighed, being the black sheep of his family still bothered him after all this time. Because of it, he felt a need to prove himself to everyone. So, this was not just about Hagan. It went deeper. "I don't have time for this." He spoke out loud, shaking his head to clear his wayward thoughts. "Something must be wrong if Sari is calling the troops back home," Avery thought, scratching his chin. A brief knock on his door pulled his head out of his thoughts. "Come in." He looked up to see his assistant peeking her head in.

"Mr. Jaymes, I was hoping for a moment of your..." Lorena Patton stopped mid-sentence as she frowned looking at the files scattered all over the floor.

"A slight accident Lorena, nothing to worry about. What can I do for you?"

"Well, to be honest, Mr. Jaymes, I have some concerns regarding Kayla Meyers."

Avery maintained his composure. Lorena was bright, and a good administrator. She was thorough and paid attention to detail which is why when she wasn't chosen as Abraham's administrative assistant, he requested her to become his. But still, she was miffed about being overlooked. Everyone in the office was aware of the feuding between the two assistants. But today, he just didn't want to hear it right now. "Lorena look, I know you two don't see eye to eye, I get it but for the sake of—"

"Mr. Jaymes, please hear me out." She raised a hand, halting his words. "I haven't said a word to her. However, I've been noticing things missing."

That caught his attention. "What type of things?"

"Well, a couple of weeks ago, I was down in the mailroom. I heard her tell the young man who delivers our mail that everything should go to her first and then she would distribute it to us. She told him it was to help eliminate the junk mail, but I had my suspicions. I always felt she was just plain nosy."

"Lorena, part of Kayla's duties would be to manage incoming correspondence," he said, sitting back, relaxed.

"Agreed, however, I believe these would not fall in the category of junk mail," she said, handing him several large and small envelopes.

Reaching out to receive them, his face contorted into a scowl, seeing one envelope marked private to him but already opened. The other one was from Keturah with no postmark on it at all. "Did you open these?" he questioned.

"No, I didn't. I found them like that in the shred bin last Friday. I had thrown an important paper away and rushed down to the shredder room to retrieve it. Since Kayla was off for the week, I used her key and opened the bin, and these were on top opened." Lorena pointed to the envelopes.

"The last person who signed the log was Kayla, so I figured either she placed them there or is aware of who did."

Looking through the envelopes, he even found one marked private sent to him by Sari Jaymes a week ago. "Did you go through any of this?" he questioned.

"I did, Mr. Jaymes," she said, looking down at her hands. "People believe I'm jealous of Kayla because she was given the administrative position over me, and I'll admit, I have been. So, I didn't want to come to you without solid proof of my concerns. At first, I thought most of it was junk mail, but when I saw pictures and even legal documents, that's when I became concerned. I gathered everything I could and planned to come back the next day to see if I could retrieve any more, but it had already been destroyed."

"Lorena, thank you for bringing this to my attention. I will handle things from here."

"Can I at least help you pick up these files off the floor?" she offered as she moved towards the pile bending over to retrieve them.

"No, that is my mess. I'll handle it. Thanks."

Giving her boss a quick nod, she exited his office.

"So, the mouse finally gets caught," Avery said. He had known for several months Hagan and Kayla were in cahoots but had no idea to what extent. Something about their interaction with each other made him suspicious from day one. It was only when people kept stating they couldn't reach him, he had security put a trace on all his calls and Abraham's. It was then he discovered Abraham's calls were routed to her phone. What she didn't know was every call had been recorded. But rerouting his and Abraham's mail was a new low even for Hagan.

Looking at the large envelope from Keturah, he poured the documents out on his desk. She had written a letter stating she had signed the annulment.

*"Abraham, here's your ring and jewelry as well as my signature on the divorce papers. Congratulations, you're a free man. There are a few things I'd like to discuss with you, so if you can fit it in your schedule, please call me."* He muttered, curious as to the few things she wanted to discuss. It was odd. He knew Abraham received the annulment papers but had said little about it. Avery searched again for the wedding ring, and jewelry Keturah said she enclosed, but it was nowhere to be found. "Kayla, not only are you a liar but a thief as well," he said, throwing the letter down. If he could throw her butt out, he would. Picking up his phone, he hit the intercom button. "Lorena, I'm going to be out of the office for a little while."

"What about your meeting with Mr. Taylor, should I reschedule it?"

"Oh, I forgot about that. No, don't reschedule, but inform him I'll be running late."

"Okay, anything else?"

"No, thank you, Lorena."

"Sure, thing, boss." She disconnected.

He sighed, shaking his head. He needed to contact Brad from security in the Canaan office to see what they could do about tightening security, seeing some of his staff couldn't be trusted. He was about to make the call when he eyed the envelope from Sari. With a sigh, he dumped the contents on his desk. "Pictures?" He frowned, remembering Lorena did say she saw some photos. He pulled out the first one, and his mind exploded, looking at one of the images showing a very pregnant Keturah. Flipping it over to see if there was any date on it, he then began to rummage through the rest of them until one photo, in particular, caught his eye. Squinting as he focused on the young blue eyes that look so much like his friends. The photo revealed the cutest little girl. He shuffled through the other photos until he saw another baby picture that was just as cute, but he had brown curly hair and gray eyes distinctive to the Jaymes' clan.

"Kedron, you'd be so proud." He choked back a low moan. The final picture he gazed at was more sobering and made his blood boil. He knew if that's how he felt how much more would Abraham feel to see his son and daughter in the arms of Carlton Parson. "Sari's right, it's time for our fearless leader to go home."

# *Chapter Five*

There was a hint of crimson in the sky indicating that evening was gradually approaching. It was going to be a peaceful night… but for Abraham, more like a vexing one. He sighed, looking out in the multicolored sky, wondering what his spouse was doing halfway around the world.

*Call her!*

He didn't dare. What would he say? Hey Keturah, sorry I haven't been in contact with you for six months, but I was caught up in work? Yeah, that was a stretch. The business merger had long been settled. Now he was just hovering around trying to help wherever he was needed.

*"More like hiding!"*

"Okay… hiding out." He declared to the placid sky. Yes, he was hiding from his twenty-seven-year-old wife, not certain how to deal with all of their issues. He fingered his wedding ring, remembering her tender touch as she put the platinum band on his finger, how those same fingers so timidly stroked his when they made love. It was those remembrances that kept him from filing the annulment papers she'd signed. He had the means to put his life back on course, but something held him back.

*"Why haven't' you told her the truth that you love her?"*

"With everything I've done, how can I now?" Abraham pondered, his backhand rubbing the stubble on his chin. "I've been gone for over six months and haven't called her once. How can I show up out of the blue saying I love you, let's make it work? It sounds crazy even in my own ears." He chuckled, shaking his head. "My beautiful Keturah. I've wronged you, but now it's time I do right by you and let you go." He sighed with the realization of what he was about to do. Reaching for his cell phone to call his attorney, his hand paused as he heard an abrupt tap on his door.

Putting the phone down, he stood up, allowing his gaze to drift to the door. "Come in!"

"Hey Abe," Avery said, stepping into the room.

"Hey Ave, we missed you at the meeting this afternoon. Anything wrong?" he asked, already feeling something off with his friend's countenance.

He shrugged a shoulder as he handed the file he was carrying in his hand to Abraham. "Sorry about that, but I was away for a good reason. You need to read this then advise me on how you want these things dealt with."

Abraham stared at the file, reluctant to even touch it. Somehow, he perceived the contents were about to change his world. He groaned heavily. "Is it that bad?" he asked, taking hold of it. "Why don't you spare me the burden and deal with whatever it is," he proposed.

Avery remained subdued as he kept his stance. Only a scowl contorted his facial features.

"It must be bad," Abraham huffed. Turning from his friend, he went back to the window and opened the folder. He proceeded to pull out a picture of a very pregnant Keturah walking downtown with Tippy and Carlton. His hands began to quiver as his throat tightened. He never dreamed Keturah was the type of woman who would have an affair while they were still married no matter how bad the circumstances were. He hated to admit it, but her betrayal hurt. He had no alternative now but to divorce her. "So, she's pregnant." His horse voice faltered as he crossed over to his desk, tossing the file on it.

"She was pregnant!" Avery walked over to him, redirecting his gaze to the other photographs.

Abraham jerked his head towards Avery. "What do you mean she *was* pregnant?" he questioned.

"Keep reading. She had twins Abraham two months ago. The same day of Ishmael's wedding."

Rooting through the pictures, Abraham came to a dead stop. He didn't have to continue calculating in his head. One glimpse at the beautiful baby girl that looked so much like Keturah with her raven-colored curly hair and long eyelashes, but had his striking blue eyes. Instinctively he knew he was the father. "They're mine," he declared with a murmur as he rifled through the photos and found his daughter's twin. A beautiful boy with chocolate brown hair, deep dimples much like his own, but like his mother, had the gray eye coloring distinctive to the Jaymes clan. He continued shuffling through the picture until he found a photo that nearly sent him over the edge. Parson holding his little girl as if he was the proud father. "They're mine!" he said through gritted teeth with his head bowed, trying to contain the onslaught of emotions tossing him back and forth like a small boat trapped in a colossal tidal wave. He crumpled the picture with his hand wishing it was the man's throat.

"What would you like me to do?" Avery already had his cell phone out his finger positioned over the dial pad.

"I want to be in the air headed for home as soon as possible. I don't care what you have to do, make it happen," he growled.

"Right away," Avery said, already punching in a number on his cell phone. He was about to make his exit to begin preparing when Abraham stopped him.

"Avery… who else knows about this?" he asked, unable to mask his anger.

Avery remained mute.

"Avery!" Abraham snapped.

"Abraham, you need to read the entire briefing," Avery responded, giving his employer and friend a somber-look before lowering his gaze and walking out of his office.

Snatching the remaining papers off his desk, he skimmed the document. As one name, in particular, stood out to him, the air escaped his lungs. He flopped in his chair and threw the papers back on his desk. With a mirthless laugh, he shook his head. "Abe, when will you ever learn?"

\*\*\*

"Abraham, you don't stand a prayer of a chance getting away from me tonight." Hagan purred, looking at herself in the bathroom mirror in the executive washroom, admiring how desirable she looked. She had already informed Ishmael that she and his father would have their own plans this evening, which included an unscheduled stop at her loft where she planned on seducing the man's socks off... not to mention a couple of other clothing items. She grinned at her own cleverness. They had called a truce after Ishmael's wedding. They had even gone out several times since the newlyweds had been back from their honeymoon. She had played nice with Abraham, coddled his male ego from time to time. All to fattening him up for the slaughter. She didn't care what she had to do to win him to her side. As long as he ended up beside her the end justified the means.

Giving herself one more glance over in the mirror, she winked at herself. Although in her late forties, she could still give a younger woman a good run for their money. She turned to the side admiring how her tight-fitting navy-blue suit was hugging in all the right places. Smirking at herself she placed an extra coat of gloss over her burgundy dipped lips and puckered blowing herself a kiss. "Go get him tigress." Opening the bathroom door, she stalked towards her prey's office. She wanted to make a dramatic entrance but seeing that Kayla wasn't at her desk she chose to walk right in. Spotting him talking to one of his other secretaries, she leaned in, waiting for him to acknowledge her presence. When he continued talking to his secretary, she cleared her throat. His secretary raised her head and acknowledged her with a nod, but Abraham continued giving directives.

"Ms. Cobbs, have Avery come to my office shortly and make certain you postpone the rest of my appointments until the coming week after I get settled back home," he ordered, moving from his desk to one of his filing cabinets.

"Back home?" Hagan spoke up, a frown gracing her freshly contoured face. "Are we going somewhere, dearest?" Hagan asked, draping herself on the armrest of one of his winged back chairs.

"No, *we* aren't; however, I'm leaving for home," Abraham said, reaching for some files off his desk, never glancing up or acknowledging Hagan's presence.

"Home? Darling for over the last six months, this has been home." She chuckled, coming to where he stood and placing her palm on his bicep. "What's the hurry?" she purred, drawing closer.

"I need to see my children," he said, moving away from Hagan's grasp. He opened another file cabinet, and started removing selected files from it.

"Why is something wrong with Isaac? He looked perfectly fine to me at Ishmael's wedding."

"Isaac is fine."

"Oh, then is it the financial troubles Canaan has experienced under his leadership?" she questioned, walking to where he stood. His crossed looked made her hasten with a conciliatory response. "I don't mean to be harsh, Abe, but maybe he's not ready to take on such an enormous responsibility as Ishmael has already demonstrated he can handle," Hagan spoke, pretending to pluck something off of his sleeve.

Abraham drew a breath before speaking. "Isaac's fine, and Canaan will be fine under his leadership."

"Then why are you going back?"

"As I said, I need to see my children… they need me."

"Abraham, I don't understand," Hagan said, genuinely baffled.

"You don't." Abraham turned around and leveled her with a harsh gaze.

"No, I don't." Hagan walked a bit away from him, swallowing hard as she placed a shaky hand to her collarbone.

"So, you weren't cognizant that my wife was pregnant and that two months ago she had twins." Abraham's voice was dead calm.

"You mean Keturah?"

"Who else would I mean, Hagan?" His voice lifted in irritation.

"Oh…um well, I-I suppose I might have heard some news of that nature. But I don't pay mind to everything I hear." Hagan shrugged her shoulder. "But if it is genuine, are you positive the babies are yours?"

He scowled at her for a minute before declaring. "It's confirmed," he said, tossing the file folder on his desk then planted both hands on top of his head as he paused in front of his office window.

"What's confirmed, the fact she had twins or if they are yours?" Hagan acquiesced when he twisted around and leveled her with a second menacing stare. "All I'm suggesting is she's probably hoping for some money out of you, and this is her way of getting it." Hagan, now having regained her composure waved his comment off as if it were nothing. "Now, about dinner tonight, I was thinking you, me, and the kids could go to this charming little restaurant I know."

"Hagan."

"They make the best Crème Brule I've ever eaten."

"Hagan!"

"What!?"

"I'm leaving for the States within the hour."

"Whatever for?" She seized him by the arm again, twisting him around to face her.

"Haven't you listened to a word I've said? My wife had twins two months ago!"

"Yes, I heard you, and like I said, so what!" Hagan crossed her arms over her chest, tossing her head to the side to allow her long sweeping black mane to fall behind her back. "She was likely screwing around on you the entire time you were married. What's that guy's name she's so cozy with... Parson. For all, you know the babies are his."

"They're mine, Hagan." His voice raised.

"Abraham, sometimes you can be so naïve, which, I might add, is why you're in this mess." Hagan placed her hands on her hips and glared at Abraham hotly, seeing her plans going down the drain. "She's been playing you for a fool all along with the ole innocent school girl act, and you bought into it hook line and sinker. Getting pregnant was her aim from the start," Hagan said, straightening her suit jacket. "Besides, why now? You've been out of the country for at least six months. Seems rather convenient if you ask me. Just be rid of her." Hagan huffed as she sat down in his executive chair, crossing her legs.

Abraham walked away from the window to his office desk and shuffled some papers around. Finding what he was searching for, he set it aside and stored the remaining documents inside his briefcase. Afterward, he collected his suit jacket, walked towards Hagan, and bent over until they were face to face. "You're right about one thing Hagan. I can be gullible to a fault when it comes to the women in my life," he said dispassionately holding out a paper to her.

Looking at him confused, she took the paper looking at the picture of a very pregnant Keturah. Reading the damning caption at the bottom of the photo, her face reddened as she recognized her own handwriting.

"Abraham, please let me explain this..." Hagan's tone became remorseful. "I... I realize how this must look to you, but believe me, Kayla and I were trying to protect you..." she said in a small feeble voice unable to maintain his gaze.

Abraham lifted his hand to stop her explanation. "There's really nothing you can say, Hagan. You and my administrative assistant have been spying on my wife for months, and neither of you thought it prudent to say one blessed word to me," he said through gritted teeth. "I'll deal with Kayla for her role in all this later. As for you, I'm both stunned and disappointed. I hoped we were beyond this. But hiding something like this from me is inexcusable, Hagan," Abraham retorted.

"Okay fine, Abraham," Hagan fired back. "Yes, I knew she was pregnant, and I didn't tell you because, like I said, it doesn't mean the babies are yours." She angrily stood her ground.

"But what it does mean is that I've abandoned her, which casts a bad light on my character and the reputation of Canaan." He stood up and walked towards the door.

"Abraham, wait!" Hagan jumped out of her seat, rushing after him in a panic. "What about Ishmael? Are you going to leave without saying goodbye to your son?" she appealed. "How can you be so perturbed about abandoning Keturah but show no concern about abandoning Ishmael all over again?" Standing in front of him, she grasped both his arms. "The time you've invested with Mael on this project these last few months means the world to him. He's happier than I've seen him in a long time. I realize you're furious at me, and you're right I shouldn't have kept this knowledge from you, but I beg you, please don't take it out on our son."

Abraham gave a heavy sigh. "I've enjoyed this time, too," he conceded. "Mael has a wonderful business sense. I've actually been impressed watching him these last couple of months. He's done an outstanding job building his corporation." Abraham straightened and looked down at her, his mind already decided. "But you're wrong, he doesn't need me. He's his own man now. But these babies..." He pointed to the photographs she still held. "They will need their father. I won't allow another one of my children to grow up without me again." With that conveyed, he opened the door and walked straight into Avery. "Avery, we need to speak in your office." Abraham side-stepped him walking towards the elevators, never giving a backward glance at Hagan.

"Abraham, think of what this will do to our son." Hagan pleaded to Abraham's departing form.

He never responded, only stepped in when the elevator doors opened and in an instant was gone.

Hagan was close to tears when she sensed eyes on her. Turning to the side, she peered into the frigid glare of Avery. "What are you looking at?" She scoffed at him feeling she needed to discharge some of her displeasure at someone, and Avery was as good a person as any.

He said nothing, just continued to stare for a few more minutes.

"Well!?" she roared. "Are you going to just stand there with that stupid smirk on your face, or have you got something to say?"

He let out a melodramatic sigh. "Sorry I don't have time for you. I have a jet to catch, and you have dinner plans to cancel." He continued to sneer, walking out the door.

Cutting in front of him, she pointed a well-manicured finger at him and with a mouth full of spite she spoke. "You think you're something with your little title of CFO and your fancy suits. But I remember when you were nothing more than Abraham's errand boy and believe me nothing has really changed. For all you think you are Avery, you will still never be a Taylor."

She hissed like a wounded alley cat, slashing at him with her menacing words.

"Well then, I guess I'm in good company Hagan." He said without flinching. "Because from where things stand, you'll never be a Taylor either." He then side-stepped her and walked out the door.

Embarrassed and angry, Hagan looked around and realized she had nowhere to go but home. Snatching her handbag off the chair, she walked with head held high out of Abraham's office. She had lost this battle, but she was determined to win the war.

***

"Abel Nathan and Kamara Gretchen Birch... Birch!" Abraham took his fist and jabbed the interior of his car door. "I want their names changed to Taylor. My children will have my last name," he said gruffly as his heart swelled with pride beaming in wonderment of the tiny newborns in the photograph. He felt humbled by the fact that God was so gracious in allowing him a second chance at fatherhood. "Kamara!" He grinned at the little girl who had his lips and blue eyes. "I'm going to have to beat the boys off with a stick." He laughed with amusement then his mood darkened. He and Sarah had always wanted a daughter, but it wasn't meant to be.

*Forgetting those things which are behind me, I reach for the things that are before me!*

He quoted the scripture in his mind. He couldn't change the past. But he didn't have to let history repeat itself. He would be a father to these children and wouldn't let anything stop him... including their mother. He prayed Keturah would get on board with his plans. She loved him, well at least one time she declared she did. He only prayed it wasn't too late to set things right between them. "Avery, call the estate and have Consuela get in touch with her daughter Carmen. We are going to need her as the twins' nanny. Also, make sure Consuela gets the house and staff ready for our arrival. Oh, and I'll need to stop at the office and pick up a few things. I'll be working out of the smaller office in Gastonia for a while."

"Um, Abraham, there are a couple things you need to be aware of." Avery hesitated as Abraham held up his hand to take an incoming call.

"Um-hum… yeah, you heard me. They are my children, and I want their last names changed to Taylor. Do whatever you need to do, Burgess, but I want their birth certificates to state Taylor. What? That's of no consequence. Look, I don't care what we signed, we are not separating and we're definitely not getting divorced. Just get it done and call me back when it's worked out." He hung up, then looked at Avery. "How long will it take for us to get to Keturah's place? Matter of fact you should call a moving company, not that she has much anyway. Once we have my family, we'll go to the mansion and get settled."

"She's not at her apartment anymore," Avery stated.

"Fine, we'll pick her up at Gretta's house." He then frowned. "Why she'd go back to that neighborhood is beyond me. I will not have our children growing up in that type of environment," he grumbled.

"She's not there either," Avery said.

"Then where in the blue blazes is she?" Abraham barked, his patience wearing thin.

"Abraham, a lot has happened in your wife's life since you've been away," Avery said as he began to reveal the details to a very stunned Abraham.

# Chapter Six

It was a beautiful evening for dinner and a play. Keturah hadn't been out on a bona fide date in so long she felt downright giddy. Wanting to look her very best she went out and picked up a few items which included a modest strapless emerald green dress that showed off her slimming figure. Her unruly curls refused to tame themselves even with a flat iron so instead of going to the salon for hours she did a quick wash and set that left deep waves flowing in her shiny mane. Her reward for her effort was Parson's awed expression. All night he kept sneaking peeks at her and smiling. He told her she looked beautiful so many times she was sure her dark complexion redden with every compliment.

"You're going to spoil me with all these compliments you know."

"Then prepare to be spoiled...beautiful!"

Parson was so thoughtful and attentive, something her husband never truly was. To ensure they had an uninterrupted evening Parson secured two babysitters for the entire afternoon and evening. They had a wonderful time that afternoon at the play and now dinner reservations at the Pedemonte. The exclusive restaurant was situated right on Lake Norman, just outside of Charlotte. It was a perfect evening as the full moon seemed to be perfectly situated right outside their window.

"Did you have something to do with that gorgeous moon situated outside of our window Mr. Parson?" She asked pushing her hair out of her face so she could get an eye full of her handsome dinner companion. Lord knew he looked yummy in his charcoal grey suit and black shirt and tie.

"Like I told you, for tonight, I was calling in all types of favors to make this day...no let me back up...to make this *date* happen for us." He said looking intently at her.

She bowed her head and smiled. Parson had never been clearer about this evening. They weren't out for a grab and go meal or a work through lunch meal. He called it what it was a date. He wasn't ashamed of being seen in public with her, and intentionally wanted her to feel special. "Well you definitely out did yourself. Parson, this place is fabulous…thank you for bringing me here."

"It's my pleasure Tourie," he said, raising his glass to hers. "Here's to what I hope will be many more outings together." He clinked his glass to hers.

She bowed her head and blushed a little. "I think I like the sound of that." She looked at him, feeling a small spark in her heart. He made her feel beyond special. Parson had stepped up to the plate in a major way, which had surprised her and caused her heart to warm towards him. He had been a tower of strength ever since the twins were born. Abel and Kamara adored him. They always giggled and laughed when he came around. He didn't mind being right in the thick of things either by changing dirty diapers and washing bottles, even helping out around her new condo getting everything in its place. It was hard for a woman not to start feeling something for a man like that.

*What about Abraham…*

A dull ache filled her heart. She used to get all fluttery whenever she heard his name, now she felt nothing but anger, regret, and sorrow for the love that never got a chance to bloom and for her children who would never know the love of their father. It was an experience she hoped she and her children would never have in common. A hand touching hers brought her thoughts back to the present.

"Tourie, what's wrong?" Parson's brows furrowed with concern.

She just shrugged a shoulder, not saying anything.

"It's Abraham, isn't it?" he pressed.

"Yes…and no." She shook her head, allowing her curls to fall around her face and onto her shoulders. "I'm thinking about the twins, new business opportunities…you." She gave him a shy smile. "You have been such an amazing friend. I can't imagine where I'd be if you hadn't been there for us these past few months. I feel like I can never repay you for being…just being you," she confessed, a little surprised at her own honesty.

"I have a confession to make, as well. I was hoping that you were beginning to see me as more than just a friend." His gaze never left hers as he continued. "I have been so stupid, Keturah. For years I've been looking for the right woman, never realizing she was right under my nose the entire time. Believe it or not, I have Abraham to thank for this discovery." He then chuckled at the scrunched-up face she made at him. "Don't roll your eyes. I'm dead serious. If it weren't for him not being here for you, I never would have had this chance of getting to know you like this." His tone dropped as he rubbed a thumb over the back of her hand. "I guess what I'm trying to say is I care and not just as a friend. I would like us to be more to each other, and when the time is right, I'd like us to be a family."

Had she heard him, right? Parson was ready to be serious…and not just serious but family serious. This was all too much…too soon. Parson's kindness and attentiveness were definitely appealing, but deep down, her heart was still broken. As much as she hated admitting it to herself, she still loved Abraham. She knew it was foolish, but she had hoped when he had heard about the babies, he would rush home and stake his claim.

"Keturah, please say something. I'm kind of out here on a limb." He gave a nervous chuckle while continuing to rub his thumb over the back of her hand.

Looking up at him, she gave him a genuine smile and then with her other hand covered his hand that covered hers. "Parson…I truly care…" Before she could continue, a loud thump hit their table, causing her to jump. Looking away from Parson at the intrusion, her heart twisted in her chest.

"Well...well...well. I guess you don't allow any grass to grow under your feet, do you, Mrs. Taylor!" Sari Jaymes' harsh tone interrupted. "Abraham hasn't been able to think straight, let alone pick a decent wife since my poor Sarah passed away."

Startled, Keturah and Parson remained speechless as they both looked up at their uninvited guest. Keturah quickly pulled both her hands away from Parson's and slid them under the table. Her stomach turned sour, seeing her stepmother, brother Malcom and his wife, and stepson Isaac's disapproving glare.

Parson was the first one to recover and spoke up, unable to hide his agitation. "Ms. Jaymes, was there something that you wanted?"

"I *want* you and Keturah to stop making spectacles of yourselves. Many of Canaan business associates not to mention high society dine here, and I will not have the Taylor Jaymes name dragged through the mud due to your imprudence," she retorted.

"Auntie Sari, our table is ready. Why don't we go and have a seat?" A nervous Rebecca suddenly appeared by Sari and Isaac's side. She gave a quick nod of acknowledgment to Keturah.

"Yes, let's be seated," Isaac spoke up, giving a cold stare at both Parson and Keturah. "This is Dad's situation. Let him handle it."

Parson gave a hearty laugh that drew the attention of a few onlookers. "What a bunch of hypocrites you all are."

"Parson, please don't; let's just get the check and go," Keturah whispered, dreading a confrontation.

"Go? Why should we? We are at our table enjoying each other's company and our meal. I see no reason to get up and leave," Parson retorted.

"Of course, you wouldn't, Mr. Carlton Parson. As I recall, your family loves a good scandal every now and then, so what could I expect from you?" Sari quibbled. "But as long as Keturah is still Abraham's wife and a Jaymes, she will conduct herself as such."

"Abraham filed for a divorce months ago." Keturah spoke up doing her best to speak as if she wasn't affected by Sari's acknowledgment of her being part of the family. "So, what I do is no concern of his."

"Oh really, because when I saw him this morning, he seems to think otherwise, missy," Sari charged.

"What!?" Keturah's voice barely rose above a whisper as the color drained from her face.

"Oh, you didn't know your hubby was back in town? Humph, imagine that." Sari had a satisfied look plastered on her face. "I can assure you he's back, and I'm sure he wouldn't be pleased seeing the two of you in pubic holding hands declaring your feelings for each other."

Keturah rapidly shook her head. "No, you're mistaken. I-I signed all the papers, I gave them to his secretary months ago, so we are in the process of divorcing..." Keturah said in a small protest.

"No, little girl, you're mistaken. Nothing has been filed, and that came directly from your husband's lips." She gave Keturah a pointed look. "So, it might behoove you and your little play date to show some discretion because I'm sure your husband is going to hear about this." Sari then looked at Parson. "I can guarantee that he will."

Keturah's mouth went dry as she plopped back in her seat. She was out on a date while still legally married. She felt oddly like her mother, Pamela. The thought made her bow her head in shame.

"Ms. Jaymes, you are disrupting our dinner and upsetting my... Keturah, so please leave our table, or I will have you escorted out of here," Parson demanded as he stood from the table.

This time Sari's laughter drew even more attention to their little party. "Boy, please." Sari shook her head. "My first cousin is the owner of this restaurant, so the only person leaving here will be you," she charged.

"Parson, I'm ready to go," Keturah stated, standing up. She grabbed her purse and was moving from their table. She didn't care if he followed her or not, she was leaving. She was halfway to the door when she felt a hand touch her shoulder. Turning around, she saw Rebecca's apologetic face.

"Keturah, I'm so sorry. If I would have known Aunt Sari was going to make a scene...I never would have mentioned seeing you," she stated with regret.

"It doesn't matter, she would have seen me anyway, and the same results would have happened. Sari is a bitter, spiteful old woman who doesn't care about anything or anyone but herself." Seeing Parson coming her way with her wrap, she held on to Rebecca's arms with her hands.

"Becca, be careful. You don't know her like you think you do."

"I don't understand...what do you mean?" Rebecca questioned.

"Here's your wrap Tourie; let's get out of here before anything else can happen," Parson said, taking Keturah by the elbow and gently leading her towards the exit before she had a chance to reply to Rebecca's question.

There was a chill in the night air. Keturah secured her wrap around her shoulders while struggling to discern if her shivering was from the cold or knowing Abraham was back in town. Her companion remained quiet too as they headed towards the car both deep in thought of the evening's turn of events. All she wanted to do was go home, hug her babies, and think what it meant that Abraham was back in town fully aware of his children's existence but still hadn't contacted her.

"Excuse me, sir, but are you, Carlton Parson?"

At the sound of his voice, both Parson and Keturah looked up. Parson's grip on Keturah's elbow tightened as he pulled her behind him as a stocky African American man in a black leather coat and a leather cap came towards them. "Do I know you?" Parson said in a leery tone.

The man gave a nonchalant laugh. "No, sir, you don't know me," he said in a friendly manner while reaching into his coat.

"Keturah, go back to the restaurant now," Parson ordered, not sure what this guy was up to but posturing his body in a way to let the man know he was going to have a fight on his hands if he was about to come at them wrong.

"Whoa...whoa hey man, hold on, no need to get excited. I'm not here to harm anyone." The stranger held up both his hands and instinctively backed away from them.

"Then what do you want." Parson kept the edge in his tone, not for a second backing down.

"I just want to give you this." The man again reached back into his coat slowly and pulled out a white envelope and held it out for Parson to take. Parson slowly approached the man and took the envelope. Once in his hand, the man said, "You've been served." Then he turned around and made a hasty retreat.

Shocked, Parson just stood there looking down at the envelope in his hands and then back up at the man who had scurried away disappearing behind a dark-colored SUV. The letter had the official seal of the Courts of Charlotte. "What in the world could this be about?" he muttered as he felt Keturah's reassuring hand take his. Standing in the cooling night air, he opened the envelope and, in silence, read its contents. Afterward, he shoved the letter back into the envelop, gave a mirthless laugh, took Keturah by the hand, and resumed walking towards his car.

"Parson...what's happening. Why were you served?" Keturah asked as she tried keeping up with him in her spiked heels.

"I'm being sued for half a million dollars," he said with no inflection in his voice.

"What!?" Keturah stopped dead in her tracks, causing Parson to stop and face her. "Half a million dollars, but why, by who? What can they possibly be accusing you of doing?" she inquired, perplexed as to why anyone would charge Parson with anything.

Holding the letter up in his hand, he looked at her with an empty expression. "I'm accused of being a homewrecker, by your husband, Abraham Taylor."

# *Chapter Seven*

Rebecca sat quietly, watching Isaac watch his father during the board meeting that afternoon. Her soon to be father-in-law hadn't been himself since he had returned to the states and it was evident to all. He was moody and on edge. Rebecca figured it had a lot to do with Keturah, but not entirely. Canaan had taken some major financial hits under Isaac's leadership, and by the report, Abraham was receiving from the board, it wasn't an easy fix.

She knew Isaac was glad his dad was back, but having to face his father's scrutiny over his business dealings had him on edge, which meant he was crankier than usual and often took it out on her. Sighing, Rebecca allowed her mind to drift from the board meeting to the argument they had the other night when they saw Keturah with Carlton at the Pedemonte. Remembering his scathing remarks about Keturah still caused her to cringe.

"Can you believe Dad has allowed himself to get entangled with a woman like Keturah!? What is this sick hold these low-class women have over him?" Isaac stewed as he sped down the freeway.

"Isaac that's not a very Christlike thing to say," Rebecca interjected in a soft tone. She closed her eyes, momentarily wishing the evening had gone in a different direction than what it had. They were supposed to discuss setting their wedding date and possible venues, not his father's love life.

"Oh no honey, I'm right in the book. The Bible says that many good men have been reduced to a piece of bread by means of a whorish woman." He quoted the scripture verbatim. "That's exactly what Keturah and Hagan are, and if he's not careful, they'll take him for all he's worth. Then we'll all be sorry."

"You don't know if that's true," Rebecca spoke up in her soon to be mother-in-law's defense.

"Becca, don't be blind. Keturah has been planning this from the very beginning.

Getting her hooks into a rich man, becoming pregnant, and then bleed him for all he is worth." He charged as he slowed the car to take the exit leading to her high-rise condo.

"You don't know Keturah well enough to accuse her of wrongdoing," she retorted, hoping they'd drop the subject. She was tired of the conversation and just wanted to go to bed. She had hoped he'd just drop her off at the front door of her apartment building then take himself home to sulk alone. Lord knew she had a migraine from listening to him and Aunt Sari rant on and on about how low-class Keturah was over dinner. However, when he drove into her parking garage, she knew he planned on spending the rest of the evening as well as the night with her. She was doing her best to keep Isaac at arms-length at least until they were married, but choosing to be sexually active with her fiance proved to be a huge mistake. She didn't care what Tippany thought, sex before marriage was like putting the cart before the horse. It wasn't something professing Christians should do. If only Isaac was proficient in quoting those types of scriptures. She sighed and rolled her eyes heavenward.

*"Choose this day who you will serve."*

She couldn't remember the entire scripture, but she understood she needed to make a choice tonight—one Isaac wouldn't like. She felt conviction in her soul every time she allowed Isaac certain liberties, but the fear of losing him kept her from protesting too much.

*"Choose this day who you will serve."*

She sighed inward as she felt the scripture pressing down on her while Isaac continued his rant.

"Dad is the smartest man I know, so I can't fathom how he let this situation get so far out of hand." He got out of the car popping open his trunk to grab his overnight bag.

Wondering whatever happened to the chivalrous man who used to open her car door and help her out, Rebecca pushed the car door open and struggled to get herself out while he continued to fuss. "Isaac, believe it or not, your dad seems to have genuine feelings for Keturah." When he glared at her, she raised her hands to stop his protest. "I know…I know, it sounds crazy, but sweetheart, love has a way…"

"Love…Becca, don't be ridiculous." He dismissed her theory. "My dad got caught between the wrong pair of legs is all. He has always been a man of integrity, and women like Keturah know how to exploit another person's kindness." He strode away towards the elevators then halted. "Oh, by the way, I don't want you hanging around her. Keturah is not the right breed or class. I think distancing yourself from her will be for the best." He spoke, stepping into the elevator.

"What!?" Rebecca stopped talking as other tenants stepped on with them. Not knowing why, she felt the need to defend Keturah, she tried again as they got off the elevator and were walking to her apartment door. "Isaac, when we get married, Keturah is going to be your stepmother and my mother-in-law. We can't just ignore her. Besides, what your insinuating about Keturah is just not true. She really is a very nice person. I got to know her a little when we were in Chicago, and I really enjoyed my time with her and Tippany. I was even thinking of having her in some way participate in our wedding."

"You've got to be joking. Keturah will not be part of our wedding party, period." He took her key, opened her door, and strolled in her apartment, dropping his overnight bag on her couch. "If Dad wasn't the man he is, he'd have dumped her in the gutter where he found her."

"Fine, Isaac, have it your way." She threw up her hands in surrender. Dropping her purse on the coffee table, she made a beeline for her bedroom and went straight into her master bathroom.

Checking her medicine cabinet, she grabbed some ibuprofen, filled a glass with water, and downed the pills hoping they would kick in soon to stop the pounding in her head. She looked at her own reflection in the mirror and saw the tired circles under her eyes. All this arguing was wreaking havoc on her skin. Premature wrinkling wasn't something she could afford right now. With head bowed, she walked back into her bedroom.

"I know your tired sweetheart, but I was hoping not too tired for your man." Isaac's husky tenor spoke in the darkened room.

Her head snapped up to find a smiling Isaac holding his hand out towards her waiting in her bed.

*"Choose this day who you will serve."*

The scripture reverberated in her ears. "Sorry, Lord." She bowed her head ashamed for being weak but more afraid of what denying Isaac might cost her. In the worst way, she wanted to be the next Mrs. Taylor, so plastering a smile on her face, she took the hand he extended her and without protest did his bidding.

\*\*\*

Isaac readjusted himself in his executive chair and loosened his collar for the third time. He was in his executive office seated in his CEO's chair at Canaan but felt like a child called to the principal's office as his dad sat opposite of him with Aunt Sari going over the books. The board meeting was brutal. That much he expected; however, he didn't expect his father to be present. From the moment he walked in, the board members almost begged his father to return as CEO. Aware the numbers had fallen, Isaac had already formulated a game plan to quiet the fears of the board members, but with his father on the scene, the board automatically saw senior Taylor as the boss and Isaac as the lowly apprentice. As his father continued to take his time reviewing the reports, with every turned page, Isaac felt the room closing in on him. As much as he was glad to see his dad back, he hated the lecture that would inevitably take place about Canaan's drop in revenue.

"Abraham, is this really necessary to do right now?" Sari spoke up in protest.

"Sari, if you have something you need to attend to, please don't let me stop you," Abraham responded, never looking up from the reports.

"Really, you're just as ornery as ever." Sari huffed, readjusting herself in the seat before him.

"Just one more thing we have in common, Auntie." Abraham's tenor took on an amused tone as Sari glared at him then rolled her eyes looking away.

Squashing a chuckle in his throat, Isaac straightened himself in his seat. Only his dad had the finesse to put his aunt in her place with fewer than ten words. Looking up, he saw his dad finally close the report and lay it on his desk. He spoke up first, ready to lay out his defense. "Look, Dad, I know what you're going to say, and yes, you're right, the company has faced some difficult challenges, but we are still strong."

"Exactly." Sari Jaymes chimed in. "The dip in revenue is minor. As far as I'm concerned, it's nothing worth discussing." She gave a curt nod for added effect.

"Dad, you've always said a company is only as strong as its leader. I will be the first one to admit I have made some mistakes, and because of them, there has been a dip in revenue, but I have a plan to get them back as well as bring new upcoming business in the fold if you give me a chance."

"As far as I'm concerned, this is a moot point," Sari interrupted. "What we really need to be dealing with is that woman you've been with these last few months. Hagan is like a parasite trying to worm her way into this company and putting Ishmael in charge of everything. I'm warning you, Abraham, if you continue to be careless, she'll destroy everything you and Sarah have worked so hard to build." Sari shook a bony finger at Abraham.

"Thank you, Sari, for your valuable insight. However, the matter that I wish to discuss with my son doesn't concern Hagan or, for that matter, you," Abraham said, never giving the frail woman his attention.

"Fine!" she said in a huff. "I always told Sarah you had a stubborn streak in you the size of Texas, and I wasn't wrong then or now," she said, gathering her belongings and giving him a sideways glance. "Just remember who told you so when that narrow behind woman comes strutting herself in here like some proud peacock making this boy grovel for a position when he should be running the whole thing, remember you were warned." She stood up with her head held back proudly. Both Taylor men watched her pick up her purse and walked with a stiff gait out the door.

"Well, I'll tell you I didn't miss those lovely chats while I was gone." Abraham rubbed his face with his hand, stroking his five-o'clock shadow.

"I'm sure you didn't, but no matter how long you've been gone, you are still the only one I have ever seen shut down Auntie like that." Isaac chuckled as he turned around and caught his dad staring at him. "*Oh boy, here comes the lecture,*" Isaac thought to himself, straightening in his chair, ready to face the music. After a few moments with his father not saying anything, he began to fidget.
Unable to take his father's gaze any longer, he spoke. "Look, Dad, I know I messed up. I won't make excuses. I want to assure you that I do take the financial losses of Canaan, regardless of how minor, seriously." he said, adjusting the knot in his tie, hoping it would help him swallow.

"Son, I have no doubt of that."

"Dad, I know you're disappointed in how I—"

Lifting up his hands to stop him, Abraham stood up from behind his desk. "I didn't come here to criticize you or tell you what you should do next. I didn't even come back to reclaim the company," he said, coming around the desk and standing in front of his son's chair.

"What?! But I thought you were going to step back in as CEO." Isaac, thoroughly confused, stood face to face with his father.

"Canaan has a CEO—you. You were groomed for this position from day one. I just wanted to apologize for how I left. The backlash you're getting and the drop off in revenue is in response to my behavior this last year...not yours."

"No, Dad, I haven't led this company well. The people are accustomed to your style of leadership." Isaac walked away from his dad. "I'm not you. And I admit, your shoes are hard to fill."

"As you so eloquently quoted, *a company is only as strong as its leader.* You can't do this job trying to be me or copy my leadership style, son. God made you unique with qualities of your own, and the people will respond to the leader God designed you to be."

Isaac bowed his head, uncomfortable with the God talk, seeing he hadn't been on speaking terms with the Lord since his mother passed. "Sometimes, it's hard being a man of God." His voice quivered at the confession.

"You're preaching to the choir, son." Abraham chuckled, moving towards the window that looked over downtown Charlotte. "You've seen my life this past year, son. Sometimes we are not as close to God as we think, but it doesn't mean God has gone anywhere."

"Dad, the stuff happening to you was a set up by Satan himself. Keturah and Hagan are nothing more than opportunists. Mom was right to toss Hagan and Ishmael out back then, and you are doing the right thing by staying clear of Keturah." Isaac, stirred by anger, turned away from the window and paced back and forth.

"I'm pretty sure we can get our lawyer's involved, and you can get a no-contest divorce and a restraining order against her if necessary. I saw her out with that Parson guy the other night, so I wouldn't be surprised if the twins are even yours." He formed his fingers in quotation marks to emphasize the point. At his father's silence, he turned towards him, shocked to see his father's face contorted with anger.

"Son, I don't know where you got your information from, but let me be the one to set you straight. I pursued Keturah, I asked her to marry me, I slept with her fully aware of the consequences, and I got her pregnant, in that order. Then like a coward, I walked out on her leaving her to deal with the fallout of my actions."

"Dad...I—" Isaac stopped when his dad put up a silencing hand.

"No, you need to hear this. I left town because I was ashamed, not of Keturah, but because I didn't dare to acknowledge to myself, Keturah, or the rest of this family how I felt about everything."

*"He has feelings for her!"*

Rebecca's words from the night before echoed in his ears. Feeling a little remorse for his attitude towards Rebecca and his harsh assessment of his stepmother, he dropped his head. "I didn't realize...I mean, I just thought you were having a hard time coping with mom's..." He let his words trail off. He was also having a difficult time dealing with his mom's death, even though it had been well over a year.

"Zac, believe me, I loved your mother. Never wanted to love anyone else and didn't plan to. Keturah blindsided me. I couldn't handle my feelings, so I ran." Facing Isaac, Abraham continued. "So, if you're going to find fault with anyone, start with me, but leave my wife out of it."

Isaac remained quiet, chewing on his father's words. He didn't come right out and say he loved Keturah, but then he really didn't have to—it was evident in his tone. "I'm sorry if I misspoke, but Dad, you're the only parent I have left. I don't want to see you get hurt."

"Son, I appreciate your concern, but I've never been one to start something and not see it through. Whatever the outcome between my wife and me, I'll handle it," he said, clapping his hand on Isaac's shoulder. "Now, why don't you tell me some of these new plans of yours for the Canaan expansion project in the western part of the country?"

"Fine by me." He felt the tension of the moment dispel. "Why don't we grab some lunch while we're at it?" Isaac suggested as he and his father walked out of the office doors.

# *Chapter Eight*

Tippany breathed out a few steadying breaths as she walked the long hallway to the executive offices of Canaan. She had only heard rumors Abraham was back, but she hadn't been in the office much to verify it. However, after talking to Keturah the other night regarding Carlton's lawsuit and now with her own summons from Abraham that afternoon, there was no doubt. She didn't like being ordered to the office. It was unsettling. "What could he want to talk to me about?" she muttered. She knew no other reason for Abraham to want to see her except to discuss Keturah, which she promised herself she wouldn't.

*"Maybe he's discovered you and Keturah's secret. You can rarely keep anything from Abraham,"* her inner thoughts whispered.

She prayed he hadn't. She had done her best to keep her nose clean these past few months. She hadn't wanted to alert her mother of everything she had found out about Keturah being her full sister, and God knows she wasn't ready to discuss her newfound inheritance. She and Keturah had agreed to keep the lid on things, not wanting the publicity at the moment. Once everything was finalized, she would leave Canaan Enterprise. She stood in front of his mahogany door, shaking off the thought. She was going to stay cool and play the cat-and-mouse game she often engaged in with her mother, she thought, smiling mischievously.

*"It might not be that easy with Abraham."* A gentle whisper spoke.

The voice was unsettling. With one hard swallow, she straightened her clothing and gave a quick tap on the door.

"Come in."

She breathed in and out. "Showtime." With a playful smile plastered on her face, she walked into the room with a greeting already in her mouth. "Hey, Abe, what's..." Tippany's words faltered as she came to an immediate stop seeing the entire Jaymes' clan seated in his office.

"Tippany, thank you for coming on short notice," Abraham stated, never giving her his full attention. "Please have a seat. Now that everyone is here, let's get started."

"Yes, please, I have several important meetings that need my attention today, Abraham. I can't be expected to drop what I'm doing to deal with something my children can handle," Sari said, an air of superiority in her tone as she sat at the head of the table opposite of Abraham.

To his credit, Abraham wouldn't be bated by Sari. Tippany loved the way Abraham rarely lost his cool with the matriarch of the Jaymes family. She could take a few lessons from him.

"I can assure you this matter won't take long. I've decided to expand the foundation's reach and include a new mentoring slash scholarship program for young inner-city girls. It's a project my wife feels strongly about, so I intend to have it incorporated into our existing mentorship programs."

"I've never known Sarah to express any concerns regarding the mentorship of young women?" Sari authoritatively spoke.

Tippany rolled her eyes. Her mother acted as if she was the expert when it came to all things important to Sarah Taylor. Good grief, Abraham had been married to his wife for over twenty-five years—you would think there were some things they shared in private, even the great, all-knowing Sari Jaymes just didn't know.

"Correct, Sarah wasn't. However, Keturah has expressed her desire to implement a mentoring program for young inner-city girls, so I want to give her access to the funds she needs to get started," Abraham stated.

"Absolutely not. The foundation monies are tied up in other interests," Sari said, dismissing further discussion.

"Actually, as you all know the farmer's market pulled out this year due to the drought so we would have additional monies to allocate to the girls mentoring project and Keturah has already raised a substantial amount of revenue to support the girls' program as well so I feel it would actually be doable," Tippany interjected.

"Tippany, I said there was not enough revenue to support this project." Sari pinned her with a hard-cold stare."

"The books say otherwise, mother!" Tippany countered.

"Great, then it's settled," Abraham spoke up. "The Jaymes' Foundation will sponsor a mentoring project for inner-city girls, and Keturah will oversee it. I would suggest Tippany or Rebecca assist," Abraham said with no inflection in his tone.

Sari whipped around towards Abraham with fury in her eyes. "I don't need you to tell me how to run this foundation Abraham or who to place over it." Sari barked her indignation.

"Mom, please, the more support the Jaymes Foundation does in the community, the better reflection it has on Canaan and all of us," Malcom spoke up.

It was all Tippany could do to keep herself from rolling her eyes. Everything to her brother was a stepping stone bringing him that much closer to the governor's mansion.

"That's right, Mother Jaymes, helping underprivileged girls can emphasize our compassion for those who are less fortunate. It also supports the theme of Malcom's campaign," Malcom's wife Shannon spoke up.

This time Tippany couldn't help but roll her eyes. Her sister-in-law was always looking for an angle to make herself look good in the public's eyes. She could think of nothing else but getting into the governor's mansion. She and her mother had already made up a list of all the people they planned on not inviting to their first governor's ball.

"Well, that settles it," Abraham concluded.

"No, it's not." Sari stood up in an indignant stance, placing her hands on her hips. "You come in here after being gone for months issuing orders, demanding that we make room for your wife in this foundation just like that." Sari snapped her fingers." You want Keturah to have a place of prominence in this company; however, are you even aware of your wife's behaviors? While you're overseas celebrating your firstborn, she's been running around making an absolute spectacle of herself with that silly Carlin or whatever his name is," Sari retorted.

Angered, Tippany stood up and confronted her mother. "First off, mother, his name is Carlton Parson. Second, Keturah is not running around, making a spectacle of herself as you claim. Keturah and Carlton are friends, nothing more," she charged.

"Tippany!!! How dare you contradict me in this manner?" Sari yelled.

"Oh, please," Tippany retorted, pointing at her siblings. "Malcom and Shannon did the same thing, and I don't see you having a cow over it!" Tippany's voice rose as she stood her ground.

"Little girl." Sari's eyebrows and voice rose. "You better watch your tone with me, do you understand me Tippany Rochelle Jaymes? Because you have plenty to answer to me for with your uncouth behavior. Don't think I don't know what you've been doing once you clock out from here."

Biting her tongue, Tippany swallowed her next scathing comment. She hated it when her mother belittled her, calling her a *little girl* as if she were some child.

"Look Sari, as you stated earlier, you have a busy schedule, and I don't want to detain you any further. Everyone, thanks for coming," Abraham said, dismissing the group as he continued to look at some files on his desk.

Tippany remained poised although she wanted to laugh at the cold stare down her mother was giving Abraham who wasn't in the least bit fazed by it. After a few more seconds, she nodded to Malcom and then turned her blazing glare towards her. Cutting her eyes, she turned towards the door, and like little ducklings, her crew was expected to follow. Blowing out a sigh, Tippany fell in line with the rest of the Jaymes' tribe and was ready to follow Malcom and Shannon out the door.

"Tippany, can I have a word with you?" Abraham asked.

Her steps faltered as she turned towards him. "Of course, Abraham," Tippany said with some hesitation.

"What for?" Sari came back into the room to inquire.

"Sari, I realize you want to be informed regarding foundation business; however, do I also need to check with you to have a conversation with my sister-in-law?" Abraham gave her a perplexed look.

"Humph." Sari rolled her eyes at them both and walked back out the door without another word.

Tippany's belly hurt; she wanted to laugh so bad, but she maintained her composure until her mother walked out of his door, shutting it with more force than needed.

"I got to tell you, Abe, you know how to handle my mother better than anyone I know." She gave an unladylike snort and giggled.

"Yeah, well, I've had a lot of practice handling the Jaymes' women over the years...however, it seems this new generation is the worst." He dropped his pin on his desk and sat back in his chair, rubbing his temples.

"Oh, I don't' think we're all that bad," she said in a coy tone. "I personally think I'm quite wonderful." She smiled.

"Humph!" He grunted. "Typical, your generation also thinks the world revolves around them."

"Just think if it did. The world would be a much more interesting place." She winked.

"Yes, well as much as I'd like to play this game with you, Tippy I have other concerns I need to speak with you about."

"Oh, and what concerns would that be?"

"Where would you like me to start?" He stood up from his desk, turned, and look out the window. "We could talk about you and Keturah's inheriting your grandfather's estate, which includes ownership of Birch Corporation, one of Canaan's competitors. Or we could discuss what a huge conflict of interest that is." He turned to level her with a dispassionate scowl. "If that's not enough, we could talk about how in good conscience you could go for months keeping the knowledge of my wife's pregnancy from me. Or why you are covering for her while she is playing playmate with her old boyfriend." He finished, his normal warm disposition had turned cold and callous towards her.

Feeling her throat constricting, she swallowed hard. She had always had a good relationship with Abraham, but this was a side of him she had only heard about. His no-nonsense, take no prisoner attitude was intimidating, to say the least. "H-how did you know about the inheritance?" she said while turning towards the door her mother had just exited praying her mother wasn't eavesdropping at the door. Not that she ever caught her doing something like that, but she wouldn't put it passed her.

"Tippany, I wouldn't be where I am today if I didn't keep tabs on my competitors. I just never thought you and my wife would be one of them," he said, folding his arms over his chest. "Besides, I've known for quite some time that Thomas Birch was Keturah's grandfather; however, I wasn't aware that you and Keturah were full-biological sisters," he said candidly.

"Yeah, that was a big surprise for both of us." Tippany smiled with the memory of that revelatory day. "It was one of the happiest days of our lives." She gave him a lopsided grin, hoping the tension in the room would subside.

"Tippany, you're family. You're my cousin and sister-in-law; however, if I feel that I can't trust you, you won't remain in this company," he stated, turning away from her.

Tippany felt a chill run up her spine. How in God's name would she explain to her mother why Abraham fired her without exposing her own plans? She wasn't ready, things weren't in place. She needed things to remain just so, for her full plan to be put into place. Chewing on her bottom lip like she always did when her back was against the wall, she acknowledged the need to get Abraham on her side and fast. "Look, Abraham, I haven't wronged you. Before you flew out of the country, I called Keturah and told her you were at the office," she revealed as she slowly approaching the window where he stood. "So, she came here wanting to tell you face to face about the pregnancy and to tell you she would grant you the divorce. But you wouldn't bother seeing her. She wanted things to work out between the two of you…she loves you. But the way you brushed her off, it crushed her Abraham."

"Tippy, no one told me she was waiting to see me." Abraham bowed his head and sighed. "Do you really think I'm so crass that I'd not take time to see my wife? If I had known about the pregnancy, I would have never left. At best, I would have taken her with me," he said, rubbing the back of his neck.

Feeling the friction in the room subsiding, she continued. "Keturah has remained faithful to you, Abraham," she said, turning from the window and looking at the spacious office. "She thought the annulment she signed was being processed, but she still wouldn't do anything with Carlton until she had those papers in hand."

"You're sure about that, Tippy?" He raised an eyebrow.

"I am. I can also vouch for Carlton; he has not pressured her to do anything. Carlton cares about his friends and has been a gentleman in a time when Keturah needed it the most."

"Sounds like you're pretty fond of your sister's boyfriend." Abraham turned from the window and seated himself back at his desk. "Does Keturah know you hold a torch for him?"

"Carlton is not her boyfriend. They are just friends, nothing more," she reiterated.

"And what is Mr. Parson to you?" Abraham leveled her with his piercing blue gaze.

"Off-limits." She lowered her eyes from his. "*For now,*" she asserted within.

"Sounds like you and I want the same thing." Abraham flexed the tips of his fingers together.

"Oh, and what's that?" Tippany looked at him, confusion gracing her face.

"To have Carlton Parson out of Keturah's life…do you have some suggestions on how to make that happen?"

For the next thirty minutes, Tippany and Abraham discussed their mutual problem and how to manage it. By the time she left his office, she had found an ally in Abraham and became a co-conspirator in saving her brother-in-law's marriage.

*What if Keturah and Carlton find out about the dual role you're playing?*

The thought twisted her smile into a grimace. Keturah would be hurt, and Carlton would never speak to her again.

Abraham wanted Parson to keep his distance from Keturah and the children, and Tippany wanted the same thing. The more he stayed away, maybe Keturah's heart would turn back towards Abraham, although she had a suspicion that it had never ventured far from Abraham in the first place. Keturah loved her husband, and even though the man was as pigheaded as could be, Abraham loved Keturah. But that love would never be fully realized with Carlton in the picture, and that's where she came in. She didn't know when it happened, her falling for Carlton, but she knew something about him was different. He didn't see her like most men normally did…as an opportunity to gain notoriety or power as Conrad had.

*You're not Keturah, and that's who he wants, not you!* A nasty thought whispered.

The words sobered her. She didn't want to hurt anyone; just wanted to feel love like Keturah felt for Abraham and Carlton felt for Keturah. She had reached her office door when a jingle from her cell alerted her; she had a text message. She didn't bother looking at it. She knew it was Conrad. It was two in the afternoon; he was getting off work and wanted to meet up like they had been doing for the last two weeks. Shutting her eyes to keep the memories of their times together at bay, she had already grown tired of their little play dates. It was nothing more than a physical exchange that left her feeling empty and a little guilty, especially when she saw his fiancé in church. She hated being the other woman.

"Ms. Jaymes," a woman's voice spoke up from behind her. Startled, Tippany jumped, placing a hand on her chest. "Lilly, oh my goodness, I swear I'm going to put a cowbell around your neck." She chuckled, feeling silly about being frightened by her mother's secretary.

"I am so sorry. I didn't mean to surprise you. I was just trying to catch you before you went into your office." She looked back at her boss's open office door. "I don't know what happened when you all were in Mr. Taylor's office, but your mother came out furious and has been on the warpath ever since. She insisted I remain close by and tell her the moment you came from his office.

"Okay, thanks Lilly, I will handle things from here."

"You don't understand, I was told to escort you to her office," Lilly interjected.

Instead of stopping at her office door Tippany kept walking until she was in front of the executive elevator, pushing the down button she ignored Lilly's babbling. It was one thing to be summoned by the big boss, but it was another to be beckoned by her mother, who had the outright nerve to have her escorted to the office like she was a kid. So, she had two choices, she could either be the other woman for the afternoon or fight with her mother…neither choice was appealing. "Lilly, I'm sorry, but I have an important business meeting that I must attend. Tell my mother I will call her later."

"But your mother is expecting you," Lilly insisted.

"Lilly, where is Tippany?" Sari loud voice barked from down the hall.

"What shall I tell her?" Lilly turned to Tippany with wide-eyed fright.

"Tell her I'll be out for the remainder of the day," Tippany said as the elevator doors opened and she stepped in and turned around. Pushing the button door to close, she heaved out a sigh. No, she didn't like being the other woman, but it would do for now.

# *Chapter Nine*

It had been a week since Abraham's return to the states, and she had kept close tabs on her sister and Carlton's interactions. From what she could gather, Carlton had kept his distance and Keturah had become a recluse. She barely came out of the house. Tippy had to find a sitter just to get her to go get a bite to eat. She had been quiet, too quiet, which was concerning to Tippany. "You and Carlton still haven't seen each other?" Tippany inquired.

"No, we haven't, thanks to Abraham's stupid lawsuit," Keturah huffed.

"But, you two are still doing church this Sunday, right?" Tippany questioned Keturah as they sped down the highway making their way downtown to pick up Rebecca at her condo.

Keturah remained quiet, just shrugging her shoulders as she stared out the passenger side window.

"I know the kids must miss Carlton as much as he misses them. I'm surprised he hasn't even tried to see the kids?" Tippany raised an eyebrow in her sister's direction, already sure of the answer. She and Carlton had a nice long talk two days ago. He was angry with Abraham's accusation within the lawsuit but said on the advisement of his legal counsel he would stay clear of Keturah and the children for now. She just wanted to verify he had remained true.

"He did call this morning to confirm our plans to join him for church service this Sunday. They are having a special prayer for single mothers and their children. I thought I'd go...but I don't know if I should? I don't want to cause him any undue problems."

"Wait, why would you go to a service for single moms? Keturah, you hardly fall in that category."

"Don't I, Tippy?" Keturah spoke in anger. "Abraham went to all this trouble to make sure Parson keeps his distance but for what. He's been back almost three weeks, and not once has he come to see his children. But that didn't stop him from petitioning the courts so their names can be changed to Taylor."

"What!?"

"Yeah, dear ole hubby got a court order demanding the children's last name be changed."

"And he still hasn't called to discuss anything?" The anger on her sister's face spoke volumes. "I don't understand him," Tippany muttered. She agreed to be Abraham's little spy, but she had anticipated he would have beat a track to her door at least to see his children.

"How can he say Parson caused a rift in our marriage when the truth is, he never wanted a marriage with me anyway? He wants his first family, not me. As far as I'm concerned, when he went and spent the last six months overseas with Ishmael and Hagan, he made his choice."

Tippany's heart sank. She felt horrible knowing she was keeping Keturah in the dark. "Keturah...I need to tell you a couple of things," Tippany spoke with hesitation. She needed to come clean and now was as good a time as any. "I have seen Abraham."

Keturah's eyes went wide as she turned in her seat to get a full view of Tippany. "How does he look? I-I mean is...is he okay?"

"Keturah, your husband, looks as good as ever if not better, and now I know you still love him no matter how much you try and act as if you don't care." Tippany smiled, secretly feeling justified by her deceptive actions.

"Care!?" Keturah shook her head. "Of course, I care, Tippy. I've always cared, but it doesn't change the fact he left me without a backward glance. It doesn't dismiss the fact he's been back in town for almost three weeks now and has not contacted me," Keturah lashed out, slamming her fist into the car's soft leather seat.

"Tourie, I know this is frustrating…"

"No Tippy, you don't. You have no idea how hurtful this is. I thought I was moving on, getting some closure, and ready to start my life over. Maybe find love again. I haven't had a lot of people stick by me except you. Parson knows me. He understands so much about me—what makes me tick, what brings me down. He knows the sides of me that most guys don't bother with. So, to have him snatched out of my life with a stroke of a pen, it's crushing. Abraham doesn't care one iota about me. He has taken everything away from me. It's like he hates me and doesn't want me to ever be happy." Keturah was borderline hysterical. "Why did he come back, Tippy? It's not like he wants me. Why can't he just let me have some scraps of happiness, if not with him why not someone who cares for me?" Keturah hit her thigh with a tight fist then broke down, covering her face with her hands and wept.

Pulling off the highway and onto the shoulder of the road, Tippany turned the car off and pulled Keturah in the cradle of her arms and rocked her sister until her hysterics subsided. This was not a game, and no matter how much she wanted to be in a relationship with Carlton, it wouldn't be at the expense of her sister's sanity, she thought, holding on to Keturah's trembling form.

***

"Tippany, make this quick. I have a meeting in ten minutes," Abraham said in a curt tone.

"I have some information for you, but before I give it, I need to know your intentions towards my sister and the children." Tippany's no-nonsense tone rang loud and clear.

"My intentions regarding my wife and children are not really up for discussion. Now, if you have information regarding matters concerning Mr. Parson, let's focus on that."

"Abe, we go way back. You're my boss, cousin by marriage, and now my brother-in-law. I've always seen you as a man of integrity, but please understand, Keturah is blood, and I will not allow you or anyone else to hurt her. So, if you're going to be her husband, then be her husband, or get out of her life."

Abraham took a steadying breath. His anger and frustration were already at their peak, and this conversation wasn't helping any. "You're right, Tippy, we go way back so you know I've never taken kindly to threats. I would suggest you tread lightly with me."

"Well, that's too bad. I don't care what you like right now. You weren't the one trying to console your wife, who was half-hysterical for the last half hour because she feels humiliated by your blatant disregard for her feelings. You've been gone from her life for months, and now you've been back in town for almost three weeks, yet you aren't even man enough to face her, to see your own children. You don't even have the decency or courtesy to call her and see if she is okay if the babies are well or need anything. No, like some snake in the grass, you correspond to her through your lawyer, making threats and demands. I thought you were better than that, Abe."

"Tippy, I…there are things…" Abraham sighed wearily as he dragged a hand down his forlorn face. He could not explain his hesitation in seeing Keturah. Yes, he had admitted that he cared about her to Isaac, yet he still struggled to face her, to explain his absence. Knowing the pain, he caused ripped at his soul. He needed to make things right, but how?

"Look, Abe, I know what we agreed to a week ago, but as much as I care for Carlton, I will not spy on them for you anymore. I don't think it's the right way to handle things. So, if you want your wife back, you need to fight for her because frankly, she is worth it."

Abraham was quiet for several moments. Gaining his composure, he spoke, "Tippany, I apologize for putting you in a compromising position, and you're right, I haven't handled things well with Keturah or my children since my return. I need you to know I really do care."

"Abe, I know you do, but it's not me who needs to know it. Keturah does. You need to show her that you care, which is why I've decided to go ahead and tell you this. Keturah is going to Faith Temple Fellowship Church with Carlton this Sunday. She wants to go because the pastor is praying over the single mothers and their children."

"What?! Why would she want to do that?" She's not single, she knows we're still married."

"She believes you've abandoned her. She feels alone and sees herself as a single parent. No married woman should ever feel like she is a single Abe. You need to fix this."

Long after their conversation ended, Tippany's words echoed in his ears, and she was right…he needed to fix this.

That evening he was brooding and knew it. He sighed deeply while tossing his report on his desk then swiveled in his chair so he could look over Charlotte's skyline, hoping it would give him peace like it normally did…no such luck. As the soft grayish tones of the transitioning sky turned twilight, the colors reminded him of one thing, Keturah's gentle stare. Turning towards his wall, he looked at the picture of him and Sarah. They were both so young and happy. "If only things could be that simple." He spoke to her image, wishing he could hear her voice one more time.

*You've all but admitted you love her, but you're still afraid. Why?*

He wanted to escape, tell the voice he loved Sarah only, but he knew it wasn't true. He couldn't count the number of times he had stopped himself from racing over to Keturah's home to tell her he wanted a home and family with her, but he just couldn't go through with it. Which was why he stayed away so long and still hadn't connected with her.

"Lord, I'm too old for this foolishness," he spoke out into the darkness of his office.

*"She needs you."*

"Does she?" Abraham questioned as he turned and looked at the new report his investigator presented him earlier in the day. Keturah and Tippany's inheritance from their grandfather was more than he had even guessed. She wouldn't need him now for anything. If they were in a relationship, it would be on a level playing field. So, money was no longer an option. What else could he give to make her stay?

*"Love!"*

"Love!" Fisting his hand in the air, he then dropped it to his side. The affection he could give, providing for her, was not a problem. Protecting her and being the spiritual leader in their home was not a question but loving her as she wants? The thought brought a shiver to his spine. He had left town trying to get rid of the memory of her beautiful face, and the nights they shared. It made him feel both alive and afraid. Never did he believe any other woman could hold a candle to Sarah, but Keturah had wiggled her way into his heart and allowed her loveliness to grow within him.

"I'm sorry, babe," he spoke to the quietness in the room. Sometimes his beloved Sarah's presence was so strong he felt if he reached up, he could feel her soft curls caress his face. He had always felt Sarah's quiet presence when he was having a difficult time. "I will always love you, Sarah...but this thing with Keturah." It was all he could say. Breathing out, he decided to take a drive to clear his head, and if he just so happened to end up driving past Keturah's street, then so be it.

*Later that same evening.*

"Oh Parson, thank God you came." A grateful Keturah hugged Carlton as soon as he came upon her porch. The babies are in my room. We've been in there for hours."

Carlton hugged her back, letting out a chuckle. "Calm down Keturah. I'm sure it's not a prowler or anything, maybe just a bat caught in the attic," he said in a nonchalant tone.

"You know two weeks ago there was a prowler who broke into a home two blocks from here, and they were robbed at gunpoint."

"Which is why I don't understand your need to remain in this area, Keturah. It's unsafe," Parson charged, letting her go and moving them both into her home. Once in, he secured the locks and looked around. "Ah Keturah, why are all the lights off and windows open?"

"Well, I thought if it were a burglar, I would try and make them think no one was at home. If it was a bat, I prayed it would just fly out of the house."

"Tourie, you're a treasure," he jested then suddenly stopped as he heard a scratching sound.

"Parson, that's it, that's the sound I keep hearing. It sounds like someone is trying to open the window," she whispered.

Putting his finger to his mouth, he hushed her while trying to listen. "You go in the bedroom with the babies and keep as quiet as possible."

"Should I call the police?" She clung to his arm, nervous at the sound.

"In this neighborhood. Please, it will take at least an hour before they process your call."

"This apartment is part of the regentrification project in this area. If you want a neighborhood to begin to thrive again, people like you and me have to be willing to take a risk and move back into the area," Keturah stated while shrinking behind him.

"As much as I would enjoy debating with you about this, we currently have a situation here."

"Okay, fine. I will go into the bedroom until you give me the all-clear sign." Keturah quickly shuffled to the back bedroom and shut the door. Walking towards the bassinets, she looked in on the twins. "Sleeping sound as usual." She smiled, touching Kamara's baby's fine hair. Never did she think she could fall in love so completely until the birth of her little ones. She'd do anything to protect them. Startled by the chimes of her cell phone she fumbled with her pants pocket to retrieve it. Not recognizing the number, she clicked over before it could ring again and disturb the babies. "Hello?"

No answer.

"Hello, who is this?" she asked again as she simultaneously heard a knock on her door. Moving quickly, she threw it open. "Carlton, what was it?" She asked forgetting about the unidentified caller.

"Tourie, everything is fine." He chuckled. "You must really be scared to call me by my first name."

"I wasn't scared, just concerned." She smiled back as she placed the phone back up to her ear only to hear a dial tone. Shrugging, she clicked off and put the phone back in her pocket.

"Humph." He gave her a sarcastic look then came further into the room to look at the twins.

"Well?!"

"Well, what?" Parson asked while looking at Abel.

"What was making the scratching noise?"

"I think it was a branch banging at the window." He said smiling down at the boy.

"Parson, do you honestly think I can't tell the difference between a branch hitting my window and a burglar?"

"Follow me, my dear." He took her by the arm and led her to the dining room window. As they approached, a weird scratching sound began banging at the window.

Keturah paused, but Parson proceeded to drag her along. "Tourie, its nothing but a branch," he exclaimed as he pulled the curtain back to reveal something black with hair, letting off a high-pitched squeal.

Screaming Keturah forcefully snatched him back.

Losing his footing, he tumbled backwards, both of them falling on her couch.

"Tourie? What heck are you doing?"

"I'm saving you from the blood-sucking vampire bat."

"Okay, you've been watching too many scary movies. It's just a common fruit bat that flew in when you opened the windows." He broke out laughing while standing up, pulling her up with him.

"I don't care how it got in. Get it out of my house, or the kids and I are staying with you."

"Yeah, I don't think so. Your husband would probably have a cow if he knew I was here this late."

"What makes you think he cares?" she said, looking around the house for the flying intruder.

"Most men don't sue you for half a mill if they don't care," Parson said in a gruff tone.

"Parson, he doesn't care. I haven't heard from him since he's been back. Not even for the sake of seeing his children. I wish..." She held her peace to keep from saying something she'd regret. "Anyway, I'm sorry for all of this."

"Hey partner, we'll get through this. What's the saying? What doesn't kill us only makes us stronger." He chucked her under the chin. "What do you say we solve your bat problem first, then maybe you can make some cocoa, and we can solve your Taylor problem?"

"Sounds like a plan. Only you solve the bat problem by yourself because I'm staying in the bedroom with the babies."

"Chicken."

"Whatever. Broom and the mop are in the kitchen." She pointed towards the kitchen then quickly ducked when she thought she heard wings flapping. "Oh my God, I left my bedroom door open." She screeched, making a beeline for her bedroom.

"Women." Parson shook his head as he headed towards the kitchen.

# *Chapter Ten*

It was Sunday morning, and the small hillside church was packed with single mothers. Maybe Tippany was right. She wasn't a single mom, but right now, she felt like one. She felt alone, unloved, and unwanted, at least by her husband. She shook her head, trying to get her mind to focus on what Pastor Mathison was saying.

"Too often, we seek from people what will and can only come from God. Anything else is a cheap substitute." Pastor Mathison's words arrested her attention, and she tuned out everything else around her.

"Look at two very different women in the bible Jesus encountered, the woman at the well in John the fourth chapter, verses four through forty-two and the woman with an issue of blood in Mark chapter five verses twenty-five through thirty-four. Both were in need—one had a physical issue, the other an emotional one. Often times, when we feel that things are beyond our ability, that's when we decide to go to God, like the woman with the issue of blood. She tried all the remedies of that time, went to all the doctors, and still couldn't get the help she needed. It was when at her wit's end she thought within herself, 'If I could just touch the hem of Jesus' garment, I'll be made whole.' Her faith in Jesus' ability made her whole. But brothers and sisters, when it comes to emotional issues, why are we so reluctant to seek out Jesus?"

Many in the pews around her and Parson gave a chorus of amen, as did she.

"Jesus had to seek the woman at the well out, much like he has to do with us today. The Bible commands us to love him with our whole mind, body, and soul, but how can we if our minds and emotions are tied up in knots because of what someone else has done to us?"

Keturah shifted in her seat as she felt conviction begin tugging at her heart.

"To make matters worse, we often don't turn to God but to other people hoping the next person can fix us, and when they can't, we go to the next, then the next and the cycle continues to repeat itself. Just like the woman at the well, she tried to cover her brokenness with a lot of religious jargon and if she'd had her way, all she would have had that day was a nice conversation and left the well in the same emotional condition...but Jesus refused to allow her emotional scars to remain, so he spoke to it and out of her brokenness came salvation not only for her but also the entire town."

Keturah could feel the moisture collecting at the corners of her eyes. She had given up on her marriage and on trusting God to fix it. In her mind, it was easier to walk away and let it die than to ask God to breathe life into it.    So, lost in thought, she didn't even notice everyone was now standing.   She rose quickly, listening, as Pastor Mathison concluded.

"What are you looking for someone to do? Only God can heal, restore, replenish, and recover those things you value or that seem lost.   Will you allow your brokenness to heal others around you?   Sisters and brothers. Won't you let God take the heavy burden you've been carrying today?"

A familiar melody about placing your all on the altar of prayer was softly playing in the background as the preacher made a plea for those to come to join him at the altar.

With tears streaming down her face Keturah was up and moving towards the altar like so many others. For so long, she wanted closure to her broken childhood, wanted someone to validate her worth like the woman at the well looking for men to do what only God could. She wanted her dad to do it, but he was gone, so she looked for Abraham to do it. Yet he would never be able to...no man would. Only God could handle the monumental task. With shaky hands, she lifted them over her head along with her tattered heart, and this time fully surrendered her past, present, and future to God. "Thank you, Jesus!" she murmured over and over again, as peace flooded her soul.

Feeling a hand touch her shoulder, she instinctively grabbed what she knew were Parson's fingers and squeezed. She was too overcome with emotions to speak. When she turned around, she could see tears glistening in his eyes as well. Smiling, she hugged him tight. "I love you, brother."

"Love you too, sis," he said, placing an innocent kiss on top of her head.

Still hugging each other as they walked back to their seats, she looked around as they slowly moved up the crowded aisles. Movement in the back of the church caught her attention. She stopped suddenly, anxiety gripping her heart. "It couldn't be." She whispered.

"What did you say?" Parson asked.

"Nothing," she said, straining to see if it truly was Abraham she saw or just her imagination…but whoever it was, he was gone now. *Stop being foolish*, she inwardly chided.

"Hey, how bout I take my niece and nephew and my best girl out for a bite to eat," Parson asked.

"If we can eat Thai food, you got yourself a deal," she said, smiling as he rolled his eyes in mock disgust as she knew he would.

"I swear you're not from the south at all." He chuckled as they both headed for the nursery.

\*\*\*

A warm late September breeze filled the sky, but Abraham couldn't enjoy it. He was too angry to see the beauty of the day. His thoughts centered on his wife's activities Friday night. "Blasted!" He struck the steering wheel, unable to contain his rage at the thought of seeing Parson coming out of Keturah's home late at night.

"I told that jerk what would happen if he didn't stay away from my wife, and I'm going to make sure he pays the price for not listening," Abraham growled as he waited for his driver to pick up the phone.

"Good afternoon Mr. Taylor."

"Change of plans, Carlos. I need you and Avery to meet me at Faith Temple Fellowship Church on the south side of town on McCarthy and Fifth right now."

"I will be there in fifteen minutes Mr. Taylor."

"Good." He clicked off with his driver, then made a second call. At the beep, he left a voice message. "Chancellor Mitchell, this is Abraham Taylor. You must call me back this afternoon the minute you receive this message." He said in a brash tone then hung up. "If Parson thinks he's going to have a relationship with my wife while Canaan foots the bill, he's crazy," he griped. He was not known for fits of jealousy, but it enraged him knowing Keturah would welcome a man like Parson in her life. "Does she even know he's been in and out of relationships with multiple women, and he professes to be a Christian man?"

*"Judge not lest you be judged,"* a soft voice whispered.

Conviction settled over him like a cool blanket, dousing some of his fierce anger. Hadn't he been the one to place Keturah in this predicament by not being around? He was wrong for cutting off communication with her. He just wanted a little time to sort out his feelings, and with her underfoot, it was impossible to do. If he told her he loved her, she would have expectations, and he didn't know if he could live up to them. But he could see now that he had stayed away too long and let the fox into the hen house. "Well, that changes today!" He wasn't ready to tell Keturah the extent of his feelings, but he definitely planned on stringing a certain fox up by his tail.

*Remember where you are!*

He was in a church parking lot plotting to beat the crap out of his wife's would-be suitor. This was definitely not how he saw his weekend going. His plans were to see her and his children at her new apartment and talk with her civilly. Help her understand what was going on in his head for the last couple of months. He was sure if he could just spend some alone time with her, take hold of her delicate face, hold her in his arms, and kiss away all her worries, they'd make amends…start over and be the family they both wanted to be. Then Parson emerged from her apartment, all smiles. Abraham hadn't slept a wink since as murderous thoughts kept sleep at bay. He didn't know why he didn't just wait for her at her apartment after church, but he just couldn't wait any longer. He wanted to claim his wife and children and scurry them off to his home on the hill where nothing and no one could separate them again.

"You're acting like a jealous teenager," he griped at himself. Spotting the two coming out of church still hugged up on each other with his children in their carriers was the final straw. "I pray Carlos gets here quick because if he doesn't, I'm going to jail," Abraham muttered as he swung open his car door and got out. With a forceful slam, he stalked towards the couple, quickening his pace with each stride.

\*\*\*

Parson carried Abel while Keturah held on to Kamara's baby carrier. His arm was protectively circled around Keturah's small waist. To the outsider, they looked like the perfect little family.

Something about that made Parson's heartstrings sing. Why hadn't he swept Keturah off her feet when he first had the chance? Back then, he knew she was interested in him, but he was looking for easy pickings. He had no idea that Keturah was the total package. With things out of sorts between her and Abraham, he might get a second chance, and he wasn't going to be a fool again. He knew he shouldn't be so possessive, but this was beginning to feel like his family since the day he rushed her to the hospital to deliver the twins.

He was the one in the waiting room…God only knew where the high and mighty Abraham Taylor might be. Probably off conquering another company or something, while his son and daughter were being birthed into the world. Abraham didn't deserve Keturah, and as far as he was concerned, now that the children were born, lawsuit or not, he was going to make every effort to make this readymade family his own no matter what. A low growl made him look in Keturah's direction. "Sounds like somebody's hungry." He chuckled.

"You know, a gentleman wouldn't have mentioned that," Keturah quibbled with a playful shove.

"Oh, really? And what else would a gentleman not do?" he inquired, smiling down at her.

"A gentleman would not prey on another man's family!" a male voice barked.

Parson jerked his head up and froze as did Keturah as the angry tenor of Abraham came barreling down on them. Parson, who was the same height as Abraham but not even close to his build, dropped his hand from around Keturah's waist and swallowed hard. Abraham looked as if he was about to knock his head off. It was only his pride that kept him standing tall and proud in the face of such a menacing opponent. He knew he needed to say something, but before he could, Abraham was toe to toe with him.

It was Keturah who broke the intensified moment.

"Abraham, what are you doing here?" Keturah interjected.

Nothing was said as the men stood there in a silent challenge sizing each other up. It wasn't until Abel began to whimper that an unspoken challenge was broken. Ignoring the animosity evident in Abraham's glare, Parson turned towards Keturah.

"The babies are really tired and hungry. We should get them home," he implored.

Abraham took a threatening step towards Parson and said in a barely audible voice, "You forget your place, boy. This is my family, and if anyone is going to make sure they get home, it will be me...are we clear?"

"Abraham, please don't make a scene," Keturah begged as she looked to the side and saw several members of the congregation looking on at what was occurring. "Please let's just go, and we can talk later in private."

"You and the kids will ride with me," Abraham demanded, never taking his eyes off Parson.

"Oh, really?" Parson feeling a sudden wave of boldness now that people were witnessing the confrontation challenged him. "And how are you going to do that, Mr. Taylor? You plan on throwing Keturah in the passenger seat and strapping the kids to the roof of your two-seater? Or maybe you'll just cram them in the trunk... I'm sure they'll still be breathing by the time you make the drive back to Keturah's place."

"Parson, please don't," Keturah begged.

Abraham took another step towards him, clenching and unclenching his fists.

"Oh, what, do you plan on hitting me now because I spoke the truth?" Parson said, ignoring Keturah's plea as he continued to taunt Abraham. "You have some nerve issuing orders to this woman like you've been here for the long haul when in truth, you've abandoned her. Now you want to play the jilted husband role and step back in her life as if nothing happened. Suddenly you're the world's greatest father. But where were *you* when your babies were born?" He poked Abraham in the chest with his finger. "See, I know where I was...in the delivery room holding this woman's hand, letting her know it was all going to be alright. I don't get men like you. You have it all, but you'd allow this treasure to slip through your fingers."

"Parson…Abraham, please stop this," Keturah said with a catch in her voice on the verge of tears.

Abraham looked at Parson's finger poking him in the chest and slowly looked back at him. "Parson, if you don't get your hands off me and give me my son right now, I promise you'll get more of me than you can handle," Abraham said in a quiet threatening tone.

Parson felt the hairs on his arms rise. Slowly he back away from Abraham placing some space between them.

"Gentlemen, please." A man from the church stepped in between them, three others flanking both Parson and Abraham's side. "This is not the proper time or place to settle your differences. The lady has asked you both to stop several times, and besides, you don't want to do this in front of the children, so please go your separate ways, or we will be forced to contact the authorities."

"That won't be necessary!" Abraham said firmly. "I'm taking my wife and children home right now." Holding out his hand to Parson, he spoke with controlled fury. "My son…please."

Knowing that he didn't want the authorities involved, Parson looked at Keturah for the consent of which she quickly nodded. Reluctantly he placed Abel's carrier in Abraham's hand.

Gently taking his son, Abraham immediately turned away and stalked towards a black limousine that appeared out of nowhere.

"Keturah, I'm so…." Parson began to say.

"I'll see you later," Keturah said stoically as she hurried to catch up with Abraham and her son.

As the crowd started dispersing, Parson watched the only good things to come his way in a long-time step into the limo and ride right out of his life. As the door shut, blocking his view of Keturah, he now had a full view of Abraham and another man about Abraham's same height glaring at him. Abraham tapped the hood of the car, and it pulled off.

The man with eye's the same color as Keturah's got in the driver's seat of Abraham's Mercedes coup while Abraham maintained his stance glaring back at him.

It was at that moment that Parson realized he had poked the bear too many times. Abraham took out his cell phone and started punching in numbers, then got into the passenger side of his car and they pulled out behind the limo. The look Abraham leveled him with made him realize the lawsuit would be the least of his worries.

# *Chapter Eleven*

Tucked away safely in the confines of Abraham's limo, Keturah looked out the back window and watched the hillside church disappear in the distance. Her eyes then fell on the silver Mercedes coupe following close behind them. Shivering, she rubbed her hands back and forth over her arms, but her chill had nothing to do with the temperature in the limo. She dreaded the confrontation, sure to come with her estranged husband. This time she wouldn't have Parson as her buffer. She was thankful Abraham wasn't in the car with her now. She didn't think her sanity could take another cold, impersonal stare down he gave her in the church parking lot. She wasn't naive enough to think another battle wasn't on the horizon today, but she'd deal with it when it came; right now, all she wanted to do was get home, settle the kids so they could finish their nap and shut out the rest of the world…mainly the angry men in her life. The buzz within her pocket let her know a call was coming through. Taking the phone out, she was quite relieved to see it was her Aunt Adelle Jenkins calling and not Parson.

"Hi, Aunt Delle, how are you?"

"How am I? Honey, how are you?"

Keturah bowed her head and shut her eyes. She could tell by her auntie's tone she was aware of what happened. Church gossip was the worst. "I'm okay…I take it you've heard," Keturah assumed.

"I didn't get my foot in the door of my house good before the calls started coming in about your brawling suitors in the church parking lot." She laughed. "Serious though, Keturah, are you alright?"

"Auntie, I'm so embarrassed." Keturah tried to keep the emotion out of her voice but failed. "I'm sure after the spectacles we made of ourselves, Lord, I'll never be able to show my face there again." She huffed. "Here, you have two Christian men ready to brawl in public?" She complained while swiping at a slow-rolling tear.

"Honey, don't you worry about it. Besides, your Uncle Emory is having a talk with your husband as we speak."

"Oh, Auntie…I wish Gretta was still alive. I know she would have known what to do." Keturah's voice cracked at the admission. It was times like this when losing her grandmother hurt the most. She needed her wisdom, relied on her guidance when confusion and uncertainty obscured her way.

"I know, baby. I miss her too."

"Shoot, Abraham and Parson wouldn't have dared behave that way in front of her. Gretta would've taken her purse strap and beat them both." She chuckled, imagining Abe and Parson trying to dodge a butt beating by an eighty-year-old woman.

"Yeah, I could see her beating their behinds while quoting scriptures." Adelle laughed.

"If only she was alive. I would never have married Abraham, and none of this would have happened." Her tone was full of sorrow and regret.

"I know things are tough right now, Keturah, but when you look at the negative, you can't see the positive either, honey."

"What positives?"

"Offhand, I can think of two beautiful blessings."

Keturah looked down at Kamara and Abel. Her heart melted as it always did when she looked at her adorable twins. They both bore a strong resemblance to their father but her as well. "I can't imagine life without them. I can't even understand how you can love two human beings so fully in such a short amount of time," Keturah gushed as she rubbed Abel's soft crown.

"Yeah, they have a way of getting up under your skin and lodging there forever,"

Adelle commented.

"Aunt Adelle, I think they are the only two good things that came out of our marriage."

"Keturah, I know things seem so out of focus in your life. But remember, God is always a present help in times of trouble. Trust and lean on him—not your feelings or fears but Him."

"Thanks, Auntie, I'll try, but sometimes it is so hard to believe good is coming. Right now, all I want to do is run and hide from the world."

"There is no place better to run than straight into the arms of Jesus, Tourie," she admonished. "Listen honey, I have to get dinner started, or that old grumpy-gus of an uncle of yours will have a fit." She chuckled. "I just wanted to make sure you're alright."

"Thanks, Auntie. I'm better now after talking with you. Besides, the car is pulling to a stop, so I must be home anyway. I'm going to get the babies settled and lay down. I don't care what their father wants to do, it will have to wait until later."

"Okay, sweetie, call if you need me."

"I will, Auntie. I love you."

"Love you more."

"Impossible." She smiled as she heard the soft click. Closing her eyes for a moment, she tried to reclaim the peaceful presence she had felt in the church that morning and release the tension within her neck. "Lord, I know what happened this afternoon was only a distraction, but I won't forget my promise to you. I'm going to pass this test," she said with determination in her voice. "I don't know what Abraham wants, but I'm going to get through this day with your help," she promised herself.

An opening then slamming of the car door jerked her eyes open. She was startled to find herself face to face with Abraham. "When did he get in?" she wondered to herself, taking a quick glance at her watch. She then lifted her head to look out the car window. Realizing she wasn't at her home or even in her neighborhood she became alarmed but didn't want to show it, so she tried to play it casually. "Where are we?" She managed to keep her voice from trembling.

"Downtown!" He said with an edge in his tone.

"Oh, I see." She simply said not looking directly at him. Her traitorous heart sped up as the scent of his cologne invaded her nostrils. He looked good, better than she had remembered. His tailored blue suit fit him to a tee. His time overseas had tanned his skin to a perfect bronze color, causing his brilliant blue gaze to take on an even greater intensity than she remembered. She bowed her head feeling both attracted as well as jumpy in his presence especially in such close quarters. "Why didn't your driver just take me home first, it's closer?"

"I told him not to."

"But why?" she asked feeling the car moving again but not in the direction of her apartments.

At the same moment, a call came in. Checking his suit pocket, he pulled out his cell and took the call ignoring her question.

She wanted to take his phone and hurl it out the window she was so angry. "God, I'm trying my best to win this test, but he is making it so difficult."

"Listen, either you fire him, or the university can find another funding source. It's that simple Larry," Abraham said in a clipped tone. After listening for a while, he spoke. "No, unacceptable. In no way do I want him near my wife. Well, reassign him then to a satellite campus in Timbuktu. Frankly, I don't care—just make it happen," Abraham barked.

Keturah's eyes went wide with fright. She knew he had to be talking about Parson. "Abraham, you're being unreasonable!" she interjected. "It's bad enough that you have a bogus lawsuit against him; now you're trying to take his livelihood away?"

He lifted a silencing hand in her direction. "There is no funding for the mentoring project until he's gone, are we clear? Good! No, my wife won't step in because she won't be returning to work."

"What...you can't speak for me! How dare you!" Was he insane? He had been back in her life for less than an hour and was already wreaking havoc? What right did he have in telling her employer that she wouldn't be back to work? Unbuckling her seatbelt, she reached for his phone, but her hand was met with his steel grip and a warning glare that made her flinch.

"Hold on Larry." Covering the mouthpiece of his phone, he ordered, "Sit back and put your seatbelt on now." He commanded.

*You're not winning the test this way!"* a gentle reminder intruded into her angry thoughts.

"Abraham's not making it easy," she thought. Angered, she jerked her arm from his firm grasp and slouched back in her seat staring anywhere but at him.

"Keturah!" he growled.

Giving back her own defiant glower, she snatched the seatbelt, jerked it over her lap, and strapped herself in. "Satisfied!" she fired back. She definitely wasn't going to win the love test today.

Finishing his conversation, he clicked the end button and returned his cell to his vest pocket. Rubbing his hands over his face, he laid his head back and shut his eyes to Keturah's pouting face. But she was having none of it.

"Abraham Nathan Taylor, I cannot believe what I just heard. I would never have thought you to be a vindictive man, but having Parson fired is petty and makes you look small."

Abraham continued in his relaxed position, saying nothing, unmoved by the harshness of her chastisement.

"Oh, you are so pigheaded," she said in an exasperated tone. "Parson and I have worked hard on this deal, and to allow a disagreement get in the way of something that will benefit at-risk kids in the community is just irresponsible. Besides, Parson's done nothing to you to warrant such an attack."

Suddenly Abraham jerked his head off the headrest, unbuckled himself, and came almost nose to nose with a shocked Keturah who instinctively sunk deeper in her seat to keep out of his reach.

"That dear is where you're wrong, dead wrong," he belted out, anger evident in his tone and face. "Any man who'd move on another man's family warrants what I did and more. It speaks to the man's character or lack thereof Keturah. I won't have anyone like that working under me or be near my family. So, if this relocation is a problem for your little playmate...too bad!"

Keturah just stared at him in disbelief. She couldn't believe his callousness in the situation. Was this truly the real Abraham Taylor, the man she still loved? Tears sprung from her eyes as the realization of her inward confession settled in the pit of her soul. Yes, after all this time and all the craziness he had put her through, she still loved the brute. The moment she laid eyes on him in the parking lot, her hopeless heart began beating like crazy. Nevertheless, this was a man's life and her friend. She couldn't allow him to hurt Parson. "God, please help me get through to this stubborn man." She pleaded to God in her mind as she tried to think of another way to approach the subject. "Abraham, Parson, and I are friends. He came by to take me to church, that's all,".

"Is that all he did, Keturah?" Abraham asked in a skeptical tone.

"Yes, that's all!" she said with an exasperated breath.

"And what was he doing Friday night at your apartment?" Abraham's stone-cold voice matched his glacier stare.

"Friday night?!"

"That's right. I saw that conniving jerk creeping out of your house! What was he doing there?" Abraham demanded.

"Well, he came by because...". Keturah stopped mid-sentence. "Wait a minute, how did you know he was there? What were you doing...spying on me?"

"Answer the question, why was he there?"

"I don't owe you any explanation, Abraham. But if you were so worried, how come you didn't come to the door instead of spying around like some snoop," she challenged.

"I saw what I needed to see. Parson has no integrity. He wants you and my children, and he's not getting either," Abraham said through gritted teeth. "I told him what would happen if he didn't keep his distance, and it's a promise I intend to keep."

"Abraham, not everyone has a hidden agenda. Parson is a friend; someone I can count on in a pinch."

Abraham looked at her for a long moment before shaking his head and giving a mirthless laugh. Placing his elbows on both knees, he rubbed his closed eyes with his fingertips while he spoke. "You are so delightfully charming, Keturah. At times I almost forget just how immature you really are."

She gasped. It was as if he slapped her in the face. She had thought they had moved beyond this age thing. Yet, in the end, he still felt she was a child that he was embarrassed by. *Test failed... Sorry, Lord.* "I was hoping that we could discuss our differences, but I realize that's not going to happen. Tell your driver to turn this car around and take me home right now!" Keturah demanded.

"No!"

"Excuse me," Keturah said in an elevated voice.

"I said, no!" He spoke in a calm tone.

"This is kidnapping!" she yelled.

"Oh, well." He sat back and began to flip through his files.

She wasn't in control, and she knew it. Abraham had a look on his face that she'd seen before. He wasn't going to budge and pushing him would only make him dig his heels in deeper. Ten minutes of silence passed between them before she spoke again.

"Listen, Abe, it's the children's feeding time, and I like keeping them on a tight schedule. So why don't we just go back to my house, and I can take care of them, and once they're settled, we can talk…okay?" She hoped she was getting through seeing as he looked as if he was considering her words.

"You're not breastfeeding?" He lifted a brow at her.

"What? I uh…well, yes, but…"

"Well then," he said in a matter-of-fact tone and went back to reading the file.

"But I…" She knew there was a protest in her, but her curiosity about how he knew she was breast feeding the children got the better of her. "How'd you know that?"

Again, he looked at her for a long moment before speaking. "I believe when we last parted, you were a B cup, and judging from what I can see now, you're definitely not that anymore," he said with a smirk allowing his eyes to linger at her chest longer than she thought necessary.

Shifting uncomfortably under his gaze, she tried to develop a new argument. "But I don't have my breast pump, and were still driving." she said in a small voice.

Abraham looked at her for a moment then hit a button on his side of the door. "Carlos, how long until we arrive?"

"Ten minutes sir."

"Thank you, by the way could you slow down a little."

"Right away sir."

Keturah could immediately feel the car reduce its speed. Still feeling a need to protest she stated. "I still don't have my breast pump."

"Tourie, as you are well aware, Taylors like things straight from the source," he suggested, his eyes taking on a different type of intensity that never wavering from hers.

His look caused something in her chest to flutter. This chemistry between them was the one part of their relationship that seemed to be in sync no matter how bad things were between them. To be honest, it was a part of their relationship she had missed. The way he could caress her skin with his eye or set her heart on fire with a mere word, with a snap of his finger, she was ready to receive his affection.

"In that case, these two definitely are their father's children," she said softly with a hint of a smile.

*"He's breaking down your defenses, watch yourself."*

"Indeed." His tone was husky.

A tiny whimper snapped her mind back to the task at hand. She looked down at Abel, who was stirring. Soon both babies would be up, and she needed to get them fed. With a sigh, she began fiddling with her shirt buttons under the watchful eye of her abductor. "I guess it would be too much to ask for you to be a gentleman and go back to what you were doing." She requested.

"No, it wouldn't be too much to ask from a gentleman, but I'm not a gentleman, I'm your husband," Abraham said with a lopsided smile on his face then to press the point further, he closed his file, tossed it back into his briefcase and gave her his undivided attention.

Abel continued to whine, so to keep him from going into a full-blown wail, she sighed, gave Abraham one final defiant glare, before positioning Abel so he could be fed all under Abraham's unwavering gaze.

Allowing her mind to drift while Abel nursed, she again found herself wondering about the next step. "Lord, what am I going to do?" she wondered. Her perfectly plotted out life was now thrown into shambles. Gretta was gone, Parson was likely out of a job, and so was she, and she needed a job until all the legalities regarding her inheritance were finalized. Her marriage to Abraham was in limbo. What a mess. The only thing she was sure of was that she would do anything and everything to protect her children.

Looking down at her sweet boy, she nuzzled his soft fuzzy crown. She so wanted them to have a better life than she did. She gave a heavy sigh. "Lord, you know what the future holds for us. Please show me what direction to go. Show me how to raise these sweet treasures you've entrusted me with." So accustomed to talking to God in this manner, she forgot she had spoken out loud until Abraham commented.

"It's not just on you, Keturah. I'm just as much responsible for them as you are," Abraham charged.

Hurt by his harsh retort, Keturah fired back. "Look, Abraham, I know this was not part of the deal. You didn't want any strings attached to our arrangement, so I don't expect you to obligate yourself to us. I'll take care of the children, and I won't take legal action or drag you and your company's precious reputation through the mud. You have my word."

Abraham slammed his hand on the seat, startling Keturah and the babies. "Why do you women think that you can take a man's children from him just like that?" He snapped his finger to emphasize his point. "You act as if we have no feelings about seeing our kids or that we're happy when you try to play the martyr and do it all on your own. You, Sarah, Hagan, you're all alike. You take over our role as the father in our children's lives then blame us when everything goes to hell. I allowed this same thing to happen to my two older sons and look where they are now? Warring over the company like they were outright strangers. It makes me sick. But I'll tell you one thing, it'll be a cold day in hell before I allow it to happen to these two. I'll fight you tooth and nail Keturah! I'll take you to court if necessary, that I promise!"

Stunned by his outburst, Keturah hadn't noticed the car had come to a stop. Abraham immediately got out and slammed the door. She had never seen him so angry, especially not with her. His abrupt exit jarred both children awake. Startled, they began to whimper then loud wails erupted.

Abel, with his belly full, was the first to calm down then with two more sniffs closed his eyes and was on his way back to sleep. Kamara was not so inclined. Hungry and cranky, her cry became louder and more demanding, which again woke Abel up, and he too resumed crying all over again. Overwhelmed, Keturah could feel herself coming unglued. Silent tears streamed down her face as she pacified Kamara enough so she could nurse her. There were so many things she'd wanted to yell back at Abraham. How angry and hurt she was for him, leaving her alone for the majority of her pregnancy and the first six weeks of their children's lives. His blatant disregard for her feelings their entire marriage, and now he wanted to come in and take over and be in charge of everything, including her.

Suddenly, out of nowhere, an image of her mother popped in her mind. Keturah didn't remember much of her mom, she was so little, but one memory that always surfaced was how unhappy she was. Always crying over her father.

"I won't become her!" Keturah gripped the leather seat, feeling a little woozy but angry at the same time. No, she would not be like her mom. Placing Kamara back in her carrier, she then grabbing her phone, speaking to Google Assistant she requested. "Find a taxi service." She was ready to call the first one listed, then realized she had no idea where she was. Looking out the back window, her eyes went wide. The limo was parked outside of the biggest house she had ever seen.

"Where in the world am I?" she spoke in quiet awe, intimidated by the grandeur of her surroundings. The limo was parked alongside a circular driveway, that had a beautiful, bronzed colored statue depicting a woman sitting at a gushing well. The mist from the fountain illuminated by the sun's rays sparkled like diamonds in the sky as the droplets returned to the base of the fountain. There were no other homes surrounding them, just a well-manicured lawn and acres of woodland. As for the mansion settled on the land, she had never seen anything like it.

The sandstone colored exterior with dark brown trim arched windows resembled a Mediterranean style castle with its circular columns and arched shaped custom windows making her wonder what the inside looked like. "Stop it!" She reprimanded herself. "You need to find out where you are," she was saying just as Abraham's silver coupe pulled up alongside the limo. Avery quickly exited the car once the motor was shut off.

Although they were cousins, she never said much to Avery. An occasional nod would be given but nothing else. Today things were going to change, she determined pushing open the car door. She hadn't anticipated how hot it was outside or the fact that she hadn't eaten. No matter, she'd eat when she got home. "Avery, may I have a word with you?" she spoke out, holding onto the car door as she stood to steady her wobbly legs.

Startled, Avery quickly turned towards her. "Mrs. Taylor, I didn't realize you were in there."

Apparently, neither did Abraham seeing he left them in the car. "Yes, I umm...I..." She was beginning to feel a little lightheaded, but she pushed on. "I was wondering where the person driving this car went. I would like to go home." She tried to make sure her tone was clear even though she was struggling to stay lucid.

"Um, are you alright? Where is Mr. Taylor?"

"Off having a man tantrum somewhere, I guess. To be honest, I don't know nor do I care." She knew she was wrong for saying it, but she really didn't care. "I'm ready to go home. The twins and I...we..." A nauseating feeling swept over her causing Avery's form to come in and out of focus.

"Keturah, you don't look well," Avery stated, coming towards her. "Abe, come quick!"

Turning Keturah saw a blur that looked like Abraham running towards her along with someone else, but before she could say anything else, her legs began to buckle, and she found herself sliding to the ground.

"Tourie, sweetheart," Abraham said.

"Abe...babies... home...I'm tired," she heard herself say before everything in her world went dark.

# *Chapter Twelve*

Abraham walked through the large kitchen in search of his head of staff, Consuela Duran. His mind was a blur with unexpressed emotion. He didn't want to fight with Keturah or anyone else. He just wanted to hold her and his children in his arms from the moment he stepped foot in Charlotte but after Avery told him of all the secrecy and deception from Hagan, his staff as well as his own wife, he didn't know how to deal with it all, so he did what he always did, he pulled back and threw himself into his work…and prayed. He shook his head, trying to forget his friend Emory's challenging words while in the car after collecting his wife and children.

"You can't have it both ways, Abe. Either be her husband or be her ex. In either case, this disappearing act that keeps her on pins and needles while you try to decide if you want a wife or not is over. She's not the same mousey, lovestruck girl you left to fend for herself." Emory stated.

"This is between me and my wife, Em."

"No, Abe, you lost that privilege of saying that when you bailed on her. Besides, who do you think has been picking up the pieces of her heart after your abandonment? Did it ever occur to you how vulnerable she was after Gretta passed, and then you just left her because she was an inconvenience to you? Sorry man, but your days of calling the shots in my niece's life are over."

They were the last words he heard before Emory abruptly hung up on him. He only got a moment's reprieve, though. Before he could exhale, his phone was ringing again. "Aunt Sari, God, help me." He sighed.

"Let it go to voicemail?" Avery suggested.

Abraham gave a mirthless chuckle. "She will just keep calling until I answer, so might as well get this over with." He nodded as Avery answered the call.

"Abraham, what in the blue blazes is the matter with you!"

"Hello Aunt Sari, how are you?" Abraham's tone dripped with sarcasm as him mind wandered, thinking about his precious cargo seated in the back of the limo in front of him.

"Don't get mealy-mouthed with me. What in heaven's name were you thinking? Going to that church and acting a fool over that girl? My God, have you lost the good sense the Lord has given you?"

"That girl happens to be my wife, and I don't give a..." Abraham swallowed hard, keeping words he knew were crass out of his vocabulary. "I did what any man would do when his family's well-being is at stake. If the means and method I used weren't to your liking, then that is unfortunate."

"What's unfortunate is the way this is going to look to our business associates, especially those high and mighty Christian organizations you're so fond of. How do you think they will feel knowing that Canaan's founding CEO was not only dealing in questionable business practices with organizations that don't support Christian principles but to push matters further you come home and start a Sunday afternoon brawl in a church parking lot?"

Sari's words were harsh but accurate. He had messed up big time and was doing more damage to his reputation and the company's image every day. He had to stop the hemorrhaging. "Look Sari, I realize this situation is a mess and will only get worse if played out in public. So, I've decided as of today to distance myself and work out of the Gastonia office indefinitely until I can get things straightened out." Apparently, his words appeased her.

"Well, I tend to agree and think it best for the time being," Sari concurred.

"Fine, it's settled. Goodbye, Aunt Sari," he said, clicking off.

"Are you sure this is a wise move, Abe? I realize things are chaotic, but once everything settles down, it will get better," Avery assured.

"From your mouth to God's ears, Ave." He blew out a breath, then continued. "Tell the driver to pull off at the next turn. I'm taking Keturah to our home. Then I'll need you to go to the office and collect several files." He was hoping to reason with Keturah, on the drive home but the only thing he ended up doing was losing his temper.

"Mr. Taylor...you called for me?"

Startled, Abraham quickly swung around to see his house manager Consuela come up behind him.

"Oh, sir, I'm so sorry. I didn't mean to startle you," the middle-aged Hispanic woman said.

"It's okay, Suela, I...". He chuckled as the muscles in his neck relaxed. Moving towards her he opened his arms for a hug. "It's good to see you."

Her face broke into a genuine smile as she returned his embrace. "It is good to see you as well. It has been some time."

"It has been too long." He smiled, releasing her and looking around. "I've missed this place. It's hard being here sometimes..." He decided not to finish the thought.

"I understand.... It's been worse not having anyone around," Consuela confessed.

He nodded his head in understanding. Neither he nor Isaac had come home since Sarah had died.

Of course, he kept in touch, but rarely did he visit the staff. "Well, all of that changes today. My new wife and children will be moving in today, and I will be working from home for a little while until they get settled and then out of the Gastonia office. I hope you were able to get everything ready for them."

"Oh, yes! Avery called last week, and we all have been working tirelessly, getting everything prepared." Consuela smiled; her enthusiasm could barely be contained. "Where is the new Mrs. Taylor?" she asked, looking around.

"Well, she is out in the car with the babies. I wanted to make sure everything was ready. Come on, I'll introduce you," Abraham said, guiding Consuela outside. As they walked, she caught him up on all the goings-on regarding the staff and her daughter Carmen's so-called romance with Carlos, his driver. Outside at the main entrance, they continued their conversation until Abraham looked up and saw Avery drop everything trying to catch Keturah, who looked as if she were falling. He was already running to his wife's side even before Avery called out to him. The babies must have awakened as he heard their tiny cries from the car. "Avery, Consuela, take the children inside," he said, scooping what looked to be a very pale and lifeless Keturah in his arms.

"Keturah sweetheart, what's wrong? Are you in pain? Honey, talk to me."

"Home...babies...so tired," Keturah said in a faint voice before passing out completely.

"Tourie...honey!"

"Carlos, come...help Avery with the babies." Consuela took charge. "Mr. Taylor, let's get her inside out of this hot sun. Take her to your room, and I'll call for the doctor," Consuela said as she rushed back towards the house with Avery, Carlos, and Abraham all carrying their precious cargo.

"Father, I know I haven't done right by Keturah or our family. Please give me the chance to set things straight," he said, looking down at how frail she looked. As thoughts of Sarah's last moments flashed in his mind, he shook his head to clear it. "You have a lot of life left in you, Keturah. We have a lot of years ahead of us. I don't plan on raising these babies by myself. So, whatever is going on in you, Tourie, you got to fight, honey. You hear me? You got to fight," he said, holding her close as he carried her up to their bedroom.

It was evening. The beautiful blue afternoon sky was now a turbulent gray. A storm was brewing, you could smell it in the air. The doctor had come and gone. His prognosis was Keturah was dehydrated, and her blood sugar was low. She needed rest and to take better care of herself, something he and Consuela assured the doctor would happen. She was weak, so the doctor suggested she sleep and eat a good meal before nursing the children. Carmen, Consuela's daughter, had arrived around five that evening from the university. Although his house manager insisted that she and Carmen care for the twins, Abraham refused. "I'll take care of them, Consuela. You haven't seen Carmen in a while, so go and spend time with her. I will ring you if I need to." He smiled.

"As you wish. Shall I do anything for Mrs. Taylor?"

"I think she'll be sleeping for a while. I'll be upstairs in the sitting room with the children, that way I can keep an eye on Mrs. Taylor as well." As an afterthought, he turned and stated, "Please have the chef set aside some dinner for Mrs. Taylor. I know she'll be hungry when she wakes.

"Right away Mr. Taylor." Consuela turned and left the room to follow his directives.

"Well, I guess it's just us," he said, walking over to the identical bassinets and looking down first at Abel, who was sleeping with his thumb stuck in his mouth. He shook his head and smiled, recalling Isaac doing the same thing at his age. Sighing, he moved to look at Kamara, who was wide awake, taking in her surroundings with a curious eye.

His heart melted. With both awe and pride, he gushed over his baby girl. "How's my Mari girl doing?" He cooed, picking up his daughter and gently nuzzled her soft black curly crown. "She's perfect Lord…just perfect," his voice wobble as his eyes glistened with tears. His emotion could not be contained as he examined her tiny hand that gripped his finger. God had been faithful to his promise. Chuckling at the strength of her grasp, he kissed her fingers. "I can see now that you're going to be a handful." He spoke and was rewarded with her tiny smile. Thoughts of Sarah drifted in and out of his mind. She so wanted to give him a second child. When they first got married, they dreamed of having a house full of children. She especially wanted a daughter. He always told her it didn't matter to him what they had as long as the child was healthy, but deep down, he wanted a little girl too. Then Isaac was born, their miracle child. Sarah was ecstatic; they both were. God had kept his promise. He had miraculously given them a son. However, Sarah's body had gone through so many changes birthing Isaac, he'd never think of wanting her to go through it again. No, Ishmael and Isaac were enough. But somehow holding this little one in his arms was like a healing balm to his very soul.

"Father, thank you for these precious gifts." He prayed, placing her tiny head under his chin, bouncing her as he strolled towards the large bay window overlooking his yard.

The lightening was pulsating in the sky, and the breeze coming through the window alerted him to the rain sure to follow. He held tight to his baby girl, wanting to shelter her and his son from every storm, every possible danger she and Abel could ever face.

*"To protect them, you'll need to be present for them and their mother,"* a quiet voice whispered.

"She's going to fight me every step of the way Lord."

*"Show her the other side of you!* "God's voice echoed Sarah's dying words to him.

He bowed his head. He had denied his first wife her last request and was denying his current wife her only request.

*"Show her the other side of you"*, echoed in his ears as a low moan coming from the monitor caused his head to turn. Keturah was waking. Turning away from the window, he moved towards his bedroom. With a new resolve in his heart, he was determined no matter how hard it would be or how long it would take, it was time he held on to his wayward wife and reclaim her as his bride.

*** 

A loud crack of thunder startled Keturah awake. Disoriented, she lifted her head off the pillow. Her mind was groggy, and her body felt heavy, but overall, she was rested. Another loud clap of thunder brought her upright into a seated position. It was then she realized she was in a stranger's bed. "Where am I?" she wondered, realizing she must have fallen asleep. Scratching her head while taking in her unfamiliar surroundings, she looked at the massive room she was occupying. It was very modern, yet not overly masculine, something she couldn't picture her husband sleeping in. The bed faced a larger set of French doors leading to a balcony which displayed an evening sky dark with ominous storm clouds. A shiver ran down her spine. Placing her hand on her bare shoulder, she realized her church clothes were gone, and she was now wearing a blue colored silk negligee. "I'm sure I have Abraham to thank for this!" she deduced into the quietness of the room. As shadows danced on the walls, and the lightning continued to illuminate the sky, her children's faces popped in her mind.

"Kamara, Abel!" Panic to locate her children had her on her feet and moving, but where…where were her children? Running towards the first door she came to, she walked through it, and a small hallway opened up into what appeared to be a nursery bigger than her entire condo.

The room was dimly lit, and soft music played in the background. Two cribs were sitting in the middle of the room. Going to the first crib, her heart sank when she found it unoccupied. Checking the other and seeing it was empty as well, her heart thudded against her chest. She was about to go into a complete panic when a hand touched her arm. Frightened, she turned and was immediately relieved to see Abraham cradling Kamara in his arm. A tiny bottle was stuck in her daughter's chubby cheeks and with wide eye fascination Kamara's innocent gaze followed her father's every move.

Before she could even ask, Abraham placed his hand on the small of her back and guided her towards the door he had just come through. The large room had a huge flat-screen TV and a dark leather couch. This room was definitely masculine in its decoration but wasn't cluttered. He had two recliners facing the TV as well and what looked to be a double bassinet beside one of the recliners. Going to the bassinets, she saw a contented Abel quietly napping.

"How long have I been asleep?" Keturah asked while stroking Abel's soft crown.

"A couple hours. You missed dinner, but I'll call downstairs for the chef to bring you a plate." Abraham walked to his desk and picked up a phone.

"That won't be necessary. I'm not hungry," Keturah claimed just as a loud grumble from her abdomen refuted her statement.

"Keturah, you have to eat. The doctor said—"

"Doctor, what doctor?" She looked at him, perplexed.

"You don't remember fainting after you arrived?"

"No." She looked confused.

"Well, you did. The doctor came over, and he said you needed to take better care of yourself Keturah and recommended not breastfeeding until you ate."

"Well, I feel fine, and I'm quite capable of taking care of the twins." She wrapped her arms around her waist, affronted by his remarks.

"Abel and Kamara have already been fed and changed, so there's no reason you can't eat a good meal," he pressed. After speaking to someone about sending a tray up to the master suite he hung up. "It will be here in about ten minutes". Striding back to the couch with Kamara in tow, he sat down by the bassinet and indicated for her to have a seat next to him. All she wanted to do was grab both of her babies and run as fast as she could. Her intent must have shown on her face.

"Keturah, you might as well sit down and relax. It's storming outside, and there's no way you're going out with our children in this weather," he stated with finality.

Feeling trapped, instead of sitting she began to pace. "You can't just keep me here against my will Abraham. That's called kidnapping and believe it or not you are subject to the law," she protested.

"Good thing I'm friends with a judge," he said sarcastically.

"I'm serious. You don't have the right to keep me here."

"Fine, you can go when it's not storming, but the twins are remaining here."

"Oh, no, they aren't. How dare you…" She stomped.

"How dare I what?" Abraham said in a calm tone, his eyes fastened on Kamara's chubby cheeks gulping down her milk.

"How dare you act like you have the right to boss me around?" she declared.

"The last time I checked, I'm still your husband and the head of our family."

"Family?" Keturah snorted in disgust. "Abraham, how can you call us a family?'

"Everyone in this room is a Taylor; hence, we are family."

"I don't know what type of family you were raised in, but in my house, family sticks together." She gave him a fierce gaze. "So, where were you *Mr. Family Man* for my pregnancy, their births, and everything else leading to this moment? For the majority of our marriage, you've been absent. Then suddenly today, you appear dishing out orders and telling me how things are going to be from now on?" She threw up her hands dramatically. "Well, I'm sorry to inform you *Mr. Taylor*, but our business arrangement is over, and all bets are off." She said crossing her arms and leveling him with a fiery glare. "I realize the children complicate things, but the babies are here now, and we don't need anything from you. I'll give you a quiet divorce, I'll even leave town, you won't be bother by us any further that I can assure you."

He continued to remained quiet...too quiet for her liking. She watched as he took the bottle out of Kamara's mouth and placed a cloth over his shoulder. He then placed her on the cloth and stroked her back until she gave a pronounced burp.

"That's my girl." He smiled as he placed her back in the crook of his arm and rocked her while she watched, eating up his every word. "Look at those pretty eyes of yours. Daddy's going to have to get a bodyguard for my pretty Mari to keep would-be suitors at bay," he cooed.

It was obvious that Kamara was destined to be a daddy's girl. *"How lucky you are to know that your father loves you."* Keturah thought, feeling the emotion rise in her throat.

"Keturah, honey, what's wrong?" Abraham looked at her with worry. "Are you feeling okay? Please come and sit down," he pleaded.

"Do you think my father ever held me when I was Kamara's age?" she said, her voice sounding far off as she spoke. Had her father, Kedron Jaymes, ever held her or spoke to her like a proud father holding his princess? How she would've loved to think so. For one brief moment, she envied her own daughter. Would Kamara and Abel be angry with her for taking their father away? How would she explain to them Abraham's absence in their lives? How could she shield them from the embarrassment and deeply embedded hurt they would feel believing their father didn't care?

"Tourie."

Feeling his hand caress her cheek brought her mind back to the present. Instead of drawing away from him like her muddled thoughts were telling her to, her rebellious body leaned in towards him, soaking up all the affection he offered. Turning her around to face him fully, his thumb swept away the tears staining her cheeks. She wanted to remain vigilant, but after all this time, he remained her one weakness. If only he'd stop touching her face, making her remember how good it felt being close to him. Like a bee lured to the sweet nectar of a flower, she couldn't resist him...even though she knew she should. So, when his mouth pressed down on hers first gently at first then more demanding, she felt her last band of resistance break.

"Tourie...I've missed you," he whispered just above her lips, then moved away.

"No...please don't go," she spoke out, then covered her mouth, feeling humiliated for her need of him. Even after everything, she still longed for the affection of her husband.

Taking her hand in his, he kissed her palm. "Baby...I'm not going anywhere." His eyes sparkled, reflecting his own desire. Turning from her, he placed Kamara back in her crib.

*"There is no turning back from this,"* a whisper within her heart spoke.

As he cared for their daughter, Keturah had a brief reprieve from his overpowering presence. It was now or never—she was either going walk away or continue this dangerous dance they were embarking on. Looking at him as he turned back around, she moved towards him first. She had made her decision. There would be no going back. Whose need was greater she couldn't tell…all she knew was when he took her in his arms, she never wanted to leave them for it was the safest she had felt in months. Their past, present, and future all seemed to collide trapping them together in this moment.

She could feel herself being lowered to the floor, then the weight of Abraham pressing her down into the lush carpet. All protest was lost. Longing mixed with weariness, pain mixed with pleasure and desire overpowered any reasoning she had left as everything seemed to tumble together as they reenacted their marriage covenant.

# *Chapter Thirteen*

"Mmm." Tippany gave a contented sigh as the robust aroma of her caramel mocha latte relaxed her tense nerves. She hated being sneaky. It made her feel like she was becoming more like her mother every day. The very thought brought a sudden chill down her spine. Shivering, she shook the frightening thought out of her head. "I'm nothing like *her*," she refuted. Closing her eyes, she allowed her mind to conjure up an image of her real mother, Pamela Birch, in her thoughts. She and her biological mother both shared similar features. They had the same radiant smile, long thick raven-colored hair, slender build. The other thing they had in common was their desire for other women's men. She sighed at that truth. Her biological mother wanted her father even though he was married to Sari, and she wanted Parson even though he was in love with Keturah. "I should just stay clear of him." Tippany agonized within herself. A sudden buzzing sound from her purse brought her back to the present. Reaching in her purse she retrieved her cell phone. Her heart immediately warmed when she looked at the caller I.D., "Hey Parson. Where are you?"

"I'm stuck in traffic. I wanted to call so you won't worry."

"Oh, you are such the gentleman," she flirted. "No worries, I'm just enjoying this beautiful weather. By the way, I'm going to order you a cappuccino since I know how much you despise plain coffee. Do you want extra whipped cream and caramel in yours?"

"Awe, you're so wonderful, darlin. See you in a few," he said, clicking off.

"Yes, Carlton Parson, I am," she said to herself, knowing he didn't really mean anything by the term of endearment, but it meant the world to her. Something deeper like love was something she could only hope for down the road.

*"What about you and Conrad?"* Her conscious nudged.

She sighed regretfully at the thought. She was no angel, that was for sure, but something about Carlton made her want to be a better person. "Carlton just needs some time away from Keturah, so he can see the big picture. A picture without Keturah, just me." Tippany sighed quietly as images of them dancing together swirled in her head. She just knew it could work out for them. But it seemed some of her plans backfired. First, the lawsuit and now the showdown in the church parking lot. Holding her forehead with both hands, she fully regretted the mess she had created for Carlton but mainly for herself. She cringed as her thoughts drifted back to where she was and what she was doing when Carlton called frantic after his run-in with Abraham.

Normally after church, people ate a good meal with family and friends; however, for her, a casual hook up with her ex was becoming a regular occurrence. She never planned on seeing Conrad Jessup again, let alone allow him back in her bed, but she was bored, and sex was something he was really good at. To be fair to herself, she only attended church that Sunday because she felt guilty for spying on Keturah. Then she spied Conrad, who looked delicious in his dark blue usher suit; like a glass of cold water, she drank him in. She'd be lying if she said she wasn't trying to get the attention of her playmate when she dropped money into the offering basket. She had caught the eye of several young men in the congregation, but he never looked her way.

After church, she went home and hadn't been there a good ten minutes before he was knocking on her backdoor. Smiling nonchalantly, she walked to the door, opened it and was greeted by his seductive smile. He walked in, shut the door behind him, picked her up, and made a beeline to her bedroom. Conrad hadn't changed—although he was good in the sack, there was nothing between his ears that could hold her attention for long, but he was perfect for his little goodie-two-shoes fiancée Cassandra Robertson, the bishop's daughter. Tippany chuckled, knowing full well he wasn't getting anything from her. She would be a chaste bride for Conrad...the louse. Shame she didn't know what a sneak her husband-to-be was. Cassandra was just as clueless, if not more so than Conrad. She understood why he chose her, she made him look smart.

Tippany laid back in her bed, her body content but her mind racing to keep her conscience busy. She had had her fill of Conrad, now he needed to leave immediately, which is what she told him, but he insisted he needed to take a shower first before meeting with his fiancé for their appointment with the wedding planner. Conceding, she allowed him to freshen up. It was out of sheer spite that she eyed his suit and decided to douse it once or twice with one of her heavily scented perfumes. Cassandra would likely not even notice, she was so dense, but Conrad would know and be forced to sit there the entire time with his stupid little bride-to-be smelling the scent of the woman he had been with that afternoon.

"Serves you right, jerk." Stretching in bed, she chuckled to herself until a familiar jingle on her cell phone cause her to bolt straight up. "Carlton!?" Grabbing the sheets, she immediately covered her bare chest as if to shield him from her sin. She wanted Carlton to think well of her, not as if she was some slut who couldn't keep her skirt down. The thought was sobering. It dawned on her this was the Sunday she had informed Abraham of Carlton and Keturah's whereabouts. Her curiosity would not allow her to let his call go to voicemail. Wrapping the sheet around herself, she exited the bedroom with her cellphone in hand. "Hello...hello Carlton?" she said, clearing her throat so it wouldn't sound so raspy.

"Tippy, I'm on my way to your place. I need to talk with you, do you have the time?"

"You're coming here...now!" She panicked feeling the need to shower to cleanse her of her sinful behavior. "How close are you?" Tugging the sheet around her tighter, as her heartbeat hammered in her chest. "Oh God, if he bumps into Conrad, how will I explain?" she wondered, quickly, she tried stalling him. "Well, I'm just getting up from taking a nap...Umm...w-what's going on?

"He's got her Tippy. He came to church and hauled her and the children away like you would a prisoner."

"Wait...who hauled who away?"

"Abraham!"

Loosening the grip on her sheet and sighing, her pulse began normalizing. She should have known this had something to do with Keturah. Carlton was protective to a fault when it came to her sister. *If only he'd be that way with me.* She momentarily allowed her mind to wander with the possibility. "Carlton, Keturah is still his wife, and he does have a right to see her."

"I know that, but she didn't want to go. She only went because he was making an enormous scene in the church parking lot. Since she's left with him this afternoon, I haven't been able to get in touch with her at all. He's probably blocking my calls somehow. What if he's holding her against her will or using the children to keep her in line? We've got to get to her, Tippany."

"Carlton, please calm down," she rolled her eyes. "I've known Abraham all my life, and kidnapping his wife is not his style. Why don't we meet somewhere and…"?

"What the heck babe, my clothes smell like your perfume!" Conrad yelled from her bedroom.

Her eyes widened. Quickly muting the phone, and whirled around yelling back at him, "Shut up and get out of here, you moron."

Shocked and angered, Conrad fired back, "Fine then, I'm leaving… you are so schizo." He fussed, tugging his suit coat on, and marched towards the back door. "I swear if the sex wasn't good, I wouldn't even bother with you."

"Get out!" Tippany stomped her foot, pointing to her back door.

"Oh, by the way, I left you a little gift in your bathroom. He blew her a kiss then quickly shut the door to keep the silver salt shaker she threw from connecting with his head.

"Tippy, are you still there?"

"Yeah, I'm here," she was saying, rushing towards her back door to secure the lock. Thank God she hadn't given the idiot a key. "Look, you are more than welcome to come over here if you want." Remembering Conrad's last words, she paused. "On second thought, I have to go out, how far are you from our favorite spot?"

"Twenty or so minutes."

"Great, see you in twenty." Clicking off, she dropped the cell phone on her counter and ran into the bedroom. Discarding her sheet, she moved into her bathroom for a quick shower but came to a complete halt. "Oh, you have been busy...haven't you." She fumed glaring at a broken condom he had draped on her counter, then in her favorite lipstick wrote on the mirror, *you might want to check yourself darlin.*

"You disgusting oaf," she muttered through gritted teeth trying not to curse but was sure she was going to lose the battle. Thank God she had told Carlton to meet her elsewhere.

A horn honking in the distance brought her mind to the present time. Shaking her head to rid herself of that afternoon's events, she patted her purse and felt a little relief, knowing the day after pill she just purchased was tucked safely inside. With Conrad, she kept a regular supply on hand. She knew if she wanted to be part of Carlton's world, she would need to clean up her act. She was trying, hadn't been scoping out anyone—well except for sleeping with Conrad, but she wasn't really counting him, especially after the stunt he pulled today. Conrad was nothing more than a quick fling she had already written off, and no one would be the wiser.

*What about Cassandra?*

She dropped her cup on the table, causing the hot latte to splash on her hand. The sudden image of the woman's face unnerved her. Looking around to see if anyone had noticed, she grabbed a napkin and dabbed at the spilled liquid. Most of the time, when she heard that soft voice, she ignored it, but not this time. "Keturah!" she bit out in quiet annoyance.

Never had this kind of thing bothered her before until she started getting closer to her big sister. Keturah's genuine faith couldn't be disputed and honestly put hers, and the entire Jaymes clan to shame. No, she wasn't as demonstrative in her faith as Keturah, but that didn't mean she wasn't cognizant of God's voice.

"What Conrad and I do as consenting adults is our business. Besides, it's my body, and if I'm old enough to feed it, clothe it and keep it safe, surely, I'm grown enough to determine whether to have sex with someone or not," she reasoned.

*You are not your own. You've been brought with a price.*

Squeezing tight the tissue she had mopped up her spill with, she closed her eyes to ward off the sensation of tears gathering behind her eyes, as shame and guilt for what she had done began closing in on her. "Why did I sleep with Conrad? What type of bride will I make any man if I can't get it together?" It was her mother's words but her voice. She hated it when her mother talked like that, but deep down, she believed it too. Beating herself up wouldn't change what she had done.

*You got to fess up when you mess up!*

It was a little saying she remembered her pastor would always tell the congregation. "God, I messed up!" The words came out barely above a whisper, but they were completely sincere. "I want to be a better person, like Keturah. Don't give up on me." After a moment's thought, she added, "And help me not give up on myself." Not knowing how to end this type of conversation with God, shrugging, she said what came naturally. "Okay, bye for now." Breathing deeply, she let out a cleansing sigh.

"Hey, beautiful." Carlton came from out of nowhere, swooped in, and gave her a quick kiss on the cheek before sitting down.

"Oh, wow…hey there," Tippany said, swiping moisture under her eyes and returning her sunglasses to her face. "I was beginning to think you had gotten lost."

"Yeah, traffic was murder, but it was good because it gave me a chance to cool down and think." He took his seat and took a long sip of his latte. "By the way, thanks for this." He raised his drink in salute of her.

"You're welcome, and what were you thinking about."

"I think I might have bitten off more than I can chew with Abraham. What do you think I'm up against?"

*The fight of your life*...she thought but said, "A great white shark." Smirking at his scrunched-up face, she added. "Let's see what we can do to get you out of these deep waters."

# *Chapter Fourteen*

The sun shone bright and sat high in the blue sky. The storm from the night before had passed. Abraham looked out at the fresh new day, dreading what lay ahead. Looking back at the bed where Keturah was still sleeping, he sighed. She might have been agreeable to the passion they shared last night, but during the light of day, she would, no doubt, blame him for taking the advantage. But he couldn't help himself. As she laid in his arms last night looking down at her, he knew she was where she belonged with him as his wife and the mother of his children. So, no, he wouldn't let her go. From the minute he laid eyes on her and the children, his desire to reclaim his family nearly consumed him. Besides, Ishmael and Isaac didn't need him, they were men who would soon have families of their own. They were making choices on their own without his guidance.

Ishmael was more than capable of handling business matters. He proved that on several occasions. "Baby, you might not think so, but you and the twins need me." he declared to her sleeping form. He didn't care how spunky and independent she'd become over the last few months in his absence. He hadn't realized how much he missed her and planned to enjoy reacquainting himself with her every chance he got. He could tell by her response to him she had missed him too. It would be an adjustment, but with time they would be okay.

*"Yes, time and some much-needed distance from Carlton Parson."* an inner voice charged.

Clenching his fist, he tried to still the building anger. Parson was nothing more than a parasite, slithering his way in and leaching onto his woman when she was most vulnerable. He had told him to stay away, had threaten to taking him to court, but still, the man persisted. The showdown in the parking lot had been the final straw. Parson would regret his interference in a very costly way, he vowed looking at Keturah one last time as he walked out of the room to check in on the twins. Heading towards the nursery, he was met by Consuela.

"Oh, Mr. Taylor, God has been so gracious to bless you with such precious gifts. Come see them. Oh, they are so beautiful," she gushed as she led her boss to the cribs. "They wake up smiling."

All thoughts of Parson faded the moment he laid eyes on his son and daughter. Consuela was right, these two had to be the happiest children he had ever seen waking up. Turning towards her with a smile, he said, "They are indeed a blessing, although I'm not sure if that's a smile or gas." He chuckled as he pried his pinky out of Kamara's mouth. Looking at her, his heart filled with pride.

Swatting her boss playfully on the arm, she also laughed. "It's not gas, that is pure joy."

It hadn't even been twenty-four hours, but somehow the entire household had become enamored with the twins. Kamara had already wedged herself right in the middle of her daddy's heart, and so had Abel with his quiet demeanor. "Consuela, you don't think this will be too much for Carmen to handle? After all, she still hasn't finished school?" Abraham asked, making a funny face at Kamara and was rewarded with a big toothless grin.

Rolling her eyes and waving her unoccupied hand in the air, she said, "Carmen can handle it. Besides, she needs to focus on her career instead of having silly notions of marriage to that grease jockey." She said tersely.

"Suela, when are you going to give Carlos a break?
He's a good man. You know he and his family have also worked here for years. I consider them just as much part of my family as I consider you."

"Humph." She rolled her eyes.

"I think you're just mad because at the holiday party two years ago, people raved about Carlos' mother's red velvet cake," Abraham jested.

"Mr. Taylor, you know well, and good that was my mama's recipe, and Rita sashayed her hips in my kitchen, copied it, and said it was her own." Consuela wagged her finger at Abraham while picking up Abel in her other arm.

Abraham knew he shouldn't tease about the long-standing feud between his house staff for the last two years. The two matriarchs were still not on good speaking terms, which had wreaked havoc in the love lives of their children. Carlos Alvaro and Carmen Duran were made for each other just like he and Sarah were. Nothing was going to keep him from Sarah all those years, and he highly doubted if the tactics of Consuela and Rita would keep their children apart for much longer. "Oh...Consuela, speaking of the holiday. I think we will hold Thanksgiving dinner here after all."

"Splendid, Mr. Taylor. Oh, we haven't had an opportunity to celebrate since Mrs. Sarah..." Consuela stopped herself, a heavy cloud of sadness draped her expression.

Squeezing her shoulder, he kissed the graying crown of his housekeeper's head. Sarah's passing had impacted them all but especially the staff. Sarah had celebrated every season, every holiday. She was always throwing parties and hosting events. The staff loved her, and she had loved them.

Staff had come and gone, but it was the Alvaro, and the Duran families that had been with them the longest. Consuela had been Isaac's original nanny, who also had a flair for cooking. The Duran's had five children, of which Sarah made sure every one of them had the opportunity to go to college. Even during lean times, the two families had stuck to them like glue. So, when Sarah died, it was a great loss.

"You're right, it has been a long time since we have had anything to celebrate in this house, Consuela, but it seems fitting with the newest Taylors joining us that we celebrate life instead of mourning the dead."

"You are so right. Although God has taken your lovely wife, he has been so gracious to us as well. You now have another beautiful wife, and now these two adorable babies. God truly has blessed you." She swiped at the moisture collecting under the rims of her glasses then smiled up at him. "Okay, boss, I am ready to spend tons of your money...so what will be the theme of this year's dinner party?"

"Consuela, you know I'm not good at these things." Abraham put his hand up and back away for his overly enthused housekeeper.

"Okay, then I will ask the new Mrs. Taylor for the theme of the party."

"Great idea. As a matter of fact, you can help her plan the entire event." This was perfect. What better way to allow Keturah to begin understanding her role in his world than allowing her to throw her first dinner party? "I will see if she is up so I can introduce you two as well as let her meet the rest of the staff."

\*\*\*

*It was a beautiful day. The sun was high in the sky, causing the white sand to glisten against the backdrop of the blue ocean.*

*"What a lovely day!" Keturah thought, lying in the sun.*

*Children's laughter filled her ears. Turning towards the commotion, she saw six of the most adorable children jumping around a man's legs, all begging to be the next one hoisted on his shoulders. One lone girl vying for her father's attention kept pulling at her father's pants leg. "I want up daddy, when will it be my turn?"*

*"Come, daughter, my arms are big enough to carry you too."*

*With a toothless grin, she took his big hand, and in an instant, she was securely seated on her father's shoulder happy and content.*

*Suddenly, it was no longer the toothless girls face Keturah saw but that of her own.*

Startled by the image, Keturah jerked herself awake. "I was dreaming" she said groggily. It was morning, but the drapes had been drawn to shield her from the morning sun. Keturah, not wanting to but needed to get up, moved the heavy comforter off her shoulders and pushed herself upright. As the cool air hit her, it was then she realized she was bare. Covering herself, she twisted to see where Abraham was. For the first time, she could ever remember, she felt relief that he was not beside her after they had made love.

"God, what have I done," she berated herself. She knew she should have been stronger and told him, no, but the truth was she just didn't want to. She loved the pigheaded man. Thinking back to the dream, she wondered what it meant. The man in her dream kind of resembled her dad but looked a little like Abraham as well. "Lord, what are you trying to tell me," she mumbled as her jumbled thoughts went back and forth.

"I'm not sure what God is trying to tell you sweetheart, but I know your daughter and son's fussiness is trying to tell you they are hungry," Abraham quipped, standing in the doorway looking relaxed.

It was only then she recognized the faint cries of her children. Looking at the clock on the nightstand and seeing it was a little past eight, she was astonished that she had missed one of their feedings. "Oh, my Lord, I didn't know I slept so long." She tossed the covers off of her, moving quickly towards Abraham.

"Whoa, Keturah slow down. Kamara and Abel are fine."

"No, I have them on a regular schedule. I don't want to mess up their routine," she said, trying to dodge the hands that were trying to keep her in the room. "Please, Abraham, I've got to feed them."

"Okay, but as much as I like your current state," he eyed her with a smile, "I don't want to introduce you to the nanny in your birthday suit, so you might want to slip something on."

Looking down at herself and gasping, she moved out of his reach and quickly shuffled her bare feet back to the bed in search of her nightie, but after throwing the covers back, she saw nothing. Too embarrassed to ask him where it was, she dropped to her knees, hoping it would be under the bed while wishing that either she or Abraham would somehow disappear. Suddenly something cool and silky covered her shoulders as the scent of her husband's aftershave wafted to her nostrils.

"You are tempting me something, awful woman." He uncovered a shoulder and placed a lingering kiss. "You better be glad our children need you more than I do right now, or you would be my Monday morning breakfast." He pulled her up as he stood, helping her get the robe he gave her on.

Turning around, unable to look him fully in the eye, she mumbled, "I think last night was a mistake, and until we get things settled, we shouldn't do...um...we should keep things uncomplicated." Feeling his fingers under her chin prompted her to look up.

"You can keep things as uncomplicated as you need to, but I'm not confused as to what I want," he said, bending his head down towards hers ready to kiss her.

Keturah turned her head. She wanted...no needed to keep her wits about her. She needed to stay in the present. "I'm glad you're not confused, Abraham because I sure am. I'm confused about everything. About us, about you leaving me here for months and not responding to any of my texts, emails, calls...nothing. There was no communication between us for my entire pregnancy." She said knotting her robe as she moved out of his reach.

"Keturah, I realize I have a lot to make up for," Abraham began.

Putting up her hand, she stopped him. "You don't have to. I don't want anything from you. This has been a crazy ride. This marriage in such a short time has gone through so many ups and downs that I'm dizzy from it all. All I want is to get my babies and move on. I think it's the best thing for us not to bring children up in something that was built on a lie," she said, pushing past him and walking towards the door.

"So that's it. You want to take our children and go hide somewhere and live off your newly found inheritance? Is that your plan, Keturah?" His facial features harden and his body stiffened with his accusation.

He caught her off guard with the mention of her inheritance. She turned towards him with suspicion in her eye. "What do you mean?"

"Keturah, it is rare that I ever come into a situation without knowing what's at stake. I've known about your inheritance from Thomas Birch for some time. I know about your grandfather's company and the CEO position that has been offered to you. I also know of the marriage stipulation attached to your inheritance."

"So, I guess you've been doing your homework since you've been back," she said sarcasm dripping off her words. "So, what's your point?"

"My point is you still need me." He eyed her. "So, let's make this work."

"Abraham, all I want are my children, and we will be out of your life. You said you only wanted a marriage of convenience. Granted, we blurred the lines. But there will not be any further complications. I will pack up and leave, and you'll never see me again."

"And therein lies the complication," he said, moving towards her and pulling her into his arms. "I have no desire for you to go. I want you and the children here with me."

"Why?" she pleaded. He seemed on the verge of saying something, the one thing that could make all the difference to her, to their marriage, but suddenly she saw him back away.

"I want to see them grow. I want to be the one to place Abel and Kamara on my shoulders, so they will know that their father loves them," he said in earnest. "Look, I know yesterday I said hurtful things, and I shouldn't have. I have no desire to take the kids away from you, but please Keturah, don't take them away from me."

"And us...what happens to us? Am I supposed to watch you love your kids and...?"

An urgent knock on the door had them both turning their heads.

"I am so sorry Mr. Taylor, but this little one is not willing to take a bottle," A concerned Consuela said.

"I'll take her." Keturah held out her hands to a very fussy Kamara. She hardly had her in her arms before she was trying to nurse through her robe.

"She definitely knows what she wants." Abraham laughed. "By the way, this is Consuela Duran, our housekeeper, cook, and makeshift nanny." He smiled affectionately at her.

"It's nice meeting you," Keturah said as she shifted Kamara around so she could nurse her. "Is Abel back in the nursery?" Keturah said, turning towards Abraham but was surprised to see he was gone.

"Yes, he is in the nursery, but it is this way." Consuela pointed towards the hallway she came from.

"Oh...I see. Where did Mr. Taylor go?" she asked, saddened that he was unable or unwilling to answer her last question.

"Oh... probably taking care of some business, a merger likely." Consuela waved a dismissive hand.

"Yeah…probably," she said, following the woman out the door thinking if only she could get him to finalize their merger.

***

"This is ridiculous!" Moving from one side of the hall to the next Keturah, lost in a corridor of mahogany colored doors scratched her head. "Does one person really need this many rooms in a house?" She shook her head-turning one way then the other trying to figure out where she was and where her babies were. Consuela had been so helpful with the babies that morning, she decided to take a tour of Abraham's home. She never expected to get turned around and unable to find her way back to the nursery. As she walked down another hallway, she saw a door slightly cracked. Thinking it must be the door she came out of, she quickly moved towards it and walked in.

"Oh my God…I'm so sorry." She shut the door on the passionately embracing couple, turned, and walked in the opposite direction embarrassed that she hadn't thought to knock first.

"Mrs. Taylor, please wait, don't go." A young woman's voice pursued her.

Not wanting to stop, but knowing she should, Keturah slowed her rapid gait until the woman was at her side. "Mrs. Taylor, I am so…so very sorry about that."

Still reddened by what she saw, Keturah turned slightly towards the woman and was surprised to see she didn't appear to be much older than Tippany. "I'm the one who is sorry. I should have knocked instead of just coming in on you like that."

"Mrs. Taylor, this is your home. You have the right to come in any room you choose," she said graciously. "Please accept my apology. I just got home last night, and I haven't seen Carlos in so long that…well, you know." She shrugged.

"I do understand...All too well," She thought to herself, smiling as she extended her hand.

"Oh...my name is Carmen, and it's a pleasure meeting you, Mrs. Taylor." Taking the hand offered, she smiled.

"I'm a little embarrassed to ask you this, but where exactly am I? I left the nursery while the children were napping to take a look around, and now, I'm lost," Keturah confessed.

"Oh, this is the south wing where all of the live-in staff reside." She pointed to a large door that Keturah was sure she had walked through. "You must have come in this way; it connects the south wing to the north wing."

"Carmen...Carmen Duran, your Consuela's daughter, right?"

"Well, umm yes, but Alvera is my last name now." She gave a timid smile.

"Alvera..." Recognition began to dawn on Keturah. "Oh Carlos Alvera, Abraham's driver and you are married? For how long?"

"Just a couple of weeks." She blushed.

"And from what your mother says, you're in college studying early childhood education so you can become an elementary teacher? That's a lot how are you managing both?"

"Well, that's a little complicated," she whispered, leaning in towards Keturah.

There was something about this girl she was instantly taking a liking to. "Okay, I'll bite, why is it so complicated?"

"When I'm talking to my mother and Ms. Jaymes, I'm taking early childhood education. In their minds, I would make an excellent teacher, and that's what they felt I should major in," she said tight-lipped.

"And what do you want to major in?"

"Child psychology!"

"And what is your current major?" Keturah gave her a knowing look.

"Child Psychology!" she smirked back.

"I knew I liked you." Keturah laughed. "So why all the secrecy? Just tell your mother that you want to be a psychologist…"

Carmen looked around to make sure no one else was in the hallway she then pulled Keturah to the side in a conspiratorial huddle. "My mom doesn't know I already changed my major or that I got married a few weeks ago." She scrunched her face up as Keturah's eyes went wide.

"What!?"

"I know this is bad and you're probably wondering who is this wild child Mr. Taylor chose to be the full-time nanny for your children."

"Whoa…whoa…wait...what?" Keturah stood back from the young woman with a frown etched on her face. This was the first she had heard of this. "Since when did Mr. Taylor make this decision?"

"Oh, no…open mouth insert foot." She lightly bounced her palm off her forehead. "So apparently Mr. Taylor hasn't mentioned this to you yet."

Keturah shook her head no. Feeling defensive as she folded her arms across her chest. She remained silent, not sure of how to respond to the news.

"Mr. Taylor had contacted me while he was out of the country, letting me know he would need me to return home and be a full-time nanny once he returned to the states. Which kind of places me in a pinch. I hadn't completed all of my classes technically. I mean, I would have if I was still in the early childhood education program, but the accelerated child psychology program required more time, so I'm a few credits shy."

"So, what you're telling me is that Mr. Taylor had planned for you to come here then take the babies out of the country with him?" Keturah licked her lips and tried to remain calm. Was this his plan all along, to take her babies away from her, and replace her with this...this woman? Keturah's liking of the woman began to diminish.

"Oh no, not at all. He told me that you would likely want the children with you at all times even when you and he went out of town, so he needed a live-in nanny," Carmen said softly.

Detecting a hint of moisture collecting in Carmen's eyes, Keturah relaxed her defensive stance and move closer to the young woman giving her shoulder a supportive nudge. "Let me guess, you having to go out of town not only takes you away from finishing school but also from Carlos?" Watching her nod in the affirmative Keturah continued. "So, you got married to keep you stateside."

Tears dropped off her long black lashes. "I really do love Carlos, and I didn't mean to cause any trouble. I just want to finish what I started and live the life I feel I was meant to live, not what someone has dreamed up for me. I know I shouldn't have used marriage to get something I wanted, but I felt I was out of options."

She wanted to grab the girl by the shoulders and tell her she knew exactly how she felt, but wisdom cautioned her. This was not some random woman she met at a coffee shop; this was one of Abraham's employees...for that matter, her employee as well. This woman could be a possible ally, but she would need to tread lightly until she could determine who she could trust. "Carmen, God has a way of working things out for our good. So, have you met the twins yet?"

"I was just on my way to the nursery when I got sidetracked." She gave a shy smile.

"Good, you can show me how to get there from here and tell me more about yourself?"

"Okay." She gave a genuine smile as they headed towards the north wing.

# *Chapter Fifteen*

"Hey, Consuela, long time no see." Tippany greeted the housekeeper with a quick hug. She had called and texted Keturah to see if she was okay but got no response. Now that it was mid-week, she came out to the Taylor estate to check on her personally.

"Miss Tippy, it's good to see you and Mr. Jenkins. It has been quite a while since seeing you as well."

"Yes, it has been a while, Consuela." Emory chimed in shaking the woman's hand as she extended it to him.

Tippany didn't know if bringing her Uncle Emory was a good idea or not, but when she mentioned going to check in on Keturah, he insisted on coming. "Lord, please don't let Abraham be home." She thought as she gave over her outer coat to the housekeeper.

"Emory, Tippy, this is an unexpected surprise. What brings you here?" Abraham's deep tenor spoke from behind as they entered the foyer.

"Shoot!" Tippany muttered to herself as she spun around to see Abraham approaching from his study, holding a squawking infant in his arms.

"I was coming to check on Keturah and of course..." She pointed to his arms. "Umm, if I had to guess that wail sounds like Kamara."

"You guessed, right. She wants her meal, but Abel is not quite finished," he spoke, his focus fully on pacifying a fussy Kamara. "Besides her crying, everyone is just fine."

"Forgive me if I don't take your word for it, but I'd like to see Keturah for myself." Emory's hard glare never flinched even as Abraham's eye's narrowed.

"Why would you think otherwise, Emory?" Abraham met his gaze with a hard glare of his own.

"Maybe because of the way they got here." Emory moved forward, hands at his side, keeping his eyes straight on Abraham. Her uncle's words held plenty of malice. Tippany cringed. She wasn't sure if they were still on good terms or not once Abe had left town, and Sari announced that Canaan would be backing Malcom for the governor's seat. Her uncle had run a good campaign, but without Abraham's support, his dream of living in the governor's mansion plummeted. "Guess he's not over it," Tippany muttered, not looking forward to any confrontation at the moment.

"If my intentions haven't been clear, let me make them clear for you now. I have always been protective of my family. Keturah and the twins are part of that family, and anyone, friend or foe, who tries to interfere, will regret it." Abraham's tone held no malice, but his meaning was clear. Shivering, Tippany embraced herself with both arms and lowered her gaze from his domineering one. This was the Abraham she was hoping not to see today.

"Then let me make my intentions equally clear." Emory planted his feet and fisted his hands. "While you were gone, it was Adelle, Tippany, myself, and yes, even Parson, who were left to pick up the pieces. So, you can save the cavalier speech for someone who's impressed by it."

"Is this really about Keturah Em, or are you just still furious because I didn't hold your hand as you ran for governor?"

"Ha-ha." Emory, mocked. "You know Abe, you are and will always be an arrogant jerk...you know that." Em came to sit on the couch next to where Abraham stood. "You are living proof that God loves all kinds."

Chuckling, Abraham sat next to Emory. "He has to, otherwise what chance would either one of us have in making it in?"

They both laughed...the tension in the room lessening.

"At least you got Sarah up there pulling for you, probably Gretta too. Me, well..." Emory shrugged."

"Uncle Em, you know good, and well, my dad's up there rooting for you too." Tippany sat on the other side and gave him a quick kiss. After a few moments, she noticed how quiet he was, Abe too. Bringing her head off his shoulder, she eyed them. Both men were making faces trying to keep from laughing. "Ugh!" She pushed on his arm as a howl of laughter erupted from both of them. "You two know my dad might have made it end, so stop it," Tippany said laughter in her voice as well.

They all knew how Kedron Jaymes had left this earth. Reportedly in the arms of Delilah...literally, he was fooling around with a woman called Delilah Chambers, who was married to a pharmacist. For a while, people wondered if the jilted husband did something to her father, but the investigators said there were no signs of foul play.

"I guess I missed the joke, what's so funny?" Keturah appeared in the room arms wrapped around her middle with a cautious look on her face.

Everyone remained silent. No one really wanted to open up that can of worms about her father.

"You haven't missed anything, Tourie," Abraham spoke up as he stood to hand off Kamara to her open arms. "Em and Tippany just stopped by to see you and the twins."

With a raised eyebrow, she studied the group who didn't want to make eye contact. Shrugging, she turned her attention and smiled down at her daughter, who was already trying to nurse through her shirt. Kissing her fuzzy crown, she turned her attention to Tippany. "Well, a visit will have to wait until this hungry girl is feed. Uncle Em, can you stay for a little while?" She righted her daughter on her shoulder to stave off her whimpering.

"Actually Tourie, there is a business meeting that your uncle and I need to attend at the office. Now that Tippany's here, I can take Em back in town, giving you and Tippany some time to visit until I get back."

"Okay, that's fine with me," Tippany said, smiling as she walked over to Keturah and took Kamara out of her hands kissing her tiny face.

"No, it's not," Keturah snapped. "I don't need a babysitter, Abraham. I'm capable of taking care of myself and the twins despite what you think."

"I never implied otherwise," Abraham said in a calm tone.

"You never imply anything. You just issue out orders and expect everyone to obey. I've only been here a couple of days, and you have everything regimented and scheduled out for the children and me."

"Keturah, you are overreacting. If you want the children's schedule-adjusted, we can talk to the staff later when I return." Abraham's tone was firm.

"No! We'll discuss it now. I'm not a member of your board, I'm not one of your employees, and I'm definitely not your doggone servant, so you don't get to dismiss me."

"Fine, Keturah, I will clear my schedule for the rest of the day so we can talk." He huffed fling his hands out from his side, then turned to go into the study.

"You know what, go to your precious meeting," Keturah consented. "Tippany, will you please help me get the babies ready? I'd like to return to my home right now." Keturah turned towards the direction she had come.

"You are not taking my children away from here." Abraham raised his voice coming back towards her.

"Oh yes, I am, and unless you want the newspapers and all of your ritzy little friends to know how you abandoned me so you can run off and have an affair with Hagan, you better stay out of my way." Keturah retorted as fire blazed in her gray eyes.

The two stood glaring at each other, locked in mental combat, neither one aware of the two other figures backing out of the room.

"Uncle Em, I didn't want to drag you into this." Tippany rocked a grumpy Kamara in her arms. "I just wanted to see for myself that Keturah was okay." Tippany woefully looked at her uncle, surprised to see a smirk on his face. "What's so funny?"

"This is a side of Keturah that I'm all too familiar with." He chuckled again then put a consoling arm around Tippany. "Let's go visit my great-nephew."

But what about you and Abraham's board meeting?" She asked allowing her uncle to steer her in the direction of the nursery.

"Yeah, that will be a cakewalk compared to this."


***


Abraham looked at the fury on his wife's face and heaved a heavy sigh. He had put this conversation off way too long. Did he really think she would ignore his six-month absence and just start over? His wife might be naive, but she wasn't dumb. He exhaled slowly as he took cautious steps towards her. "Tourie, is that what you think I've been doing all this time? Cheating on you?" He stood there looking at her, seeing the hurt in her eyes was unbearable.

"It's not what I think...it's what I know!" she belted out, turning from him with arms crossed and shoulders back.

"Then, honey, you don't know a thing about me. Unlike Parson, I respect the sanctity of marriage."

"Does Hagan?" Keturah fired back. "The last time I recall, it was Hagan you were passionately kissing while we were on our so-called honeymoon. It was Hagan's arms you were entwined in at Ishmael's wedding two months ago while I was having your children, and it was her the tabloids deemed as the next Mrs. Taylor."

"Tabloids?!" He threw his hands in the air in complete disgust. "Keturah, why do you insist on reading trash!"

"Up until four days ago, I have not heard from you, and your family hasn't kept in touch with me. So, if it wasn't for this trash as you call it, I wouldn't have a clue to any of your whereabouts," she accused.

"Look, I can explain everything if you give me a minute." Abraham pleaded.

"You can?" She folded her arms with a perplexed look on her face. "You can explain your six-month absence in a minute, how?"

He rolled his eyes. "Well, of course, I can't explain everything, I didn't mean it like that. I realize there is no simple explanation for my absence." He rubbed a hand over his head. "I just wish you had confided in me in the first place. I wouldn't have left."

Placing hands on hips, she glared at him. "I tried calling you countless times, but you never returned my calls. I even came to your office before you left for Madrid, and your secretary had me sitting there like a fool for an hour. It was only when your administrative assistant Kayla came to your office, that I was then informed you had already left," She swiped at a tear. "I was tired of waiting for you. Tired of being the one person in your office, no one respected. So yeah, I left you in the dark. I signed the divorce papers and put them in an envelope along with your ring. I took nothing from you, although you took everything from me."

"Tourie, I'm sorry. There is nothing I can say or do that will excuse my behavior," he simply said, giving up trying to defend himself, remembering scriptures about agreeing with one's adversary quickly. He just never thought it would apply to him and his wife.

Hugging herself around her waist, she paced and talked. "You know, even though I was angry and humiliated by how you treated me, I still reached out to you on the day of the twins' birth to tell you. Because despite everything, I still felt you had a right to know. So, I asked Parson to call you, but even then, you wouldn't respond." Her tears wouldn't be quenched as they streamed freely down her face.

He bowed his head, knowing he had messed up. Walking over to the mantle, he looked at all the family pictures spread across it. For the first time, he noticed how empty it seemed without her and the twins smiling faces. Keturah had a right to be angry, but he couldn't' allow her to believe his leaving had anything to do with some relationship with Hagan that didn't exist. "Tourie, I know I have a lot to answer for, and I will, but honey, you've got to believe me when I say I'm not in a relationship with Hagan," he said, looking away from the mantle and directly into her watery gray eyes. "I don't doubt she wants the title of Mrs. Taylor, but it's already filled. I have a beautiful wife and a family that I want to watch grow."

She shook her head in disbelief ready to walk away when he held on to her shoulders, turning her around he caressed her face with the back of his hand, then placed his forehead on top of hers and spoke in a whisper.

"Keturah, please. I know I won't get any husband or father of the year awards, but please give me a chance."

She sighed heavily then looked up at him. "And you can assure me that there is nothing between you and Hagan?"

"Keturah...my relationship ended with Hagan over thirty years ago."

"But what about the pictures of you two going out together and dancing all hugged up on each other." She charged while fighting her tears as she pulled back from him.

"Keturah it's the tabloids job to sensationalize their stories. Yes, Hagan and I have gone out to dinner but it was with Ishmael and Marlana. The four of us have gone out to black tie affairs but they were all business related."

"And that's all it was...business." She looked at him with misgiving.

"Keturah as God as my witness, that's all it was honey. I have no romantic feelings for Hagan." He pulled her back into his arms...kissing the top of her head. "Now I want to know something from you."

"Yes." Keturah responded her face pressed into his chest.

"What's going on between you and Parson." Immediately, he felt her back stiffen before she pulled out of his arms.

Placing some distance between them, with her back turned to him she spoke softly. "I work with Parson, he's my friend." She said without elaboration.

Closing the gap between them, he stood in front of her and looked at her keenly. "Is that all he is to you Keturah...a friend and a co-worker?"

"Well, yes, I mean Parson and I care for each other's wellbeing." She said casually then, lowered her lashes unable to bear his piercing gaze. "Not once has he tried anything. We were waiting for the divorce to be finalized before exploring anything more." Her voice trailed off, realizing how her words sounded in her own ears.

"Do you love him, Keturah?"

"I...um?"

Taking her gently by the shoulders, Abraham tilted her chin up so she had to look him in the eye. "I want us to work Keturah but I need to know. As I told you, I feel nothing for Hagan. Can you stand here and say the same about Parson?" he challenged with a raised eyebrow.

"I don't' know what to feel Abraham." She turned from him. "A week ago, I was making plans for the upcoming holidays for me and the twins?" She sighed as she ran her fingers through her loose curls. "Now your back and you're saying you want us to be a family. But what I want to know is why? Is this just an extension of our previous agreement that will terminate once you settle this business deal?"

"My business overseas was settled months ago. There will be no more arrangements, no more contracts between us. I want a real marriage. But if this is going to work, I need to know your true feelings for Parson." He allowed silence to fill the room before he spoke again. "Do you love him, Keturah?"

"Yes..." she blurted out nearly choking on the confession as she pulled out of his hold. "And no," she said softly. "I will always love Carlton Parson for how he came to my rescue when I needed his friendship and support, he gave it freely." She spun back around to face him. "So yes, I love him for all of those reasons, Abraham...but I'm not in love with him."

"Okay...I can work with that." There was more he wanted to know, but for now, he'd leave it at that. "Keturah, this is on me. I..." He sighed. He felt hypocritical. Here his wife was truthful about her feelings for Parson but he still couldn't tell her about still being in love with his dead wife. How could he explain his torn heart when it made no sense to him? "Look, I know this isn't going to be easy. But if you are willing to stay...then so am I." It was all he could offer for now. He prayed it would be enough.

Keturah lowered her head and hunched her shoulders. It wasn't a yes but it definitely wasn't a no. He'd take it.

Later that afternoon, alone with her thoughts, Keturah sighed, looking out the window. The sky was filled with a mixture of grayish colored storm clouds that were billowing back and forth in the September sky. Much like her turbulent relationship with her husband. For now, she and Abraham had come to a truce. Yet like the sky ready to unleash a torrential downpour, a similar storm was barreling down on them. Abraham wanted her trust and fidelity, but those two things he couldn't demand or buy, they were something a good husband earned. He had lied, manipulated, and abandoned her. A sudden flash of lightning caused her to step back. It was the first signaled the storm was on its way. "How fitting," Keturah said spitefully turning from the window, then jumping back startled by Consuela's quiet presence in the room.

"Oh, Consuela, I didn't hear you come in," she said, trying to banish the hateful thoughts she was having towards Abraham.

"I didn't mean to startle you, dear. I was just coming to check and see if you were alright."

"I'm...I..." Suddenly she could no longer see the aging housekeeper clearly but only a blurry figure coming closer as her lips began to tremble.

"There...there...my dear. It's going to be okay!" Consuela said as she engulfed Keturah in a loving embrace. It was like coming home when she was younger and had a bad day. Her Gretta was always there with a warm smile and a loving hug. Today Consuela was her Gretta, and she needed every ounce of the comfort this woman was offering. Unable to hold on to her pride or dignity, Keturah cried for the girl who had lost everything.

"Mrs. Taylor, this seems to be a rough time for you and Mr. Taylor right now, but you must know that Jesus loves you, and he will help you through this trial."

"Help us...how can he? This mess can't be fixed, Consuela. Abraham and I..." She swallowed hard, trying to control her wayward emotions. She had to keep reminding herself that these people...although nice...were still Abraham's employees and he could do no wrong in their eyes. She needed to mind her words. "Mr. Taylor and I are so different. I just think those differences are too great to overcome."

"Mrs. Taylor, there is nothing too hard for God, nothing he can't get you through if you trust Him."

She knew she shouldn't tell Abraham's employee personal things about them. It wasn't wise...but she needed someone to talk to. "Things between Mr. Taylor and I are complicated..." She let the words trail off. How could she explain their current situation without revealing the truth about their prior arrangement? It made her look like the gold-digger the tabloids believed her to be.

"Mrs. Taylor, I know you are a woman of faith. I hear you pray while in the nursery. I see you read your Bible. I've heard you singing to your children songs about the love of God and the Lord's tender mercy. I have also heard Mr. Taylor praying in his study for guidance and to be the provider and protector of his family and to honor God all the days of his life. Our God is not deaf, Mrs. Taylor. In Psalms, the word says, 'When his people pray for help, he listens and rescues them from their troubles.'"

"Well, I definitely have some troubles I need rescuing from," Keturah admitted with a wobbly smile. "I'm just not certain what his answer will be."

"True, we don't always know how God will answer," Consuela said, moving from Keturah and looking out the nursery window appearing to be lost in her own thoughts. "Sometimes, we have a death grip on our plans and cringe at the very thought of God, not allowing them to come to pass."

"You sound so much like my grandmother right now," Keturah chuckled while swiping at a tear with the tissue she had in her hand. "She always would say 'baby girl, you gonna have to give up them plans of yours, or you and God are gonna bump heads and honey believe it or not his head is harder than yours."

Both women laughed.

"Your grandmother was wise."

"She truly was. I just wish I would have listened to her more, especially when it came to life and matters of the heart," Keturah confessed.

"Mrs. Taylor, what person do you know, thinks rationally when it comes to love? We always think we know what is best for our lives and believe if God would just keep in step with us, our lives would be great."

Keturah had often thought like this when it came to Parson and Abraham. They both had some great and not so great qualities. If somehow, she could blend them both together and get one great guy, her life would be wonderful. "I guess I do feel that way." Keturah conceded.

"It sounds like you and God were having similar problems," Consuela said, turning around looking fully into Keturah's face, her own eyes glistening with tears. "Remember how God spoke to the prophet Jeremiah when they watched the potter working with the lump of clay on the wheel. He said to Jeremiah, *Can I not do to Israel what the potter does with his clay*," she said, touching Keturah's shoulder. "We are the clay, not the potter. We can be so busy trying to fix things we forget we're supposed to be on the potter's wheel."

"I know, I know you're right." Keturah closed her eyes and sighed, shaking her head in acknowledgment of the truth. "I'm just afraid that if I don't do something, everything will fall apart."

"It might, but Mrs. Taylor remember, if the clay falls, you're still on the potter's wheel, and you're in his hands, which is the safest place to be. All God really needs us to do is remain flexible as he shapes us into what he wants us to be."

A loud wail from the monitor alerted them to one of the twins waking up.

"Kamara!" they both said at the same time, laughing.

"That little girl is going to give her daddy a fit! Mark my words," Consuela said, shaking her head as she headed towards the nursery.

"Consuela."

"Yes, Mrs. Taylor?"

"I've been missing my Gretta for a long time, but today, that ache lessened a little." She smiled as a tear traveled down her face. "Thanks."

With a smile and a nod, the woman turned and disappeared in the other room.

\*\*\*

It was at least an hour's drive into the city to Canaan Enterprises. Driving from his home into downtown Charlotte Abraham watched the blue sky replace the gray storm clouds hovered at home…for now, he had averted a storm between him and his wife. Now he needed to do damage control with Emory.

"Look, Emory, I get it. You and Adelle both have every right to be angry with me, especially the way I've handled things so far with Keturah. I don't know if I can make you ever understand why I did what I did. I don't even know if I understand why I did it myself." Emory kept his eyes straight ahead and said nothing, but Abraham wouldn't be deterred. "Sarah was my forever wife Em. We had planned so many things together, but I never thought I'd have to plan on living life without her." He sighed with the confession.

"I know if I lost my Adelle, I don't think I'd be able to clothe myself, let alone keep myself going." Emory chuckled at his own confession.

"Yeah, some parts of my life will always seem lost. You know Sarah told me she was dying. She had this feeling our move here would be her final one. Within my heart, I knew it as well, but I couldn't accept it." He shook his head, surprised at the moisture collecting in his eyes.

"Death always takes us by surprise even when we know it's coming eventually for all of us," he said, patting Abraham on the shoulder to console him.

"Yeah, I guess. I always run towards a fight, but this time knowing she was going to leave me here on this earth alone, I just couldn't bear it... so I stayed out of town going from one doctor to the next hoping they would tell me something different. Everyone gave me the same eerie message. Go home, be with your wife, enjoy the time you have left." His jaw clenched at the memories. "I hated their pity. I wanted to shove it down their throats as far as it could possibly go. I didn't need sympathy, I needed answers, a solution." He gripped the steering wheel, increasing his speed as they went along. "Then, you called." His Adam's-apple bobbed in his throat, thinking back to that fateful day. "You said two words, come home."

"Abe, sometimes you need a person in your life who can help you see what you already see. Like you said, you already knew Sarah was dying and there was nothing anyone could do but accept it."

"Yeah, I know."

Both lost in thought they drove in silence until reaching the interstate. Emory finally spoke up.

"Abe, Sarah, as wonderful as she was, is gone. Nothing can change it. I need to know where Keturah fits in? Are you here to stay, or is this some territorial thing for you?" Emory, seeing the look in Abraham's eyes, raised a hand to stop him from interrupting. "Wait, here me out. Keturah was devastated when you left without a word. She came to your office to make things right, tell you about the pregnancy but your assistant kept her waiting and then she was told you had left. Your staff doesn't respect Keturah as your wife because you don't. Keturah is a Jaymes but so very different from Sarah. She hasn't had paparazzi following her, she doesn't know how to ignore the gossip, you haven't been there to guide or protect her. She's vulnerable now more so than ever with the babies. As her uncle, I need to know you are going to be more to her than Kedron was to her mother," Emory said with an edge in his tone.

"You have always been a good friend to me, Emory. Heck, I think you're closer to me than my own biological brothers. You've always stuck by me, and I hope you still feel that you can. You're right I haven't been the best husband to Keturah. But I'm nothing like Kedron."

"Aren't you? Just like Kedron, you love two women and you're unwilling to let go of either one of them," Emory faulted.

Sighing heavily and trying to keep his temper in check, he gave a sideways glance at Emory. "I have told Keturah this, I don't know how many times and I can't believe I have to tell you, of all people the same thing. I have no romantic feelings for Hagan. What happened between us was over thirty years ago. It was a mistake; one I will never be able to live down. As I told Keturah and I am telling you now, I wasn't overseas having an affair with Hagan. I was getting reacquainted with my son," Abraham entreated.

"I'm not talking about Hagan," Emory threw back.

"What!?" Abraham again gave him a sideways glance.

"I'm talking about Sarah. You are still in love with your first wife, so where does that leave Keturah?

His words were like a sucker punch he hadn't prepared for. It was nothing but the grace of God that Emory's phone rang before he had to answer the jeering question. It was also a blessing that they were minutes away from Emory's office. He only prayed the call lasted as long. Once again, Emory saw what others didn't or at least was too polite to mention. He hated the comparison Emory had made regarding him and Kedron, but in a sense, he had pegged him right. He was in love with two women, Sarah and Keturah, and he had no desire to let either one go.

# *Chapter Sixteen*

Usually, Parson felt relaxed when hanging out with one of his old fraternity brothers, especially Robert Hines, but today he was on pins and needles, watching the lawyer read over the legal document he was served, Rob remained stone-faced while reading the charges. His lack of expression made Parson wonder if he should be more worried than he already was when meeting with Abraham and his attorney in two days. After scrolling over the last page, he breathed out a heavy sigh and laid the document down.

"Wow, you sure did tick off the wrong husband," Rob said, throwing the papers down on his cluttered desk.

"No kidding, Captain Obvious," Parson rebutted. "My question is, what can I do about it?" Parson stood suddenly, pacing back and forth. "Abraham is relentless in his attempt to ruin me even to the point that I've been suspended from the mentoring project that I've worked years to create. My boss has strongly suggested that I consider being transferred to one of their smaller satellite campuses. If that's not bad enough I've received a directive from dear ole dad, to come home so we can talk."

"What can you say? When it rains, it pours!" Rob pushed himself from his desk and blew out a sigh.

"That's the understatement of the year." Parson went back to his seat and sat down, crossing his leg over his knee. "What I need to know is what are my options?"

"Well, that depends."

"Depends on what?"

"Is it factual? Have you interfered in this man's marriage and alienated him from his wife?" Rob questioned.

"The only person who has alienated Keturah is Abraham Taylor. He has neglected Tourie from the beginning."

"Okay, maybe he did, but did you actually carry Mrs. Taylor in your arms through the streets of Chicago?"

"He left Keturah stranded on the street. I only carried her back to her hotel so she wouldn't have to walk back to the hotel barefoot."

"On the same day in question, did you also buy Mr. Taylor's wife a low-cut dress for a party?"

Rolling his eyes, Parson thrusted himself out of his seat again agitated by the report. "I invited Keturah to a fundraising event last year. She didn't have an appropriate evening dress to wear, so I brought one for her, and besides, she didn't think it was low cut, those are Abraham's words." He refuted.

"Did you introduce yourself to Mr. Taylor as Mrs. Taylor's date for the evening?

"Well, yes!" he rubbed his hand over his forehead and then pinched the bridge of his nose.

"Also, was it your idea to share your suite with Mrs. Taylor?"

"Rob, where was she supposed to sleep? In the street?
She told me she had already checked out of her room. I had an adjoining room with another colleague. I was going to share his room so Keturah could stay in mine," Parson stated. "But in all fairness, all this stuff you're mentioning occurred before I knew Keturah was married to the man."

"Okay after you were made aware, she was married to Mr. Taylor and he requested you to keep away from his wife, did you keep your distance?"

"What gives Rob! You make me sound like some conniving jerk." Parson ran a hand through his hair. "Yes, I stayed away until he left town."

"So, during her husband's time out of the country, what was your relationship with Keturah?"

"We are friends, Rob. I did whatever I could to help her during this difficult time. She felt abandoned by her husband and needed support, and I gave it."

"Okay, and when she asked you to inform Mr. Taylor that she was having his children, did you do that?"

"Yes, I called."

"What message did you leave?"

"Look, I called the jerk, his secretary said he wasn't available. I told her his wife needed to speak with him. She repeated he was out of town," he said in agitation.

"So why did Mrs. Taylor ask you to call, instead of calling herself? Maybe we need to look at this from the standpoint of her leading you on trying to have her cake and eat it too." Rob theorized and began writing something down.

"I'm going to stop you right there. This is between Abraham Taylor and me, we are not dragging Keturah into this mess.

"Yeah, um, I think it's a little late for that. Look, man, most of the time, I would say you could just blow this off. But Abraham Taylor is the type of man who loves a fight, and he has the money and influence to drag this out forever. Can you say the same?"

Remaining quiet for a while, Parson paced back and forth a few more times before blowing out a defeated breath. "Look, Rob, you're right, I don't have the money to duke this thing out with Taylor. He has all the cards in his favor. But the one thing I will not do is drag Keturah's reputation into this. She is a wonderful woman. She just had the cutest twins. She has been through too much for me to try and save my skin by throwing her to the wolves—we have to find another way," Parson pleaded.

"Hey man it's your life, we will play this out the way you want, but it's going to be pretty hard for me to sell that you are innocent of these charges when it's clear you are in love with this man's wife."

Blowing out a long sigh, Parson flopped back down in his chair and placed his hands on his knees. "Is it that obvious?"

"Yeah…it is." Rob stood up walked over to his counter and snagged two bottled waters. "Look, I know this is really none of my business, but man, how did you end up here?" He asked handing Parson a bottle.

"Thanks!" Parson took the water then asked. "What do you mean?" Parson appeared confused at his friend's question.

"Dude, you were the best of us. Ricardo, Jonny, Trevor the rest of our frat brothers… you were then and always, preacher boy. You use to always get on us about being a person of integrity. So how did that guy end up getting involved with another man's wife?"

"Whoa!!!" Parson held up his hand to his friend. "Let me get some things straight. I admit, I do love Keturah, but we have been good friends for a long time. I didn't start having romantic feelings for her until her husband left the country. Keturah had an arrangement with her husband. They both had agreed to dissolve the marriage after Abraham just completed his business deal."

"Oh…I see."

"No, you don't. The only reason Keturah even thought of doing a crazy thing like this was because her grandmother was ill. Abraham promised to take care of all her medical expenses. The marriage was to be in name only, and after a year, they'd go their separate ways."

"Well, it might have started out in name only, but their twins sure say otherwise. But this still doesn't explain how you got here," Rob persisted.

"Keturah signed the divorce papers and gave him his freedom the day he left town. She earnestly thought they were through. She intended to have the children and take care of them herself without his assistance. I guess that's when I started to play more of a role in her life, but it was because she didn't have anyone else, well accept her sister Tippany. Rob, she needed my help, and since we always had each other's back, I didn't see the harm in it."

"Then one thing led to another and…"

"No, we never crossed that line. We hadn't even discussed having a relationship with each other. I wanted to, but Keturah didn't feel free until she had the divorce papers in hand. We had no idea what the holdup was."

"Not that I'm a religious fanatic like you are, but even I can see it was God's divine intervention."

"Maybe your right," Parson said. "All I know is things were going great, and then wham…now I don't know what to do about the lawsuit, about my feelings, my future…" Parson allowed his words to trail off.

"Look, I don't know about your feelings or future, but I do know we have our work cut out for us if I'm going to keep you from losing your shirt."

"Well, what do you think I should do?"

"There are two things you need to do up front. The first thing we need to do when we meet with Mr. Taylor and his attorney is to see if we can settle this before it gets too far out of hand."

"I think I would rather go through Hell Week again at our fraternity than meet with him."

"Agreed," Rob said. "Now, let's see what we can do to get you out of this mess."

"Oh, what is the second thing we should do?" Parson inquired.

"Not we, just you." Rob clarified.

"Okay, what is the second thing I need to do?"

"Like you always told us, preacher, you better get on them ashy knees of yours and repent before God!" Rob said, laughing.

"Oh, you're just full of wisecracks today, aren't you!" Parson groused as he gave a sideways glance at his friend.

"Well, I occasionally have my moments," he said while still chuckling. "Okay, now let's get to work."

"Let's!" Parson said, yet inwardly, he couldn't help but feel convicted that his unsaved frat brother gave him the same advice he had given them so many years ago. However, unlike his frat brothers, he planned on heeding the advice.

# *Chapter Seventeen*

It had been a gruesome week, Abraham thought lying fully awake as a contented Keturah sighed in her sleep draped across his chest. The house was quiet; even the twins had finally settled down and fallen asleep. Peace was everywhere except within his soul. As he absently traced imaginary circles on her bare shoulder, his thoughts drifted back to the volatile meeting he had with Parson that afternoon. He felt his shoulders tense as the memory of Parson's self-righteous arrogance bombarded his thoughts.

*"Do you even love her...or are you capable of loving anyone?" Parson taunted.*

*Abraham knew he was trying to get a rise out of him, but he wouldn't bite, not yet, but Parson was treading on dangerous ground. "The intimate details of my relationship with my wife is not your concern. The issue on the table is your inappropriate interaction with my wife," Abraham charged.*

*"Is this a game to you?" Parson snapped. "You play with Keturah's heart like its nothing like she's a simple pawn in your game. Keturah has feelings. She's warm and considerate, kind, and giving. If you're not going to be the husband she needs, then walk away."*

*"You and your family have made a string of bad business decisions lately, haven't you? To my understanding, your family's business is suffering pretty badly."*

*"W-what?" Parson seemed taken aback by Abraham's abrupt change in topic.*

*"To keep from going under your father has cut all non-essential spending, hasn't he?"*

*"Where are you getting your information from and what in the world does this have to do with Keturah?" Parson charged.*

*"It has everything to do with Keturah." Abraham pushed forward on the table while his attorney eased back in his chair, already knowing Abraham was about to play his hand.*

*"I don't see how my family's business has anything to do with this conversation." Parson sat back in his chair, trying to look unruffled but instead appeared nervous.*

*"Okay let's move on...your uncle is the chairman of the board where you work, is that correct?"*

*"Yes...but so what?"*

*"Your last place of employment was in Arlington, where your aunt was on the trustee board...correct?"*

*"What if she was? It's not like you haven't used your influence to help your family get to where they are in life. So, what is your point?" Parson pointed out.*

*"Okay, let me get to the point."*

*"Please do," Parson rebuffed.*

*"You have and will likely always be a womanizer. I believe the last woman you were involved with; her father owned a major textile company."*

*"I know where you're trying to go with this, and you're wrong. For your information, I ended the relationship with Melody Ingstrum, not the other way around. So, your barking up the wrong tree," Parson bit out.*

*"Actually, that's incorrect." Abraham turned to Parson's attorney and inquired. "Mr. Hines, were you aware you are Mr. Parson's third attorney? He gets a new attorney every time he changes states. Apparently, going after wealthy men's daughters is a rather costly bad habit he has yet to break."*

*Parson clearly rattled, gripped his chair yet held his peace, and said nothing.*

*"What Parson, you don't want to interject, tell the man I'm lying?" Abraham challenged. "Yeah, I didn't think so."*

*"Mr. Taylor, Mr. Parson has made me aware of his past indiscretions. But before you sling any more mud, maybe you want to take your jacket off before any of it ricochets on you. My client was not aware that you and your wife were not legally separated. But why would he question it? You, by right, abandoned your wife while she was carrying your children. There is documented proof of the multiple times she had tried to call you, the numerous messages she had left you. You never responded to any of her calls," Mr. Hines said, throwing the damning documents in front of him. "If you look down at the last page, you'll see the last call was the day your wife delivered your children, made by Mr. Parson."*

*It was Abraham's turn to sit up and take notice. Grabbing the papers, he checked a long list of calls made that he never received. He could try to argue the point, but he already knew that Hagan and his administrative assistant Kayla had those calls intercepted. "There was a reason I didn't return those phone calls of which the reason has been dealt with. But the phone calls are not the issues at hand." Abraham tossed the papers back at the lawyer.*

*"Okay, fine. Then let's proceed with the issues at hand." Parson's lawyer challenged. "Keturah had signed off on a legal document your lawyer drafted, and you had already signed months in advance. Your intent was clear. This was nothing more than a marriage of convenience. When she became inconvenient, you threw her to the side. You abandoned her throughout the entire pregnancy. The only person who didn't was her friend and co-worker Carlton Parson."*

*"According to state law, these divorce papers are null and void the moment Keturah became pregnant. Regardless of her knowledge of the law or lack thereof, she is still legally married," Abraham's attorney Todd Burgess spoke up.*

*"You're right, she is still legally married to your client. But my client is not the cause of the problems in this man's marriage. Mr. Taylor willfully abandoned his pregnant wife to go off and have a romantic fling with his former mistress Hagan Zarah. That is the real cause of his marriage's dissolution. And I will be happy to tell the court and the public just that," Hines retorted.*

The meeting went downhill from there. Shouting ensued, security was called. The only thing resolved was Abraham's determination to wring Parson's scrawny neck if he ever came within a hundred yards of his wife and kids.

*"Blessed are the merciful for they shall obtain mercy."*

The scripture again rung in his ears and settled on his restless heart. He knew he needed to forgive and move on, but it literally pained him to do so. Parson and his lawyer had crossed the line, and he was ready to wage war.

"Abraham.... what's wrong?" A groggy Keturah lifted her head off his chest and looked at his tense face.

"Nothing, go back to sleep," he said with a tight voice.

"You've been like this ever since you've come home, but you won't tell me what's wrong. Why?" Keturah pressed.

He couldn't hold it any longer. "I met with your would-be boyfriend and his lawyer today, and let's just say things didn't go very well," Abraham growled.

"Parson is just a friend. I don't know how many times I have to say it."

"You can tell me all you want. I was sitting across the table from Parson, and I know he has feelings for you."

"So, what if he does? You might be able to control some things, Abe, but you can't control the way a person feels." She moved away from him and sat up, running a hand through her unruly curls.

"So, that's it." Abraham jerked his head off the pillow and sat up to look at her. "I just need to get over the fact this man has a thing for my wife. Like I told you Keturah, I might be a lot of things, but a fool is not one of them."

"Abraham, you have told me in many ways you aren't in love with me. I get it. I'm not even sure why we still come together like this other than out of basic need."

Abraham hated the way her words sounded. When he came home that night, he wanted...no needed her desperately. "Keturah I..." He was at a loss for words.

"Look, let's allow our attorneys to work their magic regarding our marriage's legality, and then we'll get a legal divorce," she said plainly.

"And what about the fact that we have children Keturah not to mention you said you once loved me? Does that no longer factor in?"

"Children of divorced parents live normal lives. It happens every day. We will work things out," she said, lying back down and turning her back to him.

"And what about your feelings for me?" he asked softly.

"I'm a big girl. Besides, isn't the saying, time heals all wounds?" She sighed. "I'll be fine, Abraham."

"But I won't, Keturah," he said, allowing the statement to trail off as he laid down beside her.

Keturah remained silent for a long time before clearing her throat and speaking. "Abraham, what are you trying to say?"

"I don't want a divorce. I don't want you or the children to leave. I want our family to stay together," he confessed.

"Then why did you sign the divorce papers? Why did you give them to me if you didn't want a divorce?" Her voice trembled as she turned to look at him.

He turned away from her, unable to look at the tears flowing down her face. He had caused this woman so much pain, would it just be better for him to let her go? The thought was so alarming he felt his heart accelerate with the notion. It was time for him to be honest. So, with a silent prayer, he began. "I have only been in love with one woman…Sarah. She was the only one I knew how to love…wanted to love. I don't know how to hold on to you without letting go of her, of everything we meant to each other. I don't think I could do that," he whispered.

Taking his chin, she gently pulled his face towards hers. "I'm not asking you to give up Sarah's memory for me." Keturah turned Abraham's face towards her, shocked to see moisture in his eyes. "I'm just asking you to expand your heart a little to include me in it," she said, kissing him tenderly.

"Be patient with me, Keturah. I know things have been chaotic, but I promise I'm willing to do what it takes to make this work," he said softly. He began planting gentle kisses all over her face in a tender gesture, then gazed intently at her mouth. Lowering his head, he kissed her passionately, expressing in action what his words could not yet convey.

*Two weeks later….*

"Marriage counseling." Abraham sighed inwardly as he shook his head looking at the various diplomas littered over the walls of the counselors' office Keturah had scheduled for them. He said he was willing to do what it took to keep his family together, but marital counseling?

"Abraham, please sit down; you're making me nervous," Keturah stated, taking a seat after signing them in.

"Lord, they allow anybody these days to set up a practice," Abraham bemoaned, reading the academic diplomas displayed on the marriage and family therapist office walls. "masters in divinity, masters in counseling. Probably some online school, no doubt," he muttered to himself. He wasn't thrilled about this whole counseling stuff, especially talking about their private matters to people he didn't know. God knows he didn't have the time for it. He just told Keturah he'd do it to satisfy her. He never thought she'd find a therapist so quick. He gave his word he'd come, so there was no escaping it. His intent would be to attend the first few sessions, but after that, forget it. "Can we get started?" Abraham asked Keturah looking at his watch. It was already three o'clock. He hated missing the corporate staff meeting for this foolishness, but Keturah insisted.

"Why are you in such a rush? One minute you don't want to come, and now you're all rearing to go. If you're not going to be fully engaged in this process Abraham then…."

Rolling his eyes, he sighed. His wife had been so defensive as of late. He could hardly make a comment before she was biting his head off. It seemed as if everything he said set her off. "I'm not trying to back out of anything, Keturah. I just asked if we can get started," he said with a slight irritation in his tone.

"You're the one who said you wanted to work on our marriage. So, I go and find someone to counsel us, and now you're ready to back out as soon as it becomes inconvenient for you?" She frowned at him.

"Keturah, I'm here, aren't I?" He raised his hands exasperated by her wary tone. "I'm not trying to get out of anything, okay?" He raised his hands in surrender, wishing he hadn't opened his mouth.

"We'll see." She gave him an annoyed scowl, then folded her arms across her chest and went back to reading her magazine, muttering something under her breath.

Dropping his head back, he looked at the ceiling. *"God, what am I doing wrong?"* He tried appeasing Keturah by coming home early; most nights, they would even eat together. Yet she still was very much on edge around him. The times they spent in the nursery with the babies were the highlight of his day. It was the only time he could visibly see Keturah relax in his presence.

*"Husbands, in the same way, be considerate as you live with your wives and treat them with respect."*

As the scripture reference rose in his mind, he sighed. Things were so different with Sarah, he fussed in his head.

*"You're not married to Sarah!"* Again, the familiar voice admonished.

Heaving a deep sigh, which won him another dirty look from Keturah, Abraham looked up just in time as the office door swung open. A perky young couple stepped out and greeted them.

"Mr. and Mrs. Taylor? Hi, we're the Shaffers'. I'm Harry, and this is my wife, Tamara," he said as they extended their hand towards them.

"Hello." Keturah stood up smiled as she shook hands with them.

Abraham gave a curt nod as he shook the man's hand, assessing him from head to toe in the process. "I have more years of marriage than this man has lived. What can he tell me? If anything, I should be counseling him," Abraham grumbled within himself.

*"Humble yourself under God's mighty hand that he may lift you up in due season."*

Abraham cleared his throat and did his best to clear his mind to keep from entertaining thoughts of grabbing his wife's hand and make a run for the door.

"Mr. Taylor, why don't you follow me and Mrs. Taylor you can follow my wife, and we'll meet up in say about a half-hour or so."

"But I thought this was something we needed to do together?" Keturah timidly questioned.

"Oh, don't worry, Mrs. Taylor. We'll all come together later. Harry and I like to do things a little differently. We first meet with our couples separately so we can get a feel for the people you are individually and then as a couple," Tamara interjected.

Abraham looked at the apprehension etched on his wife's pretty face. It was the first time Keturah seemed unsure about this whole counseling mumbo jumbo. He told her they should have gone with someone more experienced, but she wanted to take this route. He was about to encourage her to back out, but she spoke up again before he could utter the words.

"Okay, I guess we need to start somewhere." She gave a nervous smile to the Shaffer's and then Abraham before turning around and disappearing behind a door Tamara directed her in.

"Well, I guess we'll take this room," Harry said in a friendly tone directing Abraham to follow him through a door opposite the one Keturah and Tamara entered.

The room Harry led Abraham to had no desk or couch, just two comfortable chairs, and a coffee table. Abraham gave another sigh, but this time of relief. At least he wasn't expected to lie down and share his deepest secrets, something he definitely had no intention of doing anyway.

"Mr. Taylor, I never thought in a million years I would ever have the opportunity to meet you. This is truly an honor." Harry smiled enthusiastically.

Suspecting what the man was about to say, Abraham braced himself as he sat stone-faced in front of his would-be therapist.

"I went to several of your Man-Up conferences, and it has really made a huge difference in my life."

"Great…glad to hear it." Abraham gave a fake smile while inwardly he thought to himself, "*And you're going to mentor me regarding my marriage. Wonderful!*"

"So, Mr. Taylor, why don't we sit and talk about why you're here."

Feeling like a total idiot for allowing his wife to talk him into going to some stupid psychotherapy, he gave a heavy sigh. "Why does any man do something crazy like come to therapy when there is no need?" Abraham paused for added effect. "To please the wife."

"Listen, man, say no more. I understand all too well the unspoken power of a wife. Tamara can get me moving in multiple directions just by her tone." He chuckled.

"I'm really just here because I told Keturah I would try counseling, but I'd much rather be on the golf course."

"Look, to be honest, Mr. Taylor…"

"It's Abraham or Abe, there's no need to be so formal." Abraham quickly interjected, thinking he was going to steer this man clear from his personal affairs.

"Thanks, Abraham." He smiled before continuing. "I would love to go out on the golf course with you or even shoot a couple hoops with the youth at our church."

"Then why are you cooped up in here with me?" Abraham jested, feeling a little more relaxed than when he initially arrived.

"My wife put her heart and soul into building a successful counseling practice, but she didn't feel that it was complete. She said there was a certain dynamic she wanted to bring to her clients and thought that I was the missing piece to the puzzle."

"So basically, she sweet-talked you into becoming her partner," Abraham stated with a raised eyebrow.

"Welp, it's not the first time, and I doubt it will be the last," he said, reclining in his chair with his feet propped up. "I have told my wife a thousand times over that men don't take kindly to that touchy-feely stuff as women do."

"Yeah, good luck trying to get that revelation across," Abraham said sarcastically.

"I remember one time telling my wife that I didn't need to express my feelings because she and I were one, and she was the perfect expression of my emotions. You know the whole bone of my bone flesh of my flesh thing."

Both men broke out into laughter.

"I thought I was very profound...even poetic," Harry said, wiping tears out of his eyes.

"Yeah... what did your wife say?" Abraham inquired, swiping at the moisture around his own eyes. This guy is not so bad... he's rather refreshing, Abraham thought.

"Well, my wife has not always been saved, so I'll tell you the PG version of what she said. She looked at me as only a black woman can and said, You're full of crap!"

Again, both men laughed.

"Like I said, that was the PG version." Harry emphasized with his fingers.

"Your wife sounds a lot like my Sar..." Abraham stopped mid-sentence clearing his throat. "Wives can be something else."

"God calls them a good thing, but sometimes..." Harry shook his head without finishing his statement.

"Yeah, trust me, I get it." Abraham huffed.

"Well, I know we both would rather sit here and discuss sports, politics, or anything else but our feelings, but Tamara would kill me."

"Alright, well, we might as well get this over with," Abraham conceded as he sat comfortably in his chair across from Harry.

"I know you're a busy man and probably are missing a board meeting or something like that just to sit down and talk with me so I won't waste any more of your time. Why do you feel your wife wants you to participate in marriage therapy?"

That caught him off guard. He had fully intended to blame this on Keturah being young and inexperienced in the heart; however, Shaffer beat him to the punch. "Well, as you said, my wife thinks we needed it, and this being her first marriage, I thought if it made her feel better, I'd do it for her so…. here I am."

"And, in your opinion, your marriage is fine?"

Abraham twisted in his seat. "It's not perfect, I guess it could be better. We haven't been married long and now have children in the picture. I just think Keturah's on edge because of all of the sudden changes occurring in her life," Abraham acknowledged then added, "But hey that's the nature of the married life. You have your occasional ups and downs." Abraham eased himself back in his chair, thinking, "*Before this session is over, I'm going to school this young buck on a few things regarding marriage.*"

"Well, put Abraham." Harry nodded towards him with a smile. "So, you mentioned your wife is young and on edge? What's causing that?"

"Well, you know who I am and the notoriety that comes with it. I have business ties all over the globe. I can't stay with Keturah as much as she would like. I have been out of the country for several months, and I think now with the twins, she's just worried about what will happen to our family with me traveling so much. I have assured her countless times that we're okay, but..." Abraham shrugged his shoulders. "Here we are."

"Were you out of town much during the pregnancy?"

"Um yeah. Canaan was developing a new business venture overseas, and we were at a crucial time in its development."

"Oh...I see." Harry nodded, writing on his note pad.

Abraham again readjusted his position in the seat and unloosened his necktie. Maybe this wasn't going to be the cakewalk, he thought.

"What other things have made Keturah on edge?"

"Shortly after we were married, her grandmother died. Up until then, it was just the two of them," Abraham said, feeling guilty that he had left her to deal with the pain of her loss on her own.

"So, it sounds like she has had three major events happen in a short amount of time. You two were married, then her grandmother dies, and then she discovers she will be a mother herself. Wow, that's a lot to absorb. How long have you and Keturah been married?"

"I guess maybe a little over eighteen months." Abraham took a stab in the dark. He actually couldn't remember.

"So, on your anniversary, what plans did you make? Especially with the children coming. Did you talk about how often you would be out of town? Did you discuss her fears or what she would need from you?"

Abraham's head was spinning. He had no answers to the questions Harry was asking because he had not been there. With every second, Harry was proving exactly why he did need this marriage counseling mumbo jumbo stuff. "Look, I won't lie to you. I don't have the answers to your questions. My marriage to Keturah.... well, it's complicated."

"Would you say the same thing about your first marriage?"

"I'm not going to talk about her with you." Abraham's tone suddenly took on a gruffness. He quickly stood up, moving away from the chair towards the door then stopped himself. Remembering he told Keturah that he'd try, he fisted his hand and placed it in his pocket, while rubbing his other hand over his shaven head, now a little embarrassed for the outburst.

"Okay, let's talk about your current wife. Do you love Keturah?" Harry said in a calm tone.

Still shaken by the mention of his first marriage, Abraham felt his throat constrict. He tried to speak intelligible words expressing his true feelings for Keturah. "I...um. I want our marriage to work. That's why I'm here." It was all he could manage.

"Okay, we will start there."

"Good." Abraham regained his composure, moved back towards the chair, and sat down.

"But before we do, I'm curious about something," Harry said philosophically as he twisted the top of his pen lid.

"Okay, what is it?"

"When I asked you about your first marriage, you said, 'I won't discuss her with you,' and when I asked you how you felt about your second wife, you said you wanted to make your marriage work?"

"I don't see the problem. As I said earlier, I'm here to make my marriage work."

"Yes, you did say that, but I'm just not clear on which wife you are trying to appease, Sarah or Keturah?"

# Chapter Eighteen

"Hey stranger, I haven't seen too much of you lately," Tippany said as Carlton came over to their table, swooped in, and gave her cheek a quick peck before sitting down.

"I figured I better give you and Keturah some distance if I didn't want to add a restraining order to my list of accomplishments this year." He rolled his eyes, then sighed.

"I thought as much. I was wondering if we are still on for Isaac's and Rebecca's engagement party, or are you planning on ditching that event as well?"

"I don't know Tippy, I'm in enough hot water as it is. I don't think it's good for me to stir the hornets' nest," he said grumpily. "Besides, it's still a month away. If you need to, you can find another date."

"Look, this thing between you and Abraham is ruining everyone's life, and it doesn't make sense. You are my date. You said you'd take me, and I won't let you back out. Besides, you can't stop living life because of your problems with Abraham."

"Easier said than done." He sighed.

She hated seeing him this depressed. She wanted the fun-loving Carlton she was falling in love with, not this morbid woe is me person sitting across from her. "Carlton, life is a gift, and you have to be willing to enjoy it, embrace every moment of it, regardless of the difficulties you face," she encouraged.

"Easy for you to say, you're not unemployed, with a half a million-dollar lawsuit hanging over your head."

Tippany remained silent. She didn't want to pitch her idea at him yet, so decided, she changed the subject. "How is the job hunting going?" she inquired.

He sighed, his dejected look saying it all. "I didn't even get through the second set of doors. I mean, I am totally qualified for the job, but when I got to the interview, the man's secretary told me the chairman of the board would not meet with me. When I tried to give her my references and resume, she said it wouldn't be necessary. I already knew what that meant." He tossed his phone on the table in frustration. "I'm being blackballed, thanks to your brother-in-law."

"Are you sure that the chairman wasn't just busy, or maybe they already filled the position?"

"Tippy, I know how this game works," he said, spreading his hands in front of him. "Besides, my aunt Helena is friends with a few people on that board. She already called me this week asking what was going on with me and that Taylor woman. Rumors are beginning to surface. Before I got here, my dad called again. He needs to see me." Carlton sighed again. "I can only imagine what that means."

At first, she thought to hold off discussing her plan, but if his family came through for him, he might be alright and not need her help. Nervously she bit her inner lip. *"There is no time like the present!!!"* she thought straightening in her seat. "Um...I think I have a solution to your problem, Mr. Parson," she said.

"Oh, do you have half a million dollars stashed somewhere on you?" He gave a mirthless laugh.

She actually did and more, but she wasn't ready to reveal her inheritance's details, not yet. "No, but I do know some things about Mr. Taylor that you don't."

"Really, and what's that?" Carlton said, looking at the menu in disinterest.

"He won't sue you if you're part of his family." Her voice quivered a little as she made the statement.

He frowned at her first then dropped his head back, releasing a great big belly laugh drawing some unwanted attention from the other patrons in the restaurant.

"Carlton, stop that." Tippany admonished him with a slap on the wrist.

"I'm sorry Tippy, but that's hilarious," he said, wiping the tears from his eyes. "Abraham doesn't want me anywhere near his family, so how in the world would I con him into adopting me?" He continued to chuckle, picking up his menu and looking over it again.

"You know, there are other ways for you to get in his family?" she suggested picking up the menu as their waiter came to take their order. Parson stopped laughing, put his menu down, and gave her a curious stare. It was her turn to play it cool, and that's precisely what she did. "Humm, I think I'll have the chicken cob salad today, oh, and topped it off with a zesty vinaigrette. I'll also have the chicken linguine and the white wine sauce, please," Tippany said casually, seeing she had his undivided attention.

"Tippy, what are you talking about?" he said, ignoring the waiter who had turned to him, waiting for his order.

"Aren't you going to order something?" she asked innocently, batting her eyes at him. One thing Tippy knew how to do was hook and reel in a man.

"Fine, give me whatever she's having," he said flippantly to the waiter handing him the menu, his eyes never leaving Tippany's face. "Now, tell me what you're talking about."

"Well, Mr. Parson, have I got a proposition for you," Tippy said coyly taking her napkin off the table and placing it on her lap. She so did love this cat and mouse game, especially since she was so good at it. She had her fish on the hook, now it was time to reel him in.

\*\*\*

Parson in the worse way didn't want to be in his hometown of Lumberton, Louisiana. It wasn't his favorite place. He had worked hard to be at the top of his class in academics and athleticism to obtain a scholarship and leave the memories of this place along with his troubled past far behind. This was where his problems with the opposite sex first started. It was the one thing that seemed to follow him no matter where he went, and sadly his women trouble always seemed to bring him back crawling to his family to save his skin. He hated having to face his father's disappointed glare because once again, he needed his help. When would he learn? He absently stared at his hands to avoid his dad and siblings' eyes, after they had just finished reading the charges of the suit brought against him.

"When will you learn CJ? I have warned you of the consequences that could incur if you kept messing around with all these women. Now you've gone and fooled around with the wrong man's wife," Carl Parson Jr. bellowed. "Abraham Taylor is no one to play with!"

"You don't think I know that?" Parson snapped at his oldest brother. It was bad enough Parson had to ask for help from his family but didn't need to be lectured about his past. He had moved beyond that but leave it to his big brother to rub his mistakes in his face. "This issue is being blown out of proportion by Mr. Taylor," he charged.

"So, this is all a lie, right, bro? You didn't buy his wife a dress or refer to her at the Chicago benefit as your date?" Junior accused.

"Junior, we don't' know all the facts," Charles Parson, his other brother, spoke up.

"Charlie, have you not read the appendages to this suit?" Carl threw it down in front of him. "He was with her throughout her pregnancy, he was at the birth of this man's children, two months later they were out in public on a date the same day he was served these papers.

Anyone in their right mind would have stayed away from trouble, but not our baby brother. After all of this, Taylor still had to confront him at church of all places because he couldn't stay away from his woman! But you dare to sit here and claim your innocence to us?"

"Every one of those events can be explained," Parson defended.

"Okay, son, then why don't you explain it to us?" Carl Parson, Sr. finally spoke up. "Because the information in this lawsuit is damning. And regardless if you want to speak about it or not, you have a history of fooling around with women, trifling with their feelings."

"Dad, I know my history, but it's just that—history. I am not the same man I was before. I care for Keturah, and we both thought her marriage to Mr. Taylor was over, and the divorce was in the process of being finalized. The man had already signed the paperwork months ago, showing intent."

"When you go to court, and he sues the pants off you, you might not want to lead with the fact that you care for his wife," Junior said sarcastically.

"Junior, that's enough," Charles spoke up.

"Maybe you should focus on your own affairs Carl and stay out of my business," Parson hotly stated.

"I'd love to, but I can't because I'm too busy putting out fires that your indiscretions have caused for this family," Junior charged.

"What are you talking about?" Parson questioned.

"Son, you've said enough," Carl Sr. stated.

"No, Dad, I haven't said enough. We've always covered for CJ. He walks around with hardly any responsibility. He relies on the family's name and money to make things good for him. But he could care less about the cost of his actions or those behind the scenes cleaning up his messes."

At that point, his father and brother Charles hung their head.

"I want to know what Carl is talking about," Parson demanded, looking at his father and brothers. His father and Charlie hesitated, but Junior had no problem speaking up.

"The last two years have been rough. That last girl you were with, her father was ready to run your name through the mud and would have if we hadn't stepped in and squashed it. But this thing with Taylor's wife has repercussions."

"What repercussions?" Parson was almost afraid to ask but needed to know how deep this thing had gone.

"Well," Charles began. "We lost three prominent clients last week. Once they heard of your involvement with Taylor's wife, they've pulled back questioning our integrity."

"What!?" Parson said.

"Several other smaller organizations are working with Canaan Enterprise, who are also threatening to pull out of projects we've been working on setting up for months."

"That's a real nice way of explaining it, Charlie."
Junior's cynicism was evident in his tone. "The bottom line is no one wants to do business with us because you're in bed with Taylor's wife."

Before Carl could say another word, Parson was up and out of his seat, grabbing his brother by the collar and pulling him to his feet. "You better watch your mouth, Junior. I'm not in bed with any man's wife. We've never done anything other than talk on the phone and be friends with each other. She's not like that, nor does she want that."

Carlton Julius Parson, take your hands off your brother and sit back down in your seat right now," his father commanded.

Parson gave his brother one last threatening look before letting his collar go and taking his seat.

"Is that what you plan to do when Mr. Taylor's lawyers get a hold of you? Lash out? Believe me, son, his lawyers are going to scrutinize everything you've done with Keturah and any other woman for that matter," his father reprimanded.

Parson remained mute remembering his last meeting with Taylor and his lawyers didn't go well at all.

"Yeah, CJ, and it's not like you haven't given Taylor's lawyers plenty of material to use against you," Junior mocked.

"Junior, shut up," his father warned. "Your list of indiscretions isn't short either, and neither is mine. On your mother's death bed, she warned me that I wouldn't get away with flipping my nose up at God's design of marriage, that I would see the reward of my ways. Well, I see it in all of you." His father took his hand and wiped it down his face. His sons sat quiet, momentarily all lost in their own thoughts.

"Dad, I know I've disappointed you in the past, but I swear, I have not been improper with Keturah. I do have feelings for her, even before she married Mr. Taylor. To be honest, I was thinking of marrying Keturah, but then I got entangled with Melody." He bowed his head in regret. "As God as my witness, I haven't done anything with Mr. Taylor's wife."

"Well, son, the God you say you serve will have to help you out of this one, because I can't." He sighed heavily. "I just don't have the resources to bail you out of this, not this time, son." The senior Parson with a heavy heart heaved a deep sigh.

"But dad, this will financially destroy Carlton if Mr. Taylor pursues this." Alarmed, Charles spoke in his brother's defense.

"What would you have me sacrifice? The business is already in financial trouble. What's left?" Carl Sr. proposed.

*I highly doubt if Abraham will sue his future brother-in-law.*

His conversation with Tippany earlier that week came floating back to his mind. She had proposed to him, said they could have an arrangement mutually beneficial for them both. For the first time, he understood Keturah's plight leading to her decision to marry Taylor. Now that the word was spreading he was on Abraham's hit list, no one would hire him. His dad's backing, he thought, was his last resort, but without even his family being able to bail him out, he was in trouble. What seemed crazy when Tippany initial asked, seemed very promising now.

# *Chapter Nineteen*

"So, you will be at Rebecca's bachelorette party next week, won't you Tourie?" Tippany inquired as she walked down the hallway to her office. She was looking forward to doing something fun. She needed to. After not hearing anything from Carlton, her spirit was down. It had been a week, and he still hadn't called her.

He probably thought she was crazy as a loon, and she was beginning to feel the same thing. She had done many questionable things in her lifetime, but she had never proposed marriage to a man before. She had tried to erase the impulsive gesture from her mind the entire week, but it haunted her still. "No one will ever know I did something so desperate!" She told herself. She only prayed Carlton would be a gentleman and not mention it to anyone, especially not Keturah. Although she knew they were going to the wedding together, she still knew her sister held a torch for the man. It would crush her to know that she was taking things with Carlton much further than even Abraham imagined.

"I don't know," Keturah stated. "The babies are teething and cranky. Besides, I know Isaac is not my biggest fan."

"Look, I know Isaac can be difficult, but Becca's our friend and truthfully your future daughter-in-law, so it really wouldn't look good if you didn't show up."

Keturah heaved a weighty sigh. "Well, when you put it like that..."

"You and Abraham are going through an adjustment phase in your marriage. You're getting to know his lifestyle and family better...and that alone has its own challenges. Just hang in there and keep trying," Tippany said while fumbling for her keys as she reached her office door. Finding them, she took out the key, put it in the lock, and was surprised to find it already open. "I could have sworn I locked this door," she muttered to herself.

"What did you say?" Keturah asked.

"Nothing… listen Tourie, I know things might look bad right now, but things have a way of working out. Just don't give…" Her voice trailed off. Walking into her office, she was greeted by the angry glares of Conrad's fiancé Cassandra Robertson, her parents, and none other than her mother.

"Come on in here, little girl and have a seat," Sari said tersely, sitting behind her desk as if she owned the place.

"Tourie, I'll call you back…okay, bye!" Placing her phone in her purse, she moved forward in the room, trying to gather her wits about her. The Robertson's being in her office could only mean one thing—she and Conrad had been caught.

"Do you happen to know who these people are…little girl?" Sari interrogated.

"Stop calling me little girl, I have a name mother. Besides, I'm far from being anyone's little girl," Tippany protested.

"Oh, I know your name and exactly what you are." Cassandra, full of spite, looked at Tippany with contempt. Cassandra's mother glared at her as well, holding on to her daughter's arm in support.

"Oh, you do?" Tippany had turned towards the woman who looked to be on the verge of tears. "Do tell, exactly what type of woman am I?" Tippany stared the woman down.

"Tippany Jaymes," her mother admonished.

Ignoring her mother rebuke, Tippany folded her arms across her chest and gave Conrad's aggrieved fiancée a challenging glared. If her mother was bold enough to open her office to these strangers and put her business out in the street, she didn't mind giving them a good show.

"You're a whore!!!" Cassandra screeched. "The Bible says many a good man has been brought low by the likes of a whorish woman, and that's exactly what you are." She shook her slender finger at Tippany.

"Okay, I can live with that." Tippany smiled nonchalantly, moving further into her office. "But who's the good man I brought down?" Tippany put her hands on her hips and looked with a matter a fact expression at her accusers.

"You know darn well who I'm talking about. Conrad's a good and decent man, but you can't leave him alone, you keep enticing him, chasing after him, giving him no peace. He told me everything last week. How in a moment of weakness he caved after you threw yourself at him several weeks ago," she cried, placing her hanky to her nose as her parents consoled her.

"How in the world is Conrad going to put up with her until death do they part?" Tippany thought, shaking her head with a chuckle.

"Do you think this is a funny matter, young lady? Do you know how distraught our daughter, our entire family has been? How can you stand there casually, acting as if this means nothing? You've destroyed two lives, and you don't have the decency to even show you care?" Bishop Robertson chastised.

Tippany rolled her eyes at the bishop. His words were laughable. She already knew the truth. Conrad had told her about the money the bishop had paid him to marry his daughter. Cassandra was such a homely looking girl. Conrad saw her as a quick way to rise to the top of the social ladder, and she was an easy meal ticket...even if she wasn't easy on his eyes. He would put up with her as long as he could fool around.

"It's probably why she's not married now! So busy bothering someone else's man, that's how women like you are," Mrs. Robertson spoke up.

"Bishop, Mrs. Robertson, and Cassandra, I am so sorry about all of this," Sari said apologetically. "My daughter is young and immature, not like your Cassandra. I've done all I know how to keep this girl on the right road, but she is a product of her father's spoiling. I only hope you can find it in your heart to forgive my failure," Sari patronized them.

They nodded in the affirmative, while Cassandra still dabbed at her eyes. Tippany scowled at her mother, then looked at the rest of her accusers and shook her head. She was tired of their presence in her office and was ready for them all to leave. She also planned to give Conrad a call and read him the riot act. The thought brought a smile to her face.

"Tippany, wipe that stupid grin off your face and apologize to this family right now!" Sari ordered. "Bishop Robertson, I can assure you, her actions will not go unpunished. We will make restitution in any way we can."

It was that statement that made her realize what this was about. Malcom needed the ministerial vote. What better way to get it than to have the head of the committee in your back pocket? Sari Jaymes, forever the diplomat. Tippany chuckled.

"Tippany Jaymes." Sari slammed her hand on the desk with a scrawl on her face. "I am your mother, and you will do as I say and show this family the respect they deserve. You will apologize, and you will never see Conrad again. He is off-limits. Do you hear me? Off-limits," she commanded.

Flinging her Coach bag on the coffee table, Tippany placed her hands on her hips and glared at her mother and then the Robertson's. She remained quiet just long enough for the silence to create an eerie discomfort for everyone before she spoke. Holding her head, high Tippany looked at each one of them in the face. "I apologize to you all," Tippany said, then glanced towards her mother, who gave a curt nod of satisfaction. "I apologize that Conrad didn't think enough of you to stay out of my bed Cassandra. Bishop Robertson, I'm also sorry that the money you paid Conrad to marry your daughter wasn't enough to keep him from cheating on her before they were married."

"Tippany!!!" Sari bellowed.

"Oh, how dare you speak those lies!" The bishop bellowed.

"It's not a lie. Conrad told me himself the last time we were together, which was only a couple days ago, not weeks like he told you, Cassandra." Tippany said, without batting an eye.

"You hateful tramp!" Mrs. Robertson charged.

"You should know Mrs. Robertson. After all, isn't that what really keeps a man? At least that's what my mother said you did to keep ole bishop here." She winked at the bishop who turned a deep red.

Mrs. Robertson's pale complexion turned ashy white as she looked in horror from her daughter to her husband.

Having had enough of her cat-and-mouse game, she went to her door. "Finally, I apologize because I don't have the time or patience to put up with your crap a moment longer. Please get out of my office, or I'll have security come and collect you," Tippany said, opening the door and nearly had to jump out of the way as the family rushed out. Shutting the door after they exited, Tippany turned around and felt a hard-stinging blow to the left side of her face knocking her off balance. Clutching the door frame with one hand while holding her pulsating cheek with the other, she turned her furious glare at her mother, who stood before her seething with rage.

"When I tell you to do something little girl, you better do it," Sari barked and raised her hand to slap her again; however, her hand was blocked mid-stride as Tippany grabbed and steadied her arm.

"If you ever hit me again, I will slap you back," Tippany threatened. Taking her mother's arm, she forcefully flung it hard against the woman's chest, causing Sari to stumble backward.

"You meandering little ingrate how dare you handle me like this? I'm your mother, but you treat me with no respect at all," Sari charged. Your father would turn over in his grave to see the vindictive little whore you've become.

"Sari Jaymes, you are many things, but my mother, you are not!" Tippany retorted, crossing her arms over her chest.

"What are you talking about?" Sari's eyes narrowed at her daughter's words.

"You know exactly what I'm talking about. You've always known I'm not really your biological daughter. Keturah and I are full-biological sisters, and you said nothing about it...why!? Tippany shouted.

Sari gave a chuckle that didn't resonate on her face as she walked back further into Tippany's office. "Your birth mother Pamela Birch was nothing but a two-bit tramp from the ghetto. She was a common maid that your daddy couldn't keep away from. I didn't care if he had his fun with her, she was less than nothing. As long as he kept his affairs private, but no, your mom wanted more," Sari said nastily. "She claimed to be in love with your daddy, and he was too stupid to see she was nothing more than gutter trash."

Shutting her office door, Tippany walked towards her purse on the coffee table and pulled out her compact. Looking in the mirror, she could see a tiny red mark on her fair complexion. Her anger grew even more, looking at Sari, she challenged her belittling remarks about her birth mother. "Did it ever occur to you my mother loved my dad, and dad loved her?"

Sari turned towards her with the most hateful look on her face. "Do you realize the only thing separating you from being the spitting image of your mother is your skin's fair complexion? Because with that one exception, in every way you have become your mother," Sari hissed. "Despite all my efforts to keep you in the right class, you always felt more comfortable mingling in the trash."

Her remarks stung but not as bad as they had in the past. She had stopped loving this woman when she was a kid. The only thing that made her tolerate her then was her father. When her mother placed her in an out of state private finishing school, she welcomed it. Even a short reprieve from Sari's scrutiny was better than dealing with her daily criticisms. She never understood why she couldn't please her mother like other daughters, but now she knew. "Did you ever care about me? Or was I just the pawn you used to keep daddy in line?" Tippany asked, no emotion resonating in her voice.

Turning her back on Tippany, Sari collected her purse then turned around and spoke. "You have made a mess of your life, but I will not allow you to ruin Malcom's chances to reach the governor's mansion," Sari said. Walking pass Tippany towards the door, she placed her hand on the doorknob. "I have decided you are not capable of making sound decisions. Therefore, as trustee of your inheritance I have contacted our lawyers and have amended the terms of your trust fund."

"You can't do that, mother! Dad's attorney said I will be eligible to have full access to my trust fund when I turned twenty-seven or before if I got married." Tippany charged.

"Yes, he did indeed say that," Sari stated calmly. "However, I took it upon myself to incorporate some minor stipulations that would prohibit you from accessing your trust fund prematurely."

"Things like what?" Tippany eyes narrowed as she looked at her mother, suspiciously.

"Well, things like you needing to finish graduate school, securing a job, demonstrating sound judgment. Oh...and marrying a man with the means to provide for you. Have you been able to do any of that?" Sari questioned.

"I swear I hate you, and I will never forgive you for all the hateful things you've done." Tippany venomously shook with rage.

Allowing a smug look of superiority to grace her face, Sari waving off her daughter's words. "Your apartment, car, and personal expense will be paid, but outside of what you get here, you won't get a dime more. You will not retain sole control over the rest of your inheritance until you reach your thirtieth birthday, or you marry a respectable man. Seeing how much damage you've done to your reputation, I'm sure the latter won't matter. So, if I were you, little girl, I'd fall in line." Her words echoed as she walked out the door.

Tippany stood in defiance without flinching at her mother's threat. Slamming the door behind her mother's exit Tippany collapsed to the floor in a fit of tears. Shame, fear, and frustration all at once pounced on her petite frame. Her mother would have her accounts closed before the day was out; she had done it before. She was tired of living under her mother's mercy. The only bright side of the whole ordeal was grandfather Birch hadn't placed those types of stipulations on the trust fund he left her. She could have full access to it at twenty-seven or sooner if she was married. "Keturah, you don't know how lucky you really are," she pouted. Keturah, already being twenty-seven and married to boot, gained immediate access to her share of the Birch estate left by their grandfather, but with her just turning twenty-four meant she had a few more years to go.

She wanted to have a fit, but she needed to be smart and get some money out of her accounts before her mother would make good on her promise. Grabbing her cell phone, she opened her bank app. Punching in her account number, she felt a cold chill across her shoulders when the words "access denied" popped up on the screen. She tried to get access to her credit cards, but the same message scrolled across the screen. Pulling her knees up under her chin, she rested her cell phone and forehead on them. What was she going to do? Yes, grandfather Birch had a monthly stipend allotted to her, but that, along with what she made here, wouldn't allow her to live in the type of comfort she was accustomed to.

"God, what am I going to do. I can't live like this, or with this woman a moment longer," she cried out as a familiar jingle drew her attention to her phone.

Looking at the caller ID, she perked up. It was from Carlton. Breathing in and out, she tried to steady her nerves before clicking over and answering. "Hey, stranger, how have you been?" She tried to sound cheerful as she wiped the tears from her eyes.

"I'm okay, but you sound like your crying. Is everything alright?"

"Yeah…just allergies, they chose to act up today," she lied.

"Well, from the way you sound, those allergies must be giving you a beating." He chuckled.

"Yeah, I guess so," she said, picking herself off the floor, looking again for her compact. "So, how was your visit with your family?" Tippany asked, heading towards her desk. It was silly—she knew Carlton couldn't see her, but she still felt the need to check her appearance to make sure she looked her best.

"Not good."

His tone was so mattered of fact she didn't know if there was a need to ask him to elaborate. There was a long drawn out silence between them that made Tippany uncomfortable. She didn't know what to say or how to help him. Shoot, she couldn't help herself after this last bout with her mother. Of course, she could always seek help from Keturah. Her mind was bouncing around from one thing to the next, so it was no wonder she hadn't heard what Carlton said.

"Tippany, you haven't heard a word I've said, have you?" Carlton chuckled.

"Hmm…" She sighed. "Oh Carlton, I'm sorry I didn't. I just had a run-in with my mother, and it left me in a daze." Emotion clogged her voice as she decided to be truthful.

"Trust me, I understand." He gave a long pause again before speaking. "I've been trying to think of a way to ease into this conversation of the marriage proposal you talked about last week," he said abruptly. "At first, I was going to attempt to ask you what your ring size was as a backhanded way of saying yes. But even in my ears, it sounds pretty lame."

"Size eight." Her pulse raced as the words left her mouth. Could this really be happening?

"Tippy, there're some things you need to know about me...about my past." He hesitated. "There are some things I've done that I'm not proud of, but I would rather you hear it from me...no one else. This is not how I thought I would go into marriage, but I want you to know the type of man you're getting involved with."

"*If you only knew!*" she thought, knowing she'd need to come clean about Conrad. "I have a lot to share with you too, Carlton."

"Listen, they are calling my flight number, so how about we meet up for dinner tonight? I think we have a lot to discuss."

"I agree," she said, wrapping her arms around herself.

"Okay... it's a date. Pick you up around eight?"

"Perfect... I'll see you then."

"Bye."

Hanging the phone up, she reclined in her chair, her stomach still doing this funny little dance. "Mrs. Carlton Parson." She tried the title out to see how it fit. Picking up her phone, she spoke into the receiver, "Yes, this is Mrs. Parson speaking, yes, I'm Mrs. Tippany Parson." She smiled, liking it more and more each time she said it. Suddenly her cell phone buzzed. Quickly she looked at the caller ID.

"Keturah!?" Biting her lower lip, she wondered if she should pick up. She never gave it a second thought as to what this would do to her sister. It was such a long shot he'd actually accept she didn't consider how this might impact their relationship. God knows she didn't intend to hurt her sister, but there was no way she would leave a good available man on the table, especially now. Not wanting to douse her happy moment, she decided to let the call go to voice mail. Looking at her face in the small, compact, the imprint of her mother's fingers could still be seen on her face. "I've taken my last blow from you, Sari Jaymes. From now on, Mrs. Tippany Parson will be calling the shots. She smiled at herself as she thought of the dazzling red dress, she would wear for her fiancé that evening.

***

"As I said before, Carlton, I think it would be hard for Abraham to explain suing his own brother-in-law." Tippany played with her wine glass, trying to get a feel for where Carlton's mind was. He had been unusually quiet when he picked her up for dinner. "What's *he thinking?"* She bit her bottom lip anxiously. His calm demeanor was nerve-wracking. The plan she had conjured up was perfect. He could save his reputation and avoid going to court, and she would get a steady stream of cash they both could live comfortably off of. But the long lingering silence had her as fidgety as a four-year-old. Maybe he didn't think her scheme was as appealing as she did now that he had some time to consider everything. Unable to take the silence any longer, she was about to speak when he broke his silence.

"I love Keturah, Tippany." His face appeared tormented with the confession.

It was definitely not what she wanted to hear but nothing she didn't already know. It was only her own love for her sister that made her not walk the road of bitter envy. "I love Keturah, too, though not in the way I know you mean." She gave a light smile.

"I don't know when I started loving her. She was always just my co-worker and friend. But this summer, when we spent time together, she showed me a side of myself that I never thought I wanted, not really. I never wanted to settle down or take on the responsibility of a family. Now, I really do, but it was with another man's wife." A mirthless chuckle escaped his lips.

"I know you love Keturah. I saw you fall in love with her this summer. I think if her divorce had been final, we wouldn't be having this conversation," she said honestly.

Slapping his thigh, Carlton looked up. Tippany didn't have to wonder what he was thinking now. It was written all over his face.

"Everything was perfect, and now this." Raking a hand over his beard, he blew out a breath. "Look, don't think I'm not grateful for the offer, it's just..." He let his words trail off as he bowed his head.

Her perfect plan was unraveling. Maybe this was the way her biological mother had felt seeing her man's heart cling to another. She'd have to remember this feeling and never cause any woman this type of pain again. "Look, Carlton I..."

"I'll marry you, Tippy. If you're still willing. I just wanted...I needed you to know the truth about how I feel."

Her mouth was still open as she stared at him in disbelief. This roller-coaster ride he was taking her on was wreaking havoc with her nerves.

"Well, this is a rare moment, indeed. I've never known you to be quiet for this long, I must have really shocked you," he jested. "Well, what's the verdict? Am I still worthy of your proposal?"

"Well, as long as we are taking this honesty route, I need to tell you a couple things as well.

*"I love you, Carlton, and I have for a long time. I don't want to marry you to get my inheritance. I want to marry you so I can have the privilege of being your wife, have your children."* If only she could be bold enough to say what was truly in her heart. Instead, she swallowed hard before speaking. "My past is not so squeaky clean either. I've been seeing a guy and…" She paused, trying not to put herself in a bad light. "Well, let's just say I completely understand the position you're in. You and I aren't that different when falling for someone who's unavailable."

"So, I guess in some ways, we do make the perfect pair." He smiled, reaching for her hand.

"Well, I have to admit, for snagging a husband, I don't think I've done so bad." She smiled, allowing the warmth of his hand to warm her heart. Her eyes lingered on his lips, maybe a second too long.

"I'm definitely not complaining, either." A smile parted his lips as he looked into her inviting eyes. Cocking his head to the side, he looked at her intently.

"What…what is it?" Tippany asked nervously.

"Over the years I've gotten to know women pretty well, and if I'm reading things right, I don't anticipate this being an *in name only* marriage.'" He curled his pointer fingers like quotation marks giving emphasis to his words.

"Hmm, sexy and smart. I really am getting the total package, aren't I." She flirted, allowing her gaze to speak her intentions as she sipped her wine and licked the residue off her lips.

A slow smile began to emerge as he began admiring the beauty of his future before him. "So, when exactly do we plan on making this arrangement official?" he asked, sipping his drink.

"How does this weekend sound?" She raised a suggestive eyebrow towards him.

"Sounds like I'm getting married."

# *Chapter Twenty*

"Keturah, this entire discussion doesn't make any sense!" Abraham threw up his hands in frustration.

"Well, it makes perfect sense to me!" Keturah said with an obstinate look.

"Our children can't even say mama or dada yet, why in the world are we discussing if they will one day speak in a heavenly language or not?" He looked at the counselors for support. But they both just sat there tight-lipped. Abraham knew he wasn't going to get any help from them. "Keturah, please, be rational?"

"Oh, so I'm not rational because I want our children to experience God's presence. I would think being the head of our home, you would want your children to have an authentic relationship with God." She huffed, folding her arms and turning away from him.

"I cannot believe I am missing an important board meeting to sit here and have this conversation with you." Abraham shot out of his chair and paced the floor, rubbing the palm of his hands deep into his eye sockets.

"Oh, so going to a stupid board meeting is more important than the spiritual welfare of your children." Keturah raised her voice, her hands on both hips.

"Honey, I just don't see how this is relevant right now." He pressed the words out through clenched teeth. They had been in counseling sessions together for three weeks now, and it seemed like the only thing they ever did was argue. How could this possibly be helping anyone except the Shaffers', who were getting a good chunk of money to hear their private affairs spread all over the place? *And she doubts how I feel for her? Would a man who didn't feel something allow his woman to put him through all this?"* he thought to himself as he heard his wife continue her tirade.

"It's very relevant!" Keturah said, "I should be able to discuss the important things to me with you. One of those things is the spiritual environment our children will be raised in. I want our children to experience God's full presence, and that can't happen while attending the stale church you go to. Last Sunday, I even heard the crickets yawning."

"Keturah, I have gone to that church for years. Dr. Evans is very sound in his theology, and his teachings are practical."

"And his delivery is boring, and so is the worship if that's what you want to call it." Turning towards the Shaffer's Keturah stated, "You should hear what they do to praise and worship songs…ugh, I can't stand it." Keturah shivered in disgust.

"You are so melodramatic, Tourie." Abraham waved her off.

"No, I'm not. No one even moves in your church. Not the pastor, not the worship leaders, let alone God. I could hear Elder Rogers now…. excuse me, Jesus, I'm going to have to ask you to take a seat as we don't allow roaming up and down the aisles as per our church policy," Keturah mocked.

"Well, just because we believe in having decorum in our church and not a block party you can hear two miles away doesn't mean we don't worship or that the presence of God is not there. Oh, and by the way, just because you're loud and unorthodox doesn't mean you're having some Holy Ghost party as your generation calls it."

"Okay, this is good…this is very good," Tamara stated.

"So, Abraham and Keturah, I hear you sharing how important passing your faith to your children is to both of you," Harry stated. "Now Abraham, what did you hear Keturah say to you?"

*Oh…so now you find your voice?* Abraham wanted to say. "She wants me to exercise my spiritual language…I guess I don't know," he responded wearily.

"See, that's exactly what I'm talking about—he doesn't listen to me. He feels that I'm beneath him and have nothing to offer." Keturah's voice began to quiver, and before long, she began to cry.

Looking dumbfounded, Abraham replayed his words in his mind. Not once did he say anything of the sort, they were discussing the gift of tongues...weren't they? He swallowed hard; this was not working at all. He was about to say something to the counselors in that respect when Harry held up his hand to silence him.

"Keturah, why do you feel that Abraham sees you as beneath him and have nothing to offer?"

"Because he does, they all do." She sobbed.

"They? Who are they?" Tamara chimed in.

Abraham stopped his pacing and looked at his young wife, not sure of what she was saying.

"It doesn't matter," she said, trying to regain control.

"It really does matter. Keturah, you matter." Tamara said.

Keturah's head abruptly shot up as she looked at Tamara. "I've never mattered, not to him." She pointed an accusatory finger at Abraham. "Not to my grandfather, and definitely not to my father. All the men in my life have always been ashamed to openly love me, and now I've married a man who feels the exact same way."

Had he not been holding onto the fireplace mantle; Abraham might have fallen to the floor with his wife's confession. Keturah was in shambles, and he wasn't that far from it himself. Hadn't he realized by now how fragile his young wife was and like a bull in a china shop, he had pillaged through her life not thinking of how delicate she was.

Gretta was the only mother and father she had, and when she died, he was her lifeline, but she needed him to be more than an occasional lover, but his own problems kept him at bay. He only gave her what he wanted her to have, never considering what she needed. "Maybe if I had been exercising the spirit of discernment more often, I wouldn't have put her in this position." He inwardly chided, feeling the shame of failing his wife.

"Abraham, I would like you to tell us what you are hearing Keturah say about the men in her life…including you," Tamara requested.

With his elbow resting on the mantle, he allowed his fingers to massage the pulsating pressure mounting in his head. What could he really say? He shrugged a shoulder and looked away, staring at a blank wall and, in some ways wishing he could become part of it.

"Abraham, you and Keturah have been dancing around this subject far too long," Harry interjected. "You're not arguing about theology or whose faith tradition is right. Those are the safe things to argue about. Be present, hear her words, and respond," he encouraged.

Abraham sighed. How many times had Sarah said similar words? *I don't want you to fix it, just listen, be present at the moment with me.* In some respects, she and Keturah were cut from the same cloth. Eyeing his wife's weeping form, he needed…no, wanted to make things better between them. Moving from the mantle, he slowly approached her. He couldn't tell her everything, not yet, but he could extend an olive branch. Sitting beside her with elbows on his knees, he steepled his fingers in front of him, praying he'd share something insightful. Her back was turned to him, but he knew she was aware of his presence.

"Tourie," he said softly, reaching out and stroking her curly hair, wrapping several of the silky strands around his index finger. "I know it's hard for you to believe this, but your dad loved you very much. I remember one time you came for an overnight visit. You were almost three but just as independent as can be. You used to love climbing on high things." Abraham chuckled, remembering the time they met in the recreation center when she had climbed up on a rickety chair to paint some high corner of the wall. "I think you wanted a cookie, so you were pulling yourself up on the counter when you lost your grip. It happened so fast. I saw you fall, but I couldn't get to you. Then from nowhere, your dad was there diving to catch you. I'm not even sure how he reached you in time, but somehow, he had. By the time I got in the room, your dad was on the floor covered in cookies, and there you were sitting on the top of his chest, eating one and just laughing." He turned to look at Keturah, whose stormy gray eyes were fixated on him. She was hanging on to his every word. "That night when we came back from the emergency room—"

"Wait, I thought you said he caught me. Why did we go to the emergency room...did he hurt himself?"

"Oh, your dad hurt himself, alright, but he was more afraid for you than himself. The doctors told him children were resilient, and you were fine, but Kedron worried the entire night. He kept going in your room and shaking you, making sure you were okay." Chuckling, Abraham looked into her teary face and saw a hint of a smile. "I remember telling your dad, the man that marries you would have his hands full."

"I wonder if that classifies as a self-fulfilling prophecy?" Harry chuckled.

"Harry!" His wife scolded, tapping him on the knee. Of which he immediately held his hands up in surrender. "So Keturah, what are your thoughts about what Abraham shared?"

Sniffing while wiping her tears with a tissue that she continued to fold, then refold she finally spoke. "Well, it's nice to know my dad seemed to care when I was a baby." A puzzled look crossed her features. Turning to Abraham, she inquired. "How do you know all this?"

He bowed his head and cleared his throat before answering. "Kedron and I had similar situations. He wanted to spend time with you, and I wanted to spend time with Ishmael, so we would go to our family cottage on the gulf and take you guys up there. We had some wonderful times."

Keturah's face hardened as she sniffed and nodded her head. "So, you both took your children of adultery to a secret hideaway to spend daddy time with them. Did it make you guys feel better? Did it ease your conscience?"

"No…it wasn't like that at all." Abraham defended.

"Really, Abraham, then what was it like?" Keturah jerked herself off the couch and stood over him, her arms folded defensively across her chest. "You didn't dare parade us around like we were part of your real family—no, we were just your side chicks' misfits."

Somehow Abraham had stepped into a hornet's nest and had no way of gracefully stepping out of it. Thankfully Harry and Tamara interrupted.

"Keturah, this story seems painful for you. Can you share with us why?" Harry requested.

"I am tired of being somebody's secret love child, secret granddaughter, secret wife. I've had my fill of it, and I won't do it anymore." Her nostrils flared as she spoke with fire in her eyes. "And I'll tell you another thing, Abraham Nathan Taylor." She pointed at him. "It will be over my dead body before I let you or anyone else put Kamara and Abel in that position."

Abraham never took well to being threatened by anyone, but the fire and spunk his wife was showing him now inwardly made him smile. He loved a good fight. He hadn't felt this alive since dodging hot food and silverware hurled at him by Sarah after she found out about Isaac and his hunting mishap. Keturah's fierce vigor to live independent of him didn't deter him one bit, it only ignited a greater fire in him in making sure he kept his woman by his side.

# *Chapter Twenty-One*

"You're being ridiculous, it's only a building." Keturah scolded herself, yet her butt still remained plastered to her car's seat. She didn't know why Abraham insisted she meet him at Canaan today to discuss her thoughts regarding the girls' mentoring program. He was primarily working out of the satellite office. They could have discussed it there, so why did she have to come to corporate headquarters? She had promised herself never to set foot back in this place. Yet here she was sitting in her car looking at a vast building and wondering what her husband could possibly want her for that Monday afternoon. A knock on her passenger side window jolted her out of her brooding.

"Mrs. Taylor, is everything alright? Can I help you with anything?" A tall man in a security uniform asked.

"I-I was just looking for a place to park." She gave an awkward smile then questioned in the back of her mind how he knew who she was.

"Mrs. Taylor, you don't have to look for a parking spot. You and all the family park in the garage. There is a designated spot for you right next to your husband."

"Oh, I didn't realize that."

"No problem, ma'am. Just drive to the gate, use this key, and follow the arrows leading to the fourth level, and you will see your spot. Here is your security code granting you access to the private elevator, which will take you straight to the executive floor."

"Thank you...thank you so much." With a timid smile, Keturah took the key from his steady hand.

"My name is David, ma'am, and I'm happy to serve you. If you need anything else, just let me know.

"You've been very helpful David, thank you,"

"My pleasure, Mrs. Taylor. Have a great day." He nodded before walking away.

Maybe she shouldn't have felt unnerved by his friendly hospitality, but for whatever reason, she did. The last time she was in this building, no one even recognized her, let alone acknowledged her as Abraham's wife. Pulling around to the parking garage, she stuck the badge that the security officer gave her in the slot. Immediately an automated voice said, "Welcome, Mrs. Taylor." The gate raised and allowed her to pass. Slowly driving up the winding concrete ramp, she reached level four. Abraham's silver Mercedes coupe could not be missed, nor could the rest of the family's luxury cars. She never really thought of having one of those expensive beauties. All she needed was a safe, affordable car to get her and the babies back and forth. Pulling her car up alongside Abraham's, she was somewhat embarrassed by her reliable Ford Taurus with a rust patch forming on the side. In fact, as she looked around, her car had to be the worst vehicle on the entire fourth floor. "Maybe when I get a moment, I'll get something nicer," she contemplated out loud as she stepped out of her car and ran smack into Tippany.

"Hey, sis, I didn't expect to see you here today." Keturah was first startled then smiled as she was embraced by her sister."

"Likewise, what are you doing here?" Tippany asked.

"Abraham summoned me so…here I am." Keturah gave a shoulder shrug.

"Oh! Okay, well, great, glad to see you."

"So, how was your weekend?" Keturah fell in step with her sister.

"Oh, nothing exhilarating," she said in haste. "Hey, by the way, when are you going to get rid of that hunk of junk you call a car?"

"I will have you know that old faithful here has gotten me to many places this past year."

"I don't know about faithful, but I definitely would say you're right—she is old...very old." Tippany wrinkled her nose and got a playful shoulder push from Keturah.

"Well, she might be old, but she still has a good couple of miles left in her."

"Why don't you just ask Abraham to get you another car? I mean, he has a dozen or so. Just pick one from the garage or at least let Carlos drive you here."

"Carlos already has a lot of things that he does for Abraham. Being my chauffeur doesn't need to be one of them. Besides, the car seats are already in the back, and I wouldn't want to go through all that hassle."

"Okay, but you better not let Abraham catch you driving this thing...he will have a fit. Oh, better yet, let him catch you. Just make sure you tell me about it. I'd love to post his reaction." She winked, causing them both to laugh as they entered the private elevator."

"So, what are your plans for the holidays?" Keturah asked in a nonchalant manner as they sped their way to the executive floor. "Anything pressing?"

"Umm, can't really say right now, Keturah. I might have a couple plans in the works. Why, was there something you had in mind?"

Again, she shrugged. "Oh, I was hoping you and maybe even Parson might go out to dinner."

"Carlton is off limits!" Tippany said forcefully, causing her sister to turn towards her with a frown. "I mean, you know, because of the pending lawsuit. I-I thought there was to be no contact between you too?"

"I know, but it's the holidays, and I would hate for Parson to be alone. He has lost some very significant family members over the years around this time, so he often takes the holidays hard."

"Keturah, Carlton is a man. You can't save him from every hurt. Besides, you have a husband who is trying to make things work between the two of you. Why jeopardize all of that just so Carlton can have a turkey dinner?" Tippany minimized her sister's concern.

"I'm not trying to be his protector, just his friend." Sensing an edge to her tone, Keturah tried to steady her rising heartbeat. She had always known Tippany was attracted to Parson, but it seemed like something more was going on… something Tippany was trying to hide.

"Well, friends don't allow their wealthy husbands to sue them."

"So, you're saying the lawsuit is my fault?" She turned towards Tippany to look her in the face. However, Tippany wouldn't look back at her. "Tippany, are you blaming me for this situation?"

Sighing heavily, Tippany turned her attention towards Keturah. "At this point, it doesn't matter whose fault it is Keturah. The bottom line is you can't have it both ways. You can't work on your marriage and arrange play dates with Carlton. No matter how innocent you might feel it is, in the end, Carlton will get hurt. If he's truly your friend, then his best interests should be your primary concern."

Keturah was about to respond when the elevator doors slid open, and a smiling Abraham was waiting on the other side.

"Hey, sweetheart," he said, kissing her on the lips before greeting Tippany. "Hey, Tippy, I trust your weekend went well," he inquired.

"What do you mean?" She asked with wide eyes.

"The meeting in Vegas…I trust everything went well?" He scrunched his eye at her curiously.

"Ahh, the meeting, yes, it went great." Tippany fidgeted with the fringe on her purse. "Hey, listen, I need to get moving. Keturah, we'll talk later," she said. Stepping off the elevator, she looked to her left, and her face turned pale. "What's he doing here?" Tippany spoke in a small voice.

Abraham turned to see who she was referring to. "Oh, that's Conrad Jessup, my new personal assistant. Your mother highly recommended him, and so far, he has shown great initiative. I'll introduce him to you."

"I can't right now. I have an important phone call to make." Tippany abruptly turned around and quickly headed towards her office.

"What's up with her today?" Keturah spoke, watching Tippany's hasty retreating form.

"Who has ever been able to discern what is running through the Jaymes' women's minds?" Abraham sighed as he steered Keturah to his office.

"And just what is that supposed to mean?" Keturah quickly retorted.

Raising his eyebrows, he scratched his head, then placed an arm around her shoulder. "So dear, how has your day been so far?" he asked, ignoring her last comment.

"Okay, I guess." She absently shrugged her shoulders, feeling uncomfortable. This new public display of affection Abraham was assuming with her lately was offsetting. Funny what a difference a year made. She would have been on cloud nine if he had done any of this last year, but now somehow, she couldn't help but feel he had some hidden agenda.

"You seem as if you have the weight of the world on your shoulders, Tourie. What's the matter?"

The intensity of his gaze made her tense and retreat. Something she was becoming very good at. Every time she had shown her true feelings, he had used it against her. Well, she wouldn't be that vulnerable again. Some lessons weren't worth repeating. "I'm just feeling jittery, I guess. This is the first time I've been away from the twins…I guess I miss them."

"Well, I hope you know that they are in good hands. Consuela and Carmen are excellent caretakers."

"I guess."

Chuckling, he pulled her along. "You first time moms are all alike. I couldn't get Sarah to leave Isaac's nursery when he was firstborn. She was afraid she was going to miss something he did. We had cameras installed all over the house and in our bedroom."

Feeling her ring finger where her wedding band used to be, she hesitated before speaking. "Well, you can never be too cautious. What if a burglar came into your house or a bird flew in the window?"

Sighing, he reiterated. "New mothers. Anyway, I want you to meet our newest employee, my executive assistant, Conrad Jessup. Conrad, this is my wife, Keturah Taylor."

"Ma'am… it's a pleasure to meet you." Conrad extended a hand and smiled.

"Likewise." Keturah greeted him and stepped a little closer to her husband.

"Mr. Taylor, I have Joslin and Associates on hold. Are you still planning to meet with them at eleven-thirty? I can tell them you got tied up and will need to reschedule at a later date."

Smacking his forehead, Abraham sighed heavily. "I completely forgot about that meeting today."

"Let me reschedule it," Conrad suggested started picking up the phone.

"No, this is my fault, I can't put it off again." He sighed. "Honey, I'm sorry, but I'm going to need you to do this meeting with the board for the girls' mentoring program without me."

"What! No Abraham! I can't," Keturah said frantically.

"Conrad, have the car sent up, and I'm going to need you to attend this one."

"I'll take care of it, sir. Mrs. Taylor, it was a pleasure," Conrad stated before leaving.

Taking Keturah by the hand, Abraham led her into his office, shut the door, and hugged her tightly. "Tourie, stop worrying; you'll do fine."

"Abraham, I can't do this. The only reason I came was to listen to you, not make a presentation to the board." She complained. I mean, just look at how I'm dressed." She gazed in the mirror, wishing had thought better of wearing the soft, comfortable maxi dress. Yes, it fit her nicely but was definitely not something to wear for a formal presentation before the board. "I'm a mess. I'm not ready."

"Sweetheart, you look fine, and besides, you know the girls' mentoring program inside out. This project has been in your heart and soul for years. Who better to pitch this than you? Besides, you and God make a majority, and if that shouldn't ease your worries, more than half of the board is made up of people with the same last name as yours."

Keturah sighed. "But what about lunch?" She looked up at him, her gray eyes hopeful and expectant.

"I'll make you a deal. You pitch this project for me like I know you can, and I'll go pick up the kids, and we will all go out somewhere and celebrate...no nannies, no drivers, just the four of us... deal?"

She sighed again and nodded in the affirmative and was rewarded with a mind-blowing kiss.

"That's my girl." He finally released her gently, holding on to her chin. "Then maybe when the kids fall asleep, you and I can have our own private celebration," he said just before kissing her again.

"I guess you, sir, have yourself a date for the afternoon." She smiled, looking forward to the second part of their deal. Maybe this new Abraham wasn't all bad.

***

Keturah didn't care how many of these people shared her last name; she felt like she was in hostile territory. Sari was the meanest of the bunch, followed by her own stepson Isaac. If their intent was to embarrass her, they both would receive an A for effort. But they didn't know how bad she wanted the girls mentoring program to succeed. So today they had met their match.

"The mentoring program for young girls is necessary because young women have to be capable of supporting themselves and their families. Women who can excel in business and finances can determine which direction they want their life to go. They can have a better quality of life."

"Humph, maybe we should have enlisted this program a while back... maybe twenty-seven years ago to be exact," Sari stated sarcastically.

Tippany gave her mother a hateful glare, but Keturah kept her composure. She knew what her stepmom was trying to say backhandedly about her mother. Swallowing the hurt, she decided to use her mothers' story to her advantage.

"You're right, *Mother* Jaymes, I too often wonder what would have been if women like my biological mother Pamela Birch had better opportunities than the ones presented to her. But she is not alone. It was my grandmother's story, but I'm sure many men and women can identify with my mother's situation. Mothers who didn't have the opportunities or advancements many of us in this room were blessed with. No matter how hard they worked or how many jobs they took on something or someone in their home suffered." Keturah allowed her moment of silence to speak for her before she continued. "I am the product of a single parent, and when my mother died, I was raised by a single grandmother. Though I'm blessed, and can say this is not going to be the story for my children, I would think an organization such as the Sarah Jaymes Taylor Foundation would feel it a privilege to have young girls model the same courage and determination my cousin did. Sarah stepped out on an unknown path to challenge not only herself but to set an example for her family and others who'd one day follow in her footsteps." The room was quiet after Keturah took her seat, even Sari had ceased her cackling.

"As eloquently as you have stated your case, Keturah, this organization still has to consider the best utilization of our funds and where disbursement would do the greatest good. I know Rebecca has the final voice in our decision, but I honestly feel that the mentoring for males has been a well-established and proven benefit for that population," Isaac said diplomatically.

"Agreed. We can't save everyone," Sari chimed in. "I think the girls' mentoring group will need to sit on the back burner for now."

"Well, I disagree," Tippany spoke up. "We know the mentoring for males will be successful, so why skate by on past accomplishments. If the boys' mentoring program has any merit of which it does, then it should be duplicatable and adaptable for young girls."

Another board member spoke up. "As a single mom, I understand the difficulties a woman has in making decisions that can critically impact her family. I had the fortune of having a husband who was well versed in business and finances. His voice still rings in my ears when I'm about to make a substantial purchase." Clearing her throat, she continued. "I have sons, so they have greatly benefited from the boys' mentoring program. But I also have young nieces as well. Who's going to mentor them?"

"Look, we all know that the decision we make today is going to leave someone out. But I agree with Sari and Isaac, the boys' mentoring program is tried and proven. Why mess with our success?" another man stated, receiving several nods from other members.

"Well, it seems that many feel we should continue to stay the course and fully fund the male mentoring program," Rebecca said, her voice a little low but clear. "I heard everything everyone said. Each side had valid points."

Keturah sighed inwardly. There was no way Rebecca was going to side with her. She was more concerned about being the next Mrs. Isaac Taylor to cross her fiancé. It was okay, she had her own plans, and with her grandfather's company, she would make a foundation of her own to make sure girls would have the support they needed.
She would hear Rebecca out and then do things on her own.

"Keturah, I want to thank you for your passion for this project. Girls often don't get the resources needed to make changes in their lives. I appreciate your willingness to support them, and you will have this foundation's full support as well," Rebecca said with a genuine smile, shocking her and everyone else into silence.

Keturah sat there with her mouth hanging open. It wasn't until she heard Tippany's undignified "yippy" that kicked her back into reality. "Thank you, Becca."

Rebecca nodded with a smile, which slowly vanished as she heard Isaac standing and pushing his chair in with more force than needed. Sari had her mouth twisted so tight you would have thought she had just sucked on a lemon.

It was a funny sight, but no smile came to Keturah's lips. She knew how much this decision had cost Rebecca, who watched first Sari, then Isaac leave the room without a backward glance at her.

"Men are such jerks," Tippany said within earshot of Keturah.

"Yeah. I just hate what this might do to Isaac and Becca's relationship." Keturah sighed, watching Rebecca quickly get up and trail after her intended.

# *Chapter Twenty-Two*

"I will not marry anyone who doesn't respect me, Becca, period." Isaac's tone rang loud and clear through the phone.

"But Zac, baby, I do respect you...I love you." Rebecca's tearful admission was heart-wrenching. For two weeks, she hadn't seen Isaac, apparently her punishment for siding against him in the meeting. On the advisement of Aunt Sari, Rebecca was to stay in the office as she would be too busy with the girls' mentoring project to attend. It was Isaac who told her, but she could hear Sari's voice through and through. "When are you coming home?"

"I don't know."

"I miss you."

"I miss you too. Look, I got to go."

"Will you call me tonight?" Rebecca pleaded.

"We're five hours behind you, it will be too late."

"No, it won't, I'll wait up for you." She assured.

"Alright, I'll try to call."

"Okay, and Isaac, I truly love you." Her hand gripped the phone. She closed her eyes and prayed he'd say it back. She needed to hear him say the words.

"Okay, talk to you later, babe. Bye."

The dial tone buzzing in her ear signaled he had hung up without saying he loved her. It crushed her soul. Allowing her head to fall in her waiting hands, her gut twisted as her heart broke. She had been a wreck since the day he had left.

He barely had spoken to her, didn't even kiss her goodbye. She hated, despised that day. She'd give back the position of committee chair in a heartbeat if she thought it would help. But the damage had already been done. She had gone against the family, and now it was time to pay the piper. She was about to give in to a full-blown heart sob when her phone rang. Looking at the caller ID, her eyes went wide. Grabbing tissues and blowing her nose, she then dabbed at her eyes as best she could. Breathing in and out a few times to squelch her sobs, she counted to three then in a cheery voice she picked up. "Hey, Dad Taylor, how are you?"

"Hey, Becca, honey, how are you?" Abraham's deep tenor spoke. "What did I tell you about that dad Taylor business? It's just dad."

She chuckled. "Some habits are hard to break... I'm doing okay, Dad."

"Ahh, I know what that means. You miss that son of mine, no doubt."

"Yeah, I do." She swiped at a wayward tear.

"I'm surprised that you didn't go down there with him. Hawaii is beautiful this time of year."

"Well, since the foundation is taking on the new mentoring project, he and Aunt Sari thought it best that I stay here and oversee things." She swallowed hard. Isaac didn't say he was going to Hawaii. She would have loved to go there with him. He must really be angry with her. So, caught up in her own miserable thoughts, she hadn't realized how silent the other end of the line was. "Hello, Dad, are you still there?"

"I'm still here, hon. Listen, I just wanted to call and say thank you for backing Keturah on the project. It meant a lot to her and me as well. Whatever you need to make this work, you have my full backing."

"Thanks, Dad. I really appreciate your support."

"By the way, I think Isaac made a wise decision when he placed you in that position. You're going to do us real proud."

"Thanks, Dad." Her voice choked as she struggled to keep her tears at bay.

"Well, sweetie, I have a couple of phone calls to make. Talk to you soon…bye."

"Bye Dad." Laying her head on the desk, she gave in to her sobs. She missed her natural father, dearly. When she was brought into the Taylor fold, Abraham immediately treated her like family. When her father died last year, Abraham stepped in and gave her the love her real father would have. With things the way they were between her and Isaac, she felt as if she would lose not only a fiancé but also another father. "I should have stayed away from Keturah like Isaac wanted me to. If I had, we wouldn't be having these issues."

*"How so?"* an inner voice spoke.

"Well, I wouldn't have stopped having sex with Isaac, which I know is another issue he has with me. Even though I told him why he still feels slighted."

*"Go on."*

"This whole issue with Keturah, he feels she a negative influence on me as if I'm a child and I don't know the type of people I should keep company with. I mean, she's practically my mother-in-law."

*"So, Isaac's issue with Keturah is that she's encouraged you to honor Me by following the scriptures?"*

She didn't know when she recognized she was having this conversation with the Lord, but it was happening, and it was real. "Lord, I really do love you, but I also love Isaac, and I really don't want to lose him. He's my heart and soul."

*"You shall have no other gods before me!"*

Her head immediately popped up off the desk. She was about to protest but hesitated. Was she acting as if Isaac was a god to her? She loved him, of that she could not deny, but was she genuinely worshiping him...was that the way God viewed it? "God, I'm not trying to worship Isaac. I just feel that when I'm with him, everything comes together like he's my soul mate, and to have him is to have everything I've ever desired...is wanting that so wrong?"

*"For what shall it profit a person, if they gain the whole world, and lose their soul?"*

The scripture rose in her heart like a lost memory. She had done so much to show Isaac how much she loved him and wanted to please him that her love for the things of God had grown cold. "Maybe Isaac was right, maybe this time apart will do both of us some good." She dabbed her eyes with the last tissue in the box. Standing up, she went to her private bathroom and splashed cold water on her face. She had done enough sulking; it was time to get to work.

Later that night, when Isaac didn't call or text her, she turned over, prayed for his safe return, and went to sleep. It was the best night's sleep she had had in months.

*** 

He probably shouldn't have stayed the extra week in Maui, but after the meeting was over, he felt the need to relax, think things out. It didn't help matters any when he got a call from his father, tearing into him because of his treatment of Becca.

*"I thought I raised a man, not some sniveling boy who picks up his toys and leaves because he can't get his way. If I were Becca, I'd tell you to take a long walk off a short pier."*

*"Dad, you don't understand. I want a wife who will support me."*

*"Do you think your mother agreed with me all the time? She was my greatest support and critic. She had no problem telling me she didn't like what I did or wasn't in agreement with my choice."*

*"Yeah, but she didn't openly dismiss you and side with the enemy."*

*"Enemy!? Since when did inner-city girls or my wife for that matter, become your enemy?"*

*Hearing the anger rise in his dad's voice, he thought again of his words and decided to carefully choose them. "Dad, all I'm saying is that I expect Becca to give me her support when I feel strongly about something."*

*"Are you talking about supporting you or obeying you…because those are two separate things, son. Maybe you're right in taking this break. You and Rebecca need this time apart so you can decide what you both really want."*

That conversation happened a week ago. He had never stayed away from Rebecca this long. In the three weeks of separation, they had only spoken a handful of times. Although she had texted him daily, he only texted her once or twice a week. However, this last week she hadn't texted him at all, which was troubling. He was the one giving her the silent treatment, not the other way around. Deciding to extend an olive branch, he texted her before his plane got underway that he was coming home. He fully expected her to come and pick him up, then they could go someplace quiet and talk. So, he was shocked to find not only hadn't she texted him back, but he needed to hail a cab to get back to the office. It was mid-week. Assured she would be in the office; he had the cabbie take him downtown. He gritted his teeth to control his tongue with the cab driver, who took every alternate route imaginable to make the drive longer.

By the time he reached the executive floor, he was angry having to lug all his bags to the regular elevators as the cabbie refused to go in the parking garage. The peace offering, he was going to give Rebecca was off. Instead, he opted to give her a piece of his mind for not responding to his text. Going directly to his office, Isaac deposited his luggage, then made a beeline for his would-be fiancée's office. With a quick knock on the door, he came in shocked to see her holding a meeting with Keturah, Tippany, his Aunt Sari, and a few more.

"Oh, hello, everyone. I'm sorry, I didn't realize you were in a meeting," Isaac said, looking in Rebecca's direction, inwardly sighing. "I definitely stayed away too long.", he thought, as he remembered the last time, she had that form-fitting red business suit on not to mention the fun he had in helping her out of it. The woman looked incredible in just about anything, but that suit was his favorite. "Becca, when you're finished, I'd like to see you." She gave a curt nod and turned her attention back to her meeting. Definitely not the greeting he had hoped for.

# *Chapter Twenty-Three*

Rebecca took several deep breaths before knocking on Isaac's door. After having prayed and fasted for the last week, something she had never done, she knew what she needed to do. Isaac's lack of communication spoke volumes. Although she loved Isaac with her very soul, she would not be married to a man who did not respect her. Although she wanted to be the next Mrs. Taylor with everything in her being, that didn't mean she was okay with being mistreated. She looked at her engagement ring. It had almost graced her finger for a year. It was a promise of things to come. However, him leaving town and not communicating with her was not something she would tolerate—not in their engagement and definitely not in their marriage. Tears stung the back of her eyes as she slowly slipped the engagement ring off of her finger and placed it in her pocket. By far, this would be the most challenging conversation she ever had with her fiancé.

"Don't' do it, Becca, if you issue him demands and ultimatums, you'll lose him forever and then what? You'll be an unhappy, unemployed old maid...like many good Christian women." Fear screamed inwardly at her.

Fisted raised ready to knock, Rebecca momentarily hesitated on hearing the tormenting thought.

*"Trust in the Lord with all you heart and lean not to your own understanding in all of your ways acknowledge him, and He will direct your path."*

The scripture in Proverbs rose in her heart and felt like a salve on a fresh brush burn. "I can do this," she whispered, then with two brief knocks, she walked in the door to look at the face of her sulking fiancé.

"Did you stay in that meeting extra-long just to annoy me?" Isaac groused as she walked through the door.

"Everything's not about you, Isaac."

"Oh, really? You used to think it was." He looked at her crossly. "Which herein lies the problem. You've been different towards me lately, and I don't like it. I want to be intimate; you want to give me a Bible lecture. I want you to support me in a business decision, you jump ship to the other side. If you're doing this now as my fiancée, what am I to expect when we're actually married?"

"So, are you saying for me to be your wife, I'm not to have a mind of my own? I'm not to have my own feelings, my own thoughts? Everything is about you and only you. What about how I feel? What about what I want is that even a factor?" Rebecca charged.

"Don't be absurd; that's not what I'm saying, Becca."

"Then what are you saying, Isaac?"

"I'm saying my wife needs to respect me, support me, and follow me. That is what I want, that is what I expect, and that is what I require—the question is, can you do that? Because if you can't..." He didn't finish the threat, but his meaning was flagrant.

Unshed tears that she could no longer hold began to spillover on her cheeks. Isaac had given her a lucid account of the type of wife he wanted and expected of her to fulfill his laundry list. She closed her eyes as the tears fell and whispered a quiet prayer.

"Lord, I so badly want to be this man's wife." The truth of her confession almost broke her.

Hearing her words, Isaac smiled confidently as he moved around his desk to stand before Rebecca. "That's my girl," he said smugly as he bent his head down and kissed her passionately. When he finally released her, she had an awed look on her face.

With a small smile, she looked into his eyes and said with all sincerity. "I love you, Isaac. I always have, and I likely always will." She took his hand, brought it up to her lips, and kissed it slowly. Opening his hand, she placed his engagement ring in his palm and closed it. Quickly she turned from him and walked out of his office door before losing it entirely.

"BECCA!" a perplexed Isaac called after her.

She heard him, but she kept moving.

"Rebecca, what's wrong?"

Vaguely recognizing Ishmael in the hallway, she pushed past him. On finding the office door, she was looking for without knocking barged her way in only to see Tippany passionately kissing Carlton.

"Oh my God, Tippy, I'm so sorry I just-I —" Suddenly covering her mouth, she ran to the office's private bathroom. She could hear Tippany calling after her, but her nausea could no longer be contained.

Tippany found her bent over the commode emptying the contents of her stomach. After several minutes of uncontrollable stomach spasms, she flushed and sat indecorously on the bathroom floor with her knees pulled up and her arms circling them.

"Rebecca, are you ill? Do we need to call an ambulance? Do you want me to get Isaac?"

"No… No… And definitely, NO!" She sniffed as she shook her head from side to side as if in agony. Tippany momentarily stepped back out of the bathroom door. Rebecca could hear her talking to Carlton in hushed tones. The only thing she for sure could make out were the words, *I'll see you at home.* Apparently, Tippany's relationship with Mr. Parson had taken a turn that Rebecca wasn't aware of. Hearing what sounded like a parting kiss, Rebecca repositioned herself on the floor. Tippany entered the bathroom and sat down on the white marble tile floor beside her.

"Okay, Becca, I would say spill it, but it seems you already have," Tippany jested. "Seriously, level with me... what's going on?"

"I'll tell you everything on the condition you tell me what's up with you and Carlton?"

Breathing a heavy sigh, Tippany remained silent for a moment. "Okay, I'll tell, but you can't breathe a word of this to anyone...not even Isaac." She charged. Then with a big smile that covered half of her face, she held out her hand, displaying a modest diamond on her ring finger. "It's official!"

"Oh my God...Tippy, you're engaged to Carlton?" Rebecca mustered up her enthusiasm to give her friend a hug.

"Thank you...but I'm not engaged," she confessed.

"Oh?"

"Carlton and I got married last month in Vegas."

Rebecca's eyes widened as she looked at her friend in disbelief. "You what?! No, sir!"

"A little over three weeks ago. Remember when I told you I had to go to Vegas for a business meeting. Well, the business meeting part was true, but it just wasn't the only thing that I was doing while in Vegas."

"Does Keturah know? Better yet, does your mom know? Oh, and does Carlton know your true feelings for him?"

"As you said earlier, no... no... and definitely, no." Tippany squeezed Rebecca's shoulder and giggled.

Rebecca found herself scrunching up her face as she looked at her friend. "The way you two were all hugged up on one another when I walked in, I think it would be hard for him not to know your true feelings."

"Well, what can I say? Men are dense." She rolled her eyes, smiling.

"Amen to that!" Rebecca said, causing them both to chuckle.

"Now it's your turn, Becca. Spill the beans. What's going on with you? Why are you so upset?"

Turning to Tippany, she showed off her ring finger minus her engagement ring.

"What happened to your engagement ring Becca, did you lose it?"

"No, I didn't lose it. I gave it back to Isaac."

"You did what?! When?" Tippany's eyes widened in disbelief.

"Isaac gave me a list of demands regarding the type of woman that he wanted to marry. I came to the realization that the woman he listed and the woman I am are not the same, so I gave him his ring back."

"But you two love each other?" Tippany said in a small voice.

"No, Tippany. I love Isaac, and Isaac loves himself. I need to find the man who loves me just as much as I love him."

"Becca, what are you going to do now?" Tippany held her hand concern riddled her face.

Rebecca looked at her friend with watery brown eyes and, with a wobbly smile, confessed, "I'm going to have his baby." She broke down in tears again as Tippany consoled her. Lifting up her head, she spoke.

"It's ironic, you know. I can be his girlfriend, lover, bedmate, and now even his baby's momma." Looking at Tippany, she then said, "If I can be all that to him, why am I not good enough to be his wife?"

*** 

*What just happened!* Isaac sat back in his executive chair, staring at the elaborate engagement ring that was still warm from Rebecca's finger. "What just happened?" was all he could mutter.

"I'd like to know that myself," Ishmael said from the doorway. "It's not every day you almost get run down by a crying female coming out of your office, or is that an everyday occurrence for you, bro? I got to say when it comes to women, you haven't lost your touch."

"What do you want, Mael?" Isaac bit out in no mood for his older brother's queer sense of humor or timing.

"Is that any way to greet your brother who came halfway around the world just to invite you to lunch."

"I highly doubt you came to the states to do that. Besides, I'm not in the mood."

"I can see that. Looks to me like you need more than lunch, maybe a stiff drink."

"I don't drink," Isaac lied, knowing full well he had a fully stocked bar at his home and even had a little something in his office refrigerator.

"Sure, you don't, baby brother, but by the way you're looking at that ring, I'd say you're going to need a drink and then some…so come on, let's go."

The old adage saying misery loved company must be right. Why else did Isaac find himself grabbing his coat and followed his brother out the door.     But before he shut the door, he looked back at the sparkling diamond marquise ring resting on the desk and not Rebecca's hand. He went back over and picked it up, placing it in his coat pocket, wondering if it were possible for his life to ever be whole again.

It was nearly one in the morning when Isaac stumbled out of his cab and into the high-rise luxury condo. He didn't remember how he got to the tenth floor or why his keys weren't working. He knew the occupant was long asleep by now, but it didn't keep him from banging on the door.

As the familiar feminine voice from within the condo spoke to him, his resolve, his demands, his tirade turned to a sobbing mess.

"Becca, please, honey, please let me in," he shouted as he pounded both of his fists on her door.

Suddenly the door flew open. Isaac stumbled in towards her, practically falling into her arms, knocking her off balance in the process.

"Becca, please don't go." His words slurred, and his breath reeked of alcohol. He heard her gag as she dragged his uncoordinated body over to her couch, deposited him on it, and then ran back to shut her front door. Once closed, she placed her hand on her hips and glared back at him.

"Zac, you're drunk...what in the world did you come here for?" she demanded.

Initially, he came over there to demand that she take her engagement ring back and beg for his forgiveness. After all, he was Isaac Taylor. Women were hounding him all the time. He had to keep most women at arm's length. She didn't know how good she had it.

Ishmael had said the same thing and suggested that they go out clubbing and have a good time. He had thought about it, but at the last second, he decided not to.

Instead, he planned to come over and hash it out with her. But now that he was here, seeing her lovely face, made him long for her more. Those weeks away from Becca were horrible; he missed her so desperately. But he had to teach her a lesson, but the only lesson learned was by him. He hadn't come home as the conquering hero he thought himself to be but conquered.

"Becca, please don't leave me. I'm sorry...I don't understand what is happening...you're leaving me, mom left...I don't understand. Why do you want to leave me?" he said, sobbing loudly while holding his head in his hands.

"Look, it's late...and you're drunk. I will get you some coffee and call you a cab," Becca said with finality in her voice as she moved from the door into her small kitchen.

"Lord, why is everyone leaving me," he muttered.

*"I will never leave or forsake you."*

The still small voice in his head whispered to him, causing a calm, peaceful comfort to wash over him. The tormenting feeling lifted off him as he drifted deeper until nothing but a warm blanket of comfort engulfed him.

The morning seemed to come around fast...too fast for Rebecca's liking. She forced her eyes open and stretched her legs although she really wanted to stay in bed. She was earnestly contemplating doing just that when the caress of a familiar hand slid over her bare thigh. Startled, she shot straight up in her bed, shocked to see Isaac resting comfortably, nestled beside her. Having passed out on her couch last night and he was too heavy to move. Tired, she decided to just let him sleep it off and would send him packing in the morning. Angry at him for taking the advantage she was about to wake him, but then her stomach began to flip flop.

Before she could say or think anything, a wave of nausea forcefully greeted her stomach, making her scramble to the bathroom before it was too late. Her dry heaves were at their worst in the morning. When one set passed, another wave was right there to greet her. At one point, she thought she was going to hyperventilate when a cold, moist towel touched her brow, and a gentle hand rubbed its way up and down her spine.

"Take it easy, Becca, I got you," Isaac's voice comforted. Pulling her sweat-drenched hair off her face, he guided her back onto his lap. Becca allowed her arms to rest on the toilet seat while Isaac gently spoke to her as the last waves of dry heaves begin to subside.

"Baby, how far along are you."

"At least two months." She spoke, her raspy voice was barely above a whisper.

"Why didn't you say anything…have you seen the doctor?"

She shook her head, no. "I took the test last month, I wanted you to be the next person to know. But you wouldn't speak to me." The confession unleashed a dam of emotions she had been holding back for weeks.

"Baby, I'm so sorry for everything I've done… everything I've said. Sweetheart, please forgive me."

"Isaac, I can't be all those things you said you wanted yesterday. I deeply love you, but I do have my own opinions, I do have my own thoughts, and when they don't line up with yours, I don't want us not speaking for months at a time" she cried.

"Becca…I don't want that…I just want you."

"But you said you wanted a wife that would…"

"Baby listen to me." Isaac interjected pulling Rebecca around until they were face to face. His own tears seemed to catch her off guard.

"After you left my office yesterday, I went out with Ishmael and his wife, Marlana. She is a perfect description of the type of woman I told you yesterday I wanted. She catered to Mael and laughed at his jokes, but to be honest, she seems dull and uninteresting. The saddest part is my brother doesn't respect her. I went back to my office and got good and drunk, but I couldn't shake the feeling that if you are not in my life, it will be the biggest mistake of my life."

It was the words she longed to hear, but he needed to know her love came with a price tag. "I love you so much, Isaac, and you know that, but I can't be with a man who won't respect me or my opinions."

"I realize that, Becca. I was so stupid, insulting, and wrong for trying to silence you. If you honor me by becoming my wife, I swear on a stack of King James Bibles, I will never do that to you again."

"Isaac, do you really want to marry me, or is it because you now know that you're going to be a father?

"You're the only woman I've ever wanted to mother my children. You're the only one I want to call my wife. Please, Becca, take me back?" He said, hugging her with an intensity she had never felt before.

"Isaac, how could I do anything else but take you back? I love you," she said, holding on to him, praying that this would not be a deal-breaker for them. "But there is one other thing I need for you to be okay with."

"Name it, sweetheart!"

"We can't have sex again until we are legally married."

Isaac's hold on her lessened. Leaning back to look in her face to see if she was really serious, he cocked his head to the side as if to read her mind. "Honey, we put that cart before the horse a couple months ago. Are you serious?" Isaac gave a nervous chuckle.

She chuckled too and winced. Her throat was still raw. "I realize that, but I want our marriage to honor God. We can't do that if we're not following his Word. Agreed?"

He sighed heavily. "You're right, agreed." He drew their foreheads together. "So, I guess make-up sex is out of the question too?"

"Zac!" She shoved his arm.

"I know...I know." He sighed again. "So, since we aren't going to make up like we usually do, how about we get some breakfast and plan our Christmas wedding?" he asked, kissing the side of her neck.

"You mean Christmas engagement, don't you?" Becca questioned, struggling to pay attention to his words. His gentle back rub and soft caresses were messing with her resolve to stay chaste.

"No babe, I mean a Christmas wedding. There's no way in the world that I can wait until after the New Year to hold you in my arms again. Sixty days max is about all I can do, and that's stretching it meaning our wedding will be right around Christmas time."

"Okay, I accept your terms and your deadline, Mr. Taylor. And if my head wasn't just hung over a toilet bowl, I would seal the deal with a kiss."

Scrunching his nose up at that idea, he countered. "How about you get back in bed, I'll fix us breakfast then I'll take notes of all the things you want for our wedding?"

Smiling lovingly at him, Rebecca said. "I'd say that sounds like heaven."

# Chapter Twenty-Four

"Good morning, sleepyhead." Carlton playfully kissed Tippany's nose and then nibbled on her ear.

Smiling, Tippany stretched out in her husband's arms, and lazily yawned. "It was an even better night." She playfully kissed his chin, then wrapped her arms around his neck to kiss him more passionately. They had been married for almost a month now, and the only other person who knew it was Rebecca. Keeping secrets was hard, but this secret was downright delicious.

"What is going through that pretty little head of yours?"

"I don't know, maybe I'm just happy we decided to do this."

"You mean this right here…" he left a trail of playful kisses from her neck to her bare shoulder. "Oh yeah, I'm glad we decided to do this, this morning, last night, yesterday afternoon…."

A small decorative pillow bopped him in the head, causing them both to laugh.

"I know what you mean, Tippy. I'm glad we decided to get married too. I mean, if anyone would've told me I would be married and happy three weeks ago, I would have told them they were crazy...but here I am…happy." He kissed her nose, which led to a series of kisses. Out of breath, they both stopped and just stared at each other for a moment, then Tippany spoke.

"Let's play hooky today. Let's stay in bed. We can order in and watch movies all day or do other things." She wiggled her eyebrows.

"Mrs. Parson, as appealing as that sounds, today's the day we tell Keturah as well as the rest of our family and friends about us."

"Do we have to?" Tippany pouted, pulling the lavender-colored sheets over her head.

"Yes, we have to." He chuckled, pulling the covers down to expose her face. "You know in this town secrets don't last long. Do you really want Keturah to find this information out from someone other than us?"

"You know I don't. It's just right now in this space, everything seems so wonderful. But when others are included in this little circle of ours, it will become a disaster."

Carlton pulled his wife closer to him and held her for a while before speaking. "Tippy, people will come in and out of our circle, but what we cannot allow is for people to come between us."

Twisting out of his arms, she propped herself on her elbow to look him in the eye. "Excuse me, Carlton, but have you met my mother? She can turn a baby bear against his own mother. What chance do we have against her?"

"Well, I already had a run-in with your mom, and if I do say so, I think I held my own."

"You keep thinking that," Tippany started getting out of bed, baring her scantily covered form to her husband as she walked into the master bathroom.

"Listen, you weren't there, and like I said, I did well on my own against her," he said, walking in the bathroom just as she stepped into the shower.

"Carlton, all I'm saying is you don't know my mother like I do."

"And all I'm saying is neither one of you know me," Carlton said, stepping into the hot sprays with her. "I can hold my own in a street fight, and I can hold my own with a bully, male or female."

Closing the gap between them, she draped her arms around his neck and stood on her tippy toes. "The only thing I need you to hold right now is me."

He eagerly complied.

\*\*\*

Her sister's message sounded cryptic. Keturah knew something was up. She could feel it for the last couple weeks, and somehow, she knew it had something to do with Parson. She hadn't seen or heard from him at all, no emails or text—nothing. Whatever Abraham had said to him when they had met must've put the fear of God in him because he was keeping his distance. Maybe it was all for the best. Her and Abraham's current arrangement seemed to be working out so far. He was staying home as he promised, coming home from work at a decent hour, spending time with her and the children, even sticking it out in counseling sessions. Everything was picture perfect—a little too perfect for her.

"Why can't you just be happy?" she questioned herself. Something about Abraham's behavior felt too perfect as if he was an actor on a stage giving his best performance but his true nature was still shrouded in darkness. "Lord I'm tired of the secrets, and it seemed like the Taylor Jaymes clan is full of them. If we are ever going to be a true family, we all need to begin to walk in truth."

*"You can't handle the truth."* The words from an old movie she watched rushed through her mind.

"I can do all things through Christ, who strengthens me," Keturah spoke to herself to fight back the sudden fear that grappled with her mind. She said the scripture verse three more times as she sat in the little café. By the time she had spoken it the fourth time, Tippany, along with Parson, were walking in the door.

Keeping her hands folded on the table, Keturah smiled as the two waved at her and came towards her table.

"Hey, Tippany, hey Parson." Keturah stood to give both of them a hug. "Long time no see stranger," she said, smiling then taking her seat. It was good to see them both. The three of them hadn't been out together in a long time.

"It's good to see you too," Carlton said with a smile. "I've—"

"How are the kids? I hope they are both over the sniffles?" Tippany abruptly chimed in.

"They are both doing well, and I know they'd love to see you both." Keturah smiled outwardly, but on the inside, her nerves were doing a jittery dance. Something was definitely going on.

Taking Tippany's coat, Parson helped her in her seat, and that's when Keturah noticed the ring on her sister's finger. Instinctively, Keturah knew they had gotten married.

"Thanks, Carlton." Tippany smiled up at him.

"You're welcome." He gave a warm smile back.

"So, when did you two tie the knot!" Keturah asked once Carlton was seated.

The couple looked at each other wide-eyed then looked back at her. Tippany began to fumble over her words as she tried to answer. "Yes...yes we did, but how did you know?" she asked with a nervous titter in her voice.

"Your ring." Keturah nodded towards her hand.

"Oh," Tippany said softly as she looked down at her wedding ring.

"We haven't told anyone or announced it yet. We wanted you to be the first to know," Parson said slowly.

"Oh, I see," Keturah said, looking down at her cup of hot chocolate. "I didn't realize you two had feelings for each other." Keturah creased her eyebrows at both of them, trying to understand when all this happened.

"Oh...we don't," Parson spoke up quickly.

Keturah noticed how his quick response caused Tippany to drop her gaze and look at her hands. Parson didn't realize how his words impacted his new bride. He might not have romantic feelings for Tippany, yet and still, she had deep feelings for him, Keturah surmised as Parson rambled on about their marriage arrangement.

"So, you guys decided to have a marriage of convenience. I thought after seeing how disastrous my marriage turned out, you wouldn't have taken the same route."

"Keturah, we might be sisters, but I'm not you. Carlton and I have an understanding. We were open and upfront about everything. We know what we're doing and what we're going after. The damage your husband and my mother have done has no quick fix to it. We had to get creative, and so this is what we've come up with. I'm sorry if your high standards cause you to disapprove." Tippany's condescending tone was evident to all.

"Tippy, come on. Don't be like that. Keturah is not giving us a hard time, she's just telling us her experience."

"Tippy, you're right, we are not the same, but we are sisters. So, I understand you, and I see more than you realize." Keturah knew her words were going over Parson's head, but she also knew Tippany understood. "When all is said and done, I don't want my sister nor my friend hurt."

"Tourie, thanks for being a friend. You have always looked out for me; this time, I'm returning the favor." Parson covered her folded hands with one hand and held Tippany's hand with the other. "I promise I won't let anything bad happened to Tippany or our friendships."

Keturah smiled at them both knowing that something had already happened to their friendships, and the saddest part was they all knew it.

# *Chapter Twenty-Five*

As the day continued to unravel, so had Keturah's nerves. After Tippany and Parson's earth-shattering revelation regarding their impromptu marriage, the tension between the two sisters was obvious. Deciding to skip lunch, they drove directly to the attorney's office in separate cars, much to Keturah's relief. "Arrangement my eye." Keturah fumed. She could tell just by the way the newlyweds were interacting that this was no marriage of convenience.

*"They've consummated their marriage."*

With the words still ringing in Keturah's ears, she suddenly gritted her teeth as a jabbing pain shot up from her tailbone and raced up her spine. As the pain began to subside, she felt moisture trickle down the side of her face. She couldn't tell if the tears were from the pain still pulsing in her body or her hurting soul. She shouldn't be angry, Tippy and Parson both had a right to find happiness...*just not with each other*. Hitting the steering wheel with her fist, she cried out. "God, it's not fair. I waited, I obeyed, and I still lost. It's just not fair. Abraham gets what he wants, and so does Tippany...well, what do I get out of this deal?" she sobbed. Hearing the familiar jingle of her cell, she forcefully swiped at her tears and quickly answered.

"Hello, oh hi Beth, yes, I can come in. Can Dr. Stalworth just tell me over the phone? Oh...I see, okay, yeah, I can make it on that day. Okay, see you then...bye." She blew out a long sigh, "It's never good when the doctor asks you to schedule an appointment," she muttered. Glancing momentarily at her almost flatten stomach as the familiar flutter made its presence known. Chuckling, she already suspected what her doctor was going to say. "Well, I guess I'm getting something out of this deal, after all."

At the attorney's office, things went from bad to worse as Keturah, Tippany along with Parson and members of her grandfather's board of directors discussed her grandfather's last wishes regarding his company and who would ultimately head it.

"Frankly Keturah, I think you trying to run grandfather's company would be too much on your plate," Tippany stated. "I mean, you have the twins, and your mentoring programs, not to mention playing the role of Abraham's wife. I just don't see how you could possibly do all that and be effective in running our grandfather's company. Now my husband Carlton, on the other hand, has the experience, and I think he would make the perfect candidate for CEO."

Their lawyers, and the board of directors of Birch & Associates, were not impressed by her sister's suggestion. From what she gathered, the attorney of their grandfather's estate said for them to maintain controlling rights of their grandfather's business Keturah would have to step in as CEO. It was a role of a lifetime, and she quickly accepted it. It was only after she was given the details that included her relocating to the gulf shore, she thought it might have been better to consult Abraham before accepting. "Well, if we had begun couple's time once a week like we told the Shaffers' we'd try to have, I could've been discussing this with him. But he kept putting me off, always had some important business to deal with." Keturah said defensively as she drove into Canaan's parking garage, pulled her old jalopy alongside the row of expensive Taylor Jaymes cars. The board of directors at Birch & Associates needed to know if she would accept the position. She wanted to tell them yes but knew this decision was too big to make without Abraham. She dreaded this conversation, knowing it was a lot to drop on a person all of a sudden. Her tummy fluttered again. She covered her belly with her hand. "Maybe I shouldn't tell him everything at once." She winced, knowing how keeping that type of secret when over the last time. Sighing heavily, she stepped into the elevator and let the doors closed. "God, please let Abraham be in a good mood." she prayed as the elevator whisked her up to the executive floor. A chime indicated she was at her destination. Immediately the doors slid open, and Keturah stepped out and headed directly for her husband's office. Conrad was not at his desk. Seeing no need to wait for him to announce her, she bypassed his station and went straight into Abraham's office.

"Abraham, Conrad wasn't at the door, so I...." Keturah came to an abrupt halt as she looked up to see Hagan seated comfortably behind Abraham's desk.

"Why hello Mrs. Taylor, how pleasant it is to see you again." Hagan said casually.

Caught off guard by Hagan's presence, Keturah's level of discomfort rose quickly. She did her best to calm herself, although she was sure her discomfort made Hagan relax all the more as the woman leaned back in Abraham's chair, crossing her legs like she owned the place.

"Oh, Hagan...hello. Umm...where is my husband?" Keturah asked the annoyance evident in her tone.

"In a meeting with our son Ishmael." Hagan let the words come out of her mouth like a soft purr.

"When will they be done?" Keturah hated the smug tone in Hagan's voice. She hadn't even realized they were in town...but she was sure Abraham had known.

"Allah only knows. Abe is so excited to have Mael at his side again, they could be in there for hours. It's so rare that he has his two favorite sons working side by side with each other. Who knows how long they'll be?"

"Oh, I hope not, Mother Hagan. I feel so light-headed today. I think I need to eat something very soon," another feminine voice rang inside the room.

Keturah turned to see Ishmael's wife, Marlana, in the opposite corner. She was as beautiful as ever, but her normal vibrant bronze skin tone looked a little dull.

"Hello Marlana, I didn't see you. Are you okay? Do you need some water" Keturah inquired?

"No need, Father Abraham's boy has gone out to bring me something."

"Abraham's boy?" Keturah looked confused as to who she meant.

"Yes, what's his name? Connor, or Cobbler...something like that. Anyway, he should be back, although it is taking him a rather long time," Marlana said in a flippant tone.

"Keturah be a dear and go fetch Marlana something won't you," Hagan ordered.

There were a lot of things Keturah had done that day and would likely have to continue to do before the day was out, but *fetching* her daughter-in-law something to drink would not be one of them.

"If Mar—"

"Mrs. Taylor, hello. I wish I would have known you were in here; I would have gotten something for you to drink as well," Conrad said, coming in the door, holding two drinks in his hand.

"Oh, that is not necessary, Conrad, but thank you. And thank you for taking care of Mrs. Taylor." She gave a tight smile to Conrad as he served her daughter-in-law the drink.

"Of course, that's what he's been hired to do," Hagan said in a thoughtless tone.

Conrad's back stiffened, but he managed to maintain his smile as he served both ladies.

"Ah Conrad, has Carlos come around for us? I'm ready to go back to the estate."

This time Keturah's back stiffened. She prayed they were talking about some other place she didn't know about in some other state. "Please, God, don't allow Abraham to be so inconsiderate as to allow Ishmael, Marlana, and Hagan to stay at our house." She begged inwardly.

"I hope you don't mind having guests for the holidays Keturah. When I told Abraham that there was a mix up with our reservations because of some ridiculous computer glitch, he was so gracious in accommodating us...he did mention it to you, didn't he?"

"Father Abraham is so generous. He told us his house was our house," Marlana said sweetly.

"And since the east wing is practically empty, he said there was no need for us to stay anywhere else," Hagan added. I hope this won't put you at an imposition knowing how quickly the holiday season is coming."

"If Abraham has okayed it, then who am I to object?" Keturah said, showing no emotion on her face. "Conrad, may I have a word with you?"

"Certainly Mrs. Taylor." Conrad nodded to Keturah. "Ladies, I will check and see what the hold-up is with the car," he said as he was leaving the office with Keturah right on his heels.

"Conrad, where is Mr. Taylor?" Keturah no more than said his name when Abraham came from one of the conference rooms surrounded by both his sons. They were in deep conversation, and he would have walked right past her if she hadn't stepped in front of them.

"Keturah!?" He stepped back, startled at her sudden appearance. "Honey, what are you doing here?"

"Well, I need to discuss some things with you. I called your office in Gastonia, but they said you were here, so I came here but found your office was occupied with what I was informed will be our house guests for the holidays." Keturah spoke in a nasty nice way.

"Yeah," Abraham, looking guilty, responded.

"Dad, we need to get going if we're going to make the meeting this afternoon in Vegas," Ishmael spoke up from behind him.

"You're leaving for Vegas?!" A wide-eyed Keturah questioned.

"Mael is right dad, we do need to get going," Isaac confirmed.

"Yeah...um look Keturah, some unexpected business came up that I have to attend to. We will discuss this when I come back." He sidestepped her as he headed towards the elevators.

"What about Marlana and Hagan? Not to mention, we have counseling scheduled for tomorrow. Will you at least be back by then?" Keturah was frantic at this sudden change without being consulted.

"Keturah, this business meeting is important. I'll be back in a week or so, but I will call you tonight so we can discuss things."

"But what about your house guests? Who's supposed to accommodate them while you're gone...hum?" She pressed, knowing she was definitely not up to entertaining her would-be rival.

"Keturah, please." Abraham's stern tone was heard by all. Taking her by the arm, he pulled her to the side and lowered his voice. "I know this is sudden, but I need you to work with me. You know do what the Shaffers' always suggest give and take a little. I will be back next week. In the meantime, Marlana and Hagan will be taken care of by Consuela and the other staff...okay!"

He wanted her cooperation and didn't care how she felt about the debacle he was leaving her in. Like Tippany and Parson, all Abraham cared about was his needs. It was time she stopped worrying about everyone else. It was time Keturah cared for her children and herself. Having resolved it in her heart, she looked up at Abraham and gave him a confident smile. "Okay, darling, have a great trip."

Standing on her toes, she kissed him tenderly. Pulling away she caressed his face then walked away. Turning to Hagan and Marlana who were standing in the doorway of his office, she smiled. "I guess I'll be seeing the two of you at home." With that, she turned and walked towards the elevator. When the doors opened, she walked in and never looked back at the people staring strangely at her.

\*\*\*

Repositioning herself in Abraham's executive chair, Hagan placed her hands behind her long flowing mane and stared at the ceiling somewhat perplexed. "You know that stepmother of yours is a very odd duck," Hagan spoke out loud, then stood up and paced back and forth in front of the executive office window. Abraham hadn't made many changes to his office suite. The warm brown tones and dark burgundy furniture spoke of Sarah's love of mid-eastern design.

"She certainly has no class. I cannot imagine why Father Abraham ever married her," Marlana said placing her bare feet on the wine-colored, soft leather sofa, while sipping her fruit smoothie.

"I do." Hagan stood walking over to Sarah's portrait and staring at it momentarily. "When Sarah was Keturah's age, she was a different woman than the one in this picture." Hagan genuinely smiled at the memory. "She was young, energetic, and idealistic. She was going to do it all, be it all, then Abraham came into the picture and changed everything." Turning to her daughter-in-law, she gave a knowing smile. "Men have a way of doing that with their women."

Marlana blushed. "You're right. I was going to be a model and run the circuit as long as my looks would allow, but then I met Mael, and my whole world tilted. I didn't think I wanted children, and even if I did, I didn't want them this soon." Marlana gently laid a hand on her flattened abdomen with a smile. "Then I got Dr. Omar's call..." Marlana's face went from happy to puzzled. "Mother Hagan, why don't you want Father Abraham to know that I'm expecting yet?"

"Oh, I have my reasons, dear." She stopped her pacing as she stood in front of his office window, looking at the Charlotte skyline. She had a plan that this was going to be her son's office one day…one day soon, she hoped. Then they'd all be sorry for running her and Ishmael out of town. "You just focus on doing all the doctor has instructed. Especially when it comes to eating. I know models are used to starving themselves, but you can't do that anymore, you have my grandchild's welfare to concern yourself with," she said kindly.

"I have already told my agent not to book any more showings for me. I am going to follow the doctor's instructions; I just pray I don't turn so round that Ishmael runs from me." Her voice faltered as she looked down at her hands.

Hagan looked intently at her daughter-in-law, something in her voice, something familiar. "Everything is going well between you and Ishmael, isn't it?"

Marlana hunched her shoulders, but it was a long time before she responded. "I worry too much, is all."

"About what, Marlana?" Hagan frowned not liking the turn their conversation was taking. She hated to think that Ishmael had picked up not only his stepfather's business savvy, but also some of his more deplorable habits like cheating.

"It is probably nothing. Lately, Mael has been coming home very late. But at times when I call the office, I'm told he is not there. He once told me that he wasn't going out for lunch because he was swamped, so to surprise him, I picked up some lunch and went to the office, but he wasn't there and hadn't been in the office that entire morning."

"Well, he could have stepped out for a quick bite."

"His secretary said he wasn't scheduled to come to the office until around two that afternoon." Her voice trembled as she looked everywhere but at her mother-in-law.

All the signs were there. From not being where he said he'd be, to even coming to the office late, in every way, Ishmael was acting like his cheating stepfather. She had hoped she had done a better job of sheltering her son from her husband's sleazy behavior, but apparently, she hadn't. Hagan looked again at the picture of Sarah hanging over Abraham's desk. The smile she once had was replaced with a frown. If Ishmael had had the opportunity to be raised by his birth father, he wouldn't have picked up his stepfather's sordid ways. In fact, he wouldn't have had a stepfather. This was all Sarah's doing. Her hatefulness had permanently altered her son's moral compass.

"Mother Hagan, are you, all right?" Marlana came up behind her mother-in-law, extending a gentle hand on Hagan's shoulder.

"Oh, I'm sorry, what were you saying?" She recovered.

"Do you think everything is okay and that I'm worrying for nothing?"

She looked at her daughter-in-law and saw herself. Her mother-in-law blamed her for everything when all she really needed was a friend and some guidance. Well, Hagan was determined to be the friend that she wished her mother-in-law would have been to her. Taking Marlana by the shoulders, she encouraged her. "Don't worry, I will talk to my son. Everything is going to be okay. You and Mael just need guidance from those who love you most...Me and Abraham. Now let's find out where that car is and go to our temporary home."

# Chapter Twenty-Six

A month had passed since Ishmael, with his family besieged Keturah and Abraham's home causing everyone to be on edge. Keturah still hadn't told Abraham about the CEO position or that she was expecting. They were too busy snapping at each other. The arguing had escalated to the point where Abraham started spending less time at home, blaming it on his business ventures' demands. Keturah knew better but was too peeved to give the man the benefit of the doubt. Besides, his increased late nights allowed her to work at Birch & Associates and commute home without Abraham being any the wiser.

"As far as I'm concerned, Tamara, if he's not going to consult me, then I'm not consulting him either." Keturah folded her arms, turning to the side unwilling to look her counselor in the eye.

"Okay, and how is that working for the two of you?" Tamara questioned.

"Look, Tamara, I know you're a counselor and all...but you're also a wife," Keturah dodging the question as she defended her actions. "How would you feel if Larry brought his ex into your house, and if that's not bad enough, stayed out of town the entire time leaving you to entertain her."

"To be honest, I would be upset." Tamara simply stated.

"Exactly."

"So, you don't want Hagan in your home, so why don't you ask her to leave?"

"Because my husband feels it's our Christian duty to show others the love of Christ. Oh, that man!" She growled, stomping her foot. "He is so quick to quote scriptures to me about my attitude or how I should treat others, but he completely ignores my feelings?" Keturah jerked out of her seat, holding her hands out in frustration.

"So, this is not about Hagan as much as it is about what Abraham is requiring from you," Tamara probed. "Why does that bother you so?"

Whisking around, she blurted, "He tells me I have to keep my distance from Parson, yet he invites Hagan to stay in our home? What's worse, I have to play all nicey-nice with her!" The words gushed out of her mouth with such force she shocked even herself.

"I was wondering when we were going to talk about him." Tamara's expression remained neutral as she pointed towards the seat Keturah had moments ago exited.

Fidgeting with her fingers, Keturah walked over to her chair and plunked herself down in the seat, unable to look at the other woman sitting across from her.

"Do you miss Carlton?"

Keturah nodded yes while large teardrops plopped down on her hand. She was so very thankful they were doing an individual counseling session today. She couldn't bear seeing the reserved but cold glare of Abraham's eyes.

Grabbing the tissue box off her desk, Tamara reached out and handed it to Keturah. After she took three or four, Tamara returned it to her desk. "Do you feel Carlton misses you?"

"Well, nowadays, not so much now that he's sleeping with my sister." Keturah's matter-of-fact tone caused her counselor to narrow her eyes with questions. "Oh yeah, a lot has happened since our last session."

"Yes, I would say so." Tamara sat back and stretched in her chair. With hands folded, she emanated a quiet reserve allowing Keturah the time she needed to sort out the war going on within her soul.

Swiping at her tears, her voice trembled as she spoke. "Yeah, they up and got married a couple of weeks ago, and then told me before we went to discuss our grandfather's inheritance."

"Did they say why they got married?"

Shrugging a shoulder, she twisted her lips and muttered. "Well, I assume my husband and stepmother are to thank." Keturah squished her tissue in her hand, holding her bottom lip in with her teeth.

"Why them? Why are you blaming Abraham and your stepmom for something Carlton and Tippany chose to do?"

Again, she shrugged as tears of hurt flowed down her cheeks. Unable to come to terms with what could have been but now would never be.

"I want to ask you to do something for me. Will you try?" Seeing Keturah nod, yes, she continued. "Shut your eyes and let your mind go blank."

Keturah breathed out heavily then complied by shutting her eyes.

"Mentally, one by one, I want you to picture the people you love. Do you see them, Keturah?"

"Yes, I see them." Her voice wobbled.

"Good, now I want you to also bring into focus those who have not been so great to you, the people who have hurt you, mistreated you."

As images of old friends, Abraham, Sari, Tippany, Parson, Hagan, and others surfaced, her peace and joy started to leave her.

"Now, with your eyes closed, I want you to say, Jesus, I invite you into this room with me. And I ask you to help me forgive and love these people the way you have forgiven and loved me."

Keturah repeated the phrase with a quiver in her voice, as she finished the sentence the dam within her broke. As her shoulders shook and streams of tears fell from her face, she forgave those who left, betrayed, hurt, looked down on, disrespected, and rejected her.

Finally, Keturah felt a serene peace hanging heavily in the room. Keturah let the breath she didn't know she was holding escape through her lips as a wave of peace began to cool her flushed skin.

"Did you forgive everyone in the room, Keturah?" Tamara questioned.

Nodding her head yes, she reached for the tissues Tamara handed her.

"What about God? He was in the room too. Did you forgive Him?"

"God doesn't need my forgiveness. Besides isn't that sacrilegious?" Keturah looked up as she blew her nose, surprised that Tamara would even suggest such a thing.

"That is a very good Christian answer." Tamara chuckled. "But is it an honest one? Yes, He does know what is best, but it doesn't always feel that way, especially in our dark moments."

"But I feel It's wrong to be angry with God. He is the one who knows what's best." Keturah sniffed as she wiped under her eyes.

"Again, what your saying is good Christian Theology, but does it keep you from feeling angry at Him?" Tamara pushed.

"Tamara, for me to say, *God I forgive you,* is like saying I believe God did something wrong or He wronged me, and that is not true. I owe Him everything."

"You are so right, we all do. But what happens when the unexpected occurs? Your loved one dies, and God didn't stop it like you thought He would, or when that job doesn't go through, or your life is forever changed because of a decision someone else has made, and God didn't block it, what then? I know your struggling with this concept so think of it in this way. Unforgiveness robs us of our peace and joy. It keeps us from trusting fully. But when we finally forgive. We gain all that back. So, this is not about what God needs from you but what he wants to release to you through forgiveness."

Keturah sat hunched over in her seat as her mind muddled through everything Tamara had said. She wondered, was she holding God at a distance? "Maybe I do need to forgive God!" The words still felt foreign coming out of her mouth. "But how can I know...I mean, really know that His plan for my life is going to make me happy?"

"Keturah, so far has your plans made you happy?

Keturah bowed her head. None of her plans had worked out like she thought. "No, I guess not."

"God wants us happy and to experience fulfillment in this life. His word says his plans will give us a hope, a future and an expected end. But God's priority is in making us whole in our soul. He wants to bring you to a place where you won't be shaken no matter what happens or doesn't happen. That is something only God can do."

# *Chapter Twenty-Seven*

"Sloppy…sloppy…sloppy!" Abraham threw the file down on the conference table and paced back and forth.

"Dad losing the Pendleton contract is not that huge of a deal, and neither is Basco Incorporated," Isaac indicated. We knew they were not satisfied last year and were looking to jump ship," Isaac said nonchalantly. "Besides what we've done here the last six weeks more than makes up for the loss. In fact, we've gained more than we've lost and then some.

"Son, that is not the point. You sent Conrad, who is a novice at best in this business, to cover for you. He should have been there observing not trying to run that type of negotiation."

"But it was worth the risk, Dad. The big picture is that we have advanced Canaan, just like we were planning to do in the country's western part, we are right on schedule. Yes, we lost two small accounts that we shouldn't have, but when you weigh the loss with what we've gained…" Isaac reiterated.

"Son, this makes us look uninterested in the needs of our clients. Like we don't have time for them because they are small." A knock on the door stopped him. "Come in," he commanded, turning to see who it was. "Conrad, good, we were just discussing the Pendleton and Basco contracts. I would like some insight into what happened."

Conrad hesitated as he walked into the room and took a seat in front of the three Taylor men. Swallowing hard, he adjusted his tie and began. "Well, gentlemen, for starters, both companies did their interviewing process a bit differently than what I expected."

"Oh? How so?" Isaac inquired.

"Well, it was more of a round table discussion. I, along with several other bidders, were invited to discuss and brainstorm on ideas and how to make the corporation more competitive. If they liked what they heard, you were asked to bring the full presentation. Of course, we were in the running, as was one other competitor."

"And who was that?" Abraham inquired.

"Birch & Associates," Conrad muttered, not giving Abraham full eye contact.

"They're not even in our league. Since when did they start dibbling and dabbling in our line of work." Isaac grabbed his cell, ready to make a few calls.

"Since your wife became their new CEO." Conrad stated.

All three Taylor men stopped their activity and looked at Conrad intently.

"Yeah, I was just as shocked to see Mrs. Taylor in the meeting and introduced as the new CEO of Birch & Associates as anyone. I can tell you this. Your wife doesn't pull any punches, she is one shrewd negotiator."

"Dad, did you know Keturah was taking over as CEO of Birch & Associates?" Ishmael inquired. When his father didn't respond, he turned to Conrad. "When did this happened."

"Officially four weeks ago. Well, at least that was what the press release confirmed when they went public with it after this deal went through."

"Of all the..." Isaac slammed his phone on the table and was up pacing in the office then turned to his father. "Dad, how can she do this? I mean she is doing the girls mentoring project for Canaan, how can she be doing both? Besides, how much does she really know about business marketing anyway?"

If it wasn't for the fact that the conference table was made of tempered glass, it would have shattered under Abraham's forceful blow. Reaching for his cellphone, he hit one on the speed dial. "Avery contact the pilot, I want to be in the air within the hour," he clicked off then, grabbed his suit jacket and briefcase and stormed out the office door.

Ishmael, Isaac, and Conrad looked on, knowing for sure they didn't want to be in Keturah's shoes.

***

*"You must tell Abraham!"*

Rubbing her temples, she leaned her head on her fingertips, not sure how she was going to break the news to her husband when he returned home. She had no idea Canaan was going for the same bids she was gunning for. She and members of her firm went in for a presentation. She was taken aback when she ran into Abraham's assistant Conrad, coming off the elevator. They exchanged quick pleasantries, and she scurried into the elevator. Then this morning, they ran into each other again, this time there was no way to deny the reason for her presence. They were going after the same contract, and she was sure by the time her meeting was over, Abraham would know about it.

"Why didn't I just tell him yesterday?" She gave herself a silent reprimand. She was so out of it after her session with Tamara when she came home, she played a little while with the children, then crawled into bed and went to sleep. Abraham had called as usual, but she was dead to the world. Getting up late was her excuse for not calling him back that morning. Seeing Conrad today, she knew she had made one too many excuses. She tried calling her husband after her meeting, but this time he didn't pick up.

*"Ladies and gentlemen, please fasten your seat belts as we make our descent into Charlotte,"* the pilot over the loudspeaker announced.

Keturah huffed as she strapped herself in. "Time to face the music."

Rushing home Keturah ran in the house and went straight to her room for a shower and afterward she planned on spending time with her children. "Of all days to get stuck in bumper-to-bumper traffic." She fussed, allowing the hot spray to melt the tension in her neck and shoulders. She wanted to be relaxed for the kids. This was her favorite time of day. She often let Carmen go early just to spend the rest of her time coddling them. Turning the water off, she reached for her towel but felt nothing but tile. "Oh shoot...I forgot my towel," she said, stepping out of the shower, looking through her wet hair at the empty towel hook.

"Oh, well." She shrugged and began shaking herself like a wet dog would, her long, damp hair smacking her face.

"Last time I checked, I'm pretty sure we still have towels, Tourie?" Abraham's deep tenor echoed in their ensuite.

Shrieking, Keturah spun around, losing her balance in the process and was about to connect to the floor when she was pulled upright by his strong arms. Clutching on to his sleeves, her feet continued to slide as she tried with no luck to steady herself.

"Stop squirming. I've got you," he said gruffly.

Looking up at him annoyed, she frowned. "Well, if you hadn't scared me in the first place."

"Would you have rather I let your bum hit the floor?" he said, steadying her then walked away to retrieve a towel.

"I would rather you have announced your presence," she stated.

"And I would have preferred you be home when I got here. But I guess you can't be here when you're out there playing CEO." His cold blue eyes bore into hers.

She bowed her head. She had been caught. There was nothing she could do to twist out of it. "You're right, I know I should've told you. I'm sorry." There, she said it.

"So, that's it?" He tossed his hands in the air letting them fall to his sides. "I'm sorry I went behind your back babe and took the CEO position at Birch & Associates, knowing it is a conflict of interest to have this job and oversee the mentoring project at Canaan? Or how about this, I'm sorry babe because I have absolutely no business trying to run a company when I have two babies and a husband to care for at home" he yelled.

"Don't yell at me, Abe." she hollered back, storming away from him into their bedroom to retrieve her nightie. If they were going to have a quarrel, she wasn't going to do it naked. "Oh, and by the way babe, yes, this is the best I can do because you're never home long enough to discuss business or anything else." She plopped on the chaise lounge next to her armoire as she patted her damp skin dry.

"You know what, you're right. So, let's discuss it now." He plopped on the bed in front of her.

"Okay, fine, let's discuss it," she challenged.

"So Tourie, if you would have discussed this with me, I would have told you that in no uncertain terms, am I okay with you taking this position. But that's water under the bridge. The only thing I want to know now is when you plan to tell the board you're going to resign." Abraham demanded.

"Humm...let me think." Keturah tapped her chin. "I'll resign the day after Hell freezes over!?" Keturah jerked off the chaise, her towel, and nightie flying in opposite directions. " What right do you have to order me to leave my position? You might be head of this house, but that doesn't give you the right to boss me around."

"On the contrary, dearest." He stalked towards her. "Being head of this house gives me the absolute right to make decisions for this family which you are part of. So, like it or not, what I say goes," he said, lording his authority over her.

"This is the twenty-first century Mr. Taylor. Sarah might have allowed you to lord over her, but you won't be doing that with me."

"Oh, really!?"

"Yes, really!" she said in a mocking tone. "If you wanted a docile woman, maybe you should have married Hagan, or better yet followed in Ishmael's footsteps and married a snippy little princess like Marlana," Keturah said in a cocky tone, turning to her right to snatch her towel and nightie off the floor. "You'll find you won't get your way that easily with me, Mr. High and Mighty," she said sarcastically as she turned around only to jerk back, not realizing how close he was to her. Her heart rate increased as his eyes bore into hers. Throughout their marriage, she and Abraham shared many intimate moments. She was always unassuming; he was always eager but tender. But what she saw flashing in his eyes was new...and tempting. Stepping into his space, she kissed him with a longing that scared her. She had no chance to second guess her actions as she felt his strong arms lift her off her feet as he carried her to their bed.

*** 

This wasn't the shy young woman he had married a year and a half ago, or even the woman he had to drag to his home two months ago. The woman he found himself clinging to brought out the passion buried within him. She stirred his longing to be free—to live, to love, to try new things, to take risks.

Feeling his side being tickled, he captured her fingers and brought them to his lips and smiled. It was dark, the only light shining in the room was from the moon hanging in the night sky. Within the intimacy of the darkened room, he took a risk and broke a promise that he never thought he would.

"I love you, Keturah. I have for a very long time." He closed his eyes, ashamed of the emotions his words evoked in him. "I promised myself I'd never love anyone else but Sarah and then you came in and blew my world out of the water. I didn't know how to love anyone else, but Keturah, I want to learn how to love you." Before he could say anything else, Keturah's mouth found his, and in the stillness of the night, they clung to each other, neither willing to let the other go. They talked and held each other well into the night. She shared her dreams and hopes, and he shared his loss and desires for their future.

"Abraham, please try and understand why I took the position. You and Sarah loved each other, and you created Canaan for Isaac. You established Taylor International, so Ishmael could share in your dream. But what about Kamara and Abel? I want our children to have a legacy like you left for your sons. With Birch & Associates, I can try and do that. Yes, the company is small and can't compete with Canaan, but I plan to do everything in my power to make sure one day it can, so they will have an inheritance."

"Baby, do you really think I would not take care of you and make sure our children were provided for?" he questioned.

"I know you'll take care of us. But I want our children to remember me too. I want Kamara to know she had a mother who handled business. Abraham, I don't know if you can understand this, but you are a rare breed. Kamara might not find someone like you to marry. I want her to be prepared to take care of herself and marry because she wants to not because she couldn't take care of herself. That's not the legacy I want to leave her."

Keturah's words still rang in his ears the following morning. It was still early; the stars were just beginning to fade in the morning sky. Abraham left a sleeping Keturah's side and found himself in the nursery. Like her mother, Kamara was sound asleep, but not Abel. He was yawning and stretching. When Abraham looked over at him, his son greeted him with a smile. "Hey, little man, why are you up so early?" He smiled, scooping his son's wiggling body up in his arms.

"Bababababab," Abel muttered with a spit bubble smile.

"How about da-da. Come on, son...say da-da," he encouraged, but instead, his son continued to make loud screeching sounds sure to wake the dead. "You're going to wake up sissy, and that's not going to be good for any of us," he cautioned, placing a soft kiss on his son's crown, then walked out of the French doors onto their private balcony. "This was my first wife's favorite place to be. I'd always find her here with hands raised praising God for his goodness to us." He lowered his head as the memory washed over him. "I have so much history here with her and your brother Isaac. She made this our home." He walked over to the small table and chair and sat down; Abel still tightly cradled in his arms. "Isaac is going to marry and have a family of his own. It has always been my intention to give him this place. Rebecca is going to come in here and make this their home. When you get married, I pray that I'm there to witness it. However, in case I'm not, remember this, every woman wants to make a home for her family," he said, stroking his son's tiny fingers. Looking down, he wondered what parts of him would Abel remember when he was gone? "Hopefully, the good parts," he said quietly and in deep thought of what the future would hold for his two youngest.

"Here, you two are." Keturah emerged with Kamara in tow, giving a yawn and smile. Kamara tiny fingers grasped her mother's nightgown as she feasted away on her morning meal. "I was wondering if we could do a swap before this greedy little girl downs her meal and Abel's."

Sucking his teeth, Abraham looked at his wife with amusement. "You know good, and well, she is going to start squawking as soon as you give her to me."

"True, but no one in the world can get her quieted like you can babe." Keturah, now standing over him, bent down and gave him a lingering kiss.

"Flattery will get you everywhere, my love." He stroked the soft skin of her face then sought to move in closer for another kiss until a little fist hit him in the eye. "Kamara Taylor, you have the worst disposition ever." He chuckled, taking her in his empty arm as Keturah took Abel.

"Wonder where she gets that from?" Keturah raised her brow at her husband.

"Don't look at me, I was a model child."

"Yeah, right. It's not like I know anyone who can corroborate that."

"Well, you do when it comes to you. I witnessed first-hand some of your childhood behaviors, and well, I think this little girl is all you."

"Well, since you know how to handle the grownup version so well, this little darling should be a piece of cake." She chuckled as she walked back towards the nursery with Abel.

"Yeah, dealing with Jaymes' females is a piece of cake," he jested, laughing as she playfully stuck her tongue out at him. "Hey, I was thinking, why don't we spend today together, just the two of us?"

Tilting her head, Keturah stared at her husband inquisitively. "You mean like a bonafide date?" She smiled while rocking Abel in her slender arms.

He turned up his lips thoughtfully. "Yeah, why not. So, what do you say, Mrs. Taylor, would you like to go out on a date with your ole hubby?"

"Are we going anyplace special?"

"You'll just have to wait and see."

"You know this will be a first for me. I've never gone on a date with a married man before." She smiled coyly. "This should be very interesting."

"Indeed, this will be a first for me as well. I make it a policy never to get in bed with one of my competitors. But, for you darling, I'll make an exception," he said, laughing at his own joke as his wife rolled her eyes heavenward.

"Oh, to think you'll get that lucky, sir." Keturah turned and gave an exaggerated swish to her hips as she headed back to the nursery.

Abraham looked down at his daughter, who was still fussing. Smiling at her, he was rewarded with a pout followed by a quivering bottom lip. Shaking his head, he stood up before she began to wail. "Like I said, dealing with Jaymes' females is no piece of cake."

# *Chapter Twenty-Eight*

"At least it's not twins this time!" Keturah shook her head and chuckled while sitting downtown outside of the little coffee house. She had just come from the doctor's office and was still reeling from the news. Taking another long sip of her iced green tea, she mulling over her dilemma. "Lord, how am I going to run the business, keep my obligations to the girls mentor program, take care of my family, all while pregnant?"

*What makes you think Abraham will allow you to do anything once he finds out tonight? Of which, you are telling him tonight!"* Her conscious prodded her.

Her head was pulsating. Shutting her eyes, she massaged her temples with her fingertips. Last night, Abraham's confession of love changed the entire trajectory of their conversation. They had come to an unspoken truce, but she knew nothing had been definitively decided regarding her working at Birch & Associates.

"Keturah, are you okay?"

Startled Keturah's eyes popped open as her heartbeat sped up. "Parson, oh my goodness, you surprised me." She gave a nervous chuckle. "What are you doing here?"

"Well, actually, this is my neck of the woods now."

"Oh…yes that's right. Tippany's loft is right around the corner."

"Yeah, we decided it would be easier on her work commute to stay put, so I moved to her place…anyway, what are you doing down in this neck of the woods?"

She sighed…maybe this was a set-up from God. She was harboring unforgiveness towards them without a cause. It was time for her to bury the hatchet. "To be honest, I hadn't planned on coming this way, but now that I'm here, I'm glad I ran into you," she confessed.

"Keturah, I'm glad to see you too. I didn't feel comfortable the way we left things the last time we were all together. I want you to know I had nothing to do with Tippany's plan to have me run your grandfather's company."

That was Parson, always upfront and to the point.

"Why don't you sit down." She motioned towards the empty seat opposite her. While he set his drink down on the table and took the seat offered, she worked up the courage to say all that she needed to say. "Listen, I owe you and my sister an apology. You and Tippany had every right to do what you felt was best for you."

"Keturah, I know our marriage was out of the blue and a shock, especially since you and I were discussing getting closer."

Shaking her head, she tried to stop him. "You don't have to explain yourself, Parson, you have a right to live your life."

"I want you to know I truly loved you, Keturah." He lowered his eyes. "I know it's crazy to confess it now after I've married your sister, but it seems everything that has happened up until now has been crazy."

"Parson, I—"

He held his hand up to stop her. "Keturah, please let me finish. I tried to justify in my head a thousand times over, but I knew pursuing my feelings for you were wrong. If you wouldn't have been the woman of integrity, you are..." He stopped and shook his head. "Anyway, being away from you and the kids has allowed me to put things in perspective. Your husband was right. A good man doesn't prey on another man's family, especially if he is a Christian. I allowed my wants to supersede God's way, and for that, I'm asking your forgiveness."

Keturah let his words wash over her. He loved her but she now knew the only love she ever wanted was from one man, Abraham.

Being home with her husband and their children was just what their marriage needed. Even with all the disagreements and compromises it all worked together to make them stronger as a couple. So now it was finally time to let her infatuation with Parson, die. "Parson, I always said you would make some woman a wonderful husband. I guessed when things got bad between Abe and me, I made you my pretend husband. But deep down I always knew the only man I truly loved was Abraham. So, can you forgive me for misleading you?"

"I already have." He patted her hand and smiled. "Friends?"

Shaking her head, no, she held on to his hand tightly and returned his smile. "We're family now!"

"Yeah, I guess we truly are."

"Well, since that is settled, how about a favor, bro." Keturah chuckled as he rolled his eyes.

"Not even in the family for more than two seconds, and you already need me. Well, what can I do for you?"

"I need your help at Birch & Associates. Although I hate to admit it, Tippany was right. I have a lot on my plate, and now with the CEO position, I'm afraid maybe I have bit off more than I can chew."

"How does Abraham feel about you taking on such a tremendous responsibility, especially with the twins?"

"He's Abraham Taylor…what do you think?" Keturah blew out a frustrated breath. "He likely thinks I should have my head examined."

"Well, he's in good company. Keturah, being CEO is not for the faint at heart. It can be stressful, and that's with you giving it your one hundred and ten percent…"

"Parson, I want my children to have an inheritance from me. With my grandfather's company, I can make that happen. Besides, it's not just about me, what about Tippany? We both grew up not knowing anything about this side of our family." Twisting her napkin in her hand, she continued. "I just really want to make this work."

Parson was quiet for a few moments, appearing lost in thought. Finally, he looked up at her with a smile. "You know, you and Tippany are very much alike. We had a very similar conversation the day we came home from the meeting."

"I don't know how much alike we are?" She wrinkled her nose at him. "But I do know this is an opportunity of a lifetime. So, what do you say...partners?"

"I'd say, let me grab another latte, and let's talk about this brilliant plan of yours."

Smiling, Keturah got to her feet feeling lighter than she had in weeks since signing on as the CEO of Birch & Associates. Finally, her vision was starting to take form. Now, if only she could get her husband to catch hold of it.

*** 

"Mr. Taylor, here are the reports you requested regarding Birch & Associates," Conrad said, handing his boss the documents. "Oh, by the way, Mrs. Taylor called. She said something came up, and she would be an hour late."

"By the time I get out of here, we'll be having an early dinner." He sighed heavily, looking at the mountain of paperwork he needed to attend to. The way things were looking that special day he promised would be on hold at least until the evening. "I'll call her back in a few minutes. Conrad, call my attorney when you get a minute. I need to discuss a few things with him as well."

"Sure thing Mr. Taylor." Conrad said walking out of the office.

"You look like you're going to be here all night."

Looking up, Abraham smiled as both of his sons entered his office. "Not that long, I hope. So, what are you two up to?"

"Well, apparently, baby brother is planning on getting hitched in less than sixty days, and although I tried my best to talk him out of it, he still plans on going through with it." Ishmael jested.

Abraham was stunned but quickly recovered. Getting up from his chair, he walked over to Isaac, who had a sheepish grin on his face and hugged him. "Son, congratulations...and I might say it's about time."

"Yeah, well, I've been dancing around it long enough. I plan on bringing the new year in with Rebecca as my wife."

"I'd ask what the big rush was, but being the choir boy, you are, I guess we already know," Ishmael smirked.

"Whatever" Isaac gave Ishmael a shove, "All I know is the wedding is right before Christmas, of which Dad, I need a huge favor."

"Of course, anything you need, son."

"Well, because the wedding is so last minute, finding a venue is out of the question, especially around the holidays. Rebecca doesn't want anything as big or elaborate as Aunt Sari was planning. Just something small and intimate with the family. So, with that said, we were hoping to have it at the estate?"

"Son, you don't even need to ask. You have the entire estate at your disposal."

"Hey, since you're not even leaving us time to give you a proper bachelor party, I'll take us all out to lunch. At least we can give you a proper toast to your funeral...I mean wedding. We can call a few people and have them meet us there," Ishmael offered.

"If Ishmael is buying, I'm definitely in." Abraham clapped a hand on his eldest's back and moved back towards the desk to retrieve his suit jacket, resting on his chair's back. "Well, gentlemen, it's settled; let's go."

# *Chapter Twenty-Nine*

"Where is he?" Keturah looked at her watch again, wondering where her husband could be. Conrad had assured her he had told Abraham she would be late. She even called his cell to tell him she'd just meet him at the restaurant, but after an hour there was no signs of him. She had already called his cell twice, but it went straight to voicemail. She didn't want to worry or become angry, not knowing the circumstances behind the delay. Still, she was beginning to feel a hint of alarm. Determining that their lunch date was a bust, she began packing up her things deciding to have a play date with the twins, when she heard a harsh woman's voice coming from a booth behind her.

"Of all the foolish things you've done to date…this takes the cake!"

Keturah didn't even bother to look up. She immediately recognized the harsh critical nature of her step-mother's tone.

"If your reckless behavior in any way harms Malcom's political aspirations, mark my words girly you and that nitwit you married will answer to me."

There was such a lack of dialogue at first Keturah thought Sari must have been on the phone talking to her latest victim. Looking at the restaurant's wall that sported a reflective glass, Keturah could see the regal old bird pick up her purse and strut away like a proud peacock. Keturah shook her head. It didn't make any sense for one person to house that much nastiness in their soul, as her Gretta would have put it. "I'm getting outta here," Keturah concluded. "He's probably up to his neck in some meeting and totally forgot about our date." She fussed. Gathering her belongings, she stood up, ready to leave when she heard a faint sniffle coming from behind her. Peering into the booth, her heart broke seeing Tippany sitting there in tears. They hadn't spoken in three weeks, which was a long time for them. She knew she wasn't walking in forgiveness with her sister. It was time to bury the hatchet.

Swallowing hard, she moved out of her table and came to her sister's side. In a soft tone, she spoke, "Tippy…are you okay?"

Jumping at the sound of Keturah's voice, Tippany quickly looked up. At the sight of Keturah, her face contorted, and she covered her face with her hands as sobs shook her small frame.

Immediately Keturah placed her purse down and sat next to her sister's trembling form and held her tightly. "Tippy, whatever it is, it's going to be okay, honey."

So overwhelmed, Tippany couldn't talk. She just laid there cradled in her sister's arms.

Whatever unforgiveness Keturah held for her sister dissipated in that moment as nothing but compassion rose in her heart. She was about to speak again but was interrupted by a rebuking voice.

"Tippany, what in the world is the matter with you acting this way in public. Pull yourself together this instant," Sari's stern tone commanded.

Keturah normally cowered back from her stepmother, but not this time. Feeling Tippany right herself to follow her mother's command, Keturah stood up from the table and confronted Sari. "I don't know what makes you think you have the right to talk to people in the demeaning manner you do, but quite frankly, I'm sick of it. You walk around here like you're the toast of society when in all actuality, you're petty, narrow-minded, and just plain nasty. You barge around like a bull in a china shop stepping on people as if they don't matter."

"Quite frankly, little girl, you don't matter. Besides, I was talking to my daughter and not you." Sari spoke in a dismissive tone.

"On the contrary, *Mother* Jaymes, I do matter because you're not talking to some little girl. You are addressing your boss's wife, and if you don't want to find yourself having a discussion about your tenure at Canaan with my husband, I suggest you tread lightly with me."

Keturah was quite aware that people around them were beginning to stare but didn't care. It was high time this old bat ate some crow.

"Well, I didn't think you had that in you," Sari retorted with a chuckle, then turned her attention to her daughter. "Tippany, wipe your face, and let's go."

"I'll bring Tippany back to the office. I need to speak to her."

"Well, it will have to wait. She has—"

"Mother Jaymes, I plan on talking with my sister, and I will bring her back to the office when we are through. If you don't like it, again, you can take it up with my husband!" Keturah folded her arms and leveled her with an unwavering gaze.

"Might I remind you that your husband is no longer CEO of Canaan and has no authority over me." Sari reared her head back in a challenge.

"Oh…yes that's right; my husband is not CEO of Canaan, just like your son is currently not the governor of this state. It would be a shame for the press to get wind of any family dissension that could potentially hinder his political aspirations… wouldn't it?" Keturah noticed the fire in the old bird's eyes rise as she struggled to keep a venomous retort back.

Looking around at those looking at her, she centered her attention back on Keturah and somehow managed to reign in her indignation. Turning to Tippany, she spoke in a rapid tone. "I will see you back in the office." Looking at Keturah, she narrowed her eyes to slits, as she spoke in an ice-cold snarl. "Mrs. Taylor, I will see you again," she said, annunciating each word then moved past them with her head held high.

"Looking forward to our next chat Mother Jaymes." Keturah purposely elevated her tone so others could hear. Momentarily she saw the woman's back stiffen as her steps faltered at the sound of the title, but then she quickly masked her stammered gait and kept walking.

"Who are you, and what have you done to my sister?" Tippany spoke up a hint of a smile on her tear-stained face.

"I'm your big sister, remember? I'm supposed to be looking out for you. Our mom would have wanted it that way." Keturah smiled as she sat down next to her sister, and playfully bumped her shoulder.

"I wish I would've known her..." Tippany let her words trail off as silent tears rolled down her face.

An idea popped into Keturah's mind as her lips erupted into a smile. Standing abruptly, she grabbed her purse and turned to her sister. "Let's go, Tippy."

"What!?"

"Come on...you, and I have someplace to be." She took her sister by the hand and pulled her out of the booth.

"But I have to get back to the office," she said as she was being escorted out of the restaurant by her sister.

"And like I promised Sari, I will bring you back to the office when we're done."

"Keturah, where are you taking me?" She stopped mid-stride.

"Someplace where I should have taken you a long time ago." Keturah looked down at her hands, then looked up at her sister. "Now, let's go."

Tippany stared at her momentarily, then heaved a sigh, relented, and followed her sister until she reached her car. "Oh no...wait a minute. Please tell me we are not going in this car." Tippany looked wide-eyed at Keturah's beat-up ride.

"Girl, shut up and get in. This is one of the most reliable cars around."

"It may be, but I have a reputation to uphold." Tippany again looked at the car with a turned-up nose.

Keturah turned around with her lips pursed as she leveled her sister with a gaze. "You are so bougie."

"Yes, and proud of it." Tippany pulled out her sunglasses from her purse, tied her long scarf around her head, looked around to see if anyone was looking, and quickly jumped into her sister's economy car.

Rolling her eyes, Keturah was about to get in the car when she saw a woman down the street selling flowers. Looking up to heaven, she smiled as she ran over to her and got as many bouquets as she could carry.

"Keturah for heaven sakes what in the world are you doing?" Tippany looked perplexed as her sister opened her car's back door and placed the flowers on the back seat. "Why in the world did you buy all those?"

"You'll see, and you'll be glad that I did," Keturah said cryptically knowing in her heart that this trip was definitely long overdue.

It was a short twenty-minute drive to the cemetery. Ten minutes after they arrived, Keturah and Tippany were both crying as they held on to each other kneeling at their mother's and grandmother's gravesites. Tippany, with her dignified self, was on her knees with make-up smeared as she poured her heart out to the mother she had never met. Keturah heard her sister's confessions, the things a mother and daughter would only discuss. She gave her as much privacy as she could as she laid flowers on Gretta's grave. It was hard to believe more than a year had gone by. She hadn't even talked to Gretta about her beautiful Kamara and Abel. She had always come to her mother's grave, but it was harder once Gretta passed. Gretta was the only mother she had, and to know she was gone hurt deeply.

But for Tippany, she didn't have a Gretta, she only had Sari. Shivering at the thought of ever being raised like Tippany, who had all the luxury in the world, but no love. It made her understand why she wanted Parson. Someone she hoped would love her deeply.
Tippany needed to be loved right, and Parson was a good man who, given time, would be that and so much more. She was so deep in thought she didn't even hear her sister calling her name.

"Keturah," Tippany called her again while touching her hand.

"I'm sorry, I kind of zoned out. What were you saying?"

"I never knew our mother was here. She's been here all this time," Tippany expressed through her tears.

"It's okay Tippany, there was no way for you to know."

Shaking her head quickly, Tippany tried to swallowed pass the lump of emotion in her throat. "You don't understand," she finally spoke. Jumping up, she extending her hand towards Keturah.

With a curious look on her face, Keturah took her sister's hand, and stood up, puzzled at her sister's odd behavior. "What is it?"

Tippany smiled and took her under the arm, they walked a little way down the aisle and stopped in front of a headstone. Pointing to the monument, she spoke. "He knew. Dad insisted he wanted to be buried here, even put it in his will. I never understood why Sari wouldn't allow us to come here and visit his gravesite. But now...I know. Dad wanted to be with our mother." Tippany spoke in a reverent whisper. "I guess since he couldn't be with her during his lifetime, he planned to be with her in death."

Keturah squeezed her sister's hand. "After twenty-seven years, we are all in the same place at the same time." Keturah's voice broke. "We're their legacy Tippy...you and me. We lost them when we were babies. Now we've found each other, and we're together...a family. Promise me that we'll never let a disagreement or money tear us apart."

"Never...Tourie...never." Tippany dropped everything and grabbed hold of her sister and hugged her tight. "I'm so sorry we've been at odds over the company and Carlton. It's just that things are so tight right now for us. He is still trying to find another job, and Sari has tightened the purse strings. I finally told her about Carlton and me, and she went through the ceiling. She said if I ruin things for Malcom, she will ruin things for me, and I won't see a dime of my inheritance until I was thirty-five." Tippany pulled back from Keturah and bent down to retrieve her purse to grab a couple of tissues inside. "Ooh, that woman is so vindictive."

"If it's money, you don't have to worry about that. Your husband just landed a major job, and if I must say so myself, it's a pretty sweet deal."

"What? He didn't say anything to me...wait? How do you know all this?"

Keturah gave her sister a lopsided grin. "I asked him if he would be the head of the marketing for Birch & Associates."

"What?" Tippany's eyes went wide.

"Yeah. I would have given him the role of vice president, but I was hoping you'd take that position since this is a family affair."

Unable to contain her joy, Tippany started to dance around her father's gravesite singing, "I'm going to be a VP...I'm going to be a VP."

"I'm going to take that as a yes." Keturah laughed as her sister grabbed her hands and they both danced, sang, and thanked God for finding each other and their family.

# *Chapter Thirty*

Abraham hated the nagging feeling he'd forgotten something because nine chances out of ten, he had. The day had been long, but it was well worth it. Finally, his sons were settling down in life. He was glad he hadn't taken the CEO position back over. Isaac was still learning, but many of the changes he was trying to implement weren't half bad. Change never came easy. Canaan had seen many rough times, but the company hadn't sunk and wouldn't under Isaac's leadership. God had been and still was showing himself to be faithful in so many unique, wonderful ways. A knock at his office door interrupted his thoughts. "Enter!"

"Hey, boss, man. I just wanted to check to see if you needed me to take you home tonight?" Avery walked into the office and sat down.

Looking at his watch, Abraham winced. "Wow, I had no idea it was getting this late. Don't worry about it. I'll drive myself home."

"In what?"

"My coupe…ugh!" He popped himself in the forehead with his palm. "I let Mael drive it after we came back from lunch." His eyes went wide after he spoke the word now remembering what and who he had forgotten…lunch…oh my God. "I was supposed to meet Keturah for lunch." Abraham covered his face with his hands and reared back in his chair. "Keturah is going to kill me." He spoke through his hands as he slowly dragged them down over his face.

"If I were you, I wouldn't go home empty-handed. That little wife of yours has quite a bite when she gets riled up…and if you don't believe me, ask dear ole Aunt Sari." Avery snickered.

"What do you mean?" Abraham furrowed his brows, giving Avery a curious stare.

"Well, I saw her rip into Sari like nobody's business this afternoon at the Groove in the Hilton. She was steaming mad and didn't care who knew it." Chuckling, he continued. "Abraham, she did you proud."

"Then that explains it."

"What do you mean?" Avery looked perplexed.

"I got this irate call from Sari around closing time talking about honor and respect, and I better get my wife in line and up to speed with how things run...blah blah blah. After a few minutes, I did what I normally do and hung up." Abraham chuckled, planning to get the full story from Keturah if she was still speaking to him.

"Well, I think you would have been proud of your wife for standing her ground."

"Actually, Avery, I'm very proud of her, and I miss her and the kids. So, I'll take you up on your offer for a ride home with a few stops in between so I can get her something extra special." He said shutting down his computer then grabbed his jacket and briefcase.

"Okay, so we're off to the jewelers?" Avery inquired.

"Ave...I stood my wife up for lunch on the same day I told her how much she meant to me and how much I cared. I think I'm going to need something bigger than that." Abraham paused momentarily. "On second thought, let's go there too," he said as he pulled out his phone and started making some calls.

It was late when he finally pulled in the driveway with Keturah's new Land Rover. The car was a beauty, and he prayed she'd love it, although he couldn't see how she wouldn't compare to that clunker she was driving.

With two dozen red roses in the crook of his arm, and her new wedding ring in his pocket, he prayed she'd be as forgiving as she was loving. Hoping to coax her out of the house for a little while so she could drive her very expensive ride, he parked on the side of the house and went in on the back patio. He was almost on the steps when a young woman quickly blocked his path.

"Mael, where have you been, you promised you'd be home hours ago?" A distraught Marlana came out of the shadows and unknowingly confronted Abraham. "Oh, Father Abraham." She covered her mouth, realizing her mistake. "I'm so sorry, in the dim light, I thought…"

"It's okay, Mar…and what did I tell you about that Father Abraham business… it's just Dad." He extended his arm towards her for a quick embrace.

With a shaky smile, she gladly received his hug.

"Mar…is everything okay?" he questioned, noticing her teary-eyed expression.

"I'm okay, father A…I mean Dad." She timidly smiled up at him. "It's just that, oh I…I don't know, I wish Mael did more than resemble you is all."

"Marlana, my dear, that is something you'll just have to get used to." Hagan appeared from the door frame. "The Taylor men often work late and come home even later," Hagan spoke with a smile to her daughter-in-law then gave Abraham a sideways glance.

"Dad…do you think Mael will be at the office much longer?"

"Nah… I'm sure he'll be home soon." He hated letting her believe Mael was somewhere he knew he wasn't. Maybe he had to stop somewhere. He left the office at three and now it was nine at night. Abraham didn't like the feeling he was getting.

"Oh, Marlana dear, you worry too much." Hagan, emerging from the house, joined them on the deck. "Why I just talked to Mael's secretary no more than five minutes ago, and she assured me he's finishing up at the office and ready to come home." Placing an arm around her shoulder, she gave her a firm squeeze and smiled. "No man wants to see his beautiful wife sad and gloomy the minute he comes home. Why don't you go upstairs and freshen up?" she encouraged, nudging her towards the house. Hagan carefully watched her disappear in the house then she turned a worried eye towards Abraham.

She had lied...they both had. He had a nagging suspicion that he couldn't shake. The worried look in Hagan's eyes only confirmed it. Ishmael was having an affair. He gave a weary sigh.

"Abraham, we need to talk about our son," Hagan spoke in a low tone as her eyes traveled back to the door Marlana just entered. Moving forward, she took Abraham by the arm. "Abraham, I'm worried. This place is not good for our son. There are too many distractions. Maybe it's time for you to come back with us. That way, he can have your guidance and place his full attention on the business and taking care of his family."

"Hagan, Ishmael is a grown man and has his own business sense and values. What makes you think he'll listen to me?"

"You're his father, and you owe him." Hagan charged walking in front of him with her arms tightly folded across her chest. "If he had had you raise him instead of his stepfather, he probably wouldn't be mimicking some of his appalling behaviors," she accused.

"Hagan, did it ever occur to you that maybe his cheating did come from me?" Abraham said boldly, throwing Keturah's roses on the deck table and flopping down in one of the patio chairs. This was not how he wanted the evening to start out. He already needed to apologize to his wife, now he was rehashing old messes with his ex.

"No, this is learned behavior." Hagan pointed at Abraham. "He saw Jamar's whoring after other women all his life."

"And what about what he saw me do, Hagan? I broke my vows to God and my wife when I slept with you and had Ishmael. Then all the adults walked in front of him as if it were nothing. So, the truth is all of us are responsible."

"Agh!!!" Hagan's entire body shook in anger. "There you go, always protecting Sarah when the truth is, she orchestrated this entire thing."

"You know what Hagan; this conversation is old." He rubbed his eyes with the palm of his hands and then stood up. "I have a wife and two infants to care for, and I'm not about to leave the country so I can go babysit a grown married man."

"Yes, that's right, Abraham, he's a grown married man who's about to become a father...making you and I, grandparents. Is this the legacy you want for your first grandchild?

"What!?" Abraham was momentarily stunned at the news of becoming a grandfather. "When did this happen?"

"What differences does it make if he and Marlana end up getting a divorce?" She reasoned. "So, if you don't want history repeating itself, then you and I need to sit down, here and now and figure this thing out."

"Hagan."

At the sound of her name, Hagan and Abraham both turned towards the door to see Keturah standing in the doorway.

"Hey, baby." Abraham quickly stood, picking up the flowers off the table and walking towards her.

"Abraham, we need to finish discussing this," Hagan demanded.

"Hagan, listen..." He turned towards Hagan but feeling the pressure of his wife's fingers on his arm, he turned and looked at her.

"Babe, the kids are about to fall asleep, and I know you don't want to miss tucking them in." She smiled. "Go on up, and I'll join you in a minute."

"Okay." He kissed her softly, placing the red roses in her hands. Stepping to her side, he walked into the house having no desire to be a fly on this wall.

\*\*\*

Hagan glared at the couple as they exchanged a tender moment, then like a coward, Abraham ran behind his wife's skirt to avoid dealing with her. "Typical," she muttered through gritted teeth. How she could have ever loved a man like him, she'd never know. "At least Jamar had some fight in him," she muttered under her breath. Her husband was nothing but a low-down dirty cheat. In the end, he didn't even bother to hide his infidelity. He put her through hell and back, but at least he paid her well to keep up the front.

*"What about your peace?"*

Hagan turned her head in haste to keep them from seeing her tears. Ever since she came back here, she had heard that soft whisper. Peace...it was something that even with all of Jamar's money she could not afford. The price was too high. Not wanting to be bothered with Abraham's teeny-bopper wife, she turned to walk back in the house but was blocked by Keturah.

"Hagan, I would like a word with you."

"It will have to wait, I'm tired and ready to turn in," Hagan spoke dismissively as she passed Keturah.

"Funny, you didn't seem too tired a minute ago when you wanted to have a private audience with Abraham." Sarcasm dripped from Keturah's words.

Hagan decided it was time for Keturah to understand the depths of her relationship with Abraham which, as far as she was concerned, would never end. Turning back towards Keturah, she raised her chin and looked her rival square in the eye.

"Look, Keturah, you're a mother now, so this should be something even you can understand. As a mother, you will always have your children's best interest at heart. You will always make sure to protect them and make sure they have what they need. Ishmael is Abraham's firstborn. By birthright, all of this ..." She moved beyond Keturah, raising both arms to indicate the property. "Everything you see should rightfully be his. Abraham knows it, and so did Sarah. I let that little manipulator push my son and me out, and we paid dearly for it." Hagan spat, turning around to see Keturah frowning at her intensely. For a moment, she reminded her of Sarah. "Anyway, we won't be pushed out again," Hagan concluded with a defiant gleam in her eye towards Keturah.

"Hagan, you're right. Ishmael is Abraham's firstborn. But Ishmael's not Abraham's first priority." Keturah held her gaze without wavering as she spoke. "Abraham has three sons and a daughter. And when it comes to my children, you will not monopolize his time with trivial things about your grown son. Ishmael is married and, from what you say, is about to become a father himself. So, cut the apron strings and let your son be a man."

"How dare you try to tell me anything about being a parent! You know less than nothing."

"I'll give you that, I don't know much about being a mother, but I do know something about being a guest in another person's homes and when to go once I've worn out my welcome. You most certainly have worn out yours, so why don't you go back home? I'm sure Ishmael is quite capable of handling his business without his mommy."

"I'll stay in this city as long as I darn well please and you won't be pushing me out." Hagan took a step towards Keturah visibly incensed.

"I have no control over the length of time you stay in this city. However, I do have a say as to how long you will remain in my home. From where I stand, your welcome just ran out," Keturah spoke in an equally harsh tone as she took her own challenging step towards Hagan.

"Ladies…ladies… as much as I would love to watch a good ole catfight, I must insist that the two mothers in my life retract their claws and be civil." Ishmael, came out of the shadows with a smug smirk plastered on his lips, swaggered into the women's view.

"Ishmael, wherein the blazes have you been? Do you have any idea what time it is? Marlana has been worried sick," Hagan demanded.

"I am well aware of the time, mother." Ishmael's tone was as chilling as his glare.

"I realize you have numerous things to do before taking your leave tomorrow Hagan, so I'll be sure to ask Consuela to help you in any way she can." Keturah interjected glaring at Hagan then turned to Ishmael. "Goodnight, son," she said spitefully, then walked up the steps and disappeared into the house.

Amused Ishmael watched her retreating form. "I guess all the Jaymes are spunky, I can see why Dad is attracted to that little spitfire." He chuckled, but no sooner had the words left his mouth he felt a hard blow to his cheek.

"I'm sick of you Taylor men tonight, always thinking with your crotch and not with your head." Hagan walked away but found herself in her son's firm grip.

"Mother, I'm not sure what is wrong with you, and right now, I don't care." Ishmael held his mother's wrists firmly until she winced. Realizing he was hurting her; he flung her arm away from him and placed some needed distance between them.

"You were supposed to be home by six. I told you I had made reservations for the three of us to go out to dinner, and you completely blew me off." She walked behind him. "I've worked too hard to make things happen for us to allow you to screw it all up, chasing after some back-alley tail."

Ishmael whirled around to confront his mother. "I'm a grown man and will do whatever the heck I please. If you and Marlana don't like it, then you both can go to..." Before he could get the word out of his mouth, his mother's hand was coming towards his face. This time he caught it and flung it away.

"You owe me, Mael." She pointed a scolding quivering finger at his face. "You, your father, Sarah. You all owe me."

Ishmael remained mute, glaring at his mother before speaking. "Wow, Dad, better be glad he found himself in Keturah's bed last year instead of yours. No need for both Taylor men to be made miserable by the same woman," Ishmael said animosity evident in his tone.

"Ishmael!"

"What!" he said in a sharp tone not bothering to give her his full attention as he walked towards the house.

"Before you go to your wife's room, stop in mine." She turned towards her son, staring at his back.

"What for?"

"To take a shower. I can smell the scent of your whore's perfume still clinging to your clothes." Hagan said spitefully.

Chuckling while shaking his head, Ishmael turned slightly and looked over his shoulder at his mother. "You know, mom, I never thought I'd agree with my stepmother on anything, but what she said tonight was true. You've worn out your welcome. It's time for you to go home. I'll make the arrangements in the morning." He spoke in a cold tone before walking out of sight.

Hagan watched him leave and felt a piercing in her soul. "Oh, God, I'm so tired." She almost prayed but quickly covered her mouth to keep from reaching out to the only God whoever spoke to her and gave her hope. No, she wouldn't turn to God, Abraham, or her son. She swiped at her tears as her heart hardened even more. "I don't need any of you. But Ishmael, you do need me... you'll see, son." She spoke out in the quiet, darkened sky. Noticing a single rose left on the table, Hagan picked it up and inhaled its delicate scent. Feeling a slight prick to her finger, she looked down to see a blood drop forming on her fingertip. She looked at it and smiled, remembering Jamar one time describe her as a rose. Beautiful to look at but dangerous to hold. The Taylors would soon understand that Hagan Zarah was no one to trifle with.

# *Chapter Thirty- One*

Abraham wasn't in the nursery. "Maybe he heard what I said to Hagan." Keturah sighed, the thought of having an argument over his ex-lover's feelings brought a sour taste in the back of her throat. Looking down at Kamara, Keturah's heartstrings tightened as usual. She was growing so fast. She smiled, watching her little girl's restless legs move back and forth. "You'll be walking in no time." A tiny gurgling caused her to turn towards Abel's crib. Moving towards him, she looked down at him as he tossed his head from side to side and cried out. Immediately he was in her arms as she bounced and rocked him. "It's okay, my beautiful baby boy, mommy has you." She cooed while kissing his forehead. Something broke inside her heart at that simple gesture. Understanding for Hagan began to emerge. She hadn't been a mother for long, but every day since her twin's conception a tremendous love Keturah could not explain held her tight. She would work, fight, and even die for her children. The truth of that thought made her arms tighten around Abel even more.

"Maybe Hagan is taking her protection to the extreme, but a mother's love can't be turned on and off like a light switch no matter how old your children get," Keturah thought as a different image came to light in her mind. Mary, the mother of Jesus, weeping at the foot of her Son's cross, willing to give her own life in exchange for his. Tears began to roll down Keturah's face. "Father, you allowed your only son Jesus to die for all of us, even his mother, as she cried at the foot of his cross. I can't imagine seeing my son in that much pain as a mother like Mary, and even like Hagan, I would have done anything to take his pain away. But just like Mary had to commit Jesus into his father's hands. I pray for Hagan and myself that you help us commit our children into your hands...I pray in Jesus' name...Amen." She spoke into the room's darkness, allowing God's sweet presence to rest on her mind as she felt strong arms encase her waist.

"I've always known you were a special woman Tourie," Abraham spoke, kissing the top of her head, then pulling her back, so his chin rested on her crown. "There was such a kindness in your heart that I couldn't stay away from you. I had to have you, but I was afraid that people would find out that the great business guru was lovesick over his beautiful young wife." He confessed. "Baby, please forgive me for everything. Let's wipe the slate clean and start over."

Turning in his arms with a gentle hand, she caressed his face. "Sweetheart, as great as that sounds, we can't just wish everything away. Besides, you love your family, your sons, they will always be a part of you. What you had with Sarah will always be a part of you. It's those experiences that have made you the man you are…the man I love." Walking away from him, she moved back to Abel's crib and gently placed their sleeping son down. "I realize you have a lot of history with Hagan, and how Sarah's contempt drove her and Ishmael out of the home into an uncertain future. To be honest, Abraham, I'm glad you decided to come back for the kids and me. Because truthfully, I wouldn't want to be in Hagan's position…fighting for my children to spend time with their father."

"Tourie, there is so much more to the story than that." He sighed as he kissed her shoulder and turned her around to look into her eyes. "Hagan wants more from me than spending time with Ishmael. She wants Ishmael to run Canaan, but that's something I cannot give."

"But I thought the whole reason for you doing this overseas project was to bring Canaan into a foreign market so Ishmael could run it?"

"Yeah, it didn't work out well. When Ishmael converted to Islam, it made our backers here in the states nervous. I made an error in judgment, and Canaan is paying for it. That's the reason I didn't come back here and take the position of CEO. When it comes to Ishmael, it seems as if I keep making mistakes. I don't know how to fix the wrongs without making things worse."

Placing her arms around his neck, she kissed him. "There is nothing wrong with you loving your son. He is part of your legacy, no matter how he got here. The thing for you to figure out is how God wants you to participate in his life now."

Picking her up off the ground, he kissed the tip of her nose. "How is it that you're such a smart lady?" He smiled.

"Well, when I was seventeen, I heard this dynamic speaker at our high school. I think I told you about him before. Anyway, I guess you can say, believing in him and the God he serves changed my life forever."

He breathed out heavily. "Mrs. Taylor, you keep stroking my ego like that, and we are going to be adding to this little foursome." He chuckled before kissing her passionately as he carried her to their bedroom.

"Abraham?"

"Yes," he said while kissing her face then neck.

"I know my timing sucks, but I really do need to talk to you about a couple things."

"Will this conversation by any means take me out of the mood I'm currently in?" He raised an eyebrow at her.

"Yes, absolutely yes."

"Well then, can't it wait until the morning?" he pleaded trying to keep her close.

"No, it can't wait. I don't want you to feel manipulated by me, and I want to be totally honest."

"Okay." He kissed her again then let her down. "What is it that just can't wait."

"I saw Parson today!" she said, seeing her husband's demeanor immediately change, she quickly added. "It wasn't intentional, I was at the coffee shop downtown, and he came in."

"Okay!" Abraham sat down on the lounge chair in their bedroom, clearly agitated. "So, what do you want to talk about concerning him?"

"Abe, you already know what I want to discuss. There is no need for you to continue with the lawsuit against him."

"That's a matter of opinion, and it's an opinion that I don't share with you. I don't want him hanging around my family Keturah."

"As of last month, he is our family."

"What are you talking about?" He frowned, looking at her waiting for an explanation.

Instead of sitting on the bed, she sat in the lounge chair beside him. "Abe, Tippany, and Parson got married last month." She paused, waiting for her words to sink in.

"What in the blazes is wrong with Tippy?" Abraham slapped both of his thighs hard, then stood up and began pacing the bedroom floor. "Why would she do something so foolish? He can't get you, so he goes after your sister. And you wonder why I don't want him around my family." Abraham vehemently shook his head. "Nah babe, the lawsuit stays."

Keturah stood in front of Abraham and grabbed his hands to stop his ranting. "Tippany asked Parson to marry her, not the other way around."

Abraham stopped mid-stride and turned to look at Keturah, then covered his mouth and shook his head. "Why would she do a fool thing like that?"

"Because you're impossible, and Sari is a downright tyrant. She has backed Tippany up in a corner, and Tippy thought this would be the best way to get out of it."

There was more to it than that, but Keturah decided this was all he needed to know for now. "Desperate people do desperate things, Abe. She wants out from under her mother's thumb, and I don't blame her."

"But why marry Parson?"

"Why do you think...she loves him." Keturah sighed as she saw understanding illuminate Abraham's face. "She has for a long time. So, you coming back, the lawsuit, her mother pressing in on her all played a role in her decision to ask him. Besides, he was in a bad fix, so she figured what did either of them have to lose by joining forces, so to speak."

"But Parson loves you Keturah. There is no way you're going to convince me that he doesn't."

"He loved me...yes. But what you don't understand about Parson is that he loves God more with all his faults and flaws. He's repented to God and me for allowing his feelings to go astray, and now the only thing we'll ever be to each other is family."

"Family!" Abraham shook his head, walking to the bed and plopping down on it and allowed gravity to pull him on his back. Looking at the ceiling, he wondered out loud. "What type of mixed-up family is this? Half of the time, we love each other, and the other times we can't stand each other. This much bickering and discord has me wondering what type of life Kamara and Abel will have?"

"Well, maybe our first families weren't the greatest examples for us," Keturah surmised. Coming over to the bed, she climbed on top of Abraham and straddled his chest. "But the one we're making with God's help will be better."

"Yeah...maybe. You know I never thought a year ago I'd be remarried, watch my oldest sons find love, get married, and begin families of their own. If that wasn't enough, God granted me to have two more beautiful children. My only regret is I wasn't there to support you and watch Kamara and Abel come into this world." He spoke softly as he gently rubbed his wife's knees.

Bending over him, she planted tender kisses on his chin, cheeks, nose, and then lingered over his lips. "Well, Mr. Taylor, I forgive you for missing the twins' births," she said, taking his hands and placing them on her stomach. "But this little one right here, you better move heaven and earth to make sure you don't miss him or her." She smiled at the frown on his face that quickly turned to astonishment.

Propping himself up on his elbows, his eyes were wide with surprise. He sputtered his response. "W-what...y-you mean that we're pregnant?" When she nodded in the affirmative, he reached up and hugged her tight. "Honey, this is great, but when...how did this happen?"

She smiled lovingly at her husband. "You don't know?" Not waiting for a response, she bent over him, allowing their lips to touch slightly as she whispered. "Well, by all means, let me remind you," she expressed by passionately kissing him excited about their future and the second family she'd make with him.

# *Author's Notes*

**KETURAH,** which in Hebrew means incensed, fragrance, or sacrifice, married the biblical patriarch Abraham shortly after his first wife Sarah died and had six sons. Some commentators have noted Keturah to be one of the most important yet overlooked persons in the biblical text being mentioned only in Genesis 25:1-6 and I Chronicles 1:32, 33. A complete portrait has not been painted of this phenomenal woman who by God's grace her lineage includes Africans, Arabs, and possibly Greeks.

Dear Readers:

I hope you enjoyed reading Keturah II to None and found the story entertaining. If you can please leave a review on Amazon and look for another novel in the Keturah II series.

I'd love to hear from you so please feel free to join my mailing list, drop me a note, or post a message on my website.

Here's where you can find me:

www.vicstories.com
www.vicstories17@gmail

I look forward to hearing from you.

**BLESSINGS,**

*Vickie*

# Other Books by Author

Keturah the II

Shelf Life:  How to cope with prolonged singleness

www.ingramcontent.com/pod-product-compliance
Lightning Source LLC
Chambersburg PA
CBHW051333020726
47501CB00007B/2056